The
Plum Thicket

Also available in Large Print
by Janice Holt Giles:

Miss Willie
The Kentuckians
Hannah Fowler
The Believers
Johnny Osage

The Plum Thicket

by

Janice Holt Giles

G.K. HALL & CO.
Boston, Massachusetts
1984

Published in Large Print by arrangement with
Houghton Mifflin Company.

British Commonwealth rights courtesy of
John Farquharson, Ltd.

Set in 16 pt Times Roman.

Library of Congress Cataloging in Publication Data

Giles, Janice Holt.
  The plum thicket.

  ''Published in large print by arrangement with
Houghton Mifflin Company''—T.p. verso.
  1. Large type books. I. Title.
[PS3513.I4628P58 1984]   813'.54   84–12795
ISBN 0–8161–3647–5

The
Plum Thicket

One

Last summer I went back to Stanwick.

The town looked different. It was smaller, more cramped. The business section had never been longer than three blocks, but somehow they had shrunk into very short blocks now, and the buildings seemed crowded together and meager. I drove into town from the north, down the wide, white-paved highway. Small, neat suburban homes extended farther out along the road than I would have expected, but it was still only a very short way from the most distant of them to the heart of the town. So short a distance in fact that I almost passed the bank and had to turn very sharply into a parking place. The inevitable parking meter reared its hooded head, waiting for a dime. I got out of the car, deposited the coin and then stood, looking

1

at the bank.

It, too, seemed to have dwindled in size. Surely it had not always been so small, so squatty, so commonplace and unimportant looking. Oh, I knew nothing had actually changed about it. It was still the same faded red brick building sitting there on the corner where the depot road crossed the main street, and its plate-glass windows still looked out on both streets. There was still gold lettering on the windows and for all I knew the lettering still said the same thing. I tried to remember. Had the capital assets been fifty thousand dollars then?

My grandfather had been president of that bank. It had been a big and imposing building to me. There, where the parking meter was, had been built the special platform from which the governor had watched the parade on the opening day of the Reunion that summer. And there, because I had been only eight years old, I had been lifted to the bunting-draped railing so that I might see better and had been steadied on my perch by the executive arm itself. The white highway which ran directly down the main street of the town had been, then, a dirt road, oil-packed and smelly on that hot August day.

I did not go into the bank. There was no need of it. No one I knew would be inside. No member of the Rogers family had been connected with it for nearly forty years. Even that last summer, Grandfather had seldom gone to his office. In everything but name Adam had been the president. Adam . . . I walked slowly by the big window which fronted the main street. As I passed it seemed I should see his ruddy, homely face above the low curtain which hung across it. His desk had sat beside that window. He should look up and wave at me, his big mouth widening into his one-sided grin, and his hand should reach up in that familiar gesture to smooth down the unruly sweep of sandy hair which would never stay neatly combed for longer than five minutes. A strange man sat at the desk, which itself may have been the same, but the back of his head held no interest at all for me.

As I have said, the bank sat on the corner, in the middle block of the business section, where the depot road, also paved now, bisected the main street. I crossed over to the opposite corner. Here was a drugstore. There always had been a drugstore on that corner. In the old days it had been a Rexall store. Now it bore a Walgreen sign. I did not go inside it, either. But when I passed I looked in, and I saw that the old bent-iron chairs and little round, marble-topped tables were gone. They had been replaced by booths with chartreuse plastic padding. The soda fountain with its mahogany-framed mirror reaching to the ceiling was gone, too. Instead there was a long, shining, chromium thing looking very much like a bar. I wondered if the lovely old drugstore smell was gone, also. It had struck you the moment you entered the door . . . the mixture of floor sweep, piny and astringent, and drugs, a little bitter, but clean and sharp, and the sweet, sticky smell of vanilla. I supposed it must have, for no drugstore smells like that today.

I walked slowly on down the street. Most of the shops I passed were in the old, familiar buildings, but they had a new look to me. There was the usual assortment to be found in the average American small town; little uninspired dress shops with tired cotton dresses sagging from the forms; a drab, greasy-looking restaurant or two; a grocery store, a hardware store, a dime store and a department store whose name linked it with a chain of cheap department stores which stretch across the nation from the Atlantic to the Pacific. I had such a feeling of strangeness at seeing new names across the fronts of the old buildings. I felt larger than life walking down a street which had been as familiar as the palm of my hand to me, seeing only backgrounds and outlines that were familiar. Even my feet walked strangely.

Then I came to the post office, which was exactly the same, and I knew at least what had been wrong with my feet. Automatically I stepped down and landed foolishly hard

4

where there was no step. All the sidewalks had been straightened and leveled, of course. When I was a child each store had built its own walk, and one was constantly stepping up or down, from board to concrete and even to hard-packed dirt and cinders. Here, the post office walk had been down one step from the walk in front of the store next door. The leveling of the walks accounted, in part, I thought, for the faceless look of the town. All the wrinkles had been smoothed out.

I started into the post office, but stopped in the door, deciding after all not to go inside. I could see that nothing had changed there. There was the long bench against the wall where people had waited for their mail. The train from the city had gone through at nine o'clock each morning, and everyone gathered at the post office shortly afterward. The night train, going back up to the city, carried mail, too, of course; but it carried the mail away from Stanwick. It was the morning train that was important. There was the same high counter where one stood to make out money orders, and I thought perhaps the pens might be the same. Even if they were new I was certain they would still sputter and scratch as they wrote. Over the high counter bulletins were still hung, and as always there were one or two "Wanted" posters. No, nothing had changed here . . . except that Aunt Maggie wasn't there behind the bars of the small window sorting out the mail. "My prison," she used to call it. "I see the world from behind bars," and then she would laugh. It would not be her nice laugh, which was round and good and chuckly. It would be her sad laugh, which came wistfully and broken from her mouth.

The strange man behind the small window looked up at me. "Something for you, ma'am?"

I shook my head and passed on. I did not want to raise Aunt Maggie's ghost. Not just yet . . . not in the post office.

I walked on down the street to the end of the block. The doctor's office was there yet. It had been new that summer, just built, shiny and white in its fresh paint; but it had gone shabby with time, and it had a gray, scabrous look about it now. The sign hanging over the doorway was different; it bore a name I had never heard, the name of another stranger. Doctor Jim had been gone a long, long time.

It was growing late and I turned back. I thought I had better find a place to spend the night. There were people who would remember me in the town, people who might even be glad to see me, especially under the circumstances, and who would offer quick, warm hospitality; but I did not want that. I wanted to be alone . . . for that one night. There would be time later for the family friends.

I went back to the car and drove to a filling station to ask about accommodations. The filling station itself was on the corner where the old hotel had stood. When the young man had finished checking the gas and oil I asked him if there was a hotel in Stanwick. "No, ma'am. No hotel. No need of one. There's a good tourist court right on out the road, though. Nice one."

"About how far out is it?"

"About a mile. You can't miss it. Just drive on out the highway the direction you're heading . . . south. It's right across the road from the high school."

I listened carefully. Yes, that would place it almost exactly where the farm had been. I let out the clutch. "Thank you."

"Don't mention it, ma'am. Hope they got a vacancy."

I slid the car onto the highway, following its white concrete glare out of town. It had used to be deep in dust in the summertime, and the dust had whirled up over the buggy wheels when we had driven to town. It had not been a long drive even then, but now my car moved so swiftly that within seconds of leaving the filling station I was pulling into the graveled court of the Sunset Motel. I switched off the engine, but did not immediately get out of the car. I simply sat there and looked at the pink plastered walls, the neon signs which must light the place so brilliantly

7

at night, at the restaurant officiously labeled "Coffee Shoppe" in one end of the nearest building. And then I started laughing. I could not help it . . . the Sunset Motel in Stanwick! It was so incongruous . . . or was it? There had been woods here then, and a pasture and a small stream winding through it; and cows had stood in the shade of the trees placidly chewing and ruminating.

There was a vacancy and I was taken to a quite comfortable, even a luxurious room. When I had bathed and changed I went outside and, carefully watching the heavy traffic of the highway, crossed over to the other side. I had known, of course, that the school had been built where the house used to sit. When my father sold the farm he had sold it to the Stanwick school board, and while I had never seen the building, I had known the purpose of the purchase.

I looked at the building and the grounds for a long, long time. I was not impelled to move, for nothing, nothing was as I remembered it. The grove of tall, fine trees which had never let a ray of hot summer sun beat upon the house was gone. There was instead this low, functional building of brick and aluminum, sprawled out over the whole acreage which had been the grassy, unmowed yard, and nothing at all between it and the sky. One tree only had been left, and it stood in a far corner of the school yard, a very small circle of grass surrounding it. No other grass had been left. The entire place had the look of having been leveled and flattened and stripped, and where the grass had grown so thick and greenly, there was now a gray spread of gravel, neat, trim and controlled.

The land sloped a little to the right, and there, just over the edge of the slope, had been the barns, gray, weathered, old, half hidden by the pear and apple trees between. Orchard grass had grown there under the trees, waist high and so thickly twined with morning-glories that until noon of a summer day they had spread a dew-glistened blue carpet over the orchard floor. A child had run among them and her feet had tangled in the vines, and she had fallen, tumbling and rolling, with bubbles of sheer joy in her throat, thinking she would be a morning-glory, too, blue and glisteny in the sunlight. The white pavement of tennis courts glistened there now. And the old rail fence which had separated the yard from the orchard, and over which wild roses and honeysuckle had matted and clambered, was replaced with one of close-woven wire.

Back of the house, and to the left, had been the wild plum thicket, with the unknown child's grave in its dark depths, where the mourning doves had called so sadly, and the trumpet vines had bloomed so redly. What had they done with the little child's grave when they cut down the plum trees and laid out that baseball diamond? Where was the sunken slab that had marked it? And where had the mourning doves gone?

Straight back of the house had been the kitchen garden, where Grandfather had raised his fine tomatoes and lettuce, his peas and beans and carrots, and his white, pearly little onions. And then back of the garden had stretched the cotton fields . . . as far as a child's eye could see. I have heard Grandfather say that the rows in the big field were a mile long, and that it measured exactly a mile wide. That seemed enormous to me, as big as eternity . . . a square mile of cotton. The rows stretched out so long, so straight, that they disappeared over the horizon like ships hull down on the far slope of the sea. In August they were waist high, the plants heavy with tight-closed bolls, soaking up heat greedily, and slowly, slowly forcing the tight bolls into dryness that would, in October, split and spill out the snow-white fluff which was their reason for growing.

Row upon row of small new houses stretched there now, as straight as the cotton rows had been, as like each other in their sameness and monotony as the cotton bolls had been. It seemed to me that their reason for being must have been somewhat the same . . . to house and spill out fluff. But even as I thought it I knew I was only grieving with a private and personal grief. I thought how I was a child in this place, and how today I am a middle-aged woman with children who have children of their own, and how none of them have any memories of Stanwick, or of this farm and the home that stood here. Memories are not immortal. They die with each remembering mind. For the first time I wondered if I had been right in the decision I had made. I wondered if he really would have wanted it this way.

I turned to leave, saddened . . . and then for some reason, I do not know why, I walked over toward the one tree which had been left standing. Before I was halfway there, though, I was running, stumbling in the gravel, my heels sinking and turning under me. I had recognized the tree. They had left the mulberry tree . . . out of all the trees that had grown about the house, they had left the one I had known and loved the most. Its ancient, gnarled roots which had ridged the earth beneath it were now padded with a soft turf of grass, but they were still there beneath the grass, and even through my shoes I thought I could feel their grooved roughness, for my bare feet had climbed over them more times than I could remember. The packed earth under the tree, on which no blade of grass would then grow, had always been cool to my feet, even on the hottest day. It was cool, now, under the tree, when I came into the shade of those broad, flat leaves. I walked around it, touching it, feeling again the deep grain of its bark, finding again the familiar, giant knots on the trunk which had made so fine a ladder to the higher limbs. And the tree was the one thing which had not shrunk in size. Its girth was still vast, its height still towering. It was all that was left of a place and a time so very dear to me. And the thought of that, the loneliness of the thought, was suddenly unbearable and I flung my arms about the tree and leaned my forehead against it and wept . . . wept for the place and the people gone, for the happiness and the way of life gone, for the peace and the innocence gone . . . wept for the beautiful and the unrecoverable past.

TWO

To begin, I know so much about what happened that summer because of several things. First, it was in part because of the freedom which parents of that day allowed their children. We did not run on schedule. Children were part of a family, with no special timetable of their own. I was allowed to go places, stay up later at night, participate in many affairs, be present on many occasions, which would horrify the mothers of today. There were no baby-sitters, and while there were servants, it was rarely a mother's attitude that her children would be left to their care; they would naturally go where she went, do very much what she did, and be included in most of the things, saving perhaps the most formal, in which she participated. Thus I was often in a place where I saw and heard things

13

which I frequently misinterpreted and often did not understand at all.

Second, it was true because of an almost universal habit of adults. They so frequently forget that children can see and hear at all. In times of stress, anger, grief, surprise, almost any strong emotion, they are apt to forget entirely that children are present; a child becomes as inanimate and as insensible as the furniture itself, and adults will weep or quarrel, laugh or kiss before them quite uninhibitedly, belatedly remembering the child perhaps only when he calls himself to their attention. Thus things were said and done in front of me which the adults themselves probably did not realize I took in at all.

But most important, I think, is the simple fact that I was there, I was eight years old, and the events of the summer unrolled before me, around me, within me, at a time when I was old enough to bear witness to them, but not old enough yet to sense all of their meaning. There is thus in my remembering a mixture of the innocence of the child, who frequently did not understand, and the wisdom of the woman who now understands it all.

I was sent alone to my grandfather's that summer because my mother was expecting a baby. Since my birth she had lost two, but there was every reason to hope that this time, if she were very, very careful, she could bring the child to full time. She had already passed the dangerous stage at which she had lost the other two. "But you must continue to be simply a vegetable," the doctor had told her. "Rest . . . and let the child have its will."

Although my father made no burden of it, my mother knew how very badly he wanted a son. It was for that reason she kept trying so valiantly to bear him one. It was for that reason that willingly she gave herself up to the long months of nausea and illness which she always suffered and which she could never overcome; she could only endure until it had passed, and by that time the heavy weight she carried was swelling her legs and feet and ankles until she could not be on them more than an hour or two each day.

I was not sent to be got out of the way, not that at all. My mother was not like other mothers of the time. She had told me about the baby at the beginning. Without making a mystery of it, she had explained as much as I was capable of understanding, the general truth without the details, and I had been included in all the plans for it. I was sent because it was our custom to spend a part of each summer at my grandparents', and my mother and father did not want me to miss the visit which was such a great joy to me. Since Stanwick was only fifty miles from the city, and since I was eight, going on nine, it

15

was decided I should go alone.

So that is how it happened that when school was out my father went to the station with me one fine June morning and put me on the train that went to Stanwick. He let me choose a seat, advising me only to pick the shady side of the coach, and then he put my bags in the rack overhead. "How shall I get them down?" I asked a little anxiously.

"The brakeman or the conductor will get them down for you," Papa told me. "Here is your ticket, Katie. Open your purse and put it inside, and don't get it out until the conductor comes for it."

I took the stiff little piece of green cardboard and put it in my new purse. My hands were cold, and for some reason my heart was beating too fast. Suddenly my father looked very big and very solid and very desirable to me. I was afraid I was going to cry. Oh, I *did* want to go to Grandfather's, I did! But I hadn't thought how it would be to go alone like this. I felt so small all at once, so shrunken in size, and the train looked so big and filled with strange grown people. "There is drinking water at the end of the coach, Katie," my father said, "if you get thirsty. You know where it is. Shall I show you how to work the tap?"

"Yes," I said, and in spite of myself I slid my cold hand into his large, warm one.

He looked down at me soberly. "If you'd

rather not go, Katie, you needn't."

"Oh, yes," I told him, "I want to go. It's just . . ." and I motioned vaguely at my stomach.

He laughed. "Butterflies. I know. They'll pass."

He showed me how to press the tap to make the water come out of the cooler and how to release the paper cups. "The ladies' room is right across . . . remember? If you drink much water," he said, laughing, "you'll certainly need to know where it is. But don't lock the door, dear."

I had a propensity for locking myself in strange bathrooms. I don't know how many times when we were traveling I had had to be rescued. I always had to try the lock, and then I could never get it undone. "I shan't," I promised him seriously. With all my heart I meant it. It would never do to be locked in the bathroom on the train alone. I might be carried past Stanwick. I might just never be found and be left there for always. I thought how it would feel to be locked in that tiny place, with no father or mother to scream to, and how hungry I would get, and how dark it would be. I shuddered and hurried back to my seat, determined I would not even go in the bathroom unless it was absolutely necessary and then I might leave the door open a peek.

The train gave a little jerk and we heard

the conductor call out, " 'Board!''

My father bent quickly. "I must go, Katie. Be a good girl. Have a wonderful time. Give Grandfather and Grandmother my love. Write to us every week, don't forget . . ." the words trailed off.

"I won't, I won't!" My arms were around his neck, hugging him frantically, strangling him with last-minute longing to stay near.

"Katie . . ."

I let him go and he dropped a kiss on the end of my nose, hurried down the aisle and was out the door, just as the train began to move. He stood there on the platform, waving to me, until the coach had passed and left him behind. I sat very still then, huddled small and insecurely into the corner of the seat with my face pressed into the hard, green plush, trying not to cry . . . trying not to run to the door and fling myself off the train. The butterflies in my stomach were fluttering very actively.

Pride, however, came to my rescue. In a short time I sat up, straightening my red and green plaid jumper and fluffing out the crisp white ruffles of my blouse. It would not do to allow strangers to see me acting like a baby. "Remember whose child you are," my mother always said when I was trusted without supervision to my own judgments. I accepted it as an unequivocal fact that my mother and my father were very special people. I did not know how, or why, but I never once doubted it. It was a privilege to be their child. I used to wonder how other children could possibly endure not having my mother and father for their parents . . . how life could be borne in any other family than ours. But it was something of a responsibility, too. One had constantly to remember so many things.

The train was a very shabby, small one that ran as a local some hundred miles down into the country south of the city. The end of the line, and largely its reason for being, was in the coal district in the hills, but Stanwick was only about halfway, just in the edge of the hills. It was in a rather poor, flat, level farming country. The train went down each morning, leaving the city very early, and it came back late each night. Going down it consisted of the engine, coal car, baggage and mail car and one passenger coach. Coming back it actually became a freight, the passenger coach merely hooked onto the end. The engine was antique, with one of those round, inverted, bell-shaped smokestacks, and it chuffed and puffed heavily and laboriously, making much ado over its twenty miles per hour. There were frequent stops, some of them at the small stations along the way, some of them for no reason apparent to the passengers. My mother used to say, "The engineer is picking blackberries." It is true that occasionally some member of the crew had to get off and chase a stubborn cow off the tracks.

As we got out into the country I began to enjoy the journey. I had made this trip each summer with my parents since before I could remember, but it was always new to me, and it was fun, now, to be flying along. It seemed like flying to me, for the telegraph poles went by almost faster than I could count and farmhouses no more than came into sight before we had flashed past them. It was not a pretty landscape I was watching, but I did not know it then. The sandy earth was gullied and eroded, patched shabbily here and there with wormweed, broom sedge, jimson weed and cockleburs. The hills, which were here very low-lying and broad-based, were covered with scrub oak and hickory and pine, the trees themselves giving testimony to the poorness of the land. The creeks we crossed, on wooden trestles, were narrow and slow flowing, thick with the red silt of the earth they channeled. The farms were, for the most part, very poor, and the houses were mean and ugly. The towns through which we passed were equally mean and ugly, being merely more of the dreadful little houses clustered around the railway station.

Something of this I must have felt even then, for an uneasiness stirred within me and I remember thinking, when we were stopped at a station once, about the people gathered, as they always gathered, simply to watch the train go through. Why were they there? Why did they live in this small town? Why did people live anywhere they did? Why did we live in the city? Why did my father teach history in the college there? Why did my grandfather live in Stanwick on a farm? How did it happen, and why?

The faces of the people were turned toward the train and as I stared down at them they were suddenly frightening. They were all alike and they were all blank, dozens of eyes and noses and mouths, with no identity; and their anonymity made me anonymous too. That was the first time I ever felt my own essential loneliness, nor did I know it was the common fate of man. I only knew that something about the blank, unseeing faces disturbed me, and I turned away from the window, wishing the train would start.

I did not grow weary of the journey. I talked to an old woman who sat across the aisle from me, spent nickels with the candy vendor who came peddling his wares through the car, and tripped back and forth to the water cooler; and there was always the passing scene just outside the window.

Before I realized it, we had come to Fox Fork creek and then I became one immense bubble of excitement. It was only a mile to the station in Stanwick now. Fox Fork ran along the back of my grandfather's farm and my father had fished in it when he was a little boy. I had fished in it, too, and had watched this very train go chugging by. The conductor came into the coach. "Almost there, Katie," he said, and he reached overhead for my bags and bundles. "I expect your grandfather will be waiting for you."

"I expect he will," I said, and then the bubble of excitement rose in my throat. "I expect he will bring the surrey."

"Suppose," the conductor said, "suppose he brings the old farm wagon?"

I was aghast at the very idea. "He would never do that!" And then, anxiously, for maybe I wasn't important enough for the surrey, I asked, "Would he?"

"I don't know. You've got a terrible lot of luggage here. He might think the surrey wouldn't hold it all."

Oh, he was teasing. Grown people teased about the queerest things. I put on my hat, the little flat sailor that sat so stiffly atop my braids, and snapped the elastic under my chin. "How," I said, with unexpectedly clear reasoning for me, "would he know I had so much luggage?"

"Well, he knows you're coming to spend the summer, doesn't he? And he surely knows little girls have to have an awful lot of clothes to spend the summer. I don't know . . ." and he shook his head.

"Well," I said, straightening my shoulders, "the farm wagon is very nice . . ." but my voice dwindled off. It wasn't nice at all. Oh, for picnics down on the creek, yes, when we all scrambled in and sat in the hay. Nothing could have been finer than the farm wagon then. And for sitting high on the seat with Choctaw and jolting down to the grove for a load of wood, it was grand. For piling full of cotton into which one could burrow deep and softly, it was perfect. But not for being met at the station, when one had just arrived on the train. It was not nearly important enough.

The conductor laughed and patted my shoulder. "Don't you worry, Katie. Your grandfather will bring the surrey, and it will be polished and shined until you can see the whites of your eyes in it, I'll bet. I'll set your bags outside, now, but don't you come out on the platform until the train stops, hear? I want to deliver you whole to your grandfather." He picked up my bags. "Now, when the brakeman opens the door, you can come out."

The train was already slowing and to save my life I couldn't help leaning out the window a little. Not much, for if I had been told once I had been told a thousand times never to put my head out the window. But I *had* to see if Grandfather had brought the surrey. If I just put my head out the least bit I could perhaps see past the locust trees, past the platform, past the little yellow depot, to the cinder drive. But of course I came to disaster. I hit my hat against the window frame, the elastic, which was worn, snapped, and the hat flew off and out into the weeds along the track. I was horrified and my eyes filled with tears. It never paid to disobey . . . just never! Now I was going to have to get off the train, looking like an orphan child only partially dressed, and the first thing my grandfather was going to say would be, "Katie! Where's your hat?" And I should have to confess I had stuck my head out the window. Sin sat heavily on my heart.

The train stopped and I waited disconsolately. The brakeman opened the door. "All right, little girl. This is your stop." I made my way slowly to the door, out onto the coach platform, and then the conductor reached up and swung me into Grandfather's arms. When I felt them, hugging me so tightly, I forgot all about the hat. Do all children love those whom they do love so deeply and so devotedly, so faithfully and so wholly? I think they surely must. It must be a quality of all childhood to give the whole heart, unquestioningly. I was so glad, so very glad to see my grandfather again. I flung my arms about his neck and buried my face in his beard and clung to him tightly. He patted my shoulders and kissed my neck and hugged and rocked me back and forth, and then he held me off. "Let me see you! I haven't even seen you yet!" He sat me down and squatted beside me, his eyes, so brightly blue, widening in a way he had when he pretended surprise. "How you have grown since last summer. Why, Katie, you're almost a young lady!"

I stretched proudly to my full height and nodded, "Big enough to come on the train by myself."

"Of course!" His hands smoothed my dress and I clutched them. They were gnarled old hands, knotted at the joints and cruelly painful with rheumatism at times, but they were such gentle, loving hands. I felt the big mole at the base of the left thumb. "Oh, it didn't go away, did it?" We had tried a new remedy last summer. We had taken a horse-hair and tied it around the mole, and then at midnight, in the dark of the moon, we had buried it in an old stump. I had been certain it would work, for Angie had told us about it.

Grandfather shook his head. "We did something wrong, I guess. It would have gone away if we had done it exactly right."

I felt responsible, for I was the one to whom Angie had told the secret. Maybe I had got it mixed up somehow. "I *think* I remembered what Angie said," I told Grandfather.

"I'm sure you did. I expect Angie got it wrong."

"We'll ask her again, Grandfather, and this

time she can tell it to you and we'll be sure to get it right."

Grandfather shook his head. "Angie's gone, baby. Didn't your mother tell you?"

I had forgotten. Angie had died last winter. One's mind may register a fact, but one's emotions frequently lag in accepting it. Only now that I was here, really in Stanwick, reminded so suddenly that she was gone, did it become real to me. I couldn't imagine the kitchen without Angie. "Who is the new cook?" I asked.

"Lulie. Angie's girl."

"Oh. The one who lived in Memphis?"

"That's the one."

"Is she nice?"

"We-e-e-ll, not so nice as Angie, maybe. She's a young flibberty-gibbet." He paused and pulled at his beard, then he winked at me. "Choctaw thinks she's nicer."

I giggled. "She must be pretty, then."

Grandfather held me off as if seeing me clearly for the first time. "Great Caesar's ghost, Katie, you look like a chimney sweep! Wash!" he bellowed at the conductor, "you opened the window! She's all cinders and soot!"

I looked down the front of my dress. The ruffle of my blouse was all smudged and the pleats of my jumper were gritty with cinders. I brushed at them, futilely, and then I saw that my hands were grimy and black. I held them away from me in disgust and looked up at Grandfather. I had even rubbed soot on his face, I saw, for there was a big streak across his forehead. I didn't know whether to laugh or to cry. I had meant to arrive with such dignity, so properly fit to adorn the surrey. Instead, here I was, grimed and cindery . . . and minus my hat. But Grandfather looked so funny with the streak of soot across his forehead, marring his immaculacy, that I began laughing, "You should see your face, Grandfather!"

Grandfather laughed, too. "You should see your own." He took out his handkerchief and handed it to me. "Here, clean me off and then I'll do you."

The train chugged slowly and groaningly away. We watched it and waved to Mr. Washburn, the conductor, who was standing on the back platform. Then we set to wiping and smearing at each other until Grandfather said that was enough. "We'll have a wash when we get home." He settled his hat, which in my exuberance I had knocked askew, more firmly on his head, and held out his hand, "Let's go, Katie."

Grandfather wore hats with rather wider brims than most, and they were always the very palest gray in color, almost white. He had several of them, and he never wore one with a speck of dirt on it. They were always immaculate, freshly brushed, and with never too much curve to the brim. He wore a hat set a little jauntily to the right . . . not much, but enough that one knew, just by the hat, that here was a man who might go through his days doing his duty, carrying his responsibilities, but one who had a merry heart and one who would always tip his hat, undismayed, to any exigency of life.

I remembered my own hat, then. It must be rescued from the weeds. "Just a moment, Grandfather," I said, and I pulled loose from his hand and ran back up the track. The hat had come to no damage. Whisking it up I settled it on my head, and then, instead of running, I walked back, thinking, I suppose, that I had recovered decorum with the hat. Grandfather stood where I had left him, pulling at his nose, *but he did not say one word*. He simply ignored the whole incident, although when I glanced at him out of the corner of my eye his beard was twitching a little around his mouth. My own mouth twitched and we both chuckled at the same moment. We had a secret. No one would ever know I had stuck my head out the window.

The team, and the surrey, for he had brought the surrey, of course, stood waiting patiently at the hitching rail. The team was a matched pair of bays, so sleek and shiny that they looked as if they had been rubbed with oil and polished. They were never used on the farm. They were kept solely to drive, and

Grandfather often grumbled over the cost of keeping them, but he loved so well to drive a fine team that he could never bring himself to part with them. Maud and Monk were their names. Maud was gentler and prettier, but it was Monk who sparked the pace when we went spanking down the road.

While Grandfather put my bags in the back I walked all around the surrey, admiring it and loving it afresh. In recent years there has been a song about a surrey with the fringe on top. Our surrey was like that. It was a glossy, patent-leather black, with bright yellow spokes in the wheels. On the dusty country roads it got muddy and dusty, of course, but it was never allowed to stay so, and it never left the house but that it shone like a mirror. I could see myself in it, now, and when I ran my hand over its sides, they were as smooth as satin. The top was made of tan canvas, with a four-inch yellow fringe dangling all around. Sometimes, guiltily, I wondered what good it did, for unless the sun were directly overhead it shone in hotly on all sides, and rain, of course, blew in equally unhampered. It looked very grand, however.

Grandfather lifted me into the high front seat and then he went to untie the horses. I ran my hand over the leather seat . . . brown it was, with a buttoned back. Under my fingers it felt brown, thick and grainy and tough along the seams; and when I stuck my nose down close to smell, it smelled brown, the way coffee smells brown, rich and heavy and full-bodied. Leather should always be brown. Grandfather swung himself up beside me. "Ready?"

"Ready."

He took the small, light whip out of the socket and tightened the reins. He never used the whip except to flick it lightly at the horses' heads, but he never drove without it in his right hand. The reins he held, firmly, between the fingers of his left. He made a wide turn, walked the team down the drive and then brought them out onto the road. He glanced at me. I settled myself more securely on the seat and smiled back at him. I was too short to brace myself with my feet against the foot-board, but just the same I disdained the small metal handhold along the side of the seat. A lady rode firmly balanced whether she were in the saddle or on the front seat of the surrey, her own body providing her balance. I straightened my shoulders and head, drew in my waist and firmed my back. Now Grand-father flicked the whip. Monk shook his head impatiently and stretched his long, satiny legs to pick up the pace. Maud lagged a second then fell into stride with him and away we went, the team in beautiful rhythm. Their shoulders were glossy in the sunlight and the muscles of their haunches barely rippled under the skin so smooth was their gait. Their feet clopped evenly in the dust, like spaced and muffled drumbeats. The thin rubber tires picked up the dust, carried it half over the wheel and then discarded it in whirling clouds that were left to blow away behind us. The yellow fringe danced and dangled. Oh, it was grand and wonderful and lovely. Clear down to my toes I tingled with the thrill of it. I could hardly breathe for it and shivers of excitement ran up and down my back. I would not have traded places with a duchess. Nothing, positively nothing could have been grander than riding beside my grandfather, behind Maud and Monk, in that shining surrey with the yellow fringe dancing in the sunlight.

The best way I can describe my grandfather is to say that several years later when I came across a picture of General Stonewall Jackson in my history book, for one startled moment I though that Captain Chisholm Rogers, of the 6th Arkansas, had been famous enough to be included in the pages of history. They had the same deep-set eyes, held by strong, prominent eye bones, which looked frankly and directly straight ahead. They had the same thin, beautiful nose, patrician and delicately formed at the nostril. Their hair lay parted alike, a little thin and flat to the head, and their beards were simply identical twins. Under my grandfather's beard, almost wholly gray now, was a firm mouth which, when not compressed, curved softly and gently, like a woman's. I do not know about General Jackson's mouth, but from his pictures I would judge it had very much the same combination of firmness and gentleness.

Grandfather always wore, when he came into town, a loose-fitting dark gray sack coat, with trousers that matched. In those days men did not keep a knife pleat in their trousers and my memory of Grandfather's is that they were always a little baggy at the knees. He made no concessions to the seasons. The same suit served him, summer and winter. With it he wore a white shirt and a black string tie. Around home, working in the garden or about the place, he wore a gray work shirt, with a pair of old, discarded trousers. He had very small feet, which he did not pamper. On them he wore plain, serviceable, square-toed boots. Grandfather's vanity lay with his head, not his feet. He allowed himself the luxury of his pale felt hats, but he never bothered with beautiful shoes.

We made the turn at the bank onto the main street with a flourish, Grandfather dipping his whip at Adam who waved at us through the big window. I dared not risk waving in reply, but I did turn my head and smile at him. He was standing back of his desk, one hand in a pocket, the other lifted to wave. His wide mouth was spread in a big grin, as if he understood and appreciated the fine nicety with which Grandfather maneuvered the team around the turn. I had time only to see that his ears still stuck out like handles on either side of his head, and that his sandy hair still bristled upward unmanageably. It had never occurred to me that Adam was a very homely man. He was simply the next nicest man to my father and grandfather, Aunt Maggie's beau, the man she was going to marry someday, and the man Grandfather trusted so much he had given him his place at the bank.

Grandfather slowed the team now to a brisk, high-stepping trot. Here in the business section the dust of the road had been laid with a coating of oil, which, renewed several times each year, had gradually packed into a hard, flat surface. On it the horses' feet sounded with a sharp and distinct ring, not muffled as they had been in the dust. The thick, pungent smell of the oil, mixed with dust, came up to me. To this good day I associate that smell with childhood and the main street of Stanwick.

We were quickly past the drugstore, the post office, Spencer's General Store . . . but here Grandfather pulled up shortly, and edged the team in toward the sidewalk. "Choctaw!" he called. It was Saturday and a dozen farmers were loafing outside the front of the store. A man detached himself from the group and came over to the surrey. I do not know what Choctaw could have been called. He was not a farm manager, for Grandfather managed his own farm. He was not a foreman, for except in busy times there was no other help but him. He certainly was not a tenant. He lived at my grandfather's and, under Grandfather's orders, did most of the heavy work. He was paid wages, furnished with quarters and meals, and when not working came and went as he pleased. He was a big, burly man, very swarthy, with a pock-marked face and dark, cloudy eyes. He was three quarters Choctaw Indian and one quarter Negro . . . Bill Mingo, his name was, but everyone, including my grandfather, called him Choctaw. He had been with my grandfather since before I could remember. He was part of the summers, too. He came toward us, smiling at me. "Hello, Katie. You have a nice trip down?"

"Very nice, thank you, Choctaw," I said primly, but I could not resist adding, "I came by myself."

He rested a foot on the hub of the front wheel. "I heard your mama and papa couldn't come this year and there was some talk you might come by yourself. But I didn't think it likely you were big enough yet."

"Oh, yes. The trip was not difficult at all." I thought my voice sounded fully as casual as my mother's.

"Except," Grandfather interrupted dryly, "she had the window open and arrived as grimy as a coal heaver. Just look at her."

Choctaw laughed. "Well, soot and cinders will wash off. You going to stay all summer this time, Katie?"

"Yes," I said. "I can stay until our baby comes, and that won't be till September the doctor says."

Grandfather cleared his throat. "You get the manure spread on the Madame's roses before you left, Choctaw?"

Grandfather always spoke of Grandmother as the Madame. Choctaw nodded. "I got a good, heavy spread, Mister Cap. Them roses ought to do real fine this year."

"All right." Grandfather laid the tip of his whip on Choctaw's shoulder. "Don't get into any trouble tonight. Don't want to have to bail you out of jail again."

Choctaw's weakness was corn whiskey, and like most Indians he never knew his capacity. Weeks would go by without his taking a drop, and then one Saturday night he would go on a bender. He was a different man when he was drinking. He became mean, quarrelsome and troublesome, and oftener than I have fingers and toes Grandfather had gone down to the county jail on Sunday morning when the sheriff called and bailed him out. He had come to no real grief yet, although also like most Indians he carried a knife, whetted to

35

razor sharpness, and on one occasion he had carved up a Negro pretty badly. He had had to serve a ninety-day sentence that time, and it had taken him six months to pay his fine back to Grandfather. Grandmother wanted Grandfather to let him go that time, but Grandfather said he couldn't find another man if he looked for the rest of his life who could turn off the work and do it as well as Choctaw. He was worth bailing out of jail occasionally. Besides, Grandfather liked him.

He took his foot off the wheel and laughed now. "No chance tonight, Mister Cap. Lulie and me are going to the camp meeting."

"Have they started that already?"

"Just starting tonight. Was that all?"

"That's all."

We pulled away from the curb and went trotting on down the street. The end of the business section was marked by a crossroad, on the left corner of which sat the square, dingy little frame hotel, its one-time white paint peeling scabbily now. No one ever stayed there but traveling salesmen, and I have heard that they were of the unanimous opinion there wasn't a worse hotel in the entire country. It may well be.

On the corner on the other side of the street stood the church which our family attended. I never thought of it then, but I know now that it was a really beautiful little church . . . of reddish, sand-colored fieldstone, constructed with simple, plain lines, which some inspired person had kept light and graceful in spite of the stone. It sat rather far back from the sidewalk and it was overhung and framed with tall, ancient trees. The lawn was not a clipped, chastened turf, but was left, rather, to its own mixture of grass, field daisies, dandelions and weeds. They were sickled down by hand when they became too unruly. The lawn, the trees and the unadorned building gave the look and the feel of a chapel set down in a woodsy field. It was charming.

The residence section of the town took up immediately where the business section left off. But between the hotel and the first residence was a new building, one I had never seen before. "What's that, Grandfather?" I asked, pointing.

"Don't point, Katie. That's the new doctor's office."

It was a small building set flush with the sidewalk, glistening with a coat of new white paint. A sign swung from an iron standard and I read it with curiosity. James S. Davis, M.D. "What happened to Doctor Clem?"

"He thinks he's getting too old to practice any more. This young fellow's his nephew. Brought him down here from somewhere up north. Lot of tommyrot. Clem Davis is no older than I am. Plenty of good years left in him. Getting lazy is what I told him."

I screwed around on the seat and looked back at the small white building. "Does he live there, too?"

"Live where? Who?"

"The young doctor . . . there, in his office."

"Yes, he's got a room at the back. Takes his meals at Jennie's."

Oh. That was where Adam lived, at Jennie's boardinghouse. He always said that next to having a home of his own a man couldn't do any better than to live at Jennie's. "Why doesn't he live at Doctor Clem's?"

"Don't know. Doctor Clem's an old bachelor, too. Maybe he's too set in his ways to have someone else move in with him."

We had come now almost to the end of town. There were still a few houses, but they were more widely spaced and there were longer stretches of open places between them. Some of the open places were woods, some of them were pastures with cows nibbling the grass, and some were even cornfields edging up to the road. There was a long, level stretch beyond the last of these in which the woods came up on either side of the road. At the end of the woods, on the left as we were going, lay Grandfather's farm. We came to the woods and my heart beat up into my throat. I looked at Grandfather. His eyes twinkled and his beard twitched as he grinned at me. "Shall we?"

I nodded, unable to speak for excitement.

"Better take off your hat." I took it off and laid it on the floor under my feet. I clutched the handhold tightly with both hands and slid to the edge of the seat so I could brace my feet against the floor.

"Ready?"

I nodded again.

"All right. Here we go!"

Grandfather settled his hat and braced his own feet. Then he tightened the reins, leaned forward a little, flicked the horses lightly with the whip and spoke to Monk, "Let's go, boy, let's go!"

As if a spring had uncoiled in him Monk answered, reaching with his body for a lengthened step, Maud as always catching the stride from him. They flattened into a dead run, their ears laid back, their manes blowing wildly, and their tails straightened out behind them. Their feet pounded hard in the dust and sent it churning in great clouds back of us. The surrey stayed steady in the road, but it rocked and swayed like something inanimate come suddenly alive. The wind whistled against my face and felt hard and full of body. I had to set my chin stiff against my neck to hold my head forward. My braids blew straight out, like the horses' tails. Down the road we went, flashing past the woods on either side which were merged and blurred into a solid phalanx by the swiftness of our motion. Oh, it was like flying . . . like throwing all of one's heaviness away, leaving nothing but the light, freed shell of the body, like taking to the air. It was like Elijah being borne aloft on clouds of glory.

Too soon, though, Grandfather was pulling the horses up, leaning back against the reins, talking to Monk, "Come up, now, boy. Come up. Easy, easy, now, boy."

When we turned into the drive which led off the road to the barn lot the horses were walking quietly, as if the long run down the smooth stretch of road had already been forgotten, or as if it had never even happened . . . existing only in the dream.

Grandfather stopped outside the carriage house, and my grandmother came from the kitchen door to meet us. Grandfather swung me to the ground and while he lifted out my bags I stood uncertainly and watched Grandmother come through the grape arbor. I did not run to meet her.

She was a tiny woman, my grandmother, and slender to the point of thinness. She was like a small, dainty bird, her wrists and ankles delicate and almost fragile looking. As she came out of the shadows of the grape arbor into the sun she was all white . . . her hair, flawlessly dressed as usual on top of her head, her face, and the thin, gauzy stuff of her dress. Even in the sun she looked cool and remote. She came up to us. "Katherine, how nice you've come." She was the only person in the world who ever called me Katherine, just as she was the only one who ever called Aunt Maggie Margaret. She bent down and kissed my cheek. Her lips felt cool and dry. She straightened and looked at the horses. "Mr. Rogers, you've been running the team again."

Her voice was peculiarly light and staccato. My father has told me that the reason Grandmother spoke so was because she spent a part of her girlhood abroad and received some of her schooling there during her formative years. That's as may be. I think my grandmother would have spoken the same way no matter where she had lived as a child. Her voice, and the way she enunciated her words, were perfectly a part of her personality. I was fond of my grandmother . . . indeed, I think I loved her a little, with that loyal kind of love a child has for every member of his family. But I did not much like her.

She took my hand. Like her lips, her hands were always cool and dry. "Come, Katherine. I see you have lost your hat, and you are terribly grimy. You must have a bath immediately."

I sneaked a look over my shoulder at Grandfather who was following us with the bags. He winked at me and grinned. We had both been caught out.

Three

I must try to describe the house and its grounds carefully. I wish I could do it unsentimentally, but I know of course that my memories of it are colored by my great love for it.

Grandmother called the place Four Chimneys, but she was the only one who ever spoke of it so. Grandfather had no patience with giving names to places. He said it was a lot of fol-de-rol. To the rest of us, it was simply the farm, the house, the place; but whatever we called it, and however we spoke of it, it was here that the heart of the family beat strongest. My father never missed spending part of each summer there. Only something as important as my mother's health could have kept him away this year. He and my grandfather were very dear to each other, and the bond between him and Aunt Maggie was very strong; but I think it was the place itself, as well as its people, which drew him so irresistibly.

The boundaries of the place were marked with locust rail fences. My grandmother would not allow a locust tree to grow on the place. She said they were slovenly, shiftless trees; they belonged in Negro yards. It is true that they grow unevenly and sloppily, they aren't much good for shade because of the scantiness of the leaves, and their roots multiply so rapidly and so inescapably that unless controlled, locust sprouts and bushes will soon take over a place. I think it was this last quality which my grandmother really hated, though. There was something not quite nice about the trees. They multiplied and bore new shoots as rapidly as poor people and Negroes bore children. However that may be, the locust trees which my grandmother condemned had made many a mile of rail fencing.

The house was barely visible from the road, for it sat rather well back, almost hidden in a grove of fine old elm trees. One entered the grounds through a swinging gate in the rail fence and approached the house across a deep, grassy yard. The walk leading to the house was made of water-smoothed slate stone carried up from Fox Fork Creek. It moved as straight as a stretched string from the gate to the front porch.

An old well was in one corner of the front yard. It was an open well and had been hand-dug, but it was no longer used. A more modern well had been drilled nearer the kitchen. Grandfather would not have the old well filled in, however, and the housing still stood, gray and weathered, near the mulberry tree. The windlass was kept oiled and hung with rope, and an old cedar bucket was kept tied to the end of the rope. We had never used the water from the well that I could remember, but Angie had used to lower her cream and butter down into its dark depths to keep them cool.

The mulberry tree which shaded the well was a gnarled and ancient giant. Its girth had grown vast in its years of living and its bark had coarsened and roughened. Knots had bulged on the trunk as big as a man's head, and these knots were my delight, for they formed a perfect ladder by which I could climb up into the tree. About twelve feet up the tree crotched, and one tremendous limb had grown, branched at almost a complete right angle to the trunk, out from it. From this limb a wide porch swing was hung in the summer, and the ground beneath it was slick and bare of grass. The main trunk of the tree went on straight up, with limbs branching out from it. It was a heavenly tree for climbing, and the big, broad leaves made it a perfect place for hiding.

The house itself was both long and wide, almost square, looking deceptively low because of its brooding, overhung roof. It appeared to hug the ground. It was built of hand-planed poplar, which had never been painted and which had weathered as smooth as satin to a uniform, silvery gray. From the brooding roof, whose cypress shingles had also weathered gray, the four massive stone chimneys emerged, not at the sides of the house as one would expect, but thrusting tall and straight and thick through the main body, giving it a look of being anchored and tied at the center.

The front porch was little more than a portico, with lattices at the ends up which Grandmother's roses climbed. It gave upon a long, wide hall which ran the full length of the house. At exactly the center, another hall, precisely as wide and running the entire width of the house, bisected the first one. We called these the main hall and the cross hall, merely to distinguish between them. At the four ends of the halls were double doors which were thrown open in the summer, and they then became cool, breezy corridors of light, moving air. The house was definitely and effectively built for a hot climate.

Thus the four big rooms of the main house were built into the four corners of the halls. Each of the rooms was very large. I think I never knew their exact dimensions, but they must have been at least twenty feet square, with ceilings so high they were always in gloom. Built into the cross-hall wall of each room was its own huge fieldstone fireplace, and each fireplace took a four-foot back log.

To the left as one entered was the parlor. I have only to close my eyes to see every detail of it . . . the shining, random-width floor, the velvet rug garlanded with crimson roses and trailing green vines, the lace curtains and red velvet draperies tied back with silken cords. Before the hearth sat, on one side a gentleman's Victorian chair, upholstered in crimson satin, on the other side was the lady's chair to match. Between the windows was the sofa, slick and hard in the same deep red, and in front of each window was a round, marble-topped table on which sat a hand-painted china lamp. A glass-fronted bookcase stood in one corner, and in the other was Aunt Maggie's beautiful grand piano. Because I had been taking piano lessons for two years I was allowed to play on Aunt Maggie's Steinway, but only after I had showed positive proof that my hands were freshly washed.

Across the hall from the parlor was the guest room; we called it the spare bedroom. Down the hall and to the left was the sitting room, and across from it was the bedroom of my grandfather and grandmother.

In the left end of the cross-hall was the

stairway, not visible from the front door. There were seventeen stairs up, I remember, cushioned with green velvet carpeting, and the banister was a lovely, shining mahogany rail which was slicker than glass to slide down. All summer long I would have a tender spot on my posterior from hitting the stair post so hard. Upstairs were two more bedrooms, separated by a hall. Here again the house was deceiving. One would have supposed these would be attic rooms with low, sloping ceilings. Instead they were large, light and airy, and while the ceilings were lower than those of the downstairs rooms, they were high enough for comfort. These were the only two rooms which did not have a fireplace. They were heated by wood-burning Franklin stoves. The east room was Aunt Maggie's. The other had been my father's room, but it was now used as another guest room. At the end of the upstairs hall a small door led into the attic. Here were kept the usual collections of trunks, boxes, old books, piles of magazines, old clothing, and all the other odds and ends every family accumulates. It was dim and dusty, inhabited only by spiders, wasps and an occasional scorpion or centipede.

The kitchen had originally been a separate log building, some dozen or fifteen feet from the house. An open, but roofed, dog trot had separated the two. It was now closed in and was the dining room. The log walls of the kitchen had been plastered over and white-washed. It was an immense room, fully twenty by thirty feet, and the far end of it was dominated by the grandest fireplace of all. A side of beef could easily have been roasted in it, and I have frequently seen a dozen chickens on the spit, or a side of mutton or veal. Angie had used the fireplace for much of her cooking; but she had also had a big, black stove which sat in the fireplace corner. It had warming closets above, and two big ovens below. One wall, windowless, was given over to cupboards, with a dry sink, for of course there was no plumbing. Against another was what we called a safe. It was a cupboard with nail-studded tin doors, the top half divided by shelves, the lower half containing drawers. It had a wonderful, spicy smell, for here was kept leftover food; bread, cookies, half a platter of fried chicken, opened jars of jelly and preserves, single pieces of cake and wedges of pie; all the food left from a meal was transferred from the table to the safe, and a little girl, too hungry to wait for supper, could open the doors, sniff deeply of the peculiar, food-heavy smell, and take what her two hands could hold. There was always plenty, and no one ever told her she must not.

Along the third wall was a long table with benches. Angie used to sit there and peel potatoes, dress chickens, make her golden, creamy butter, mix her cakes; and she and Choctaw had always eaten there. Sometimes I ate with them. It seemed to me the food from the kitchen table always tasted a little better.

Over the kitchen was Angie's room, Lulie's now, which was reached by a stairway which went up outside, but which opened into a corner of the kitchen. Once or twice Angie had taken me up there. It was snug and untidily cozy, littered with the innumerable things she liked to have around her . . . comfortable, sagging old rocking chairs, bright, patchwork cushions, an ancient and tarnished old brass bed, gaudy calendars on the walls, and one of my grandmother's discarded carpets on the floor, its thin places covered with braided rugs. I was never very comfortable in Angie's room. It had a peculiar musky smell, which I could not identify; a mixture of woodsmoke and snuff and herbs and something else, strong and penetrating. I know now that it was merely the odor of Angie's own body, caught and held in the stale air of her room by her clothes and her infrequently aired bedding. I liked Angie better down in the kitchen, though.

There was not a clothes closet in the entire house. Each bedroom was equipped, however, with a big clothespress, or wardrobe, much larger than the average closet of today. There was, of course, no bathroom. Each bedroom had a washstand, most of them marble-topped, on which stood a tall pitcher for cold water, a small one for hot water, a wash bowl, a toothbrush mug and what, in our refinement, we called a waste-jar. These things were all of china and the sets were matching pieces. Aunt Maggie's had blue cornflowers painted on it. The spare room had green ivy. My father's had been brown wheat heads, and Grandmother's set was decorated with tiny, delicate little pink roses. Angie's last chore of the day had been to fill the hot-water pitchers. At some time during the next morning she emptied the waste, filled the big pitchers with clean, cold water and laid out fresh towels, gathering up the used ones. No nice person would, of course, unless he were ill, have dreamed of using the waste-jars during the day. There was an outside toilet, built down at the end of the garden fence and beyond the plum thicket, well out of sight of the house. For some reason, going further back than my memory, we called it Greenland. "I think she went to Greenland," was our way of explaining the necessary absence of one of us. It was at least a very unembarrassing term for a very necessary convenience.

Choctaw's room was up over the carriage house. I do not recall ever having seen it. He kept it locked and so far as I know, no one ever visited him there.

This, then, was the house to which I came that summer day.

I wondered, a little uneasily, where I was to be put. The spare room downstairs was the nicest room, but I thought it would be terribly lonely without my father and mother. Grandmother, however, led me on past it and toward the stairs. "We've put your bed in Margaret's room," she said. "She wants you with her. Will you like that?"

"Oh, yes!" I said fervently. I liked it so much I took a hop and a skip up two stairs at once. Grandmother smiled at me. "Margaret was afraid you might be lonely."

"I might," I agreed seriously, "but not in Aunt Maggie's room. Will she be home for lunch?"

"Yes."

Grandmother did not much like for Aunt Maggie to work at the post office. She thought it undignified, unladylike. But Aunt Maggie said she had to do *something*. Grandmother wanted her to take music pupils. "It would occupy your time," she said, "in a more ladylike way."

"I should go insane within a month. No, Mother, I will *not* torture myself by teaching the scales to the daughters of Stanwick."

"Well, really, Margaret, after all the money that was spent on your voice, it surely could be turned to some good account.''

Aunt Maggie had been firm. "The money which was spent on my voice was about the equivalent of what was spent on Tolly's four years at the university. I take it you do not expect any return to yourself from that.''

"Indeed we do not,'' Grandfather had said. "We were obligated to educate both of you. Emily, she is to do what she pleases with her voice. And about the work at the post office, too.''

"Very well, Mr. Rogers.''

So Aunt Maggie had taken the work at the post office. She only worked in the morning, from eight until twelve. There was so little to be done in the afternoon that she was not needed. Sometimes she seemed to enjoy the work; at other times she poked fun at it and spoke as if she loathed it. It did, however, occupy her mind and her time for a portion of each day except Sunday, and after her years in New York I am certain she liked not having too much time to brood over her defeat.

We reached the top of the stairs and Grandmother opened the door of Aunt Maggie's room and we went in. She looked about quickly, then frowned. "Lulie has laid out the wrong towels.'' Briskly she gathered them up. "I'll send her with your bath immediately. Oh . . . here is your grandfather with your bags. Put them there, Mr. Rogers, at the foot of Margaret's bed. Lulie can unpack for you while you bathe, Katherine."

"An all-over bath, Grandmother? I just had one last night."

"After a journey, Katherine, one must always bathe. Give Lulie your soiled clothing." She went out of the room swiftly, brushing past Grandfather who had stopped near the door.

He chuckled. "When you get this bath over, Katie, come on out to the barn lot. There's a little heifer I want to show you, and Rastus is waiting to see you."

Rastus was Grandfather's bird dog. When he had first acquired her two years before I had insisted on naming her Rastus, not knowing that some dogs require a feminine name, and no one had made me any the wiser. So we now had the oddity of a setter bitch named Rastus. Oh, drat a bath and unpacking. I spun around on my heels and began tearing my clothes off. "I'll hurry," I promised, "just as fast as I can."

Grandfather's voice drifted back up the stairs. "Take your time. They'll wait."

I slid out of all my clothes except my body-waist and ruffled panties, then stood, shivering with anticipation and eagerness, waiting for Lulie to come with the bath water. I stood in the middle of the room and looked all around it. I thought Aunt Maggie's room the loveliest room in the whole world. It was all pale gold and blue. The furniture, bed, chest of drawers and dressing table, were made of bird's-eye maple. Their color was that of clear, strained honey, with an amber wave in the wood now and then. Curtains, bedspread and rug were blue . . . a deep, turquoise blue which was softer than bright. There were two wicker chairs, one of them a chaise longue, which were covered with flowered chintz in which, again, the predominating colors were blue and gold. Cushions, all different shades of blue, were piled on the chaise longue, and a small table stood beside it. On it were a white lamp, with a hand-painted blue china shade, and several magazines. I knew without looking they would be the most recent issues of *McClure's, Scribner's* and the *Century*.

The arrangement of the furniture had been shifted to make room for the narrow iron bed which was always given to me, but while the chest of drawers now stood on the opposite side of the room, it still held the pair of Venetian vases and the bronze head of Wagner which Aunt Maggie had brought back with her from New York. On the dressing table were her familiar silver toilet articles, the brushes, combs, boxes and trays, and on the wall over her bed hung the watercolor of Washington Square in the springtime. The room smelled clean and airy, and very faintly like Aunt Maggie herself. Wherever she went she left a light fragrance of verbena. Grandfather always had it about him, too. I think they both kept sachets of verbena in their bureau drawers.

The sun, strained through the blue film of the curtains, lay palely gold upon the deep-piled rug, tinged only a little with green, like the surface water of a pool which holds blue depths. I stared too long at it and was suddenly dizzy, the room swirling and whirling about me. I clutched at the bed, blinking, and the room righted itself. There was a clatter of noise outside the door, and I turned. Lulie came in, with the zinc bathtub dangling from one hand and the other draped with fresh towels.

Those who say that Lulie was sullen and intractable are wrong. I know my grandmother thought so, but she expected too much of the girl. She was not as thorough as Angie, she did not see quickly what was to be done and do it immediately and efficiently, as Angie had done. After all, she was new in the house. Angie had died suddenly. There had been no thought of a new girl, no time for her to work a month or two with Angie and learn the ways of the household and the routine of its tasks. She had done domestic work all her life, but each house presents its own problems and takes time to settle into. It is typical of the kind of small annoyance she caused my grandmother that she did not, after six months, know the difference between the towels to be laid out in the various rooms. There must always be a large bath towel, a smaller one, and two linen hand towels. All of the linen in the house was white, and I do not myself know how anyone could have distinguished between the towels; but some little difference in detail, the weight perhaps or the weave, was known to Grandmother and had been familiar to Angie. Grandmother thought it stubbornness in Lulie not to learn.

She was not much like Angie, Lulie wasn't. Angie had been old, of course, and the years had added weight and corpulence until it was difficult to tell what she had been like as a young woman; but that she had not been very handsome was quite evident. Although she had been half white, she had had no white characteristics. It showed only in the lightening of her skin, which had been a dull, flat cocoa color. Her features had been all Negro.

When I think of Lulie as she was then, one picture comes immediately to mind . . . that of a sleek, tawny cat. Her skin was exactly that burnished, yellowy brown, with a high sheen to it as if it had been oiled. I remember watching her as she brought the bathtub into the room and thinking that her skin looked as if it could be sliced and eaten, that it would be thick and creamy to bite into. She was innately one of the most graceful creatures I have ever seen. Every move she made was

unconsciously beautiful, the result of her almost perfect proportions and the fine co-ordination of her body. Here again she was catlike . . . reaching, bending, walking . . . unhurried, as if the muscles of her body were lazy but stretched casually and easily at her will.

Outside of that she was not really a pretty girl. She had the usual black hair, in her case curly but not kinky, and the usual black eyes. Her Negro blood showed in the broad nose and the thick mouth. She had splendid teeth and a wide smile. She had very heavy eyebrows, and when she scowled, which she did when scolded, they came together and met with a beetling look. It was then she looked sulky and stubborn.

She laid the towels on the washstand and set the tub in the middle of the bath rug. Then she stood back and looked at me, with her arms akimbo. "So you is Katie. I been hearing a lot of talk about you." She laughed. "Your grandpa and Aunt Maggie sets a heap of store on a little girl named Katie Rogers. I been thinking to myself she must be a right nice little girl, for them to think so highly of her."

I felt suddenly shy. "That's just because I'm kin to them," I said, dropping my eyes and making circles on the rug with my toe.

She laughed again and shook her head. "No, I don't reckon that's all of it. They tell how smart Katie is, and how pretty Katie is,

and how nice Katie is. They be hard folks to fool, to my notion. Well, one thing I can see for myself they was right about . . . you is a mighty pretty little girl.''

I could feel myself turning hot and coloring. I *wished* I was pretty, but my ideas of beauty were conditioned by my mother's fair loveliness and by Aunt Maggie's dark stateliness. I was neither fair nor dark, just in between, and secretly I was dissatisfied with myself. I was too fat, too. In my own eyes I looked like a fat, very nondescript little girl. Lulie's eyes, frankly looking me over, embarrassed me and I said the first thing that popped into my head, "Pretty is as pretty does."

She drew her mouth down and scowled. "That sound like your grandmother." Then she laughed again. "I go get the water, now, sugar. You take the rest of your things off."

Lulie had placed the bath rug and the tub in the sunlight. I reached down and felt the side of the tub. It was an elongated zinc tub, shaped very much like our more modern one at home. It had been painted white, both inside and out, and in one of her artistic moments Aunt Maggie had stenciled a design of blue morning-glories all around the outer rim. I remembered when she had done it, for I had helped. We had both been interested at first, then bored as the work lengthened into a chore, so that one side was very neatly done but the other showed the effects of

haste, and even left off, abruptly, some twelve inches from the end. There Aunt Maggie had thrown down her brush. "It's too nice a day to paint bathtubs! Come on, Katie. Let's have a picnic down by the creek."

I slipped out of my body-waist and panties and stood in the sun, with that singularly light and free feeling complete nakedness gives to one. A small breeze blew in at the window and played over my body. I stood very still and let it cool my back, which was hot in the sun. But it set the down on my arms to crawling, as if tiny insects were running over them and I brushed at them and then hugged them shiveringly across my chest.

Lulie came then with bath water. I thought I was going to like Lulie very much.

Four

I saved the mulberry tree for the last. I wanted to wait there for Aunt Maggie. All morning I had run, dipping like a bee in a flower garden into the remembered sweets of the place. I had been to the pasture and had seen the new calf, a red and white spotted one, still wobbly on its legs, had patted and smoothed and hugged it. The cow had watched us thoughtfully, but not apprehensively or nervously as a younger mother might have done. She had had a good many calves and I suppose she had learned, as has a woman with her third of fourth child, that a young being is pretty tough and nothing much is going to happen to it. She kept her eyes on us, but she went on placidly chewing and switching flies.

I had been to the barn and seen Rastus.

60

"Why is she tied in the stall?" I had wanted to know.

"She's in heat," Grandfather had said casually, "and I'm going to take her to breed pretty soon. Want a nice bunch of pups this time."

I knew about breeding . . . that cows were taken to the bull, that mares were taken to the stallion, not the details but the necessity, and for Rastus to be taken away so she could have pups was perfectly natural. "I wish I could see them," I said, "but I suppose I'll have to go home before then."

"Oh, no. You'll be here. Just takes sixty-three days for a dog."

"But it takes Mother nine months!"

"I know. Takes a cow nine months, too . . . takes a mare nearly a year."

I pondered the information. It certainly was odd, I thought, that there should be so much difference. "How long is sixty-three days?"

"From now to August . . . just about the time of the Reunion."

That seemed very short. "It certainly would be nice," I said, "if mothers just had to wait sixty-three days."

Grandfather agreed.

We went to have a look at the cotton. We had stood at the edge of the field and looked down the rows which to me seemed so endless. The entire field was as level as the floor of a room, and the rows were as straight

61

as a ruler, each row exactly the same distance from the next. There was something almost profligate about the cotton field . . . an expanse, a luxury, an abundance, the plants all of a height, their leaves uplifted and outspread and all of the same tender green. I squinted down the rows, nodding my head wisely. "It's going to be a good crop, isn't it, Grandfather?"

"It's got a good start, Punkin, but it all depends on the weather."

I remembered the next most important thing. "Isn't it just a little bit weedy?"

Grandfather pulled at his beard and waited a moment to answer, weighing the question. "Maybe . . . just a little. But I think it can wait another week or two before Choctaw needs to get a crew in to start chopping."

That settled, we passed on to the garden. There I had left Grandfather pulling peas and had flitted to the plum thicket. Nothing could have made me go into that dark tunnel at night. I would not even pass it unless my hand was securely held by one of the grownups. But on a bright, sunny morning I was fearless and the plum thicket was one of my favorite places. They were wild plum trees which had grown closely and densely together, and in their effort to reach the sun in such close growth, the seedlings had shot up startlingly tall and slender. No sunlight ever penetrated their overlapping and interwoven branches, and beneath them no grass grew. The earth was dark and cool, covered in the spring with fallen blossoms and with small drifts of dried leaves in the summer and fall. An almost impenetrable wall of wild grapevine had sprawled and matted itself around the trees, forming a barrier to entrance to the grove save in one place where a natural arch in the vines made a narrow tunnel through which one could creep. After entering, it was like being in a church, dim, cool and lofty. Here, in the center, was the child's grave under a slab of field rock, slightly sunk in the ground. Gray moss had edged up over the rock. I had asked about the grave once. "It's a small child's grave," I had been told.

"How came it there?"

"The child died and was buried there."

"Was it a white child?"

"Yes."

"Did the Indians kill it?"

Grandfather had smiled at me and his eyes had rounded and widened as he drew me between his knees. "Perhaps . . . perhaps a long time ago, oh, a very long time ago before there was any town and the Indians were still here, perhaps some white people came into the country to live, and perhaps they built a log house . . . ."

"The kitchen, maybe?"

"Maybe . . . and perhaps one day the Indians came, very angry that the white people had taken their land, and perhaps they surrounded the log house and began dancing and whooping. . . ."

And we had got the feather duster and pulled out some feathers and stuck them in our hair and we had done a war dance, brandishing our tomahawks and whooping and stomping, and then we had killed off all the white people.

It was not lying . . . I insist upon that. I was too young, so Grandfather had simply played a game with me, a game which I wanted to play. At any rate I had no morbid feelings about the grave, and many times my tea parties were served from the sunken slab of field rock.

After the plum thicket I had run through the orchard, entranced by the pattern of light and shadow, darting swiftly from pool to pool of shade, locking my hands about the down-bending limbs and swinging, making them shift and change the pattern. I had played touch-and-go, touching a tree and then running, trying to reach the next tree before the count of ten. I ran through the grass, which was already ankle high, turned handsprings and cartwheels, fell and rolled and tumbled, wild as a colt with freedom. I was conscious of the sound and smell of the morning all around me; the hot, moist smell of the earth in the cotton field, dark and rich, with the field larks calling from far down the rows; the acid, animal odor in the barns, and the sweet, light chatter of the martins circling about the birdhouse; the dank, musty smell of the plum thicket, and the sad cooing of the doves; the yeasty odor of peaches and apples in the orchard, and the hum and buzz of thousands of bees around them. I was drunk on sounds and smells and light and shadow and wind and sun.

But always, in the way of a child saving the best sweet for the last and anticipating it, the thought of the mulberry tree had been drawing me on. I ran in the house. "Is it time, Grandmother?"

She glanced at the clock on the mantel. "In about fifteen minutes." She slanted her head to listen. A rhythmic thumping sound came from the kitchen. "Lulie will ruin the biscuit. She has never learned to beat them properly." She hurried from the room and I flew to the mulberry tree.

It was such a fine tree to climb . . . first up the ladder of the big knots, and then up the central trunk on the big, rounded limbs spaced at easy intervals even for my short legs. Near the top a kind of chair was formed by a limb branching off laterally. A limb from another branch curved near it and made a back rest, and there was even another one underneath for one's feet. This was my special place. Here one could sit, cradled safely, in a kind of leafy nest which shut one off from everything else . . . here one could sit and pretend. The big, broad leaves made a floor under one, and the earth and the world disappeared beneath it. Above was the sky, and there was nothing living but one's own self and the birds and the clouds and the wind and the ruffling leaves. You could look at the sky so high and blue and far away, you could look and look and look until suddenly it came right down and you could reach out and touch it, or frighteningly it closed in and you felt pressed down by it and smothered. You then had to look quickly away . . . at green or brown or the red and white check of your apron, any color but blue, any texture but space, or you would be pressed right down into the earth, like the little child in the plum thicket.

There was no end to the games you could pretend. You could be a ship, with the clouds the sea, and the wind in the tree making the ship roll with the waves. You could be a bird, a seagull, wheeling through the sky, or an eagle high on a crag. You could be Peter Pan winging his way to the pirate and the Indian maid. But always, whatever you were and whoever you were, you were high and alone and free. Not even Aunt Maggie shared the tree with you.

This morning the treetop was a crow's nest and I was the lookout, watching for the great white whale. The seas were high, the ship tossed and I clung with one hand to the spar and shielded my eyes with the other. I sighted the whale . . . a speck in the distance, and cupped my hands to cry, "Thar she blows! Off the starboard beam!" Aunt Maggie's white parasol was bobbing along the path, surging through the sea of trees.

The game was forgotten and I scurried down the tree to meet her, in my hurry leaving a red hair ribbon caught on a twig, tearing the hem of my dress and skinning the palm of one hand. None of these things mattered. I was allowed to go as far as the edge of the trees to meet her, and I would have to hurry or she would be there before me. I flew out the gate, hearing it bang behind me, and down the path, yelling, "Aunt Maggie! Aunt Maggie!" at the top of my voice every step of the way.

Only a great love could have found beauty in my Aunt Maggie's face, I suppose, and perhaps it is only given to children to love so uncritically. At any rate, I had such a love for her and my eyes did not see the dark sallowness of her cheeks, nor the forehead that was too high, nor the nose that was too thin. They found instead her lovely eyes, clear and dark and gray like clouds full of rain, which saw so much beauty wherever they looked; and they found her wide, sweet mouth which said such laughing, gay things.

She was a tall woman, surprisingly tall when

one remembered that both Grandfather and Grandmother were small people, although I think her exact height was no more than five feet seven. She was slender, without being angular, and, to her at least, embarrassingly full-breasted. She never had to wear the starched flounces in her camisole with which other women of the time, even my mother, fluffed out their blouses. I remember my mother saying to her one day, watching her dress, "Maggie, you were made to have children."

"Not, I hope," Aunt Maggie had said laughingly, "until I have a husband first."

"Well, among nice people it's considered proper to have a husband," Mama had said, laughing too. "But Adam will take care of that."

Aunt Maggie had shrugged into her shirt-waist and buttoned it swiftly and competently. "Oh, I suppose so . . . in time."

Mama had looked at her, a queer, half-hidden look from the side of her eyes. "Adam will make a fine husband."

Aunt Maggie had swirled to peek at the hem of her skirt in the mirror. "Do my petticoats show?" Without waiting for Mama to answer she had chosen a handkerchief and unstoppered her lavender water. "Yes, of course. Adam will make a wonderful husband. I am lucky that he wants to marry me."

"You are lucky that you love each other," Mama had said, softly.

Aunt Maggie had looked at her. "That's what I meant, Katherine."

She wore today a blue and white striped shirtwaist, crisp and neat, the neck high and pinned with a small black velvet bow, the sleeves firmly held at the wrists. Her skirt, held in at the waist with a black velvet girdle, was smooth over her hips, then flared, heavily starched, to her ankles. Her head was bare and the rich, red-brown hair was done in the usual bun on the nape of her neck. She dropped her parasol and received me into wide, welcoming arms, swinging me off the ground, both of us forgetting my dusty bare feet against her skirt. "Katie, Katie, Katie!" she cried, holding me so tightly I could hardly breathe, kissing me extravagantly dozens of times, down my nose and chin, into my neck and then all over again, as if she could not have enough of the feel of me. "Darling, darling Katie! You are really here! You've really come! Oh, *such* a long morning, darling! So many dull people wanting mail, and so much mail to sort and distribute. I thought we would never get through! And all the time my darling was here and I so eager to see her I couldn't wait! I wanted to throw all the mail out the window and shove all the people aside and come flying home! I wanted to say . . . do you know what I wanted to say?"

"What?"

"I wanted to say . . . 'Dear people, you are not important at all today. Today there is only one important person in the whole world!' "

"Who, Aunt Maggie?"

She hugged me tightly again. "My own darling . . . Katherine Tolliver Rogers, that's who!"

Then she set me down. "I can't believe it! Was the trip nice? Did you have fun? Were you tired? What have you been doing all morning? Katie . . . look! You've lost a hair ribbon . . . you've torn your dress . . . and I do believe you've skinned your hand!" She stooped beside me, trailing her skirt in the dust, to examine my hand. Then she looked at me solemnly. "The mulberry tree?"

I nodded.

"Ah, well. It's not so bad. We'll wash it and put a nice, clean bandage on it. Here, you may carry the parasol."

That was Aunt Maggie's way. She never scolded or fretted. And now that she was home, Grandmother would not. Even when my mother was there I was always Aunt Maggie's special charge in the summer. It was never discussed, it was simply understood.

Hand in hand we went back down the path, I under the proud shade of the white silk parasol and Aunt Maggie tall in the sun beside me; I, chattering like a monkey, Aunt Maggie interested and listening.

Adam came for supper that night. He always came to supper on Saturday night and then he and Aunt Maggie went, afterward, to choir practice. Aunt Maggie sang in the choir of the little Methodist church. My grandmother had been born and reared a Calvinist, but there was no Presbyterian church in Stanwick, so she had accepted as the next best thing Grandfather's Methodism. There were at least a few familiar similarities in their theology. Both my father and Aunt Maggie had been baptized as infants, and had then been faithfully taken to Sunday School and church all their young lives. I myself had been baptized in the same small church, long before I could remember.

Usually when Adam and Aunt Maggie went places together it was in his buggy, a stylish, high-undercut buggy with a shiny, black, patent leather top. He drove a small bay mare to it, whose name was Cindy. She was considered the fastest horse in the county, and Adam liked to let her out on an empty country road. On Saturday night, however, because the church was so near, he never brought the buggy. He and Aunt Maggie always walked unless the weather was bad.

I was going tonight, of course. Whatever they may have thought of it, in the summertime Aunt Maggie's beaux had had to get used to having a little girl tagging along. I always wanted to go and Aunt Maggie rarely refused me. Of course now that the beaux had given way to one beau, Adam, it raised no problem. Adam appeared to like having me along as much as Aunt Maggie, and I was comfortably unaware of anything unusual in the arrangement.

We had ham for supper, sliced very thin, and little green peas, and new potatoes in cream sauce; lettuce, drenched with oil dressing. We had tiny beaten biscuits and for dessert, angel-food cake with the last of the strawberries. The table was lovely, as always, with its white cloth and its cut-glass epergne, the fine English china which had belonged to my grandmother's mother, and the thin, flat silver which had also been hers. The lamp, which hung from a chain directly over the center of the table, and which burned oil, made a pale yellow light which glowed softly on the faces of us all.

I thought we were rather splendid looking ourselves as we sat at the supper table that evening, Grandfather and Adam in their coats and white shirt fronts, their hair slicked down, although Adam's was already springing up on top; Grandmother, immaculate as always in white, her black eyes bright in the lamplight . . . she did enjoy a beautiful table and well-mannered guests; Aunt Maggie beautiful beyond words, to me, in her lilac lawn. I had watched her press it that afternoon. She had discovered, to her distress, that Lulie had put alway all of my frocks unpressed. Unlike Grandmother, who would have called the girl immediately to do the chore, Aunt Maggie had gathered them all up and had gone down to the kitchen herself and pressed them. She believed that Lulie had too much to do as it was, and she never asked her to do anything for herself. She had felt the same way about Angie, of course, and one of the things I remember best is Aunt Maggie, the heat from the stove and the heat from the day sending rivers of perspiration down her face and neck, ironing all those starched skirts and waists of hers, all those ruffled petticoats. Patiently that afternoon she had ironed every dress I had brought with me. Then she had pressed the lovely lilac lawn.

I felt very proud that night in my white dotted swiss with the blue satin sash. I loved the way the satin felt, so slick and cool and shiny. I kept feeling of my sash all through supper, until Grandfather noticed and asked me if my tummy hurt. I shook my head. "It's my sash."

"Too tight?"

Aunt Maggie laughed. "She just loves the sash, Papa."

"Well, who wouldn't?" said Grandfather, "it's a very beautiful sash. I noticed it immediately. All dressed up, hummh?"

"I'm going to choir practice with Aunt Maggie and Adam."

"Oh, are you now? And what are you going to do with yourself all during the time the choir is singing those tedious anthems?"

"I shall listen."

"Listen," Adam said, teasingly, "and wait patiently for them to be over so she can go to the drugstore and have ice cream."

"Oh, now the cat is out of the bag. *That's* what you're all dressed up for!"

Lulie came in with a plate of fresh biscuits. Grandfather looked at her as she set the plate on the table. "Looks like you and your Aunt Maggie aren't the only ones dressed up tonight . . . eh, Lulie? I hear you're going out, too."

Lulie was dressed to go to the camp meeting. She had on yellow silk, only a shade darker than her skin, and as smooth as cat's fur over her hips. She had a yellow rose in her hair. She grinned widely at Grandfather when he spoke to her. "Yessuh. Me and Choctaw is going to the camp meeting tonight."

"Well, mind, now . . . you're just supposed to get *religion* at a camp meeting."

"Mr. Rogers . . ." Grandmother murmured, and then she excused herself. "Lulie . . . a moment, please."

Lulie giggled. "Yessuh. I'll remember."

She followed Grandmother to the kitchen.

We heard their voices, but not what they were saying, until Grandmother's voice rose slightly. She was saying something about the rose. Aunt Maggie sighed. "I was afraid Mother would spot that rose. Papa, you shouldn't have called attention to Lulie."

"Something wrong?"

"Lulie took one of Mother's yellow roses for her hair. Didn't you notice?"

Grandfather lifted his napkin to his mouth and wiped gently. "No. I'm sorry. Well, she shouldn't have done that. Your mother is right to scold her."

"Now, Papa . . ."

"Oh, I know, Maggie, I know. But Lulie knows how she feels about her roses."

Grandmother came back. "Margaret, I have excused Lulie. Will you clear the table for dessert, dear?"

When the table had been cleared and dessert served Grandmother and Aunt Maggie took their seats again. I remember that Adam and Grandfather talked of the strawberries and how short the season was, and Grandfather told Adam of some plan of his to try a berry that would bear fruit all summer. In a lull in the conversation Grandmother spoke. "Would you like some roses for your dresses, Margaret . . . Katherine?"

"If you have some you can cut, Mother," Aunt Maggie said.

"I shall clip the whole yellow bush," Grandmother said, dryly. "Lulie has spoiled it."

"Oh, Mother, surely not . . . with just one rose?"

"One rose, Margaret, can ruin the symmetry of an entire bush. I would rather it had none on it, now."

Her head bent forward as if it were suddenly heavy. Then she said, pensively, almost dreamily, "In the old days I should have had her striped."

It was very still in the room . . . so still that one could hear the lamp sputter a little as if the oil were running low . . . so still that the flutter of a moth's wings on the screening sounded very harsh. Suddenly in the yellow light of the lamp they all seemed to turn greenish and sickish and they began to grow in size, larger and larger, giant-size, like in *Alice in Wonderland,* and their faces floated apart from their bodies, like swollen moons, and their bodies were like paper dolls, flat and sharp and thin again the white wall. I was terrified. I felt too small. I wanted to run and run and hide. Then Adam spoke, his voice quite normal, quite effortless . . . . "It would be an interesting experiment, sir, but I doubt if our climate would nourish an everbearing berry."

And Grandfather said, "You may be right. On the contrary our humid heat might prove to be the very thing on which the vines would thrive."

Aunt Maggie brushed some crumbs from the table with her napkin and shook them into her plate. "Wouldn't it be nice if they did do well? Imagine having berries all summer."

Why, everything was all right. I took a deep, shaky breath. Nothing was wrong at all. Grandmother rose and we all followed her. She went to the door and leaned against the screen, saying fretfully, "It's so hot. Do you think it's going to rain?"

I remember the stars that night, millions and millions of them, and I remember Adam pointing with the stem of his pipe as we walked along, showing me the Great Bear, the Little Bear, the Seven Sisters and the Big Dipper. I remember the quietness of his voice as he talked, and Aunt Maggie's as she answered. I remember the sound of the crickets and the grumbling undertone of the frogs far away near the creek. I remember how warm and still the night was and how close around it seemed. I remember the church, dim because it was lighted only near the organ, and the small group of people already gathered when we arrived. I remember that Adam and I sat on the back pew and listened and how pure Aunt Maggie's voice was in the solo parts. I remember leaning against Adam, drowsily, and that he put his arm around me. But I remember nothing more. The day had been too long for me and too exhausting. So I did not have ice cream at the drugstore after all. Instead, Adam carried me home, and as if in a dream I heard him tell Aunt Maggie they shouldn't have brought me, I was too tired.

And I heard Aunt Maggie's voice, muffled but still penetrating my consciousness, saying, "I wanted her to be tired. Don't you remember what the first night away from home can be like? I wanted her to go to sleep just this way . . . so she wouldn't be home-sick."

And I felt Adam sway forward and heard him kiss Aunt Maggie, and say, "Maggie, you're so sweet."

Five

The sun awakened me the next morning, shining in a broad band across my bed. Drowsily I threw back the sheet, feeling too warm. Something crackled and I came wide awake, sat up and looked about. Aunt Maggie's bed was empty, the covers thrown back to air. The room was empty, too. When I moved to get out of bed I heard the crackling noise again, and then I found Aunt Maggie's note pinned to my sheet. "Hurry! We are having pancakes and strawberry jam for breakfast."

I remembered it was Sunday morning, and Sunday morning was very special. It was the day Aunt Maggie fixed breakfast and the three of us, Grandfather, Aunt Maggie and I ate it in the kitchen. Lulie, and Angie before her, was not asked to get up on Sunday morning. Grandmother never ate breakfast and while she appeared every other morning of the week to oversee Lulie, on Sunday she stayed in her room.

I hurried to dress, and it was while I was dressing that I noticed my hand was a little sore and stiff. It hurt when I bent the fingers to button things, but not much; and the bandage was still fresh and clean. When I was dressed, I splashed a little water in the bowl and with one hand washed my face. It was a halfway job, but I couldn't do any better left-handed. I wondered about my hair. I could comb it just fine, but I could not yet braid it. I decided finally against undoing it and combing it out fresh. I just gave it a few licks with the brush on top, and dashed for the stairs, taking the banister down.

Aunt Maggie was at the stove, almost completely enveloped in a big apron which I recognized as one of Angie's. Angie had never believed in exposing an inch of her dress and her aprons had been voluminous things. Something was simmering on the stove and Aunt Maggie was stirring, her face hot and red from the heat. Whatever it was, it had a heavenly smell. "Is that the strawberry jam?" I asked, sniffing.

Aunt Maggie turned. "Good morning, sleepyhead. That's the strawberry jam. We'll have it hot, with melted butter to pour over the pancakes. Hungry?"

"Famished." That was a book word I had

been longing to use. It sounded so much hungrier than hungry, or even starved. I had a peculiarly adult vocabulary for a child of eight, perhaps. It came from living much in the company of adults who never talked down to me, and it came from having been introduced very early to the pleasures of reading. At eight I was already a voracious reader, and nothing in my father's library was forbidden me. It was my father's theory that what I could understand I was ready to understand, and the rest would be just so many words.

Breakfast was set at one end of the long table, on a red and white checked cloth which was fringed all around. The roses we had worn on our dresses last night were clustered in a small, blue vase in the center. They had been yellow buds last night. This morning the petals had uncurled, and the pure yellow of the buds was opened now to reveal centers shaded with salmon and pink. When I looked close I could see that the color was blended into the fine texture of the petals in tiny, fine streaks. They looked almost painted on. "Where's Grandfather?"

"He's helping Choctaw feed. He'll be along."

"Did Choctaw get drunk last night?"

"I don't think so. When he brought the milk in he seemed all right."

"Have you already done the milk?"

"Hours ago."

I loved to help with the milk. It never looked like the milk we drank, later, when it was cool. It was warm and foamy and ran through the strainer in a wide stream, leaving the foam gathered in the mesh of the strainer. Once I wanted some with the foam on it and Angie had given me a glass . . . but it wasn't any good.

"Does Lulie get drunk, too?"

"She never has . . . at least not that we know of."

Aunt Maggie broke off the crisp edge of the first pancake and handed it to me. It was brown and buttery and crunchy. "Is Lulie part Indian, too?"

"No, darling."

I dipped the last of the pancake crust into some melted butter and popped it in my mouth. "Why did she go to Memphis to live?"

"Well, when she got to be a pretty big girl she decided she'd rather live there. I suppose she thought the opportunities for work were better."

"Why did she come back here?"

"Why, when Angie died, dear, she came back for the funeral, and we asked her if she would like to stay and work for us. Why?"

I wiggled on the bench. "I'm just glad she did. I like her."

Aunt Maggie turned the pancakes. "So do I. Would you like some coffee?"

I was allowed coffee for breakfast . . . very weak, more than half milk. "I'll fix it," I said.

"Better let me pour the coffee," Aunt Maggie said, "the pot is pretty heavy. You can get the milk."

But Grandfather came in before we had the coffee fixed. "Good morning, Katie. Did you sleep well? No, no . . . don't touch me. No kiss till I get the barn washed off. Maggie, a cup of that coffee would go mighty well."

"You'll just have time for one before the pancakes are ready."

Grandfather spluttered and splashed at the water shelf and Aunt Maggie poured the two cups. We took them to the table. Grandfather heaped sugar into both and we sat, sipping slowly at the hot liquid. It was so good. "This coffee is almost the color Angie was," I said.

"It is, isn't it?" Grandfather said, laughing.

"Was Lulie a slave, Grandfather?"

"Good heavens, no, child! Lulie's just about your Aunt Maggie's age. The war was over long before she was born."

"But Angie was a slave, wasn't she?"

Aunt Maggie pointed her pancake turner at Grandfather. "She's full of questions this morning, I warn you. She's been asking 'why' ever since she got up."

Grandfather rubbed the top of my head and pulled at a braid. "Well, folks have to ask questions to learn, don't they, Punkin?"

"You didn't answer yet, though."

"What was it you asked? Oh, yes . . . Yes, Angie was born into slavery, but she was freed when she was still a very little girl."

"Why?"

Grandfather looked at Aunt Maggie and they both laughed. "You see," Aunt Maggie said. Grandfather chuckled again, and then he said, "Well, that's a long story. Some other time, maybe."

"No, now!"

"You're sure you want to hear it?"

"Oh, yes!" I loved Grandfather's stories.

I settled myself comfortably, and he took a sip of his coffee. "Well, my father . . . your great-grandfather, inherited a good many slaves when he came into his property. You know that we lived in Mississippi in those days, don't you?"

I nodded. I had heard my grandmother sigh for those days too often. She had spent most of her married life in Arkansas, had come as a young wife with Grandfather to this place and had lived with him in the old log house until they built the new one; had had her children and reared them here, but the raw, new land had never become her home. It was always an exile to her. "Why did you leave Mississippi, Grandfather?"

"There wasn't much left of our place after the war, baby. Not enough for four of us boys at any rate. I was the youngest so I decided to cross the river and start fresh."

Aunt Maggie set the platter of pancakes and the bowl of hot strawberries down in front of us, poured fresh coffee, and then she slid onto the bench beside me. "Go on, Papa."

Grandfather poured melted butter over his pancakes and then drowned them in the jam. Between bites he talked. Aunt Maggie and I ate and listened. One of the nicest things about Aunt Maggie was that no matter how many times she may have heard Grandfather tell a story, she always listened as if it were the first time. She listened to everyone that way. She had a capacity for listening.

"Well, as I said . . . my father inherited a good many slaves, but he didn't believe in slavery. He wasn't particularly sentimental about it, although he was a good man with his people . . . never neglected them, took good care of them, and he never broke up families buying and selling. But as a matter of principle he was against the institution of slavery. He said it was ruining the country . . . said the slaves were actually the owners of the land . . . said it took all a man could make on a place to take care of his people. We saw it work that way. We never had any cash . . . everything had to be turned back to the people . . . clothing, food, medicine, one thing or another . . . and they increased so almighty fast. They bred like rabbits. Unless you were heartless and sold off the old ones and the weak ones, you soon had a kingdom of Negros to keep up. So . . . when we boys got up old enough to understand . . . I think I was around sixteen, he called us all together one day and talked to us about freeing them. He'd been pondering over it a long time, but since they would come to us as part of the property, he didn't want to do it unless we agreed. And we all did. He didn't have to tell us a thing about the drain they were on the place. We could see it for ourselves. So . . . at Christmastime that year he freed every last one of them . . . down to the least baby."

"I expect they were pretty glad, weren't they?"

"Glad? Well . . . yes. They didn't really understand much of what it meant, baby. They knew they'd never be sold, but then they never had been anyhow. Still, it must have made a difference." Grandfather laughed. "It was quite a mess for a few years. Freeing them didn't free us of the responsibility for them. Father paid them, and a man didn't have to work unless he wanted to . . . but he didn't get paid if he didn't work, and that was hard for them to understand. It was hard for them to learn that out of their pay they had to buy clothing, food and medicine. They had to be taught how to manage, and some of them never did learn. Some of them, doubtless, would have been glad to go back to the old days. But it was beginning to work . . ."

"What happened?"

"The war came, Katie. And wars have a way
of bringing an end to a known world. People
are scattered like chaff before the wind.
Homes are burned and fields are turned into
cemeteries. When that happened to our place,
Father couldn't take care of our people any
longer. All four of us boys were in the army,
and when we straggled home, there was only
one cabin left. We never knew what happened
to the Negroes. Angie was the only one who
stayed. She was doing her best to take care
of Father. When he died and I came to
Arkansas I brought her with us."

"How came it to be Arkansas, Papa?" Aunt
Maggie asked.

Grandfather shrugged. "I thought it offered
a better chance. The war hadn't devastated
it, for one thing. For another, when my own
regiment was shot to pieces, I drifted into
Hindman's regiment, the 6th Arkansas.
Never left it. I kind of liked the breed of men
they were. When it was all over I thought I'd
like to try the country they came from."

"Did you?" I asked.

"Did I what?"

"Did you like it here?"

"Well, puss, I've been here for over forty
years now."

"And no regrets, Papa?" Aunt Maggie
asked softly.

Grandfather picked up a fork and traced a pattern with its tines back and forth across the cloth. "Regrets, Maggie? What is regret? To be sorry? No, I've never been sorry for the move. It had to be done. We've done well here, and we've had a good life. To mourn the lost? The irreparably lost? Yes, of course. It was such a kindly world we had. Yes . . . in the still of the night, the grief came, many times. Not so much for the loss . . . but the necessity of the loss."

Aunt Maggie's head bent and I was surprised to see that her eyes had filled with tears. Grandfather looked at her. "Is it no better with you, Maggie?"

Impatiently she brushed the tears away. "Of course. Of course it is, Papa. It's just . . . just . . . just the necessity of the loss, I guess."

"Maggie . . . " Grandfather's voice was hesitant, feeling its way, "Maggie, why don't you go back to New York . . . try someone else. Try Europe if you want to. After all, Werner was just one man."

"But he was the best. When he told me I wasn't good enough . . . No, Papa . . . it's no use."

"Well, would you like to live in the East? Do something else?"

She shook her head. "No. That wouldn't be any good either. You can't warm yourself at a dead fire, Papa. You know that. No, I've chosen my way . . . I've made my move across the river . . . and so help me, I'll not regret it."

Grandfather smiled. " 'The best of possible worlds,' hummmh?"

Aunt Maggie laughed and stood and began stacking the plates. "In the way Voltaire meant it, darling, no. Actually, I suppose, yes."

Grandfather pushed his chair back. "Well, I'm going to have a look at the cotton. Want to come with me, Katie?"

I shook my head, without really hearing what he had said. I was still sitting on the bench, dreaming, lost in the feeling and the sound and the texture of the words they had used. I had a way of whispering to myself, almost silently, only my lips moving, words that were left hanging in the air . . . words that fascinated me with their sound and with their rhythm—necessity . . . loss . . . Voltaire. Words were so beautiful. I could have made a song of the "S" sounds, and the "V" of Voltaire.

Aunt Maggie was standing in front of me. "Katie, wake up. I said would you rather take some coffee in to Grandmother, or finish stacking the dishes?"

"I'd rather stack the dishes, Aunt Maggie," and as suddenly as the dream had come, it was gone. But I knew I should never forget this morning . . . the kitchen, its white-washed walls clean around us; the sun on the red checked cloth, the smell and taste of coffee and hot strawberry jam, and the words Aunt Maggie and Grandfather had said. The clock had stopped for a moment, so I could have time to gather it all up and store it away. It has stopped for me like that on every lovely moment of my life.

We went to church, came home and had dinner, rested, read and dozed in the afternoon. Grandfather prowled restlessly around. Sunday was a day which bored him terribly. He hated the enforced rest and the long, lazy dullness of it. He had gone to church faithfully with Grandmother when my father and Aunt Maggie were small, but once they had grown up, he had quit. He had said if they ever had a preacher who could make him think, he'd start going again . . . but he never really gave a preacher much chance. He was essentially a restless, nervous man, who found idleness unendurable. From the time he arose in the morning until he retired at night he kept constantly busy. So each week Sunday stretched like a long, dry desert before him. He obeyed the letter of the law, but the spirit of it he stretched pretty far. He usually wandered unhappily about the place, his fingers itching for some task . . . or he read.

He read Aunt Maggie's magazines . . . the articles, he did not care for fiction in its short form, the Sunday papers, or the books from his own excellent library. He left Aunt Maggie's novels entirely alone, it being his conviction that no one since Robert Louis Stevenson had written anything worth bothering with, and there were even some things of Stevenson's he thought pretty thin. Through the years he had accumulated a considerable library of military history. The science of war fascinated him, and he believed, entirely honest in his belief, that wars were inevitable. "Not only," he said, "because it is human nature to be aggressive, and the nature of the state is merely the nature of man in the aggregate, but because men really like war. Even Robert E. Lee was trying to gloss over his emotions when he said it was a good thing war was so terrible or men would come to like it too well. War isn't ever so terrible that it isn't the highest adventure a man ever has. Never does he live so buoyed up . . . so keenly alive in every nerve. Listen to any man who has ever fought in a war and you will hear in his voice a nostalgia, even a lovingness, as he recalls his experiences. The guns limbered . . . the sound of the shot and the smell of the smoke . . . the flag . . . the horses . . . the swords flashing. He has forgotten the death, the dirt, the disease; he remembers only the high, keen adventure of it, the taste of victory, and the good, good camaraderie. Brothers in arms . . . that is a term well conceived. As anomalous as it seems, it is on the battlefield that men come the closest to achieving brotherhood. It is the glimpsed face of death which binds men together . . . but it is death, of course, which gives life its great value. . . ." and here he would go off into philosophy.

He was familiar with, and I think could have been called an expert on, the strategy of every major campaign in military history. But it was, of course, the War between the States that interested him primarily. "We made so many mistakes," he would mourn, "so many. Gettysburg was tactically a well-planned battle . . . but Early wasn't the man for the left . . . and Longstreet was sulking. When he didn't get up in time, the center should never have been charged. It was too late . . . ." It was a hobby which he rode with great enthusiasm, and at the drop of a hat. I have often wondered if his opinion of war might not have altered had he lived to witness atomic fission.

It was at supper that evening that I finally spoke of my hand, which had grown increasingly painful all during the day. By now it was throbbing constantly and shooting small pains up to my wrist. I nursed it in my lap. "It hurts pretty much, Aunt Maggie."

"Darling!" she was all contrition, "we must look at it."

When the bandage was taken off, the hand looked red and had swollen considerably. There was a silence when she and Grandfather saw it. I knew they meant me not to be frightened, but I was when Aunt Maggie's face went white. "Papa . . . " she said.

"Yes. I'll call him immediately," and Grandfather left the room.

"Is it very bad?" I asked Aunt Maggie, wanting to be reassured.

"Oh," she said, trying to joke about it, "I've seen worse-looking hands . . . " and then abandoning the joke, "Katie . . . we must have left a little piece of bark or dirt inside the wound somehow, and it mustn't be left there. Grandfather is calling Doctor Clem. You *will* be brave, won't you?"

To be asked to be brave when one is only eight, and when one's mother is very far away, and when night is coming on, and when one knows that something is going to hurt . . . it was a pretty large order. I hid my face on her shoulder for a moment. "I'll try," I said.

"That's a good girl."

She put a fresh bandage on the hand and then we went into the sitting room. Grandfather was still at the telephone, which was the kind that hung on the wall and had to be cranked. He spoke to Aunt Maggie. "Clem isn't at home. I'm trying to get that nephew of his, now."

She merely nodded and led me to the couch. The sitting room was a comfortable room, furnished really with odds and ends. The chairs were old and deep-sunken, the leather couch sagging a little. There was a round table in the center of the room, covered with an India print cloth, littered always with papers and magazines, and the lamp which hung over it gave the best light of any lamp in the house. The walls were lined with Grandfather's books, and a braided rag rug covered the floor. Aunt Maggie and I sat side by side on the couch, her arm around me, and waited. Grandfather drummed on the slanted front of the telephone. "He wasn't at his office. Probably eating supper. I'm trying the boardinghouse. Hello! Hello, Jennie?" Grandfather always shouted into a telephone. It was as if there were no instrument and no wires and by main strength of voice he would make the listener hear him. "Jennie, is that young doctor there? Clem's nephew? Yes . . . let me speak to him, please." He turned and nodded at Aunt Maggie. "Got him, thank goodness. Doctor Davis? Yes . . . this is Chisholm Rogers. Can you make a house call right away? Yes . . . my grand-daughter is visiting us and she has hurt her hand . . . like to have you look at it . . ." There were little pauses between the words, Grandfather frowning as he listened. "Yes . . . yes, of course. As soon as possible, then

. . . thank you." He hung up the receiver. "He'll be here right away. Has to have his buggy brought around. Now, Punkin, it's going to be all right."

"Yes, sir," but I felt very forlorn, all gone in the stomach. I think my voice must have quavered a little.

Aunt Maggie smiled at me and gave my shoulders a little shake. "I'll tell you what we'll do. We'll go into the parlor and you can lie on the sofa and we'll have some music. We'll just forget that old hand for a while. Would you like me to sing for you?"

"Yes." I brightened.

So it happened that when Doctor Jim came Aunt Maggie was singing for me and I had truly forgotten my hand.

It was cool in the parlor, and the two lamps, at either end of the sofa, made a pool of light which, by the time it reached the piano in the opposite corner, was only a glow. They were beautiful lamps, exactly alike. They were tall and each stood on a brass base. They were a cloudy, milky white china, actually milk glass I suppose. But what was so exquisite about them was the way the violets were painted . . . netted together and shaded from the palest, faintest blue to the most lavish, rich purple. When the lamps were lit, the violets stood out, looking so fresh they seemed to be wet with dew, and one's hands imperatively reached to touch and gather them.

I lay upon the sofa, the violets blooming at my head and feet. The piano, across the room, gleamed blackly in the light, and Aunt Maggie, on the bench, was all flowing white draperies. She was wearing a soft, white mull dress, inset with narrow bands of net . . . no touch of color about it. The sleeves were long and full, gathered into a band of the net about the wrists, and a tiny ruching of net outlined the deep oval of the neck. It was a dress designed to bestow grace upon its wearer, and upon Aunt Maggie it did. Against the ebony of the piano she was like a Harrison Fisher drawing.

She had been singing gay things, things to make me laugh, silly verses set to music of her own improvising. She played well and easily, but not professionally well. To her the piano was a beautiful and necessary accompaniment to the voice, enriching it, sustaining it, strengthening it, but never equaling it. The voice was, to her, always the great medium of music. We had made a game of the songs, I saying the verses I liked and remembered, she developing a theme, then singing them. But my fountain had run dry, and her hands had moved idly over the keys until they had drifted, chord by chord, into some of the old ballads . . . "Annie Laurie," "The Rose of Tralee," "Vilia" . . . and she was singing "Kathleen Mavourneen" when I noticed the doctor standing in the door. I was startled, but not frightened, at seeing him. He made no move to come in, merely stood there, quiet and listening. It did not occur to me to interrupt Aunt Maggie myself, and I supposed the doctor to be simply extending the same courtesy I had been taught . . . never to disturb a musician. We had such reverence for music in our family, so much appreciation of the art of the performer, that even when I was asked to play my little pieces this same thoughtfulness was granted to me. It was the gentleness of good manners, good musical manners, and to this day I have no patience with people who chatter or eat and drink while someone is playing or singing. Music is to listen to, to hear, to absorb . . . and I do not like it as a background for conversation or for dining. The doctor would have to wait.

But he did not. As if impelled, pulled, he laid down his hat and bag and slowly left the doorway. Halfway across the room his voice was joined with Aunt Maggie's . . . "I will take you back again . . . to where your heart will feel no pain . . ." Aunt Maggie glanced quickly over her shoulder and her fingers stumbled, but not her voice. She smiled, and the song went on, the two voices perfectly blended, "And when the fields are fresh and green . . . I'll take you to your home again."

"Beautiful, Miss Maggie . . . beautiful," said the doctor, applauding.

Aunt Maggie rose and her skirts spread like

flower petals around her. "Thank you," she said.

The doctor's eyes swept over her. "You look . . . different."

"I am not wearing my prison bars tonight." Aunt Maggie said. They had, of course, seen each other many times during the few months Doctor Jim had been living in Stanwick. The doctor must have called daily at the post office for his mail, and they must have spoken together often. "Now that you remind me," he laughed, "I think I have never seen you except at the post office. But your voice. It *is* good. I had been told it was."

"It is good enough for 'Kathleen Mavourneen,' " Aunt Maggie said, shrugging, "and for the church choir."

Grandfather appeared in the doorway. "Maggie?"

Aunt Maggie turned to him swiftly. "Oh, Papa. You know Doctor Jim Davis, don't you?"

"Of course." The two men met to shake hands in the center of the room, Grandfather a head and shoulders shorter than Doctor Jim. "And this is Katie, my granddaughter, whom we called you to see."

"Ah, yes . . . of course. Well, we'll just have a look at that hand, now, Katie."

I sat up on the sofa and held it out. My heart was thudding very hard and I felt as if it were going to choke me. Now it was coming

. . . the hurting. I was terribly afraid.

Aunt Maggie unwound the bandage and Doctor Jim looked at the hand. He pressed it very gently all around, Grandfather and Aunt Maggie watching, the room grown suddenly very still. Under the lamp the doctor's hair was so black it looked almost purple. His face was lean and olive, with that kind of flawlessly smooth skin which looks rubbed, with a flush of coloring showing through on the cheekbones. When he looked up at me his eyes were very dark, almost as dark as my grandmother's, with a slant at the corners. But the thing which was unusual about Doctor Jim's eyes was that his eyelids, while being sleepy and heavy looking, had a kind of wrinkled stitch in the center which pulled them up in a triangular sort of way. It game him an odd look, a rather whimsical look, as if he were secretly amused at something all the time. "I think," he said finally, "there is something still in the wound. How did she do it?"

Aunt Maggie explained. Doctor Jim nodded. "Probably a bit of bark, then. I'll need boiling water, Miss Maggie, a good light . . . a table. Perhaps the kitchen?"

"Yes."

We went to the kitchen and Grandfather built up a quick, hot fire. Aunt Maggie arranged the table and lamp, put the kettle on to boil and then sat down, taking me on her lap. It all felt very nightmarish to me; the stripped table, the lamp, the tall doctor, the fire when the night was already so hot. It didn't seem very real. Only my own thudding heart and queasy stomach were real, solid, right at the center of me. I tried very hard to be good. I wanted so much to be brave; but I have always been short on physical courage and I had none to spare that night. When the time came and I saw the lancet and the probe, so sharp and so steely bright, I began to whimper and shrink in spite of myself. Grandfather and Aunt Maggie soothed and pled . . . "Katie, darling, it won't hurt much . . . truly it won't. It will be over in just a second. Be a good girl, now, darling . . "

Timidly I would hold out my hand, but before the doctor could touch it I would jerk it back again. Finally, losing patience after half a dozen repetitions of this sort of thing, he said. "You'll have to hold her. Just hold her tight, Mr. Rogers, and as still as possible."

At that I went completely to pieces. To be compelled, to be held, that was unendurable. I began screaming and crying and struggling, absolutely frantic with fear.

Oddly enough it was Grandmother who quieted me. She came into the room, into the midst of the uproar, and looked at us. "What *is* all this disturbance?"

Aunt Maggie was crying, too, by this time

and she tearfully explained. "Nonsense," Grandmother said, "you're all a pack of idiots, all of you. She doesn't have to be held. Katherine?" and she seated herself beside the table. There was something in her voice, so dry and calm and lightly brittle, something in her manner, so dispassionate and entirely quiet, which made me obey. Snubbing my sobs I went to her. She placed her arm about my shoulder. "When a thing has to be done, Katherine, it's best to get it over with as quickly as possible. Now, hold out your hand . . . on the table, dear, under the light. Hold very still." And I did it.

It was my first experience with the odd fact that love, suffering with one, frequently merely prolongs the suffering. That what appears on the surface to be harsh and unfeeling insensitivity may actually be kinder in the long run. Grandfather and Aunt Maggie had been lovingly suffering with me, dreading the pain for me, nerving themselves along with me to meet the hurt. Grandmother simply made me face the inevitable.

Doctor Jim held up a tiny bit of bark between the prongs of his probe. "That was the troublemaker," he said.

Grandmother patted my shoulder and left the room, saying not another word.

When the hand was dressed Doctor Jim told Aunt Maggie, "Let it soak for half an hour in the morning, and again in the afternoon in hot salts water. Don't remove the dressing. Just soak it the way it is. Do you have Epsom salts?''

''Yes.''

''Good. I'll look in again tomorrow evening to make sure the infection is checked.''

He had removed his coat to work and Grandfather held it for him now as he slipped into it. ''We appreciate your interrupting your supper to come, Doctor . . . by George, Maggie, at least we can feed the man!''

''Of course,'' Aunt Maggie said, rising hastily.

''Oh, no. No, I wouldn't think of troubling you.''

''It would be no trouble,'' Aunt Maggie assured him.

''No, I had finished . . . really, I had.''

''A glass of wine, then?'' Grandfather asked.

''That, sir,'' the doctor bowed, laughing, ''I shall not refuse.''

Grandfather poured the small glasses. The doctor raised his to the light, turning it slowly. The wine looked rich and red, the glass thin and fragile in his long fingers. ''*Aqua vitae* . . .'' he said, a smile twitching his lips, ''the water of life.'' He turned to Grandfather, then to Aunt Maggie. ''Sir . . . Miss Maggie . . . to Katie's hand,'' and because Grandfather was across the room by the cupboard, only Aunt Maggie and I heard him add, almost whispering, "bless it!"

I thought it a very queer toast; not at all like Grandfather's wives and sweethearts, and I wondered that Aunt Maggie's face should flush so suddenly red.

Six

Grandmother bathed my hand the next morning, for on Monday Aunt Maggie had to be at the post office very early. It was the heaviest mail day of the week, naturally. I watched her dress and then trailed downstairs after her. The hand was still sore and stiff, but it no longer throbbed as painfully as it had the day before. We found Grandmother in her room. "Mother, you won't forget Katie's hand, will you?"

Grandmother was stripping the linen from the beds. She was very trim and tidy in her housedress. She never wore colors. Her dresses were always black or white, but on weekday mornings, when she was busy around the house, she did wear a patterned percale, stiffly starched of course. It was always either white with a small, neat, black figure, or black with a white print. Aunt Maggie had brought her a beautiful lavender silk from New York once, thinking it would be so lovely with her white hair, and she had exclaimed over its beauty; but she had hung it away in her wardrobe and, to the best of my knowledge, had never worn it.

The beds looked very big and bare stripped of their coverings. There were two of them, exactly alike, big double beds of dark walnut, standing very tall with heavy carved posts. They were placed against the inner wall with a rather large table between them. A lamp stood on the table, and on Grandfather's side was a small tray for his watch, cuff links, and the contents of his pockets which he placed there at night. On Grandmother's side was a little clock, a very beautiful French clock, gold, inlaid with pearl. Her father had bought it for her in Paris when she was a little girl. Beside it was her Bible. The Bible, which was badly worn, had been a gift of her mother. Grandmother read the Bible entirely through every year . . . so many chapters each day, and then at the New Year beginning all over again. It would have confused her, I'm sure, to pick up her Bible and read it wherever it happened to fall open, or to choose especially a given chapter and verse. She knew exactly from one day to the next, from one month to the next, where she was in her Bible. If the Twenty-Third Psalm had fallen at any time except in July, I doubt if it would have seemed familiar to her.

There were also two dressers in the room, tall and dark like the beds, with small drawers mounted on the tops on either side. A wardrobe ranged beside each dresser. The two washstands stood under the windows. Before the fireplace were two chairs, Grandmother's small, high-backed rocker with the red plush seat, and Grandfather's big, velvet-covered Morris chair. That chair used to fascinate me, and I loved to move the rod in the grooves at the back and try it in different positions.

Grandfather's interest in military history extended to guns and he had a very fine collection of them. They were kept in a big, glass-fronted cabinet which stood in the chimney corner. I think he must have had at least fifty guns of every make and kind, from rusty old muskets to modern revolvers. He was very proud of it, and it was one of Grandmother's frustrations that he was forever taking someone into the bedroom to look at the collection. "Well, there isn't room for it anywhere else," he always said when she fussed. She saw no reason for it at all, of course, but if he had to collect guns she thought they might very well be relegated to the attic or the hall. But Grandfather would have none of that, so they accumulated in the cabinet in their bedroom.

Grandmother looked up from her task. "Of

course I won't forget, Margaret. But there's no hurry about it, is there? I want to get Lulie started on the wash." Monday was, of course, washday.

"No, there's no hurry. Just be sure it gets done sometime during the morning. Coming to the gate with me, Katie?"

I walked to the gate with her. It was my right hand which was hurt and I was troubled about writing to my father and mother. "I promised, Aunt Maggie," I told her, "and they'll be expecting a letter very soon."

Aunt Maggie pinched her lower lip with her fingers. "I wish they needn't know about your hand . . . I'm afraid your mother will worry."

"But I promised," I insisted.

"All right, dear." She raised the parasol. No one in Stanwick wore a hat in the summertime, except to church. All the women carried sunshades. "I'l send them a note. After all, your hand *is* better, isn't it?"

"Oh, it's much better. You can tell Mother so she won't worry."

"I doubt that . . . but since you promised, it can't be helped." She bent and kissed me lightly on the cheek. "Now, Katie . . . be careful. Don't hurt your hand . . . and don't, don't climb the mulberry tree today."

I solemnly promised, crossing my heart, and ran, hurrying, back to the house. I wanted to help Lulie with the wash.

All my life I have loved Monday. It has a

stir and a bustle about it quite unlike any other day of the week; a picking up, a coming to life as it were, after the hiatus of Sunday. Blue Monday, I have heard others call it. It is never so for me. I greet Monday joyously, excited by a new day and a new week, happy to be back in the rhythm of the daily routine. It was especially so when I was a child, because children, I think, live so much of the time in a jungle of feelings, and they seem to know instinctively that both rhythm and routine are safe and secure. If Monday morning had not been washday I should have been shaken down to the tips of my toes. The entire day would have been awry.

Lulie had finished the dishes and was in the wash house when I got back. This was a kind of lattice-enclosed structure near the well in the backyard. It had a brick floor, and benches all around for the tubs. At one end was a chimney, and a big, black kettle hung over the fire, suspended from a crane. The water was already steaming. The laundry was heaped in huge baskets, sorted already by my grandmother's hand. Lulie was rubbing out white clothes, bent over the washboard, her yellow arms up to the elbows in suds. "Angie always let me put them in the kettle," I told her.

"She did? You know how to drop 'em in so's they won't splash on you?"

"Of course," I said haughtily, "I've been

doing it for years."

Lulie giggled. "Not so many, I reckon. You ain't that old."

"Well, last year, anyway. And I *think* the year before."

"Well, all right. Here. Here's one of your Aunt Maggie's petticoats. Now you be careful. Shake it out so's it won't be all wadded up. And don't get soot on it, neither. I don't wanna be rubbing things out more'n once."

She sounded just like Angie . . . gruff and scoldy. Many Negro women scold in that fashion. I was too young to know, then, that it is their way when they feel comfortable and at ease with you, fond of you and willing to be patient. I only knew that Lulie set me at ease myself, and that I felt she was going to be every bit as nice as Angie.

I shook out the big, ruffled petticoat carefully and slid it into the hot suds in the kettle, poking it down into the water with the wooden paddle kept handy for that purpose. The paddle was worn smooth as steel and bleached almost white from having stirred hundreds of kettles full of Rogers' clothing. Dreamily I stirred it round and round, watching the froth of the petticoat bubble and sink, rise and bubble and sink again, feeling the slick wood of the paddle under my palm, half hypnotized by the bubbling and rising and sinking and the slow round and round motion of the paddle. I was always going off into those trances of concentration, drawn into them by movement or feeling or sound. Lulie recalled me. "Here's your little underbody."

When I had slid it into the water I went back to stand beside her. "Did you go to the meeting last night?"

She nodded. "Sho' did. Me'n Choctaw."

"Was it nice?"

"Sho' was. They commencing to get the spirit already. Was a heap of shouting and singing last night. Takes you right up and out the top of the tent, might' near. Was one woman, I dunno who she was, commenced talking in tongues and dancing and singing and shaking all over. Got ever'body started."

"You and Choctaw, too?"

Lulie laughed. "I don't reckon the old devil hisself could get Choctaw worked up, but it kind of warmed me a little."

"I wish I could go."

Lulie slewed her eyes at me. "Whut you wanna go for?"

"I'd like to see the people getting the spirit and singing and dancing. They don't do that in our church."

"Naw," Lulie said, "don't nobody but colored folks know much about religion."

"Why, Lulie?"

She shrugged. "I dunno. Don't seem to me like white folks ever get much fun out of it.

Don't let theirselves go."

"I don't believe white people think religion is meant to be fun, Lulie."

"Don't see why not. Don't see why singing and shouting and praising the Lord ain't as much fun as anything else."

It puzzled me. "Well, I don't see why not, either . . . but it's always very solemn and quiet, and . . . ." I suddenly confided, "a little bit scary."

"What's scary about it?"

"Oh, I don't know . : . sin and hell and God always watching, and everything. And if he puts down a black mark every time you do something bad, Lulie . . . ."

"I don't believe it."

"You don't believe he puts down a black mark?"

"Naw. He got too much else to do running the world. What he want to bother hisself with putting down black marks? Wouldn't have time for nothing else. He got to raise up the sun and pull it down, and raise up the moon and stars and make the rain. He got more important things to do than putting down black marks."

"But, Lulie . . . he's got to know who to save and who to send to hell, doesn't he?"

"Don't believe he gonna send folks to hell."

"Not going to send folks to hell!" I was aghast. "But it says in the Bible . . . ."

"It say in the Bible he a good God, don't

111

it? Wouldn't no good God dream up no such way of punishing folks. Naw, that some mean old man think that up. I don't believe no such. Never was nobody so mean wasn't some good in 'em, and it's my notion the Lord gonna see the good instead of the bad. Anyways, that's all in the Old Testament. That don't count no more. We is in a new . . . in a new . . .," she came out with it triumphantly, "in a new dispensation."

"How do you know?"

"It say so, right in the front of my New Testament. It say so . . . and it say don't nothing count but Jesus no more. Don't none of that old religion stuff count no more."

I was vastly comforted. Jesus, I thought, could be depended upon to understand. He was the one who had loved little children. It was God of whom I was frightened. My parents would have been horrified had they known I had these feelings and fears, but it had never occurred to me to discuss it with them. I was sent to Sunday School where I was taught by a succession of good, well-intentioned women, whom I confidently believed; and I went to church and sat there, with rapidly beating heart and sinking stomach and thought that here was just another of those inexplicable things with which one was burdened, which had to be accepted as so many other things in the grown-up world had to be accepted . . .

frightening, terrible things, but inevitable. I had been baptized, it was true, but one could fall from grace, and goodness knew how many times I might have fallen already, not knowing how to rise again. Lulie gave me hope.

Choctaw came up with an armful of wood for the fire. "Morning, Katie. How's your hand?"

I wiggled it. "It's better, thank you."

Lulie laughed. "She helping me with the washing."

"She's a big help, I reckon."

"She do fine. Run backards and forrards . . . save me steps." She looked at Choctaw from the side of her eyes and laughed again. "She wanna go to meeting with us."

Choctaw looked at me speculatively. "I don't know about that."

"I wouldn't care if you wouldn't."

"Oh, I wouldn't care. It's not that. But I don't reckon they'd let her go."

"Grandfather would," I said.

"Yeah . . . reckon he would. Miss Maggie might . . . but your grandma, she wouldn't never."

"If Grandfather and Aunt Maggie said so, she would. She doesn't say what I can do, anyhow."

Choctaw was standing on the other side of Lulie, but I saw his hand slide down the flat of her hip. Lulie hitched her hip away, but

Choctaw leaned closer and reached his hand into the suds. Lulie slapped at him. "Get your dirty hands out of my wash water!"

But leaning had brought the length of his body into contact with Lulie, and the reaching arm had gone around her. I was as quick as any other child to sense an advantage and press it home. I knew that Choctaw was barely aware of my presence . . . just enough aware of it to be a little cautious. He might promise anything now. "If you'll ask him, Choctaw . . ."

His head was bent and I guessed that he was kissing Lulie's neck. They both stood very still. When he lifted his head finally his eyes looked at me over Lulie's shoulder, met mine without actually seeing me. He had a sort of blind, glazed look on his face. "If you'd ask him . . ." I said.

The eyes cleared a little. "Ask who, Katie? What?"

"If you'd ask Grandfather if I can go to the meeting with you and Lulie . . ."

He shook his head, quickly, as if to rid it of unsteadiness. "All right, I'll ask him." And he walked away from the wash house.

"Lulie . . . Lulie," I tugged at her apron, and bent around to see her face. One breast, as ripe and as round as a melon, was still half bare, and the dress around it was wet from Choctaw's hand. She shrugged the dress into place. "Lulie, don't let him forget, will you?

He'll not remember if you don't remind him."

She took a deep breath and wet her lips. "All right, baby. I'll not let him forget."

"Promise?"

"I promise." She laughed suddenly. "You wasn't born yesterday, was you, Katie?"

"No," I said sturdily, "I'm pretty smart."

"You smart enough, you reckon, not to run and tell things you see?"

"Oh, yes," I said, adding unashamedly, "if I get to go to the meeting."

She laughed again, understanding perfectly and not minding the bit of blackmail. "You'll get to go."

Grandmother came for me then, to bathe my hand.

She had placed the basin of hot water on a low table, a chair beside it, in the kitchen. "Would you like something to read, Katherine? Thirty minutes may seem a rather long time to sit idly."

"Yes, please, Grandmother."

"Run along, then, and choose something from your Grandfather's shelves."

What should it be? I stood before the rows of books, undecided, all of their bindings, all of their titles, alluring. I cannnot remember when I did not have a love for books amounting to reverence; my passion for reading is so deep that it is actually an addiction, like the drug habit. I would read the telephone directory if nothing else were available. But not only is opening a book, any book, any time, an adventure which makes my pulse beat faster, I love books also for their own sake. I like to hold in my hand a beautiful book, feel its quality and texture, smell it and, I can think of no better word, love it. I particularly love the old leather bindings, such as those on my grandfather's shelves, and I particularly love, too, the heavy, torn paper and the exquisite type which many of them had. A beautiful book is truly a work of art.

What should it be? Scott? Thackeray? Trollope? Brontë? Tentatively I took down *Madame Bovary*. I knew Grandfather greatly appreciated Flaubert. But the text was in French. Regretfully I put it back. The Dickens shelf was next, and with a kind of homing instinct I picked out *David Copperfield*. I had read it twice already, but it was always irresistible.

Grandmother was making apple pies from the first of the early apples. Some were already in the oven, for I could smell them . . . tangy and rich with spices and butter. They made me very hungry and I hoped I could have a piece, hot, when they came out. She was finishing up two more. Grandmother did everything neatly, tidily. She worked, now, swiftly, rolling the dough, spreading it in the pans, heaping the sliced apples and covering them, then pinching the crusts together and trimming them. There were no wasted motions, and there was no untidy mess. Aunt Maggie would have had pots and pans all over the kitchen, with flour and apple peelings helter-skelter; but Aunt Maggie would also have been chattering to me the whole time. Grandmother worked silently. I turned to my book and I think each of us forgot the other.

It was Aunt Maggie who aroused us. We heard her coming down the hall, her heels clicking rapidly in her hurry, and then she came flying into the kitchen, her arms full of papers, magazines and letters. She looked hot, her hair flyaway and rumpled. "*Such* a morning! Everyone, and all their aunts and uncles wanting money orders . . . and the mail! Three sacks full, and the Sunday papers. Everyone crowding. Neither Thomas nor I have stopped for a good breath all morning." She laid the load of mail on the table and sorted through until she came to a letter which she held out to me. "Katie . . . for you."

"Oh . . ." and I started up, forgetting my hand. The wet bandage dripped a stream of water down my front and onto the floor.

"Wait, Katherine," Grandmother said, and she darted for towels.

Aunt Maggie came over and dipped a finger into the basin of water. "Why, Mother, the water is cold. How long has she been soaking her hand?"

Grandmother wrapped a small towel around my hand, and then she stooped to mop up the water on the floor. She laughed, a little uneasily. "I'm afraid I don't know, Margaret. I was busy with the pies. But the water was quite hot to begin with."

Aunt Maggie laughed. "Well, that hand has had a good soaking, I'd say. No harm done, I suppose." She took my letter. "Here, darling, let me open it for you."

It was, of course, from my mother. I read it aloud. Everything was fine . . . she and Papa were both well . . . Papa was working very hard on his thesis . . . it must be ready to present to his committee by fall . . . the kitten was polishing his nose as she wrote . . . the heat was not too bad, yet, and Papa's garden was looking fine . . . she hoped I had had a nice journey, and I must have a wonderful, wonderful time. The house seemed very big and lonely without me, and she kept thinking Katie would come bouncing into her room . . . she was feeling very specially good and the new little brother, he *was* going to be a little brother, he simply *had* to be a little brother, was behaving himself beautifully.

I had such a lump in my throat I could not go on reading. It was such a dear, dear letter, and it brought them, my mother and my father, the kitten and the big, familiar rooms, so close. I wished I could fly straight home to them . . . and the little brother. "How is my mother ever going to have this baby without me?" I said, choking down the lump.

Grandmother made a funny noise in her throat, and I looked at her. Aunt Maggie looked at her, too. Grandmother was frowning and her mouth was crimped into a tight line. "Much better without you than with you, my dear," she said. Then to Aunt Maggie, "I *wish* Katherine had more sense of the seemly. To discuss such things with a child is . . . it is," and her nostrils flared, "well, it is extremely bad taste, to say the least."

I could not allow that. "But my mother thinks I am old enough to know."

Grandmother's fingers drummed on the table top. "One ought *never* to have to know!"

"Well, really, Mother," Aunt Maggie said, laughing a little, "facts are facts."

"Unfortunately, yes. But," and her voice shook, "I will never forgive God for making them necessary . . . never!" She swept out of the room.

Aunt Maggie and I looked at each other, amazed. What on earth had called that forth? Aunt Maggie's face had a dark shine of heat on it, and her eyes looked tired, but she smiled at me. Then she raised her hands, smoothed back her hair and shook her head a little. "Never mind, baby. Read the rest of your letter."

"There isn't much more. Just give you her love, Grandmother, Grandfather, everyone . . . and write often."

"And she is lovingly, your mother."

"Yes."

"She writes such a nice letter, doesn't she?"

"Yes."

Aunt Maggie bit her lip. "Your mother is a very lovely lady, Katie."

"Oh, I know."

"And she is very wise."

"Yes, of course."

"Wiser, sometimes, Katie, than your grandmother."

I bent my head and looked at my toes, a little confused. Of course my mother was wiser than Grandmother . . . I never doubted it. Then suddenly I knew what Aunt Maggie was trying to tell me; that my mother was right to tell me, and that I must not let Grandmother's little outburst bother me. I looked up and smiled at her. "I think so, too."

The doctor did not come until after supper that night. We were in the sitting room and it had grown dark enough to light the lamp. I was standing at the open window, my elbows propped on the sill, my chin in my hand, watching the last pale glow of the sunset fade from the sky, watching it turn purple with the oncoming night. Suddenly, in the east, there was the first star. It was what I had been waiting for. It was a kind of ritual with me, to watch for the first star, and to chant to myself the old rhyme, "Star bright, star light, first star I've seen tonight; wish I may, wish I might, have the wish I wish tonight." To wish, then, with eyes closed, wish with great concentration, and to turn resolutely away from the star. For if you looked at the star again after wishing, the wish would not come true.

I always wished for very small, practical things, such as buckwheat cakes, and honey for breakfast, or for new jacks and ball, or that I might be allowed to wear my new blue taffeta to church. I never tempted the stars with a really big or important wish. One *prayed* for important things, such as the sun shining for a picnic, or being allowed to come to Grandfather's this summer, or most important of all, that the new baby might really be a little brother. I had some dim feeling that I should rely upon something greater than the stars for truly important things, so I only trusted them with small things, over which the disappointment would be very slight. I thought hard and hard what to wish. Should I wish that I be allowed to go to the meeting with Lulie and Choctaw? No . . . that was too important. My mind scurried away from it. That doesn't count, I told the star, I was only thinking. That I could have a tea party in the plum thicket the next day? That wasn't much of a wish. I could have a tea party any day I pleased without wasting a wish on it. Should I wish it would rain so I could play in the attic? But rain was something I didn't like to tamper with. It meant so much to Grandfather and Choctaw and all the other farmers. They might not like it to rain. Very faintly I heard the soft clop of horse's feet coming down the road. Oh, hurry . . . the doctor is coming. I squeezed my eyes tightly together to think faster. What . . . what should I wish? What could tomorrow bring that would be fun, but not too important? Tuesday . . . it would be ironing day. Suddenly, with relief, I wished . . . I wished Lulie would let me iron the handkerchiefs. Then I turned away from the window and opened my eyes. "The doctor is coming." To this good day I do not like to tempt life by asking too much.

Grandfather went to meet him and brought him into the sitting room. Grandmother was sewing, Aunt Maggie laid down her book. "I hope," Doctor Jim said, "this is not inconvenient for you. I was kept late out in the country."

He looked a little rumpled, a little hot, and very tired. "Was it a baby?" I asked. I was very baby-conscious.

"Katherine." It was Grandmother, admonishing.

Doctor Jim smiled at me. He had a very winsome smile. It broke and softened the lines of his face and made him look, somehow, very young. For that matter, his mouth, even in repose, gave his whole face a gentler look. It was a sweet mouth, oddly incongruous with the rest of his face, such a mouth as one sees frequently on a small boy, mobile, full-lipped, and when he smiled he was very engaging. "Yes," he said, "it was a baby," adding dryly to Grandfather, "the Thornberrys' . . . their ninth, I believe."

"And you'll never get a dime for it," Grandfather said.

"I suppose not," the doctor shrugged. "Well, Katie, let's have a look at that hand."

It was still swollen and still red, but when he pressed it, either I was much braver than I had been the night before, or else it truly was not as sore as it had been. There was, however, a slight oozing from the wound, over which he frowned. He cleansed it and shook some powder on it before bandaging it freshly. "The infection is localized," he said, "but it will have to be watched carefully. You used the hot bath today?"

"Yes, of course," Aunt Maggie said.

"Good. Continue that tomorrow."

I had my nose poked into his open bag. It was all mixed up, the smell of the bag. It was bitter and pungent and dry and musty and sharp and sweet. "What's sweet?" I asked, looking up at him.

"Anise," he said, smiling.

I sniffed again. "What's bitter?"

"Quinine."

"What's . . .?" but I could not think of the word. I wrinkled my nose trying to recover the feel of the penetrating sharpness.

Doctor Jim laughed. "I think only alcohol could cause that kind of a face."

"Katie,' Aunt Maggie warned, and I shut the bag and held it out to the doctor. "I wonder," she went on, "why doctors' bags always fascinate everyone?

"Do they?" He set the bag on the floor. "I must be the exception to the rule, then. They don't fascinate me." He moved to one of the big, leather chairs and sat down in it, leaned his head against the back of it and rubbed his hand over his face. "Lord, I don't know when I've been so tired. The heat, I suppose . . . but it's been a long day."

Grandmother laid down her sewing and slipped out through the dining room. Grandfather lit his pipe and pulled it to a glow. "You are not accustomed to the summer heat?"

"Oh, yes. Yes, it gets very hot in New York. But you have such a brilliant sun down here. I think it is the glare which bothers me more than the heat."

Grandfather nodded toward his hat which had been flung down on the table. "Better

124

get you one of those. That wider brim will help."

Doctor Jim picked it up and looked at it, turning it around in his hands. "It's a very beautiful felt. You don't get them here, do you?"

"No. I order them." He stood up. "I have a new one. Let me get it and you can try it on."

But the hat which was so right for Grandfather was ludicrous on Doctor Jim. He was too lean, too tall and angular, or perhaps he simply wore the East too obviously. He looked at himself in the mirror which hung over the fireplace and burst out laughing. "All I need," he said, "is a pair of boots and a six-shooter," and he burlesqued a bowlegged cow hand with a low-hanging gun on his hip. "No," he took the hat off and handed it back to Grandfather, "it's not for me."

Grandmother came in, then, with a tray of sandwiches, some coffee and a plate of apple pie. "Food is what you need, I think," she said, setting the tray on the table at his elbow. "I doubt you've eaten properly today."

He looked at the food. "That does look good." He sat at the table, spread the napkin and took up a sandwich, biting into it. "If I had lunch today I've forgotten it, and supper was a couple of greasy eggs the oldest Thornberry girl fried . . . and corn bread. Tell me, does everyone in this country eat corn bread three times a day?"

"Well, not exactly," Aunt Maggie said, laughing, "but we have it pretty often. I missed it in New York." The sandwich stopped halfway to his mouth and he looked at her. "I studied music there for nearly four years," she added.

He nodded. "I should have known. Come to think of it I believe I have heard it mentioned at the boardinghouse, but it didn't register at the time." He lifted his cup and drank. "There is one thing I must admit, however. You make the best coffee in the world down this way."

"But Doctor Davis," Grandmother interrupted, "you've had no opportunity to know what really good Southern cooking is. Jennie does well enough, I suppose, but no boardinghouse can offer you a really fine meal."

The doctor took a bite of the pie. "I'm beginning to think you're right."

"Are you calling to see Katherine's hand again tomorrow?"

"Oh, yes."

"Then we shall expect you to have dinner with us."

Grandfather chuckled. "Emily's pride is up in arms now, sir, you'll have to give her satisfaction."

"I shall be glad to," the doctor said.

"Is there any more of that coffee, Emily?" Grandfather asked.

"Yes, Mr. Rogers, but you had coffee for dinner and if you drink another cup now you won't sleep well tonight."

"Well, I think it would be worth it. It smells too tantalizing. Maggie?"

Aunt Maggie nodded. "I believe so. Mother, I'll get it."

"No, no. Sit still."

"Have you got pretty well broken to harness by now, Doctor Davis?"

"My name is Jim, sir. People are beginning to call me Doctor Jim, to distinguish me from my uncle. He's the real Doctor Davis."

"Well, Clem's been Doctor Davis for a good many years around here. And if folks are calling you Doctor Jim instead of 'that young squirt' it is a mark of esteem."

"I take it that way, sir. Yes, things are settling down very well, I think. Uncle Clem has been thoughtful in every way. He went the rounds of the regular patients with me, gave the people to understand they could have confidence in me. I run into a few yet who won't have anyone but him, that's understandable."

Grandfather nodded. "It takes time. It means a lot to Clem to have you come here and take over. He'd have hated having to turn his people over to a stranger."

Grandmother brought the coffee for Grandfather and Aunt Maggie, and then went to her room, nodding a goodnight to the doctor. Grandfather sugared his and stirred it. "Have you always lived in New York?" he asked.

"Oh, no. I was born and reared in Ohio. But I was in New York for about ten years before coming here. Took my training there."

"This is quite a change for you, then."

"Yes. I wondered," he said, laughing, "how the people here would take to a Yankee, but Uncle Clem said the War had been forgotten long ago."

Grandfather snorted. "Humph. Clem's a Yankee himself or he'd never have said such a thing. It will never be forgotten while any of us live who remember. What has been forgotten, however, are old grudges. A gentleman is a gentleman wherever he is from."

"It helps, though," I spoke up suddenly, remembering something Grandfather had said once, "if he is a Southerner, a Democrat, and a National League baseball fan."

There was a startled silence in the room, and my words seemed to grow very loud, spreading and rippling to the walls and back again, coming to echo in my ears. One by one I listened to them and was horrified. All at once I knew I shouldn't have said that. I knew it was something said only within the family, or, teasingly, to someone one was very sure of. I knew it was the kind of thing shared only with one's own kind . . . understood only by one's own kind. I was so ashamed I squirmed around to duck behind Aunt Maggie.

But then the doctor threw his head back and roared with laughter, and, chagrined, Grandfather joined in with his own quiet, shoulder-shaking chuckle. "You're caught out, sir," the doctor said, when he could speak, "and I can't qualify. I am frankly a Yankee, a Republican, and sir," he shook his finger at Grandfather, "if any team in the American League can't lick the best team in the National League . . ."

"Wha-a-a-t?" Grandfather bellowed.

"Oh, for heaven's sake," Aunt Maggie said, standing suddenly, her cup tinkling in the saucer, "don't, don't let's get started on the War, politics, or baseball! You'll be at sword's points in no time at all."

The doctor stood, too. "I'm sorry, Miss Maggie. But I do love a good argument, and your father tempts me."

"He does most people. He delights in duels with words."

"Best way in the world to keep your wits sharp," Grandfather said.

"I agree. We'll have it out one of these days, sir." Doctor Jim laid his napkin on the table. "I must go. Thank your wife for the supper, sir. It was exactly what I needed."

"She'll be very happy about that. We'll be looking for you, then, tomorrow evening. We eat about seven in the summer."

"I'll be here, and I look forward to it. It's very kind of you to have me."

"Nonsense. Should have thought of it sooner."

We were all standing now. Aunt Maggie put her arm around my shoulder. "Katie and I will walk you to the gate. It's so still and warm tonight, I want a breath of air."

We walked very slowly toward the gate. The moon was up, just past the first quarter, silvering the old rail fence and massing the trees down the road darkly against the lighter sky. The road itself was a white unwinding, disappearing mysteriously into the yawning mouth of the trees.

The path was crowded with three, so I stepped out into the grass, holding with my good hand to Aunt Maggie. The grass was wet and in the moonlight the dew looked like frost. I kicked my feet along and slid them and let the damp reach up to my ankles. My feet were as silvered as the grass and I thought silver must feel like it looked, gleamy and damp and cool.

Neither Aunt Maggie nor the doctor said anything . . . just walked slowly, their feet making small clicks on the stones. Aunt Maggie's starched petticoats rustled a little, and with her movements there came small, sweet rushes of the odor of verbena, mixed with the tobacco smell of the doctor — but the verbena was the stronger. Over all there was the heavy odor of the honeysuckle which covered the orchard fence, and over all the smells was the feeling of the dew and the grass and the bright gloss of the moonlight.

At the gate they stopped. The doctor propped one foot along the lowest rail and laid his arms along the top. Aunt Maggie leaned her chin in her hands. "Do you remember," the doctor said, very softly, "the arch in the Square by moonlight?"

Aunt Maggie's head bent lower. "Yes. It was frozen . . . but somehow *warmly* frozen. Do you remember it in rain? In snow?"

"In every season . . . in every kind of weather. And the green of the trees in the spring . . ."

"The tenderest green in the world. And the lights going on up the Avenue just at twilight . . ."

"And the slick of the pavement in the rain at night . . ."

"And the Italian with his hurdy-gurdy there by the Garibaldi on Sunday afternoons . . ."

"And the smell of the river on an east wind . . ."

"Yes."

Washington Square had changed much by the time I saw it . . . by the time I made my pilgrimage there and tried to recover what they had remembered. But it was not difficult . . . it was not difficult at all to close my eyes to what was actually there and see only what they had seen. Hurried as I was I chose the twilight hour, and, I'm afraid, kept a kind dinner host waiting, to stand and shut the din of traffic from my ears, to watch the lights come on and to people the Avenue with horse-drawn cabs and carriages, with ladies in long, sweeping dresses, on the arms of gallant escorts. I stook where Aunt Maggie must have stood a thousand times, and looked upon the tenderest green in the world, and I did not hear taxis and trucks and buses. I heard a hurdy-gurdy, slight and thin and diminishing as the Italian wound it slower and slower, walking away. No, it was not difficult to know what they had remembered.

But that night I could only feel the sadness in their voices, and when they had stopped talking I looked up at them. In the moonlight the doctor's face was lifted, leanly lined, coppery, sharp-drawn. It looked like the silhouette of the Indian head on a penny. Aunt Maggie's face was shadowed, her head bent yet, and the shine of the moon lay like a white wrap about her shoulders. Then the doctor lifted the latch of the gate. "Good-night . . . Maggie." Even to me it sounded right for him to call her that.

We stood at the gate, saying nothing. We watched him untie his horse and get into the buggy, heard the buggy creak as he turned it, listened to the soft, muffled clop of the horse's feet in the dust, watched as he moved down the road until finally they were swallowed up in the mouth of the dark trees.

Seven

Tuesday was such a busy day. It began at breakfast with Grandmother, pencil in hand, consulting Aunt Maggie about dinner for the doctor. We had finished except for the last bites of jam and biscuits. "Margaret, let me talk to you about the menu for tonight."

"I haven't much time, Mother."

"It will only take a moment. Shall we have chicken or guinea? The young guineas would be fine, I think."

Grandfather raised his eyebrows, but the chickens, guineas and turkeys about the place were her province, so he said nothing.

"They're so small to kill, don't you think?" Aunt Maggie said.

"What does it matter whether they're small or large to kill? I raise them for us to eat. They're as large as partridges, and half a dozen of them, done to a turn and then simmered in sherry . . . yes, I think the guineas." She jotted it down. "Biscuits, of course, and . . ." she looked at Aunt Maggie, "shall I make spoon bread or yeast rolls?"

"Spoon bread, by all means."

"I don't know. After what he said about corn bread . . ."

"My dear Emily," Grandfather said, "your spoon bread is *not* what he knows as corn bread. Maggie is right."

"Very well, then." She jotted again, then tapped her pencil thoughtfully on the table. "There are still some late peas . . . but there are enough of the young green beans, aren't there, Mr. Rogers?"

Grandfather squirmed. He never liked to have his vegetables gathered too soon. "I doubt it."

"Oh, I think there are. I noticed quite a few last week. They would be delicious with sour cream. Oh, I mustn't forget sweet butter for the biscuits. Is there enough cream, Lulie?"

"Yessum. They's aplenty."

"Good. And carrots . . . buttered or candied, Margaret?"

But Aunt Maggie hadn't been listening. She was playing telegraph with me, tapping out our secret code on my knee under the table. Once when she was visiting us in the city, I had a cold and was kept bed-fast for several

135

days. To help pass the time we had memorized the Morse Code and it had been fun to use it since then as a way of exchanging secret messages. Aunt Maggie was saying "Hurry" to me now, which meant I should finish quickly so I could walk to the gate with her. Grandmother spoke sharply. "Margaret?"

"I'm sorry, Mother. Carrots, you said? Of course."

"I said should we have have them buttered or candied?"

Aunt Maggie thought. "Candied, don't you think? With the guineas?"

"No, I don't believe so. Buttered." She wrote it down. Grandfather grinned at Aunt Maggie and she made a little face at him. Grandmother went on. "A green salad . . . and for dessert?"

Aunt Maggie stood. "I really must go, Mother. Whatever you decide to have will be fine, I'm sure. It always is."

"Just another minute, Margaret. I was thinking of an ice . . . lemon ice, perhaps. Would that be nice? With pound cake?"

"It would be perfect."

"Will you bring the lemons at noon, then? And Mr. Rogers, I shall need Choctaw to go after ice, and one of you will have to turn the freezer."

"We'll take care of the ice and the freezing, Emily. If we don't get around to it, we'll let the doctor turn the handle when he gets here."

Grandmother was shocked. "I wouldn't dream of such a thing!"

"Well, why not, for heaven's sake? He isn't royalty. I'll bet he'd think it was fun."

Aunt Maggie and I slipped out while Grandmother was still sputtering. "Well, he isn't going to have an opportunity to think it anything. You or Choctaw will freeze that ice."

Aunt Maggie giggled as we flew through the dining room and down the hall. "You and I will probably freeze it. Papa hates to turn an ice-cream freezer worse than anything in the world. He'll forget to tell Choctaw, and he'll disappear himself."

"Oh, I wouldn't mind," I told her.

"No, because you'll get to lick the dish."

But it happened that I didn't. I got my star-wish, for Lulie let me iron the handkerchiefs, although it didn't help her to get any rest. Grandmother kept us all busy trotting on errands the whole morning. Grandfather gathered the beans. He was adamant about that. If they must be picked he would do the picking himself. He also cut the salad greens. I went along to carry the basket. Then I was sent to the chicken house for new-laid eggs. In a pound cake not even day-old eggs could be used. Choctaw killed and dressed the guineas. Lulie was sent to the old well for cream and butter, while I ironed the handkerchiefs. Nothing, of course, was allowed to interfere with the ironing.

Into the bustle and stir Aunt Maggie came at noon with the lemons. We had barely finished a very hurried lunch when the telephone rang. Grandfather went to answer, but Aunt Maggie and I tagged along. He held out the receiver. "For you, Maggie. It's Adam."

Aunt Maggie took the receiver and leaned against the wall, taking up a newspaper to fan herself with. I felt sleepy and hot, so I lay down on the couch, and Grandfather came and scrooged me over. "Make room for another sleepyhead. Great Caesar's ghost, but your grandmother is in a tizzy about this dinner tonight!"

We didn't pay any attention to what Aunt Maggie was saying. I lay on my side, my cheek against the cool leather, and watched Grandfather's eyelids quiver against the light. "Choctaw tells me you want to go to the Negro camp meeting with him and Lulie," he said suddenly, without opening his eyes.

My heart jolted inside of me and then began racing like mad. So Choctaw hadn't forgotten. "Yes," I said, as quietly as I could. I was afraid to be too eager. It would go against luck.

"I'll have to think about that, baby. Some queer things happen out there sometimes."

"But with Choctaw and Lulie . . ." I began.

"That's just it," Grandfather said, "ordinarily Choctaw would take as good care of you as I would. But with Lulie, and a camp meeting, I don't know. Maybe Maggie and Adam could take you one night."

"It wouldn't be the same," I said.

"Why wouldn't it?" Grandfather opened his eyes and looked directly at me. They were very blue.

"Negroes don't act the same with white people around. I want to see them get the spirit and sing and shout."

Grandfather chuckled, and it shook the couch. "They'd do that at a camp meeting if there were a hundred white people about. Lots of white people go to watch, didn't you know that? They drive their buggies up close enough to see and hear and sit there and look on. Now, wouldn't that be fun?"

"No, sir." I was being stubborn, I knew, but this once I didn't want Aunt Maggie and Adam. I wanted Lulie and Choctaw and no white people at all.

"Well, we'll see . . . but don't count on it."

Aunt Maggie turned away from the phone. "Papa, Adam says there is a ball game this afternoon over at Cane Valley . . . a team from one of the mining towns is playing, and he wants to see a fellow that's pitching for the miners. He thinks he's pretty good. He thought Katie and I might like to, but I can't leave Mother with this dinner on her hands.

You want to go?"

"By George, yes! Let me talk to him." He jumped up from the couch and snatched the receiver from Aunt Maggie's hand. "Hello, Adam . . . you think that man's any good? Yes . . . sure. He *has!* Could we get him? Sure, sure I understand that. I think we could. Well, I want to see him myself. What time you leaving? All right, come by and pick us up then. Goodbye . . . oh, wait, Adam," and to Aunt Maggie, "anything else you want to say to him?" She shook her head. "No, that's all, Adam. We'll be ready."

Aunt Maggie kept on shaking her head. "What about the lemon ice?"

"Oh, confound the lemon ice. Tell Choctaw I said for him to do it. Maggie, Adam says that man is really good. Says he's got a good fast ball, and a slow-breaking curve that fools everybody. And," he paused to emphasize the importance of it, "on top of that, he hits around three hundred! By George, imagine a pitcher with a batting average like that. We've got to get him, that's all. We'll lose the Reunion games sure as shooting if we don't find a good pitcher pretty soon." He prowled excitedly around the room.

Aunt Maggie was excited, too, and I was hopping around the room on Grandfather's trail. You'd have to love baseball the way our family did to understand how we felt. We were a baseball-crazy family, always. I don't remember when I learned to keep a score card. I don't even remember learning. I just always knew, as I knew grass was green, clouds white and the sky blue. The first page both my father and grandfather turned to in the newspaper was the sports page. Batting averages, pitching records, percentages, especially of the National League, were common table talk with us. And my mother, who when she married Tolliver Rogers didn't know an outside curve from a fast ball, came very early to understand that unless she shared this enthusiasm with him she would be left out of an important part of his life. For not only did he coach and manage the college team, he was a part owner of the city club and he was constantly scouting for players for them. Because she loved him, she set herself the task of learning the game, and she achieved this so well that her own interest became only slightly less than his. Both my father and Aunt Maggie had been, of course, fired by Grandfather's love for the game. Grandmother never shared it. She thought it all a little childish, but she managed to live with it fairly peaceably.

What made this pitcher especially exciting, however, was a more local and personal interest. For years, now, as far back as my father's childhood, Stanwick had had a baseball team. Most small towns in those days did have one, composed largely of local men who loved to play. The merchants provided most of the financial support, which was small, consisting largely of keeping the team in balls, bats and uniforms. None of the players were paid, except the pitchers, and they were paid a rather small sum by the game. There were no traveling expenses, for they played neighboring towns, and the players provided their own means of transportation. The games were usually played on Saturday afternoon. The *big* games of the year were the three played during the Confederate Reunion in August. The Reunion itself was tremendously important. It had been instituted years before by my grandfather, but it now had the support of the entire county, and the interest of the entire state. All Confederate veterans wanting to attend could do so, and hospitality would be provided them, but it was more than anything else a reunion of the 6th Arkansas. It was held each year in the picnic grove just outside town, and it took the place of a county fair. To miss the Confederate Reunion was, in my mind, equal to missing three days in Paradise.

Because it was the host, the Stanwick ball team always played in the Reunion games. Their opponent was the team with the best standing among the remainder of the towns. For four years, now, Stanwick had won the Reunion games. But their pitcher had moved out of the county and the outlook for this year had been very shaky. Grandfather had been growing increasingly uneasy, and Adam, who loved baseball second to nothing in this world, was the catcher for the team, *and* the captain, *and* the manager, had worried almost to the point of losing weight. Now he had heard of this new pitcher. It was no wonder that Grandfather said confound the lemon ice!

"Does he work at the mines?" Aunt Maggie asked.

"Don't know," Grandfather said, "don't know a thing about him except what Adam said over the phone. But we'll find out, and we'll get him . . . one way or another we've got to get him."

"Golly, I wish I could go, but . . ." she sighed, "no use wishing. Katie, you'll have to wear shoes and stockings, and you'd better change your dress. Hurry, Adam will be here in a minute."

Poor Grandmother. We came straggling back from the ball game just in time for dinner, hot, dusty and weary, but exultant. We had got the pitcher. Grandfather completely forgot we were having a company dinner and brought Adam in to eat. Both men had their coats off, slung over their arms, and they were still talking baseball as we went down the hall. Grandfather pulled up sharply when we went into the sitting room and found the doctor there. With his usual aplomb, however, he greeted him. "Good evening, Jim. Glad to see you. Maggie, we got him! Tell you about it at supper. Emily, I'm sorry we're late, my dear. Have we delayed dinner? Give us a moment to freshen up and we'll be right with you. Adam is staying, of course."

Not by so much as a tremor of an eyelash did Grandmother show any irritation with him, although she must have been seething, not only because we were late and had probably delayed her excellent meal, but because we had kept a guest waiting and also because Grandfather had asked Adam unexpectedly. Her table was perfect, of course, and now it must be disarranged. But she spoke to Adam as cordially as if he did her a favor by coming. "How nice you can be with us, Adam. It will make our little party exactly right. There's no hurry, Mr. Rogers. You and Adam go along, and dinner will be ready when you are."

Adam himself was not at all ill at ease. It was not that he was too insensitive to be. It was simply that he had the same good manners that made no more of a situation than was necessary. He knew what Grandmother was feeling, but being inadvertently caught in an awkward spot, he lessened it by ignoring the awkwardness. He said only, "You're very kind, Miss Emily. Are you sure I'll not be in the way?"

"Nonsense, Adam," she said, "when is a

guest, expected or unexpected, ever in the way in this house? You do need a wash, though," and she laughed.

Adam looked at himself ruefully. "I need more than that," he said, and privately I agreed with him. How he was ever going to make himself presentable for Grandmother's dinner party was more than I could see. He badly needed a fresh shirt, and he was far too bulky to borrow one of Grandfather's. He was much taller than Grandfather, and he was a sturdy man, broad and heavy, where Grandfather was as slender as a whip. He spoke briefly to the doctor as he left the room, and Grandfather promised they would be only a minute or two. Aunt Maggie took me in charge.

It was nearer thirty minutes later that we went in to the dining room. Grandfather was entirely fresh, of course, and while Adam's shirt front left much to be desired, still, with his coat on, his tie retied, his face shiny from soap and water, and his hair combed, he looked much better than I had expected he would. I had had only a lick and a promise myself, Aunt Maggie scolding all the time. "How could Papa have forgotten? Why didn't you remind him? What in the world kept you so long? The game was over at least two hours ago."

"They had to see the man after the game, Aunt Maggie. And they kept on talking and talking . . ."

"Oh, I know," she was buttoning my frock, "and it doesn't really matter, except that Mother worked so hard on this dinner, and it was so important to her. Just wait till you see the table. And Papa asking Adam . . ."

I felt very guilty. I had not forgotten the dinner, ever. But it was so important to talk to the man . . . and they couldn't hurry him. Surely the baseball team was more important than a dinner party. But I was not sure enough not to fidget restlessly all the time they so unhurriedly discussed the matter with the man. "Did they really get him?" Aunt Maggie asked.

"They did . . . they really did. But Grandfather's got to find him a job over here."

Aunt Maggie laughed. "Isn't that just like Papa? Now, where is he going to find him a job?"

"He said Adam could put him in the bank if he had to."

"And I'll bet he can't even count! Come along, darling."

As accustomed as I was to Grandmother's tables, this one almost took my breath when we went in. The lamp had not been lit; instead there were candles in the prism glass holders, and a mass of her loveliest red roses in the center of the table. The cloth was her spidery one, which had come from Switzerland, and through its cobwebs the dark wood of the table shone and glinted. The service was the familiar one of her mother's china and silver, but they took on new luster, too, against the lacy cloth. None of us really graced that table except my grandmother . . . not even the doctor, who somehow seemed all dark angles and lean lines in the candlelight. Aunt Maggie looked a little flurried and I felt that Grand-father and I, too, showed the hurry with which we had dressed. Adam, of course, in no way fitted in, save in the quietness of his bearing. Grandmother, at the end of table, was exquisite, both in her dress and in her manner. Grandfather, partly to make amends I suspect, and partly because no matter how much her small affectations may have irked him occasionally, was always genuinely proud of her; Grandfather followed her lead in the conversation and baseball was not discussed.

The food was, of course, wonderful, and the doctor was satisfyingly wordless after the sherry-guineas. Lulie was trim in her black dress and white apron and she served adequately. Her concentration was a little comical to watch. So determined was she to do everything she had been told exactly right that her face was puckered into its fiercest scowl, her black eyebrows drawn beetlingly together and her mouth tightly shut. She did, once, pouring the coffee, get the pot uncom-fortably near the doctor's cheek, but no one saw her but me. Grandfather was stubborn about coffee with dinner. He liked it with the meal and he saw no reason why, in his own home, he shouldn't have it. I doubt he would have called for it that night, but apparently Grandmother was afraid he would, so it was served with the food.

It was I, in fact, who was responsible for Lulie's defection. Grandmother was busy with Adam, and Grandfather and Aunt Maggie had their eyes on their plates for the moment. I was watching Lulie and as she finished pouring Grandmother's cup, she looked up and across the table at me. I motioned toward Grandfather and then toward myself, trying to tell her that Grandfather had spoken to me about the camp meeting. I frowned and shook my head, indicating he had not yet committed himself about it. Lulie grinned and slyly winked at me, as if to reassure me. It was then that the heavy silver pot wobbled dangerously near the doctor's cheek. The warmth of it and the obvious unsteadiness of ·Lulie's hand made him draw away, and he then leaned back in his chair to wait until she had finished. He smiled at her as she murmured an apology and watched as she steadied the pot with her free hand. Following his eyes I saw, too, how gold were her hands against the silver of the pot. Nothing about Lulie was ever ungraceful, except her scowly face, and her hands now, holding the curved urn, were touched with the kind of beauty

Cellini gave to his metal work. They seemed carved and bent from the pure metal itself, with the dull yellow gleam of gold unmixed with any alloy, and their grace, holding the urn, was equally pure. The doctor stared, not taking his eyes from her hands until she had finished, and for some reason I felt embarrassed for Lulie, as if his eyes saw more than her hands. Grandmother turned to him, then, and he gave her his attention. Lulie moved on down the table.

After dinner, in the sitting room, my hand was examined. "It's mending nicely, now," the doctor said. He reached for fresh bandaging. "I think one hot bath each day will do now, Miss Maggie." I noticed that he did not leave off the 'Miss' this time, but I did not wonder why. Grown people had such queer ways with names, anyhow. Grandmother always called my grandfather Mr. Rogers, and when my father spoke of my mother to others he always called her Mrs. Rogers. It had something to do with courtesy.

"I'm afraid it had only one today," Aunt Maggie said, "she was at that ball game all afternoon."

"Well, no harm done. I'll look in again tomorrow, and if it's still improving, that will be all."

For some reason I was glad he would not be coming much longer.

We sat, the men with their cigars, talking

for a while, Adam and Grandfather finally recounting the details of the afternoon, their enthusiasm mounting all over again as they talked about the young miner. "The boy's headed for the major leagues," Grandfather said, "just as sure as you're a foot high. We'll not be able to keep him long. If Tolly sees him he'll be stealing him for his own club." He turned suddenly to the doctor, "By the way, Jim, do you play?"

"Play?" the doctor seemed startled at the question. "I? Good Lord, no. I never saw half a dozen games of baseball in my life."

Both Adam and Grandfather stared at him as if he had suddenly denied the source of life. Then Grandfather hitched his shoulders.

"Well, I suppose it's different in the cities."

Adam agreed quietly. "I believe it's true most ball players come from small towns."

"Should I learn," the doctor asked, "to be accepted in Stanwick?"

Grandfather chuckled. "No." He drew on his cigar and then looked reflectively at the ash. "I don't believe you can learn to play baseball. I think it's something inside . . . something like, well, like Maggie's voice here . . . something you're born with, a skill, a talent, a love. Oh, if you've got it to start with you can undoubtedly learn to do a great deal with it . . . but it's got to be there in the beginning. No, it's a little late for you to start,

Jim . . . but," he added, "if you've got a dollar or two to spare you can chip in and help pay that new pitcher."

"Certainly. I'll be glad to."

"And," Grandfather went on, "if you watch him pitch a few times you'll get your money's worth."

"I'm sure of it." Doctor Jim turned to Aunt Maggie then. "Miss Maggie, the evening won't be complete without some music. I've been looking forward to it all day."

"Of course." Aunt Maggie always sang when she was asked, if she thought she was in good voice. There was never any protesting or pretending. She paid people the compliment of assuming they really wanted to hear her, and she knew very well she was worth hearing. Occasionally when she knew she would not sing well she said no, and when she did, no amount of persuading would budge her. It was, I suppose, the artist's pride in her instrument.

We moved to the parlor, where Grandmother's foresight had already had Lulie light the lamps. Grandmother herself went with us only long enough to make certain the room was ready, then she excused herself, murmuring her goodnights, saying something about seeing to the kitchen.

It was such a jolly evening. Aunt Maggie sang and from her songs I knew how happy she was, for she sang only the gayest, most rollicking things. Then she persuaded Adam to do one of his funny monologues. Adam had a voice like a frog, croaky and unbelievably flat, but he could sit down at the piano and accompanying himself with a few chords, half talk and half croak the words to the bulldog on the bank and the bullfrog in the pool. When his voice went way down into his chest as it did when the bulldog called the bullfrog a green old water fool, it sent us into stitches. He did that one, and the "Camptown Races," and then the doctor and Aunt Maggie sang some duets. I remember they did "Take Back Your Gold," the doctor twirling the ends of an imaginary mustache and simpering foppishly as he offered the girl the gold, Aunt Maggie exaggerating the foolish girl's distress, in a quavering voice refusing, "Take back your gold, for gold can never buy me . . ." It was delightful. Even Grandfather contributed a small share, singing an old war ballad . . . "Lorena." How does it go? " 'Tis just a hundred months, Lorena, since first I held thy hand in mind." Grandfather's tenor was a little cracked, but it was still sweetly true.

After that I grew very sleepy and I had only the dimmest memory of more music, and of voices flowing like a dreamy river all about me. I waked a little when Grandfather lifted me and I heard him say goodnight, and I knew he was carrying me up to bed. In the way of one more than half asleep it seemed a very long time to me until we reached the top of the stairs, as if I slept and dreamed and slept again, knowing all the time we were going down the hall and up the stairs.

At the top of the stairs, however, I came awake, fully awake, for Grandfather stopped so shortly that my head jolted uncomfortably against his shoulder. I lifted it and looked, rubbing my eyes. Grandmother was coming out of the little attic door. She was in her nightdress, a white wrapper thrown about her shoulders, and she was carrying, not a lamp, but a candle. Her white hair hung in braids, ready for the night. Her face looked masked and remote, only her eyes gleaming darkly in the light of the candle. She came down the short hall toward us, walking stiffly and carefully. Then she saw us, and her mouth curved in a slight smile. "It's going to rain," she said . . . and then very softly, "I've been closing the windows, Chisholm."

Grandfather set me down. "Yes, Emily," and he went to her, taking the candle. "Katie, can you get to bed by yourself?"

"Yes, sir."

"Goodnight, then," and he bent to kiss my cheek. He went down the stairs with his hand on Grandmother's arm, and I went into Aunt Maggie's room, undressed and slipped into bed.

Perversely, now, I was not sleepy. The

music from the room below came up to me and I wished I were back downstairs. Then suddenly I sat bolt upright. She had called Grandfather by his name . . . Chisholm. Never before in my life had I heard her call him anything but Mr. Rogers. Mother said it was the old way of showing respect to the head of the house. Chisholm had sounded so strange, so very strange, coming from her lips . . . almost as if she meant another man. And when I lay down again the moon was shining brightly across the cover. It wasn't going to rain at all. The pattern of the window panes lay in long, thin bars across the white counterpane, and I traced them out to their shadowy ends, counting as my eye followed the dark lines. I remember there were eight of them.

Eight

My hand continued to improve rapidly, as frequently those local infections which flare up so suddenly and so threateningly will do. All at once the danger is over and within a day or two there is little evidence it has ever existed. The doctor had come on Wednesday, but he had then said the hand was doing nicely and he wouldn't need to see it again. "By the end of the week," he had told Aunt Maggie, "you can leave the bandage off."

It was on Friday, I remember, that the bandage was first left off and my hand felt strangely free and flexible without the hampering cloth. "Now, be careful," Aunt Maggie had warned. "When you climb the mulberry tree don't slide down any more." I had not been the least bit afraid that climbing the tree would be prohibited. It would be

155

assumed, as I myself knew it to be a fact, that I had learned the hard way to be more careful. I was cautioned about danger, always, about falling in the creek, about getting into or out of the wagon when it was moving, about snakes in the cotton rows, about the rear end of the mules; but having been cautioned, my freedom was not then curtailed by fear. When I came to grief, as I occasionally did, even to sliding into the creek one time, no one said, "Now see what you've done! I told you not to fall into the creek. You can't go there any more!" I was told instead, "Be more careful next time."

That may have been why Grandfather finally did allow me to go to the camp meeting with Lulie and Choctaw . . . or it may simply have been that I persisted so doggedly that he gave in to have a little peace. Whatever the reason he did let me go, but not that weekend. I had to wait awhile.

On that Friday I remember Aunt Maggie had come home from town a little early. Lunch, or dinner as we ordinarily called it, was not yet ready and she hurried to the kitchen, I on her heels. "I'm starved," she said, lifting lids and peering into pots. The smells from the stove were heavenly.

"What?" I asked, anxiously.

"Chicken and dumplings . . . carrots and peas . . . and, oh, Katie, guess!" She hovered over the last pot.

I shut my eyes and tried to tell from the smell. "I can't possibly."

"Corn! Corn on the cob. The very first of the season."

I flew to the dish cupboard. "Let's hurry. I'll set the table and let's hurry fast and eat." No wonder I was such a fat little girl. I was always ready to eat.

I was setting around the silver and the plates and Aunt Maggie was pouring the water, humming a sort of tuneless little song, when she broke off to ask, "Would you like to drive out into the country this afternoon?"

"Oh, yes!" I dropped the silver with a clatter and ran to throw my arms ecstatically around her waist.

"Katie! Careful . . . you'll make me spill the water." She laughed and pulled one of my braids. "You get *so* excited."

"Where are we going? Is Adam going to see a farmer?" He frequently made trips out into the country. When a farmer applied to the bank for a loan it was necessary, if Adam did not immediately know the situation, for him to look over the farm, or stock or equipment he was offering as collateral. We had often gone with him.

"Let's finish the table, dear. No. Doctor Jim stopped by the office this morning and asked us to go with him. He has to pay another visit to the Thornberrys."

My excitement died slowly away and an

uneasy feeling of disappointment took its place. I picked up the silver again and began setting it about. I knew very well how it had happened. He had come into the post office sometime during the morning after his mail . . . late, perhaps, when there weren't many other people there, or very likely no one else at all, and he had talked to Aunt Maggie through the bars of her little window. He had stood there, I could see him, so tall he must have had to stoop considerably, and dark in the dim light of the post office vestibule, with his elbows leaning on the little shelf, maybe, and one leg crossed over the other; and she had handed him his letters and the paper, and they had talked, oh, about this and that, my hand no doubt, Grandmother's excellent dinner, the music we'd had in the evening, and, of course, the weather, such a nice day. And then he'd said just as he was leaving, "I have to pay another visit to the Thornberrys this afternoon. Wouldn't you like to drive out into the country?"

And Aunt Maggie would have considered, thoughtfully, her head bent a little to one side. Deciding suddenly she would have said, "I'd love to."

The water splashed into the glasses and Aunt Maggie went on speaking. "It *is* such a nice day, and I thought you'd enjoy the drive, darling."

"*You'll* enjoy it," I said, accusingly, "you

and Doctor Jim."

"Why, Katie!"

I couldn't imagine why I had spoken so. I felt all mixed up inside, full of this sudden and unreasoning jealousy for the doctor's hold on Aunt Maggie's interest; for their sharing something which left everyone else, even Adam, outside. We had never lived in New York. I didn't even like Aunt Maggie liking him at all. I wished I hadn't skinned my hand so that he had started coming to the house so often . . . wished Grandmother hadn't been so proud of her cooking . . . wished the doctor had never come to Stanwick. It was so unsettling having him part of the summer. He didn't belong with us.

The kitchen door banged and Lulie screeched, "Get yourself outta here! What you mean sneaking into the house thisaway?" And the old yellow barn cat streaked across the kitchen and came flying into the dining room. I scooped him up as he went past. He clung, quietly, to the front of my dress, his claws digging in for safety. I stroked him, rubbing his soft, silky fur down. "I'll put him out, Lulie," I told her, and she left him to me, going back to the kitchen, muttering to herself. But I held him and kept on stroking. Once I rubbed my hand the wrong way and the fur bristled up and the cat moved restlessly. That was the way the doctor made things, I thought . . . bristly. Aunt Maggie was laying the napkins around now, and I watched her place each linen square precisely. She looked at me. "Don't you like the doctor, Katie?"

"Yes," I said, grudgingly, then quickly, "but not as well as Adam."

She laughed. "Well, Adam is pretty special, I'll admit."

"I'd rather go with him this afternoon."

"Well, darling, Adam isn't going anywhere this afternoon, not that I know of, at any rate, and Doctor Jim is, and he has asked us to go with him."

I lifted the cat and held him against my face, peering at Aunt Maggie over him. "Do *you* like him?"

"Who? Doctor Jim? What a little goose you are. I think he's a very charming person . . . very nice." She said it lightly, airily, in that offhand way grown people use sometimes when they wish not to probe too deeply into something. It hadn't the ring of honesty. It was a surface thing, tossed off from the top of her mind. But it made me feel better than if she had said, quietly and sincerely, "Yes, I like him very much."

I put the cat out and came back to the table. "If you don't like him so much, why are we going driving with him?"

She looked at me, amazed. "But, Katie, I just *did* say I liked him."

"You didn't *really* say, Aunt Maggie. You

said he was charming and nice."

She continued looking at me, and then she smiled and shook her head. "The oddest things go on in that head of yours. What is it you're getting at, Katie?"

Then I was embarrassed and ducked my head, squirming. Finally I managed to mumble, "I don't want you to like him as well as Adam."

To my great relief she began laughing, and it was her good laugh, full of fun and real humor. She sat down and drew me to her. "Look, darling, Adam is the man I am going to marry. I promise you I shall always like him best." And my troubled heart was immediately set at rest. Aunt Maggie never broke her promises. Everything was fine; Adam was not unthroned. The doctor took his place in the scheme of things, a charming, nice person, but not a terribly important one. With no further burden of worry I could let myself go and look forward to the drive into the country. It was a very nice feeling.

The Thornberrys lived on the far side of town. The doctor called for us about four o'clock. It was quite evident that he had freshly bathed and shaved. There was a smell of shaving soap and bay rum, newer and sharper than the older and more clinging odor of tobacco mixed with the inevitable doctor's smell of drugs and chemicals. He seemed to have several very handsome suits, linen at this time of the year, although to Grandmother's dinner he had worn a thin black suit of some kind of shiny stuff like stiffened silk. So far we had seen him in gray and very light tan besides. Today he had on white linen, and nothing could have set off his lean, saturnine good looks quite so perfectly. I have tried to think how it was that Doctor Jim could wear the same kind of clothing other men wore . . . my father, for instance, who always wore white linen in the summer, and Adam . . . and yet somehow manage to give the impression that they were the garments of a gypsy, or those of a Spanish grandee. I think there, just now, I have hit upon what it was. He had a gypsy look about him, a warmth of color on his dark cheeks, a restlessness in his dark eyes beneath their sleepy lids; a look of sun and sand and of wandering beside far seas and in wild places; a look of having flung himself, untrammeled and free, into wide, vast spaces. It was as if he played always to himself gypsy music, and wore a ragged cape of adventure swaggeringly about his shoulders.

Beside him Aunt Maggie denied the heat in her own white linen waist and skirt. I remember that both were hand-embroidered, the waist having a yoke of fine cutwork set in, and the skirt ending in deep, curving scallops. Neither of them wore a hat, and I remember how their hair blew and how the color came into Aunt Maggie's face when we raced the freight train, although she scolded the doctor for his recklessness.

That was as we went out to the Thornberrys'. We drove through town and turned down the depot road. As we passed the bank we could see Adam sitting at his desk in the window, but his back was turned and he was talking to a man sitting near him. He did not see us. I had a small dismal feeling of faithlessness, but I resolutely put it aside. Adam's place was secure. We crossed the tracks, and then the road turned left and followed the railroad for several miles. It was a smooth, clear stretch of road, and when a long freight overtook us, the doctor waved at the engineer, whipped up his horse and we flew along beside the train, never once allowing it the lead until the road curved away from the tracks to the right. As we swept into the curve the doctor waved again to the engineer, this time in parting, and the engineer grinned and waved back. He was used to such a race on that stretch of road. No man with a good horse could resist it. But Aunt Maggie scolded. "That was foolish. It's too hot to run your horse like that."

"But it was fun, wasn't it? We'll go slowly now and let him cool."

He had a good horse, but privately and loyally, I thought he was not as good as either Maud or Monk, or Adam's mare, Cindy, for that matter. Tactlessly I blurted out, "I'll bet

Adam could beat you in a race."

He didn't answer for a moment, but Aunt Maggie put her hand on my knee. She never said "Katie!" in that horrified way when I said or did something awkward. She merely touched me, or shook her head a little. But I knew I had been rude. The doctor laughed, then, a kind of short, snorting laugh. "I think he could, too," he said.

Trying to make amends, I offered balm. "But your horse is awfully good. What is his name?"

"Do you know," he said, suddenly gay again, "he hasn't a name yet. I only bought him a couple of weeks ago. Would you like to christen him?"

I nodded and began looking the horse over for some mark that would suggest an appropriate name, but there were none; he was allover bay, with no splashes of white, no socks, nor even a star on his forehead. Then I began racking my brain for another kind of name. It must be a very distinguished one, to make up a little for having been so rude to Doctor Jim. Suddenly the most distinguished name in my brief knowledge of distinction flashed through my head. "I know," I cried, "we'll name him General Albert Sidney Johnston!"

I looked up at the doctor to see what he thought of it, and he was looking at Aunt Maggie with a sort of wildly unbelieving look.

164

Then they both burst into shouting laughter, the kind that makes one bend double and sends the tears rolling down the cheeks. The doctor whooped and roared and rocked the buggy with his shaking, Aunt Maggie sat with her handkerchief to her mouth, her shoulders narrowed as she struggled with her own exploding amusement. Nonplussed I watched, a little hurt, and then belatedly catching the infection began giggling myself.

We had come to the old bridge across Fox Fork and the doctor pulled the horse off the road into the shade and stopped. He sat there mopping his eyes for a moment. "By George," he said finally, still chuckling, though, "how about that! The hero of Shiloh for a horse!"

"It serves you right," Aunt Maggie said; "it's a perfectly wonderful name."

"Don't you like it?" I asked the doctor anxiously.

"Oh, sure, Katie. I like it fine, but it's quite a mouthful, don't you think? How am I ever going to talk to him? 'Come up, now, General Albert Sidney Johnston.' I'll get my tongue tangled over such a long name every time I use it . . . just as sure as shooting."

"Oh, you wouldn't have to call him all of it," I said, very positively. "You could just call him General."

"Why, of course," he agreed. "Very well, then, it's settled. General Albert Sidney

Johnston it is . . . General, for short. Now, let's see," he looked around, "we should really christen him, shouldn't we? Hah, the creek." He climbed out of the buggy and began rummaging around for his bag. "I've got a drinking cup in here somewhere." He found the bag and pawed through it. "Always carry one . . . I don't care for the communal dipper most of these farm families use around here . . . ah, here it is." It was one of those little cups that are made of narrowing bands of aluminum which nest into one another. He gave Aunt Maggie his hand and then swung me to the ground. "I'll get some water. Have to do this right, Katie."

He left us standing and scrambled down the bank of the creek, dipping the cup into the water and bringing it back nearly full. He handed it to me. "Your Aunt Maggie and I will stand godparents," he said.

Solemnly I took the cup of water and walked around to the horse's head. Doctor Jim and Aunt Maggie ranged themselves behind me. I dipped my hand into the water, and then felt a little unsure and shy. "I'm afraid I don't remember anything but the naming part."

"That's all right," Doctor Jim assured me, "that's the important part."

So I sprinkled the water on the head of the horse, having to tiptoe to reach it, and intoned with as much dignity as I could muster, "I christen thee, General Albert Sidney Johnston." The horse was unimpressed. He only shook his head and stamped one forefoot to rid himself of a fly. I rubbed his nose and then turned around. The doctor had stepped closer to Aunt Maggie, and he was holding her hand. He was not watching me at all. He was looking at Aunt Maggie, and she was looking at him. I did not recall that joining hands was a necessity for godparents, but I thought it may have been. At any rate the doctor released her hand immediately and stepped forward to take the cup. "That was beautifully done, Katie. He is properly christened, now."

Aunt Maggie, her cheeks a little pink, gathered up her skirts. "I was never godmother to a horse before, but it was most impressive, Katie. I hope he has a long, useful life, Doctor, and I hope he lives up to his name."

As we were getting back into the buggy I said, "Go fast over the bridge."

"Why?"

"So it will *thunder* . . . like the Charge of the Light Brigade."

"Dear me . . . what a military young lady we have."

"Oh, she's been well indoctrinated," Aunt Maggie said. "You'll have to come out and watch the Battle of Shiloh."

"The Battle of Shiloh?"

"Oh, yes. We always fight the Battle of

Shiloh at least once while she is here . . . sometimes twice."

"But you couldn't be in it," I said, hastily, "not unless you join the Dixie Grays. We don't have any Federals . . . no one wants to be a Federal."

"Would I be allowed to join the Dixie Grays?"

"I don't know," I told him honestly, "we'll have to ask Grandfather."

"Oh, is he the general?"

"No, he's Captain Chisholm Rogers, just like always. But he was *in* the Battle of Shiloh, and he knows."

"Who else takes part in this battle of yours?"

"Oh, Adam and Choctaw and Grandfather and me . . . and Papa, but he isn't here this summer . . . and Aunt Maggie."

"Aunt Maggie, too?"

"Oh, yes. She's a very good skirmisher."

The doctor laughed. "I'll bet. I'll bet she's a very good skirmisher. Well, we'll see, Katie. I think I'd be rather proud to belong to the Dixie Grays. You let me know when the battle is going to come off, will you?"

"We will," I promised.

"Now," the doctor said, "let's see what we can do about some thundering effects."

He drove back down the road a little way to give us a good run for the bridge, and we all shouted together as we clattered down onto the wooden floor, "Cannon to right of them, cannon to left of them . . ." and made a most magnificent thundering. He was fun, I had to admit . . . almost as much fun as Adam, but, quickly loyal, I added, not nearly so nice.

At the Thornberrys' Doctor Jim said he wouldn't be long and we could wait in the buggy for him if we liked. But Aunt Maggie said nonsense, she'd known Lizzie Thornberry all her life and she wanted to see her again. "I think Katie had better stay here, though."

I didn't mind. The Thornberrys were tenant farmers and the house was a shack, one room of gray, sagging weatherboarding, with a lean-to tacked on the back. A rusty stovepipe poked itself tipsily through the roof at one end. There was no front porch and the steps were loose and drunken. The yard was spilling over with clutter and trash, corn shucks and cobs, an unricked woodpile, and a heap of chips where wood had been chopped near the door; chickens were scratching about in the dust and half a dozen hound dogs were lying in the shade of the only tree. It was an evil-looking place and some fastidiousness in me drew back from closer contact with it. The doctor hitched the horse to the tree and wrapped the lines around the whip socket. "We'll not be long, Katie."

As soon as he and Aunt Maggie had

disappeared I unwrapped the reins and held them, pretending I was driving. I clucked and talked to the horse, but I knew better than to jerk on the lines or to slap them against him. All the driving was strictly in my imagination. It was fun pretending, however, until a swarm of Thornberry children came piling out the door. They pulled up short when they saw me in the buggy and slowly walked toward me. Feeling self-conscious I stopped driving and simply sat there, the reins limp in my hands. No one spoke, neither I nor they. We just looked at each other. There were five of them, three boys, much larger and older than I, and two girls of about my size and age. They were all very shabby and dirty, their hair ragged and uncombed and their clothing all hit-or-miss. Their stares embarrassed me, but I tried to sit quietly and with as much dignity as I could muster. Gradually they circled the buggy, eying the horse, the buggy itself, and me. The two little girls whispered and sniggered, and I was suddenly aware of my fresh pink dress, my new pink hair bows, my spotless white socks and shiny patent leather slippers. I was uncomfortably aware of the difference between us and I felt instinctively that these children were my enemies, that they hated me and were poking fun at me. It seemed to me that their hatred shone in their eyes, sullen and unblinking and so offensively staring. I began to be uneasy and to wish Aunt Maggie and the doctor would hurry.

They had formed, now, on one side of the buggy, the three boys ranked closely together, when all at once the oldest boy stooped quickly and scooping up a corncob threw it directly at me. It glanced off my shoulder, but it startled me and I dropped the reins. As if it were a signal they had been waiting for all of them began throwing things, whatever they could lay their hands on, chips of wood, corncobs, small stones, and even handfuls of dirt. At first it was all done in silence. Not one of them said a word. There was just the scurrying as they ran to pick up things, and the steady pelting of what they threw. I did not scream or cry out myself, but I did get very angry. Remembering, I think it was a kind of class anger . . . the anger of the elect against the mob who dared . . . a kind of virtuous outrage that they should attack me. I grabbed the whip out of the socket and began laying about with it, not caring who I hit or where, determined only to make them feel the weight of it. There was, of course, the need to defend, and I felt it strongly. But far more important was the need to punish them for their insolence. With gritted teeth, not dodging or even feeling the chips and cobs and dust, I hit and hit and hit at them, wanting to hit as hard as I could and not caring how I hurt. They began to retreat under the whip

171

and the little girls started crying. At that the boys began yelling, and one of them ran for the horse's head. Another one picked up a limb and started beating on the horse's flanks. He reared and jerked, of course, and I had to drop the whip and clutch the reins again. I started yelling, too. "Quit that! You quit that, I tell you!"

The doctor, Aunt Maggie and Mr. Thornberry came running from the house. Doctor Jim ran to quiet the horse and Aunt Maggie flew to the buggy. She was beside me in a moment. Mr. Thornberry, apparently knowing his brood, took in the situation at once and began unbuckling his belt. "You, Thomas . . . Jed, Sammy! Come here!"

Aunt Maggie was looking in dismay at the litter in the buggy and at my dusty, grimy face. "What happened, Katie? There's blood on your forehead! Are you all right? What happened?"

Mr. Thornberry was gathering the children together, roughly, knocking them about and cursing them. I pointed at them. "They started throwing things, and then they tried to untie the horse and make him run away with me."

"Why, the very idea!"

The doctor had got the horse quieted and he came around the front wheel of the buggy. "Is she all right?"

"Just a cut on her forehead, I think."

We heard the first blows of the belt then and we looked. The children had made no attempt to escape . . . they hadn't run or begged or pleaded. They had simply herded together helplessly and waited. When it began we knew why. Nothing could have been more hopeless or futile than an effort to escape the brutal, dull, implacable anger of Mr. Thornberry. A temporary escape could only have brought it down on them more savagely. He lined them up and then, without asking any questions, without giving them any chance at explanation, he began beating the oldest boy. The flogging he gave the boy with his belt was more unmerciful than any imagination could have made it. He beat as if he liked beating the boy, as if some pleasure lay in it for him, as if inflicting pain were a joy to him, and if he could have killed him with pain it would have been a greater pleasure.

When he began on the second boy I could stand it no longer and I began crying, "Make him stop, Aunt Maggie. Make him stop."

She looked at the doctor. "Jim . . ."

Doctor Jim moved over to interfere. "Don't do that, Thornberry. Don't beat the kids like that."

The man shook his arm. "I'll take keer of my own kids, Doctor. Only way to handle 'em is to take the hide offen 'em. They was fixin' to unhitch yer horse an' set it runnin' with the little girl in the buggy, wasn't they?

Might of killed her."

"Even so, Thornberry, they're just kids."

The oldest boy, who had made no outcry of any kind during the awful flogging, looked at the doctor and, surprisingly, grinned. "You think that's a beatin', mister? You orta see what he kin do with a blacksnake whip."

His father slashed at him again with the belt, cutting him across the head. The boy ducked and cursed. The doctor's face went a sort of ash color and he lunged at the man. Taking him by surprise he ripped the belt out of his hands. "You make another move toward those kids," he said, "and I'll use this belt on you. You might have put an eye out for that boy then."

Thornberry gave ground, staring at Doctor Jim. "All right," he said finally, "have it yer own way, but I know these kids. They're the devil's own mix."

Doctor Jim flung the belt on the ground. He went to untie the horse, and then he came back and crawled into the buggy. "I ought to have the law on you, Sam Thornberry." He looked at Mr. Thornberry as if he had been a worm, too despicable almost for notice. "Your wife is doing all right and won't need me again. But I suggest you try a little kindness with her as well as your children."

The man was shaving off a cut of tobacco which he thrust into his cheek before he answered. "The way I treat my family is none of your business, Doctor. You kin send me a bill fer what I owe you an' I'll see it's paid. But you needn't ever expect no more calls from me."

Doctor Jim looked at him, then he laughed. He didn't bother to answer the man, just pulled the horse's head around toward the road. I was sorry . . . terribly sorry over the whole thing and feeling a little sick in my stomach. I wished I could have told the children I was sorry. I didn't know why I had incurred their hatred, but I had a guilty feeling about it, and even then I somehow suspected that in some way I did not comprehend, in some way beyond my control, I was the offender; that it was because of my fresh pink dress, and my new pink hair bows, and my belonging so obviously to the fine horse and the fine, shiny buggy. It was my first experience in the injustice of class distinction.

I looked back once and the man was still standing there where we had left him, his legs spraddled and one hand thrust into a pocket. I shuddered and turned around. Never had my own family, my own father and mother, Aunt Maggie and Grandfather, seemed so dear; never had our own way of life seemed so gentle and kindly. How could there be people like that in the same world as mine? It was horrible to think of boys and girls with a father like that . . . and, maybe, there were millions of them. I felt a sudden distrust of the world, and life, and people. Things were not always nice, then. They could be very, very out of kilter.

Down the road a piece the doctor stopped the buggy under a tree. "Let's have a look at Katie, now." But I was not hurt. A stone or rough cob or chip had scraped a bit of skin off my forehead and that was all. Doctor Jim cleaned it with some alcohol, which hurt far worse and made me squirm a great deal more than all the things which had been thrown. Then we drove on.

No one said much. The sun was going down and there was a bank of dark clouds in the west waiting to receive it. The air was very still, as it so often is just at sundown. The birds were twittering, that tuneless, busy twittering which is merely the making of sound before quieting down for the night, a kind of housewifely setting in order of their bird day. The doctor seemed sunk in introspection, looking within himself, moodily. Aunt Maggie was silent, too. When we came within sight of the town Doctor Jim roused himself and looked about. Then bitterly he laughed. " 'O God! O God! How weary, stale, flat, and unprofitable seem to me all the uses of this world . . . 'tis an unweeded garden, that grows to seed; things rank and gross in nature possess it merely.' It's such an ugly place to live, Maggie. People like the

Thornberrys . . . and look at it . . . look all around you. Have you ever seen an uglier land?" He flicked his whip in the dust. "Red earth, rocks, weeds, gullies, hickory trees and dull, unbending oaks. God, what I'd give for the sight of a birch! Thick, sluggish creeks . . . brackish water. I'd drive fifty miles to see a clear, swift-flowing stream again."

Aunt Maggie said nothing, but her hands which were folded in her lap tightened. The doctor went on after a moment. "And look at that town. Take a good look at it. There it squats like some hideous toad, in the heat and the dust and the rawness, crusted over with its own complacency, flicking its greedy tongue at the flies of gossip and inconsequential small-town happenings. Maggie, do you know what they talk about at that boardinghouse where I eat? Every night it's the same thing. Cotton — whether there's going to be a good crop or not, whether there are signs of drought, whether the price is going to hold, whether there might be too much rain. And then Jim Weatherbee's new barn roof . . . what did it cost? I'll wager I have heard ten different speculations about what that barn roof cost and whether it was worth it. Price Jenkins bought six cows last week. Wouldn't it have been better for him to wait? The market may go down and he could have got them cheaper. A great shaking of heads . . . a consensus, wiser, much wiser than

Price Jenkins, that he should have waited. And the women? Represented by Jennie and her daughter, of course, there is a running monologue. Mrs. Price Jenkins got the material for a new dress when she went up to the city two weeks ago. Too good to buy at the General Store now that Price has sold the cotton he held over and got such a good market for. Mousseline-de-soie, she got. Very fancy for Stanwick. Where did she think she could wear mousseline-de-soie, for heaven's sake? She'd have done better to get mull or lawn or a cotton print. And Sis Simpson is going to mismanage Johnnie right into bankruptcy one of these days, just you wait and see. The waste in that woman's kitchen is a sight to see! Lord, sometimes I think I'll start throwing the dishes and yelling at them. For God's sake what does it matter?" He hit his fist against his knee. "There is nothing on the face of this earth so ugly as a little town."

Aunt Maggie's head lifted. "Maybe . . . maybe you're right, but there's nothing so safe and friendly and kind, either."

"Who in God's name wants safety, or friendliness, or kindness?" His voice was rough with denial.

"What do you want, then?" Aunt Maggie cried at him angrily, "what is it you want, and why did you come here?"

"I came because I had to . . . do you think I would have come otherwise? Do you think

I chose to come? Do you? I came because I had to . . . and I want only to do my own work. Safety? I wanted the danger and the struggle. Friendliness? I'd forfeit every friend I ever had. Kindness? You can starve to death on kindness. I wanted . . . I wanted . . . Oh, nothing. I wanted more than the gods would grant. Leave it at that."

We were coming into town, now, nearly to the bank. I plucked at the doctor's sleeve. "Don't quarrel any more, please. It isn't nice in town."

"There!" he flung at Aunt Maggie. " 'It isn't nice. It isn't nice.' " He mocked my precise speech. He looked at me, however, and suddenly smiled. "All right, Katie. It's not been a very nice drive for you at all, has it?"

But I stoutly denied that. "It's been a lovely drive," I insisted. "Even if the Thornberry kids did throw things."

"Well, I'm glad you think so."

We passed the bank, but of course it was long since closed for the day. I turned to Aunt Maggie. "Adam doesn't think Stanwick is an ugly town, does he?"

And I could not imagine why her eyes were suddenly filled with tears.

Nine

I think it must have been about two weeks before I went to the camp meeting with Lulie and Choctaw. Time has so little meaning to a child. It is like a river flowing, with no beginning and no end. There are, of course, the long times, such as the year between birthdays and Christmases, time which stretches out so interminably that it is almost beyond conception. And there were short times, such as waiting for Aunt Maggie to finish dressing, or for Grandmother to set dinner on the table, or for Grandfather to hoe to the end of a row in the garden. These sometimes seemed very long, but at least they were measurable; there was an end in sight. Weeks were set off by Sundays in between, but the meaning of seven days was blurred. The mornings were fresh and dewy, bustly with housework and Aunt Maggie's leaving for the post office, perfect for tearing through the high grass of the orchard, for following the cows to the pasture, for romping with Rastus in the barn. The afternoons were hot and lazy, a time for dozing on the old leather couch in the sitting room, for playing house in the cool gloom of the plum thicket, for climbing up the mulberry tree to the roof of the sky.

It must have been the very next Saturday after I hurt my hand, however, that my father came, surprising us all. When he walked in that morning I had very mixed feelings at seeing him. I was delighted, of course, but underneath I was very uneasy for fear he had come to take me back with him. "Do I have to go home?" I asked almost immediately.

"No, no, baby . . . no. I just ran down to see how your hand was doing."

"Maggie was afraid her mother would worry," Grandfather said.

"She wasn't too worried," Papa said, "but I could tell she was uneasy . . . mostly afraid Maggie had minimized it. I thought the best way to set her mind at rest would be to run down and see. I stopped at the post office and talked with Maggie a minute. Let's see the hand, Katie."

I exhibited it. "It doesn't need a bandage now."

"So I see. It looks all right to me. Maggie

says the doctor has dismissed you."

"Yes."

Papa straightened up. "Is there a ball game this afternoon?"

Grandfather looked at him suspiciously. "Yes . . . but I'm not too sure I want you to see it."

Papa laughed. "Ah hah . . . so Maggie was right. You've got a new pitcher."

Grandfather fumed. "Tolly, I swear I'll disown you if you make this man an offer before the Reunion."

"You don't think I would, do you?"

"Sure, I think you would. I don't trust any man where a good ball player is concerned. But you'd better not, I warn you."

"I swear I'll not touch him. But I do want to see him. Maggie says you and Adam think he is a real prize."

Grandfather really wanted Papa to see him, of course. There was nothing he wanted more, but he wasn't joking when he warned him to let the man alone until after the Reunion.

There was time before lunch to walk with Papa and Grandfather all over the farm. We looked at the cotton, at the pastures and the cornfields and I stood between them and listened as they talked, gravely as men always talk about fundamental things . . . crops, weather, markets, health and illness among the animals, the things and the ways of the

182

earth. My father was digging the toe of his boot into the soil, kicking loose the top dirt and turning up the dark, moist earth beneath. "Look at it," he said, taking up a handful, "look at it. The source of life . . . without it, nothing. You know, Papa, I'm not sure I'm not a farmer at heart after all."

"Are you unhappy teaching?"

"Oh, no . . . no, I like to teach. Each fall I'm eager for the new term, and the hope that there will turn up a few really good minds. Even one makes a term worthwhile . . . one that is keen and fine and ready to explore. No, I like teaching. But I have to dig in the ground, too. It's a compulsion. You've seen our backyard . . . about as big as a dinner napkin, but I have to grow things there. I am forever aware of the land . . . how it's always there, never changing."

"Don't you believe it doesn't change," Grandfather said quickly. "Nothing changes more rapidly than land. Nothing has to be pampered and babied and petted and fed more. Nothing goes to wrack and ruin quicker than untended land."

"Yes, I know . . . what I meant is . . . well, it's *there,* underneath, the base of everything. All its potentialities are there, all its beauty. I think that's what draws me."

"Yes, I think I know what you mean."

"And it goes even deeper than that . . . it's a compulsion to return to the . . . the substance."

Grandfather pondered and then chuckled. "Something like Antaeus renewing his strength?"

"Precisely. Touch the earth . . . and live."

We walked on, both men silent, thinking. Then Grandfather said, "Tolly . . . speaking of beauty. Have you ever noticed how short a time one can capture and hold the emotional response to beauty?"

"Of course. Only a moment. I've noticed it often. Stand before a beautiful picture, and for a little space of time you are flooded with an awareness of color and line and perspective and something is drawn out of you. Then it passes and you must become active again. You move on. Or climb to the top of a mountain and look out across a lovely valley. The view captures you . . . for how long? Ten minutes? Thirty minutes? Then you have absorbed it, the peak passes and you are restless again, ready to descend. Oh, of course I've noticed how brief a time one stays on top of such response . . . but the moments *have* been and you are all the richer for them."

"Yes . . . yes, they are enriching. But, you know, the longer I live the more I have come to believe that it's the association of beauty and use that is really the best. To be aware of the . . . the, well, as you put it, the *thereness* of the land and its beauty, to have deep within one the knowledge of its eternal qualities, and then to add to it the very practical knowledge of use. How much richer your whole conception of beauty is when it is a part of your entire way of life. Look . . . look at that cotton field there. You have one reaction to it. You see the long, straight rows dwindling away down the field; you see the green of the plants, you smell the soil. It is beautiful to you, aesthetically, for the moment you are looking at it, and it fits into your concept of eternal values. I see it every day. I don't just look at its beauty, I make it and feel it and use it. And the sun rising and setting are a part of the rows I've plowed and the plants I've tended; and the line of that hill yonder against the sky is more beautiful to me because it is a part of the sound of the morning milk streaming into the pails; and the curve of that rail fence across the pastures, which so delights your eyes, is lovelier to me because I laid the fence and I planted the pasture. No . . . the brief moments aren't the best. The reality is in the beauty of use."

Papa was thoughtful. "What about the reality of the concept?"

Grandfather shook his head. "No, Tolly. That stops short."

"What makes a beautiful picture, Papa? Or a great book? Surely it is the artist's concept?"

"If he doesn't go ahead and paint the picture, or write the book, what good is the concept?"

"And what good would the action be without the concept?"

Grandfather began laughing. "And that brings us around full circle, doesn't it? No, I think you've chosen right, Tolly. Ideas are the important things to you. Teaching is exactly what you're meant to do. Your little backyard garden will always give you enough contact with the earth. You've got to have more action than concept in farming, or else starve to death."

We walked on and after a moment Grandfather resumed. "By the way, Tolly, there's something I've been meaning to tell you. I am leaving that little farm I bought last year, that hundred acres out north of town, to Choctaw. You and Maggie should both know of that provision in my will. He's been very faithful. I want him to have property of his own when I'm no longer here. It has no connection with this farm and will not disturb your own share of the property."

"It wouldn't matter if it did, Papa."

"No, I'm sure it wouldn't. But this place is yours and Maggie's."

We had turned and had been slowly walking back toward the house. As we went through the barn lots Papa saw the round little puff-ball baby chickens, the guineas, which were somehow always a little repulsive to me with their small, reptilian heads and mottled bodies, the young, lanky turkeys and the fat, waddly little goslings. He stopped to look at them. "Mother has quite a poultry farm this year, doesn't she?"

"Oh, no more than usual, I'd say. She always has quite a few." Grandfather started laughing. "She's going to experiment this year. Not going to have any males about the place. Going to kill off all the roosters, cocks, drakes and so forth, and buy her fertile eggs from now on. Says infertile eggs are better to eat, and she thinks the hens will all lay better. Thinks the males keep them disturbed."

Papa laughed, too. "I'd think it would be the other way around."

"So would I."

"Well," Papa shrugged, "the poor males . . . no fun, just food for the pot. Mama sure gets some funny ideas, doesn't she?" Both men were still chuckling when we went into the house for lunch.

That afternoon we went to the ball game. Aunt Maggie did not go. She had a very bad headache and she was of the opinion that sitting all afternoon in the hot sun would do it no good. She walked out into the hall with us as we left. "Don't forget this is Adam's night for supper with us," she reminded Grandfather; "bring him home with you."

"When are you two going to be married?" Papa asked.

"Oh, we haven't decided yet. There's no hurry."

Papa raised his eyebrows. "Adam is my age, and you're only four years younger. You're missing some mighty good years."

Aunt Maggie flushed and said a little tartly, "That's for us to decide, Tolly. There's plenty of time."

I sat in the back seat of the surrey this time, Papa and Grandfather up front. We would pick Adam up at the bank. As we clopped along down the road, Papa spoke again about Aunt Maggie's plans. "What is the trouble there? They've been engaged for over two years now. Is it Maggie? Or is Adam waiting to get on his feet more comfortably?"

"I don't know, Tolly. Adam is as secure as a man needs to be for marriage. He has the farm his father left him, and he manages it well. He has his salary at the bank, small but regular, and he's buying stock. He's on the Board of Directors, now. It isn't a financial worry, I'm pretty certain."

"It must be Maggie, then," Papa said. "Do you suppose she still has some notion of going back to New York?"

"No. I talked with her about that the other day. Her mind seems to be made up about that. At least she thinks it is."

"What do you mean . . . she thinks it is?"

"Well, Tolly . . . I think Maggie is trying very hard to be reconciled to the disappointment of all her hopes and plans. I think she does mean, or think she does, to marry Adam and settle down here at home; but I think she hesitates at taking the final step that would forever close the door for her. She can't quite bring herself to do that yet."

"You think she has never quite given up hope, then?"

"Perhaps. Most of us hold onto a hope, forlorn though it may be, as long as it is comforting at all. She can't yet put New York and all it meant to her, and all it was going to mean to her, entirely out of her mind."

"The doctor is from New York," I said, suddenly, apropos of nothing except that I was reminded of him.

"What doctor?" Papa said.

"The new doctor . . . the one who fixed my hand."

Grandfather then explained who he was. "Oh, Lord," Papa said, "that's all she needed to keep her unsettled. You don't suppose . . ."

"I don't suppose anything, Tolly," Grandfather said, "after all, Maggie is thirty years old. What she does with her life . . . whom she chooses to spend it with, if anyone, is entirely her own business."

"You have, then, thought this doctor might come between her and Adam?"

"Oh, no," I said urgently, standing and hanging over the back of the seat, "he won't!

189

She told me he wouldn't. She told me she was going to marry Adam and that she would always like him the best."

"The oracle has spoken," Papa said, laughing. "Well, that's a comfort, anyhow."

We were coming to the bank. "What does Adam think of this new doctor, by the way?" Papa said.

"Knowing Adam as well as you do, that's a foolish question for you to ask," Grandfather said. "The last thing he would ever do is to let anyone know what he thought of him . . . if he thought."

"Yes, of course. He was always reserved about his emotions, even when he was a little boy." Papa was quiet, thinking, and then he went on. "I remember how poor they were . . . his folks, and how he came to school dressed so shabbily, his clothes usually cut down from his father's and badly fitted. He never had any gloves, even in the coldest weather, and I can see his hands yet, the way he held them out to the stove to warm them . . . not complaining, simply warming them. They were chapped and blue with the cold. Once he got a pair of red mittens on the big Christmas tree at the church. Why, it must have been Mother who knitted them for him."

Grandfather nodded. "Once a year you could give Adam something. Everyone had a present on the big Christmas tree."

"He wore those mittens until they barely reached his wrists and they had been darned until there was very little left of the original gloves. But I don't recall that he ever mentioned being delighted with them. He had a new pair of shoes, once, too. Usually his shoes were badly worn, and these must have been the very cheapest in the store. They were heavy and tough, and they had no lining. They made blisters on his heels. But he wore the shoes until his heels calloused and no longer blistered. And his lunches . . . Papa, they were always a couple of cold biscuits put together with sorghum, or sometimes a fried egg. Occasionally there would be a cold sweet potato. If he ever minded, he didn't show it. He never tried to hide what was in his lunch bucket . . . that's what he brought it in, a lard bucket. He ate with the rest of us, just as openly. I used to want to give him a piece of cake or pie, but I somehow never did. I didn't have the courage. I think even then I knew he didn't really need them. That what he had was enough for him right then, and that when it wasn't enough, he would get more for himself."

We had drawn up to the sidewalk now, and Grandfather leaned back. "Yes, Adam gives you that feeling. And he got more for himself when the time came. He got four years at the university, two years in a bank in St. Louis, then his farm clear of debt and his present

191

business interests."

"How did he manage those university years?"

"Well, his father died. His mother died when he was in high school, you remember. All the old man had to leave Adam was the farm, but he was always afraid of debt. That was why they lived so meanly. But when he died he could leave a farm entirely free of debt to Adam. Adam mortgaged it to the hilt so he could go to school."

"So it was you who loaned him the money?"

"No, it was the bank . . . and we had good security. We loaned him exactly what his place was worth, not a dime more. How he managed to stretch it to cover four years at the university, I don't know, for it wasn't a great amount of money. Just about a fourth of what you had to spend."

"I know about those years. He waited tables and tended furnace. He joined nothing and he had no social life. He went to classes and he studied and he worked."

"Yes, that would be like him, too. He got out of the university precisely what he went there to get."

"And all that time he has loved Maggie. I think it must have begun even when they were children. I don't recall that he ever had another girl. Even when she went east to study he didn't run to someone else, did he?"

"No, it has always been Maggie."

Papa sighed. "Well, as you say, it's their affair . . . but I hope Maggie has the good sense not to let him go."

Adam came then and we went on out to the picnic grove. The ball park was merely a field beyond the grove, a meadow, with the diamond laid off at one end. The only seats were a very crude set of bleachers built back of home plate and extending only a very short way down each base line. Foul balls were a constant hazard for there were no screens, but it was part of the fun to duck and scramble when a ball was tipped off the end of the bat. Needless to say, the balls were always returned. There were never too many of them, and most of the games were played with a maximum of three balls. I have seen more than one game in which one dirty, misshapen ball was used the entire time. It made a pitcher have to work pretty hard, and even the best hit ball was apt to lob in any direction. The outfielders played in grass up to their knees, with no certainty when they started after a high, deep fly that they wouldn't end up with one foot in a gopher hole. But my father always said that if a man played good baseball under such conditions, he was a good ball player, and he kept his eye on all the small-town teams thereabouts.

The game began about thirty minutes after we arrived. The new pitcher was a Hungarian. In the mining towns they were called

Hunkies. His name was Gorchek, and he was not a very large man. He was slender, without being thin, and at first Papa shook his head over him. "I'd worry about his stamina," he said, "doesn't look as if he'd have much reserve."

"You'll see," Grandfather told him.

And as the innings passed, my father did see. The man pitched easily, with no apparent effort, and yet his fast ball thudded into Adam's mitt with a clean, sharp sound like a bullet hitting the target. He was a quiet man on the mound, no restlessness in him; he stood and waited patiently for the ball's return, and he waited for Adam's signals just as patiently. He wasted no energy on excess motion of any kind. When he had the signal he jerked his chin down, took a slow look at the bases, and sent the pitch where Adam called for it. But when he fielded the ball or ran bases, he was like an arrow released. Before three innings had passed, Papa was pounding his knee. "My God, what co-ordination! What beautiful co-ordination the man has got!" And Grandfather was grinning like the Cheshire cat. "Remember, not until after the Reunion."

Doctor Jim joined us when the game was about half over. He shook hands with Papa and sat down. "How's it going?"

"Good," Grandfather told him. "We'll take this one easily."

"Fine. I'm sorry to miss any of it, but I couldn't get away any sooner."

The doctor wasn't entirely ignorant of baseball, even if he hadn't seen much of it. He didn't have to be told what was going on, but he did talk too much. We watched baseball the same way we listened to music, with entire concentration, and it annoyed even me to have the doctor so constantly bringing up another subject. Neither Grandfather nor my father were prepared to be very courteous under the circumstances, and either their monosyllabic replies, or an increasing interest in the game made him subside after a while. He was amazed that I was keeping score. "Katie, what are those hieroglyphics you're putting down? What are those numbers, and that line across the top?"

"The man got a single, but Adam threw him out at second when he tried to steal. Don't you know how players are numbered? Two to four . . . catcher to second. You can't analyze a game after it's over without a score card."

"And I suppose it's very important to analyze it?"

Papa laughed then. "In our family it is."

We won the game, seven to two . . . a nice margin, a very nice win for the new pitcher. "How many strike-outs, Katie?" Papa asked.

I counted. "Eight."

Grandfather looked at Papa and Papa

nodded. "Pretty good. Pretty good, indeed. You've got yourself a man, Papa. The Reunion games should be a cinch."

We were all standing, stretching after sitting so long, waiting for Adam. The doctor was lighting his cigar which had gone dead. Between puffs he said, lightly, "Well, in an emergency, we could always buy the other pitchers, couldn't we?"

I think none of us was quite certain we had heard him correctly, at least not sure he had actually meant it. Grandfather stiffened and looked at my father. Papa looked at the doctor. Then he said, just as lightly as the doctor had spoken, "That isn't done, you know."

"Isn't it?" he laughed rather shortly, and shrugged his shoulders. "Winning, then, isn't the most important thing?"

"No."

"No, of course. It would have to be winning with honor, wouldn't it? But we bought Gorchek, didn't we?"

Grandfather spoke. "That's entirely different. He was in the market."

"I see. Well, I don't know the rules of the game very well." He bowed slightly, said goodbye and walked away. We could not help noticing he had difficulty with his walking. "The man is drunk," Grandfather said, and the tone of his voice was the doctor's condemnation.

Papa was watching Doctor Jim weave his way between the seats. "I think he is. I noticed that he smelled pretty strong, at once. Papa, Maggie must not learn to like that man too well. He has no principles."

Grandfather picked up his coat and slung it over his arm. "And the surest way to make her like him too well is to disapprove of him. Women always like to tuck under their wings the lame duck, or the crippled pigeon. Watch yourself, Tolly."

So Aunt Maggie was not told, at least not then, that the doctor had appeared at the ball game under the influence of drink, nor that he lacked an understanding of the most fundamental rule of good sportsmanship. But Adam was told as we drove back to town. He listened quietly, not sharing either my father's angry, or Grandfather's affronted disapproval. "He is not having too easy a time here, I'm afraid," he said finally, and dispassionately. "The ways of a small town are full of mystery to one not accustomed to them, and he is, I think, an impatient man. He has much to learn yet."

"No man," Grandfather said, "should have to learn not to appear in public the worse for drink. So far as I know it isn't done by gentlemen anywhere."

"And no man," my father put in hotly, "should have to learn fair play."

"He may not have had much experience

197

with fair play," Adam said, his voice still judicial. "He has been hurt, I think. We must not be too quick to judge him."

Grandfather snorted. "He is likely to be hurt again if he keeps up such behavior. The people here will not trust him very long."

"No . . . and they will distrust him much more quickly if we lead the way for them."

Grandfather and Papa both looked at Adam, then Grandfather tipped his hat. "Touché, Adam. We are rebuked."

We left Adam at the boardinghouse, but he promised to arrive promptly for supper, and he did, looking scrubbed and ruddy from his bath, and beautifully fresh in white linen. But of course before supper was over his tie had slipped and his suit was rumpled. There are men who simply cannot sit without their clothing sliding up and around on them, and Adam was one of them. I think it was the way he relaxed; he sat loosely and his coat and his trousers sat on him loosely, too. One has to be aware of one's clothing to keep it as fresh as when first put on, and an aware-ness of himself or his clothing was something Adam had not.

My father left on the evening train, but there was time before he left for some music after supper. He played the violin, and one which he had used as a young man at home was always kept ready for him. Aunt Maggie did not sing that night. There was only the piano and the violin, and I can see them yet, my father tall and intent, in the curve of the piano, his head bent over the instrument tucked under his chin, his long, slender fingers so flexible on the strings, and the arm with the bow curved with a special grace; Aunt Maggie at the keyboard, more than half shadowed, but the expression of her face somehow shining through the shadows, uplifted, detached from herself, carried by the song of the violin into that passionately beautiful world of music which was her home. Even my grandmother stayed with us through the evening, a thing she rarely did. She nearly always excused herself and went to her room soon after supper. She sat by Grandfather on the sofa, and I recall that once when I looked at her, her face was unguarded and innocent, her mouth soft, her eyes tender and musing. I think, while she would have sternly restrained herself from showing more affection to one of her children than to the other, my father was the one she loved best. Many mothers do love their sons more than they do their daughters. It may have been, of course, that she simply cared more for instrumental music than for the voice, and that it was my father's playing which enchanted her. But we were all enchanted . . . it was such an hour of perfect enchantment that the night, and the lamplight, the two who played, and our own bodies were all caught up and blended into a whole thing, not separate anywhere from the music itself.

It ended with our coming back as if from some far journey when my father laid down the violin. "I must go. It's almost time for the train. Thank you, Maggie. Thank all of you." For we did need to be thanked, as every real listener does. We had been a part of his music.

He would not hear to Grandfather driving him to the train. "No, it's a fine night, I'll walk. Need to walk, in fact."

Adam left with him and Aunt Maggie and I went to the gate with them. As my father told me goodbye, I heard Adam tell Aunt Maggie he was glad her head was better, and I heard her laugh and say the music must have cured it entirely, for it was all gone now.

Yes, I am sure now that it was two weeks from that night that I went to the camp meeting. I remember, now, that there was time in between for the doctor to come several times, after supper. He would drive up, as if just passing by, and he and Aunt Maggie would sit in the swing under the mulberry tree. What they said, I do not know, for I didn't approve of his coming and would not go near them; but I know they talked a lot, and laughed a lot, and sometimes sang together, and that sometimes it was very late when Aunt Maggie came to bed.

Ten

Lulie wore a green silk dress that night, as green as a greengage plum. "I likes pretty clothes," she had told me once. "I likes silk next to me. I likes the way it feels, smooth and nice, like my skin." And she held out her arm for me to feel. I had run my fingers from her wrist to her elbow, and her skin was smooth, but it hadn't the feeling of silk, I had thought. It wasn't so slippery and yielding. It was more like the firm surface of metal. It felt gold, as if it had been molded and poured and had then shaped itself into an unblemished texture and form. When I felt my own arm, the skin was soft and I thought that without looking you would know how white it was. I wished it was like Lulie's.

Lulie had made the dress and the head scarf matching it herself. She was clever that way.

She wore the scarf wrapped around her head like a turban, tied in a perky bow with the ends sticking up. She wore golden hoops in her ears and bangles on her arms, but they were not more golden than herself. Even her eyes were gold in the light. She glittered, like a piece of gaudy jewelry, and her mouth spread wide in her pleasure with herself as she paraded before Aunt Maggie and me. When Aunt Maggie saw the dress she said, "Hmmmmmh." I, too, thought that if Lulie had got it any tighter across her bosom and the hips she would have burst the seams. She turned and swirled so we could see its fold and pleats and when she lifted her arms the thin, soft silk clung to her breasts, curving around them and nesting them, suggesting rather than confining what was hidden there. Watching, I remembered the twin gold melons, and saw again the one, half bared, and wet from Choctaw's hand. For some reason I felt uncomfortable, as if I had a sure knowledge that the dress was cunningly contrived to invite and to tempt, as if already I knew that it was intended deliberately to provoke a secret stripping away, an unveiling of the rich, tawny flesh that lay beneath. "I likes my clothes to touch me all around," Lulie explained.

"In that dress you have certainly got what you like," Aunt Maggie told her.

Choctaw brought the wagon around.

Personally I felt that the occasion demanded the surrey, but I knew Grandfather would never allow that. No one ever drove the horses but himself, and even I could see the ludicrousness of the mules hitched to the surrey. Both Grandfather and Aunt Maggie went out to the wagon with us, and Grandfather spoke again to Choctaw. "You take one drink tonight, just one, and you'll have no job tomorrow."

"I said I wouldn't," Choctaw answered, a little sullenly.

"And Lulie," Aunt Maggie put in, "this is no night to let the light shine through. You stay put on a bench tonight."

"Yessum."

And then warnings to me. "You keep hold of Choctaw or Lulie, now. Remember."

Then we were allowed to go. Choctaw continued to grumble. "I don't know why I let you talk me into this, Katie. It ain't my idea of a way to spend Saturday night."

"It ain't mine, neither," Lulie said, laughing, "but look to me like she had us over a barrel."

I wiggled myself back into the space between them more securely and said complacently, "It won't hurt either of you to behave yourselves for once." I hadn't the slightest idea, outside of Choctaw's drinking, how they might misbehave, but it sounded important, judicious. Lulie laughed again.

"Ain't she a sight, though? Talk like she was growed clean up already."

"She hears too much grown-up talk. Got too many big ideas for the size of her." He dismissed me casually. "You're mighty dolled up tonight. Pretty as a picture. Ain't that a new dress?"

"It sho' is. Just got it done this evening. Come might' near not, too. That ole witch, she keep me trotting ever' minute, look like. She can find more things for a body to do."

"Where'd you get them earrings?"

Lulie shook her head and made them jingle. "I bought 'em . . . in the city."

"Bet you never. Bet some man give 'em to you."

"If he had, it would be my business, Mister Mingo."

"Well, don't lie about 'em, then."

"I ain't lied. I did buy 'em. I was just telling you, so's you'd know, what was my own business."

"What was your own business, *then*. It would be some of mine, *now*."

"Hoooo! Look who's talking. Sound like a big wind blowing."

"You try something and you'll find out I ain't just talking. You let some man give you earrings now, or give you anything, and I'll cut his heart out. I'll carve him into little pieces, and you too!"

"Aw, Choctaw," Lulie leaned behind me

204

to put her arm around his neck, "you wouldn't do that. I just teasing, honey. I don't love nobody but you. You knows that, honey."

There was a long stillness while Choctaw kissed her, and then he laughed. "I better know it. One thing I don't stand for is a trifling woman."

"I ain't trifling," and then Lulie giggled. "Ain't nobody to trifle with in this little ole measly town, even if I was a mind to."

"There's plenty, if you look for 'em, and I got more'n a halfway notion that new dress was aimed to start looking."

"No such thing." She made the earrings jingle again. "Never was a woman didn't like to look nice, and I ain't going out among these niggers down here looking any way but my best. I ain't no country nigger to go slopping around. I got style and I intends to show it."

"You sure have, sugar, and you show it plenty." They laughed and leaned together again.

I thought how strange it was they called each other niggers so easily and even so affectionately. I had been taught never to speak of them so. "No well-bred person calls a Negro a nigger, Katie," my grandfather had said. "When you hear a white man speak of a nigger, you can put him down as ill-bred. It is an insulting term, and a lady or a gentleman does not use it."

He had other ideas about the way one spoke, too. It was only one man's opinion, of course, but Grandfather held that a person's speech should not reflect his region. He believed that good diction and a quiet voice were marks of the cultured person the world over, and that whether a man came from Mississippi or Massachusetts should not be evident in his speech. Just the same, if he wasn't thinking he was apt to say it was a right smart piece from our house to town, and if a thing was really puzzling and unreasonable to him, it bumfuzzled him. What he would not allow was the soft, slurred Negro sound in our speech.

But among themselves the Negroes constantly used the opprobrious term and sprinkled it around, along with the endearments honey and sugar, indiscriminately. It somehow went well with their voices, so soft and drawly. Their voices were the color of their skin, night-soft and dark, plushy with their slurred consonants and open vowels.

Choctaw did not hurry the mules and they ambled along at their own slow pace. The wagon rumbled, for it was old, and the harness creaked, and the springs of the seat joggled us all together occasionally. The moon was not yet up, for it was past full, but there were tens of millions of stars and they looked hot and yellow and very near. I wondered why. In the winter they seemed to

206

go very far away and show only as pinpoints of icy brightness. Now they had a melted look. Maybe, I thought, they really did come closer in the summer, and maybe the sun really did melt them a little. "I'll ask Adam," I decided.

"You'll ask Adam what," Choctaw said.

"About the stars."

Choctaw looked up. "Sure is a lot of 'em tonight, ain't there? I don't know as I ever seen so many before . . . except, maybe, once. But that was in the winter time."

"When? Where?"

"In the Indian Territory. When I was a little boy."

"Tell me about it." I wiggled closer to him.

He looked down at me and laughed. "Not too big for stories, yet, are you? Well, I was a little boy, like I said, and we was moving. Had all our stuff in a wagon, about like this one, and we had it covered over with a wagon sheet. We had to camp out one night, right out on the open prairie. Cold as death, too. Had to break the ice in the creek to water the team and get water for cooking. We built up a big fire and couldn't get more'n two feet away from it or we'd have frozen. I recollect we sat around the fire after we'd eat, thinking we'd soon get out the quilts and things and go to bed, and we was just setting there, talking, when we heard a wolf howling, way out on the praire. Way off, he sounded, and lonesome. There's no more lonesome sounding thing in the world than a wolf howling, far and away on a cold winter night. Sounds like the end of time was at hand, or like you were done and buried in your own grave, and something mourning over you. It's a terrible, shuddery kind of a sound. Soon as we heard it we knew what kind of a night we had ahead of us, for he might be a lone wolf howling now, but he'd soon have a pack around him, and they'd smell the horses and us."

He clucked at the mules and shifted the reins to his other hand. "Go on," I said, feeling small and shuddery myself, "what happened?"

"My father went to get the horses and brought them right up to the fire. We pulled the wagon close and hitched 'em to one of the wheels, and we gathered up all the wood we could find. We gathered up a great pile of it, for we knew we couldn't let the fire die down till morning. And then we set down and waited."

"Just waited?"

"Just waited. Nothing else to do. Pretty soon the horses got restless and my pa told me to stay by 'em and keep 'em quiet as I could. 'Don't let 'em break loose,' he told me, 'no matter what happens.' So I stood there and rubbed 'em and talked to 'em, and Pa started laying chunks of wood around to start burning. After a time we saw the glint of the wolves' eyes in the firelight, not too close at first. Pa got him a burning chunk handy and told my brother to get him one. Next thing they had us in a ring and little by little they started closing in. Just an inch or two at a time, but drawing in steady. Pa kept watching on one side, and my brother on the other. Mama and the two girls he'd made get up in the wagon and they were setting there with a quilt wrapped around 'em, scared to death and cold, too. But there was no help for it. I remember standing there by the horses, rubbing their noses and talking to 'em, and noticing how many stars there were, and all around, under the stars and looking closer and brighter than stars, the wolves' eyes gleaming in the firelight. Seemed like a year I stood there. Every time I see a whole sky full of stars I remember that night."

"But what happened? What did the wolves do?"

"Nothing happened. When they'd get too close Pa and my brother would sling a burning chunk into the midst of 'em, and they'd run off, howling. Then they'd start closing in again. Kept Pa and my brother busy all night keeping the fire up and slinging their chunks."

"Suppose you'd run out of wood?"

"They'd have killed and eaten the horses, and us, too, maybe."

"Did they go away when it was morning?"

"Yes. Come daylight and they slunk off and we harnessed up and rolled on. No harm done . . . but it was a long night."

I always did have much too vivid an imagination, and now I could see a pack of wolves coming up out of the prairie, slinking and slavering and circling a fire, and I could feel the fear that the fire would die down and the wolf leader would spring. A line of verse began to sing through my head in the sing-songy way I had heard my father chant it . . .

"The Assyrian came down like a wolf on the fold." Over and over it repeated itself, like a phonograph record stuck in one place. It wouldn't go on to the next line, and it bothered me. Lulie shivered beside me. "I wouldn't want to live in no such place as that. Wolves and wild things coming right up on a body."

"The wolves and the wild things weren't the worst of that country," Choctaw said, "they was a natural enemy. It was some of the folks supposed to be human made it so bad."

I had heard Grandfather and Papa talk of the old days in the Territory, before Judge Parker had brought law and order into the Western District. I knew vaguely that the land had been set aside by the government for some of the Indian nations, and I could even say over some of the tribes that made a kind of song . . . Choctaw, Cherokee, Chickasaw, Osage and Creek. I knew that the Indians had been moved there from other places, and I had heard Papa speak of the Trail of Tears, that long weeping march from the land of home to the new, forsaken, desolate land which now had to be home. I knew Grandfather considered it indefensible, for like everyone else in those days, he thought it a worthless land, barren and poor and almost beyond hope. I knew that a class of renegade white people had drifted into the area and that there was no civil law in the Territory. Each nation was settled into its little division of land, and each was governed by its own elected governor, but he had authority only over his own people. No white man came under the jurisdiction of an Indian governor, and the federal court was corrupt and impotent. The country harbored so many outlaws, thieves and murderers that it had become known as the Robber's Roost. Probably no section of the United States, ever in its history, had offered refuge to so many depraved and degraded criminals, and the especially horrible thing about it was that they preyed so easily upon the guileless and unsuspecting Indians who were almost entirely at their mercy . . . selling them whiskey, cheating them of their allotment money, murdering the men and taking their women. But Judge Parker had changed all that. He was appointed in 1875 as judge of the United States District Court for Western Arkansas. The name of the court was misleading, for only eighteen Arkansas counties were under its jurisdiction, but stretching out to the west it was the largest federal court in the country, extending clear to the Colorado line. With an inflexible sense of duty and an unshakable conviction that the only way to check crime was to make punishment as inevitable as death, within twenty years and with the help of over two hundred deputies, Judge Parker had made the Territory a decent place again. He was called the "hanging judge," for he sent eighty-eight men to the gallows during that time, and he wept over each man he sent to death. However much he wept, though, when a jury found a man guilty of murder, the Methodist zealot continued to intone in stern judgment, "I sentence you to be hanged by the neck until you are dead, dead, dead."

Grandfather had known Judge Parker . . . not well, for no one had known that strange, proud figure well, but to speak to on the street when he had business in Fort Smith. Once when he was there, Grandfather had seen Belle Starr, the notorious woman outlaw. "As homely a woman," he used to say, "as ever I saw. Don't know why the papers make her out as handsome. She had a face like a horse."

But Choctaw had been a boy in those old

days and evidently the mood of reminiscence was on him. "It was Booly July was the worst of the lot," he said, "it was him and his men rode over the country looting and stealing and killing in cold blood. It was them that made an orphan of me." He stopped for so long a time I thought perhaps he would not go on, but apparently he was only sorting his memories. "The deputies were after them and they'd been hiding out in the Kiamichi Mountains. They'd ride down out of the hills, though, in raids, and one day they rode into our place. There was five of them . . . the meanest men ever lived, I guess. They made my mother cook supper for them, and then they eat, and then they took my father out in the backyard and shot him, for no reason at all but to get him out of the way. Then they had their way with my mother, right in front of us kids . . . and then they shot her, too. They rode off, laughing, and said for us never to forget it was Booly July had been there . . . as if we ever could. No, it wasn't the wild things that were the worst in the Territory."

"Did they catch 'em?" Lulie asked, after awhile.

"Oh, yes, they caught 'em. Judge Parker's men always caught 'em, in time. They were hung. But that never brought my father and mother back."

"What happened to the children?" I asked.

"We scattered . . . . went to live with our folks different places. All but me."

"What did you do?"

"I went to Fort Smith to see 'em hang. If they hadn't of hung, I was aiming to kill 'em myself, as many of 'em as I could. But they hung, and your grandfather was there in the crowd and he seen me standing around, got to talking to me, found out who I was, and then he asked the court if he couldn't bring me home with him. They let him, and I been here ever since."

I had never known how he had come to be in our family. He had just always been there. "I'm glad my grandfather brought you home with him, Choctaw," I said, feeling suddenly full of goodness.

"I ain't ever been sorry, myself," he said. "Like Booly July and his gang was the meanest men I ever run into, Mister Cap is about the best. They don't make men no finer."

"I just wish," Lulie said, "his woman was as . . . ."

"Oh, shut up," Choctaw said gruffly, "not in front of *her*."

We came to the camp meeting then. It was being held in a brush arbor in a clearing in a grove of trees, and Choctaw drove the mules into the edge of the woods. He helped Lulie and me out and we waited while he unhitched

214

the team from the wagon and tied them. I looked around, excited. There were other teams and wagons drawn about, some horses and mules with saddles, but not nearly as many as I had expected. "I thought Grandfather said there would be lots of white folks sitting in their buggies to watch," I said.

"Oh, they don't come till later. Ain't no use them coming at the commencement," Lulie said. "Don't nothing happen till folks get warmed up."

Choctaw joined us and we went into the meeting place, I walking between them, holding a hand of each. I had seen these brush arbors many times. They were used all over the countryside for summer revivals, but I had never been this near one before and I looked at it curiously. It was very simply made. The people had cut sapling poles and sunk them into the ground to form uprights. Across them they had laid more poles as rafters, and then they had roofed the whole thing with great, overlapping leafy branches. The leaves had long since wilted, but they still formed a good roof. I doubted it would keep out much rain, should it rain one night, but at least it offered shade for their Sunday meetings, which lasted all day. It was very dimly lit. A few kerosene lamps had been hung on the outer poles, and there were two more up on the platform at the front. They smoked and gave off a smarting stench and the smoke and the smell of oil and the dust under our feet and the strong smell of sweaty bodies all combined to make me feel more than a little apprehensive. I gripped Choctaw's hand tighter and hoped all these smells were not going to make me sick.

We sat near the back, for the place was already well filled and the singing had started. The seats were benches, without backs, made from rough, green lumber, and they were uncomfortably high for me, leaving my legs dangling in the air. The edge of the seat cut into my leg, too, back of the knee, but the worst thing was that sitting down I could not see a thing. I began to wiggle almost immediately. "Sit still, Katie," Lulie hissed at me.

"I can't see," I hissed back at her. "I want to *see!*"

"They ain't nothing *to* see. Now you sit still."

Choctaw looked around back of us and saw that the last bench still had some room on it. "We can move back there," he told Lulie, "then she can stand up if she wants to, and won't be in nobody's light."

We moved and the new place was fine. There was even a pole for me to lean against as I stood, and I could see everything. There was a man up front on the platform, leading the singing; another with a guitar, two women with tambourines, and an old man playing a fiddle. There was no piano. The man who was leading the singing was stocky, mud-brown, and he wore a white surplice so full-sleeved that when he lifted his arms it was as if he had spread great white wings. He had a powerful voice which boomed out over the crowd and led them with fine certainty. One of the women with the tambourines was fat, as fat as Angie had been, and when she shook the tambourine she shook all over herself. She had on a purple dress and she looked like a bowl full of grape jelly, quivering. The other woman kept her feet shuffling and her head thrown back, her mouth wide open as she sang. She was thin and the color of cold ashes, gray and bleak. The man who played the fiddle was old, like a piece of wrinkled and dried old chocolate cake with a grizzled frosting, but he grinned constantly and kept scraping away, patting out the time with his foot. The one who played the guitar was young, as black as coal and the sweat poured down his face making it shine. He hovered over the guitar as if it were a baby he was cuddling, his head now bent to it tenderly, now lifted, and when he lifted his head he fixed his eyes on the roof in a kind of entranced, unseeing look.

The people sat on the benches, and I was glad to be at the back and not caught in the middle of them, for they gave me the feeling of a black, anonymous sea, surging restlessly. In the beginning the music was spirited, fast, swingy and jolly, and the people swayed with the music, and in rhythm with each other, shoulders touching and moving together. Occasionally when a voice lifted higher than the rest, solo, they would stop singing and break into a rhythmic clapping, then it would subside and their voices would take up the hymn together again.

There was no hour of preaching, such as I was familiar with. People spoke from time to time, standing where they were and speaking without premeditation, witnessing and confessing mostly. The man on the platform in the surplice seemed to guide them. He spoke, too, in between times, and he prayed, and it was always his voice which signaled a song. Suddenly he would lift his arms, spread his wings and begin singing. After a few bars the people would join in. As time passed the songs became less spirited, sadder and more mournful. The people sang with high, ecstatic voices, full of that inexpressible sorrow which only the burden of long misery could give them. All their grief-laden past and all their unbright tomorrows were in their voices, coming from deep within and floating out in those quavering, elided notes which only Negro voices use. It comes from a black enchantment, from nothing known to the thinned-out, civilized white bloodstream, from something primeval and lost, mourned and grieved for. As young as I was I felt it frighteningly, knowing it for something as foreign as the dark continent which had bred their dark faces.

More frightening, however, was the fact that Lulie, beside me, was turning into someone unfamiliar to me. She, too, was swaying and singing, moaning in small, gasping sounds, and clapping her hands. Her face had become a mask and her eyes had a glazed look. Sweat poured down from under her head scarf, and she let it run like rivers down her cheeks. I knew she had not only forgotten me, but she had forgotten herself, who she was and where she was. Slowly she was going under the spell of the music and the shouting and the praying and the whole magic of the black enchantment. I edged nearer to Choctaw, who sat apparently unmoved by all of it, stolid and phlegmatic. Butterflies chased themselves around and around in my stomach and I hugged the post closely to stay steady on the bench. I would have given almost anything to have had Aunt Maggie and Adam somewhere near just then.

And suddenly the climax was reached. The thin woman on the platform threw her arms high over her head and began screaming. The screams poured out of her mouth shrilly and so long sustained that I thought I could see them, ribbons of screams winding out of her mouth like snakes. They seemed to have no end, winding and winding and curling and coiling, stretching and writhing even to where I stood, getting into my head and ears and mouth. Then she began to jerk, her arms and her legs moving in weird contortions and she started a stiff, doll-like dance about the platform. It was a signal for a surging forward of shouting, shaking, dancing men and women. They gathered at the front of the platform, some of them kneeling, some of them falling into the dust in a trancelike state, others continuing to jerk and shake and dance, the music never stopping, only the tempo accelerated in a kind of wild, passionate accompaniment. The mud-brown man spread his wings over the gathered ones, his face exalted and gleaming with sweat, his voice shouting praises and glory hallelujahs and amens. I huddled close to Choctaw, turning loose of the post with one hand so that I might hold to his shoulder. Something flesh and blood, something sane and real, I had to touch.

Then Lulie brushed past us, so brusquely, so quickly that she almost knocked me off the bench. Choctaw grabbed at me and tried at the same time to reach for Lulie. He called her, "Lulie! Come back here!" But the light was shining through and Lulie went dancing down the aisle, her hips wiggling in the tight, green silk dress, her arms reaching lovingly out to the vision which only her eyes could see. Choctaw forgot himself. "Goddammit!"

He tried to free himself of me to go after her, but I wouldn't let go. I clutched him tightly. "No, Choctaw, no, don't go. Choctaw!" I was screaming at him, terribly afraid he would pull loose and leave me alone. I was also crying, and my stomach was churning. "I'm going to be sick, Choctaw, I'm going to be sick. Let's go to the wagon. Please, let's get out of here and go to the wagon, Choctaw . . . please."

He finally heard me and looked down at me. "Choctaw, please let's go to the wagon. I'm going to be sick, I think." He looked again at the milling people gathered down front where Lulie had disappeared, and then he picked me up. "All right, Katie. Ain't no use trying to find her in that mess. Ain't no use trying to do nothing with her, if we found her. She's clean out of her head by now."

He carried me to the wagon and when I had finished being sick he made me lie down on the wagon seat, while he hunkered down on the floor beside me. "You all right now, Katie? You feel better?"

I did. I felt much better. Out here there were no oily, greasy smells from the lamps, no smoke and dust, no sweaty bodies packed all about. I could still hear the singing and the shouting, but it was not all around me. It was off somewhere and not beating itself down inside me. I lay still for a little while, looking up at the stars, feeling blessedly quiet, the fresh, damp air blowing against my face, the mules, tied to the back of the wagon nudging it from time to time, munching on grass. These were things I knew, smells and sounds and feelings. Not that other. Not ever that other. I sat up then and gave Choctaw part of the seat. A little timidly, feeling I may have spoiled the meeting for him, I said, "You could go back if you wanted to, now. I'll be all right here in the wagon." But I hoped very much he wouldn't.

"No. Don't mean nothing to me. I just come because Lulie likes to, and there's no place much to go. It all looks kind of crazy to me." Perhaps it was the Indian in him that made him unresponsive. He was, after all, only one quarter Negro.

"Will we find Lulie all right?"

"Oh, sure. When it dies down she'll come to her senses and go on back to the bench where we was sitting. When she don't find us there she'll know we've done come to the wagon."

We watched for a while, then, saying nothing. Looking around I noticed, too, that there were a good many more buggies hitched, and I could see the gleam of white faces in them. It somehow made me feel much better to know there were some white people there, now. They made a kind of refuge for me . . . a sort of spiritual refuge, because they were my own kind. Again I had the compelling feeling that it never, never paid to set my will against that of grown people. Just as when you disobeyed, something inevitably happened to make you sorry. Now I knew how right Grandfather had been to urge that I come with Aunt Maggie and Adam. What I have learned since, of course, is that it is one's own emotions one cannot trust. However stubbornly, or even gaily, one may set out to have one's own way, go against the will of others, cut across conventions, what one cannot foresee is the tangle of emotions which may result in regret, sorrow, fear and unhappiness. I only knew then that Grandfather had been right, and I wished I had not so stubbornly insisted on having my own way.

I grew sleepy, finally, and drowsed. Choctaw roused me getting out of the wagon. "Where are you going?" I wanted to know, immediately alert.

"I'm going to find Lulie. It's lightning over there in the south like it's going to rain soon. It's getting late and most of the excitement is over now. Time we was going. You stay here and I'll soon be back."

Well, that was all right, and I was glad we would soon be going home. Completely awake I watched Choctaw wind his way through the people to the arbor, and then disappear under its roof. Then I watched the lightning. It was the kind we called sheet lightning, low on the horizon, swelling and subsiding in an almost continuous curtain of light. There was no thunder yet, but almost certainly rain was very near.

Choctaw could have saved himself the trouble, for Lulie wasn't in the crowd in the brush arbor. A noise of some kind, a blundering and rustling behind me made me turn and look into the woods. Lulie came out of them, giggling, and entirely herself again. Her dress was rumpled and there was dust on it when she came into the light. "Where have you been?" I asked her.

"Nowheres. I come around back of the arbor to get to the wagon. Couldn't get through no other way. I knowed in reason you'd get sleepy and Choctaw'd bring you out here."

"Choctaw has gone to find you," I told her.

She climbed up on the seat. "Yes, I seen him leaving. He'll come back in a minute." She brushed at her dress. There were some leaves and tiny, dried twigs clinging to it, too. "A brush arbor's a powerful dirty place," she said, flicking them off.

"It sure is," I agreed. "What made you go down front? You know Aunt Maggie told you not to."

"I couldn't help it, Katie. Something pushing at me, something pulling, something gets inside and you don't hardly know what's going on. Something boils up, and you got to sing and you got to shout and dance and shake. You got to go . . . . just got to go.

224

You'd bust if you didn't. Bust plumb wide open. The light shines through and it's bright and white, and it's like being full of love, all melty and soft." Her voice was husky from the singing and shouting, but it was tender as she spoke, remembering.

It left me unmoved, however. I was still indignant. "Well, Aunt Maggie is going to be very angry with you."

"Aw, Katie. You wouldn't tell her. You'd not do that, would you? I couldn't help it. You wouldn't want to get me in trouble, would you?"

Stubbornly I insisted. "Choctaw didn't go."

"Naw. He don't never. He got about as much excitement in him as a snake. Pure cold-blooded, that's what Choctaw is. Anyhow, didn't nothing happen to you . . . with him along. Long as one of us stayed with you, look to me like they wasn't no harm. What you have to tell Miss Maggie for?"

"You didn't keep your promise."

"I never promised. I just said yessum. You not tell, Katie, I make you a rag doll. I make good rag dolls. Shoebutton eyes, cotton hair . . . make her a dress outen scraps of this'n if you want. Be real nice, wouldn't it?" Her voice was wheedling.

"When?" I was weakening. I hadn't brought a doll with me, and tea parties weren't the same without one.

"Tomorrow. First thing in the morning. I'll

225

get up early and make it 'fore breakfast. Might even make some on it tonight." Her voice was easy, tempting.

I gave in. "All right. Tomorrow, now, and don't you forget."

"I'll not. You see I don't." We giggled together. One way or another Lulie and I were getting to have several secrets together.

Choctaw came back then, growly and grumbly, asking Lulie the same questions I had asked, and scolding her for the same things. She made the same explanations, without having to bribe him to say nothing. He went about hitching up the team, still fussing. "You going to get in trouble, you see."

"Naw. Katie done promised not to say nothing, ain't you, Katie?"

"Yes. She's going to make me a rag doll."

Choctaw got in the wagon and turned the mules toward the road. "Just the same, you oughtn't to done it."

It was then I saw Doctor Jim. His buggy was farther back than the wagon, nearer the woods, and as we swung around I saw it. Doctor Jim was climbing into it. "Why, there's Doc . . ." I started to say, but Lulie's hand slid over my mouth and she began talking, hastily and complaining, about the lamps being so smoky and it did look to her like they could have some of those new gasoline flares, and the dust was so bad they ought

226

to put down sawdust, and did Choctaw see Sis Florine when she commenced getting the shakes . . . it was a sight to see, for sure. She laughed loudly.

It had all been a sight to me, and I was wearily glad it was over.

Eleven

I awakened slowly the next morning, with a drugged feeling of having slept either too long or not enough. Half opening my eyes, and turning in the bed, I saw that the light in the room was dim and gray. It was very early, I thought. The sun was not yet up. I closed my eyes again and hid my nose in the pillow. Something bothered me, though, something different about the day. I raised up and looked over at Aunt Maggie's bed. It was already made, the counterpane smooth and straight and the bolster in place. Things began to take shape. We had gone to the meeting the night before, and that was Saturday night. This was Sunday morning. I glanced at the window. It was raining. That was what I had been hearing. I scrambled to the window and knelt there on the bed, pulling the curtains back and looking out. The sky was resting right on top of the trees, gray and heavy, sagging with dark clouds, and the rain was coming straight down in a steady sheet. It must have been raining for hours, for already the backyard was afloat with water. I remembered the lightning last night. Choctaw had been right. It had meant rain, and this was not just a summer shower. It had set in for the day, or maybe for several days. It looked as if it might never stop. I sighed. That meant being cooped up in the house. But immediately I brightened. There were books . . . I could read for hours on end; and suddenly I remembered the rag doll. How could I have forgotten it! I began darting about, collecting clothes. I could play house in the attic, have a tea party there. It was always snug and cozy on a rainy day. The roof came right down over your head, and the rain was loud and drumming on the shingles, and there were old chairs and tables and trunks and old clothes in the trunks. You could dress up in them and play lady. It was dim in there, but never too disordered. Grandmother would not have disorder even in her attic. Everything was labeled and tagged and set neatly about. Oh, a rainy day could be fun, if you just set your mind to it.

I slid down the banister as slick as greased lightning and went tearing down the hall, sliding on the slippery floor and banging the sitting room door behind me. Grandfather was sitting at the table, a magazine in his lap. The lamp was lit so he could see to read. He looked at me over his spectacles. "Gently, Katie. You'll disturb your grandmother. She has a headache this morning."

I clapped a hand over my mouth. "I forgot. Is breakfast ready?"

"We had breakfast long ago."

"You ate Sunday breakfast without *me?*"

"Your Aunt Maggie said you should sleep. You got home pretty late last night, remember?"

"Oh. . . . But I would rather have got up."

Aunt Maggie called from the kitchen. "Katie? Come see what Lulie has made for you. Hurry!"

"It's a rag doll," I whispered to Grandfather, "I already know."

He whispered back, "I already know, too. I've seen it." His eyes rounded and widened. "It is the *most magnificent rag doll I have ever seen in all my life.*"

"Shoebutton eyes?"

He nodded solemnly, "Black as coal."

"Cotton hair?"

He shook his head. "No . . . better than that. Wool."

I let out an explosive breath. Lordy, Lulie must have laid herself all out to make that doll. I whirled and spun on my toes, coming to a sudden stop with an idea, giggling. "You know what I shall name her?"

Grandfather pulled at his beard, thoughtfully. "Little Nell?"

"Oh, no. She died."

"Little Eva?"

"She died, too. But you're getting warm." I couldn't wait for him to guess any more. "Give up?"

"I may as well."

"Topsy!"

Grandfather was overwhelmed. "How did you know she was a Negro doll?"

"Oh, I just guessed," I said, airily. "I *thought* Lulie would make her out of a black stocking."

"Katie?" It was Aunt Maggie again, so I ran, skidding around the corners.

Oh, she was undoubtedly a magnificent doll, and no stinginess about her. She was easily two feet tall. It must have taken several stockings to make her, and Lulie had stuffed her so nicely, with no bumps or lumps anywhere. She had sewed on the shoebutton eyes with white thread and had stitched her a white mouth, and tiny ears under the black wool hair. It was curly black wool, and I knew that Lulie had raveled something which had been tightly knitted, for it still had its crimps and kinks and fringes. About the hair was tied a little green head scraf, and Lulie hadn't forgotten to make the dress of scraps of her own green silk. She had even made a small white apron to go over the dress. The finishing touch was a little pair of green shoes on the doll's feet, also made from the silk.

"You like her?" Lulie asked, when I had examined the doll from head to toe.

"Oh, I *love* her, Lulie. I think she's beautiful," and then remembering my manners, "thank you so much."

But I kept my promise, too. Aunt Maggie brought a cup of coffee to the table and sat with me as I ate breakfast, and Lulie, since she was already up, went pattering back and forth serving us. Aunt Maggie wanted to know all about the camp meeting, and I told her . . . but I never said a word about Lulie going up front. I was a little afraid she might ask me right out if Lulie did, and I couldn't then have lied, of course, so I kept talking a lot, telling her everything I remembered. Lulie helped, putting in things I forgot. Remembering, it was a lot more fun than it had actually been, and I could almost forget my strange feelings and queasiness. Naturally I said nothing about being sick. I was ashamed of it. Aunt Maggie laughed at the things we told, especially when Lulie told about Sis Florine getting the shakes. She said she was glad I'd had such a good time, and she told Lulie it had been very nice of her to take me. Neither Lulie nor I said anything, either, about seeing the doctor there.

Grandmother didn't go to church that morning, but Aunt Maggie and I did. Aunt Maggie had to go because she was to sing a solo, and I went because I wanted to. Adam came for us. His buggy had side curtains and would keep us from getting wet better than the surrey. We waited for him in the sitting room, where Grandfather was reading again. Aunt Maggie was putting on her gloves, one finger at a time, smoothing and stretching them on gradually. "Is Mother's head any better?" she asked Grandfather.

He looked up from his magazine. "I think the rain is disturbing her more than her head," he said, quietly.

Aunt Maggie looked out the window. The rain was still coming down steadily. "She didn't used to dislike rainy days particularly, that I remember. Just this spring and summer. Do thunderstorms frighten her? Has she always disliked them and simply hidden it?"

"I don't know, Maggie . . . but I don't think so. She doesn't seem frightened of them, now . . . more depressed than anything else, I'd say."

"Yes . . . she seems to dread them. She starts peering at the sky with the least threat of rain."

"I know. It troubles me. But . . . ."

Adam came just then and we had to leave. There weren't many people at church, and I think the preacher shortened the sermon some, for dinner was not yet ready when we got home. Adam wouldn't come in. He said he had some accounts to run over at the bank and a rainy afternoon was a good time to do them. "But you'll be over tonight?" Aunt Maggie asked him.

"Oh, yes, of course."

He didn't come, though. He telephoned soon after we had eaten dinner and said he had to go out in the country and would probably be pretty late getting home; he had better not try to come after all. He wouldn't go but for the fact that the man had driven in in all the rain, and he needed to see the farm before giving him an answer, and he had such a busy day ahead of him he couldn't spare the time Monday. Would Aunt Maggie excuse him? Of course she did, but you could tell it gave her a dull feeling of nothing to look forward to. She turned away from the phone a little droopily. "Couldn't Adam let someone else make a few of these trips?" she asked Grandfather.

"He could, but it's his responsibility," Grandfather said. "He has too strong a sense of duty to shift it."

"Well, sure . . . duty. He also had an engagement with me."

"Oh, come now, Maggie. You and Adam have too fine an understanding for you to take that tone."

Aunt Maggie smoothed her hair, then she

laughed. "Of course we do. I'm just restless. But I do," she added vehemently, "get very tired of that word duty."

"So do we all . . . often. It remains, however, unalterable. Recognition of it is one of life's most important disciplines."

"Yes, Papa."

"Would you," I put in hopefully, "like to play house with me up in the attic?" Sometimes she did, when there was nothing pressing, and surely nothing was pressing this afternoon.

She thought for a moment. "Well, this would be a good time to write letters, and I suppose I should. I suppose it's my duty to . . . but," she added, tossing her head resentfully, "duty or no duty, we'll play house in the attic."

Grandfather laughed at her. "Against whom are you being rebellious, Maggie?"

"Myself, I suppose," she mumbled, but she was in a good humor again by the time we got upstairs.

Aunt Maggie could play just like another little girl. She had so much imagination, and she seemed to enjoy occasionally just letting it go, pretending . . . play-like, we called it. Play-like I'm the mother and you're the little girl. Play-like we're going to church. Play-like we're having a party. The things one could play-like were endless. She found a rug rolled up behind the trunks that afternoon and we laid it out on the floor for our house; and she pulled up chairs and little tables and arranged them comfortably. She dug into trunks and found dress-up clothes for me, a shiny black dress with a long train, and a wonderful feather boa for me to drape around my shoulders. There were some high-heeled shoes, too, in which I could teeter about, and a gorgeous wide velvet hat with ostrich plumes dripping over its brim. I was a very fancy lady indeed. We played-like I was a duchess come to tea, and Aunt Maggie ran down to the kitchen for cookies and milk to serve. The fun was cut short, however, for Grandfather called Aunt Maggie from the foot of the stairs. "Mary and Fanny are here, Maggie."

They were her best friends and she had to go. "You go ahead and have your tea party, darling," she told me. "Play-like Topsy is your guest."

If Aunt Maggie had never been there I should have enjoyed playing house with Topsy, but after the splendor of being a duchess, it seemed a little silly to pretend with a rag doll. "You," I told her, "could never entertain a duchess." But she could serve a duchess, so I propped her up against a chair and played-like she was the maid.

I tired of the game and stripped off my finery, soon, though. The rain was still coming down steadily and heavily. I hadn't noticed it at all when Aunt Maggie was there, but now it sounded loud through the whole attic, like tiny wooden mallets hammering against the roof. It had a sad sound, I thought, a kind of weeping, dreary sound. I might as well, I decided, begin putting things away. That was the worst of games indoors. You always had to pick up after yourself and put things away, and coming as it did after the fun was over, it was a tedious chore. With no enthusiasm for the job, I nevertheless went at it. I put the clothes back in the trunk and closed the lid. I set the chairs and tables off the rug and rolled it up, then dragged it behind the trunks where it belonged. I began setting the chairs and tables neatly against the wall. One little table I had seen Aunt Maggie get from the farthest corner of the room. When I carried it over there I noticed, shoved back into the corner itself, a small tin trunk. It had been painted several times, I saw, for the paint had scaled and both brown and blue showed through in places. It had also rusted at the corners and it was dented and battered. It had a rounded top, with leather bands across it which fitted down and buckled. I wondered about it, never having noticed it before, and then I remembered that Grandmother had rearranged the attic since last summer and that this corner which had always been crowded with heavy pieces of furniture had been cleared in the new arrangement.

Probably the little trunk had always been there in the corner, hidden by the other things. I tried to open it. The buckles worked easily enough, but I found it was securely locked and there was no key. There were several round, spreading spots on the floor near it, as if grease had been spilled and not wiped up. The trunk moved easily, too, as if it were not filled with anything very heavy. I was standing there, looking at it, curious but not really much curious, when Grandfather stuck his head in the door. "Katie? I believe the rain is slacking off a little. How would you like to put on boots and a slicker and get outside for awhile?"

"Oh, I'd love it. But I haven't any boots. I didn't even bring a raincoat with me."

"We'll find you something. I think your grandmother's boots and raincoat wouldn't be much too large for you. Come along, we'll have a nice walk."

We rummaged about in the closet under the stairs where the rubbers and raincoats and umbrellas were kept, laughing over the darkness and how we kept coming up with everything but Grandmother's boots and raincoat. We did finally find them, in the very back of the closet, and the raincoat was damp and the boots, while they had been wiped free of mud, had also been recently used. Grandfather held them out to me, laughing. "Your grandmother must have had to go to Greenland."

She was such a tiny person that her things really weren't much too large for me. The coat was a little long and the sleeves had to be turned back, but Grandfather said that was good, because I was so completely covered I couldn't possibly get wet.

The rain had slowed to a misty drizzle and we had a fine walk. I wanted to go through the orchard, but Grandfather said no, the grass was too high there, but we did go down into the pasture and it was like walking in a green sea. Our boots squished through the wet grass, shaking it and parting it and sending the drops into showers on both sides, the way ships plow through the waves, dividing them and piling them and then leaving them to sink together again. Only the grass rose behind us when the pressure of our feet had passed, but it joined as if it had never been disturbed. We went as far as the creek and watched its swift, rising flow. "It is muddying," Grandfather said. Always after a hard rain the creeks rose rapidly, and just as rapidly became heavily laden with silt. Creamy foam rinsed against the bank at our feet, and Grandfather showed me a snake, its head only a little darker than the water, going with the water, untroubled by it. "That's a cottonmouth," he told me, "very poisonous."

"Do they live in the water?"

"No. But they are at home in it. They like

damp, moist places. You'll find them curled in the edges of streams, on a submerged log, anywhere it's cool and damp. Never bother one, Katie."

"Oh, I wouldn't." I wouldn't have bothered any snake, for that matter. They didn't throw me into terror, but I had no love for even the little harmless green garter snakes which crawled sometimes around the garden. Grandfather picked up a stone and tossed it at the snake, and its head disappeared.

We went back to the house around the edge of the cotton field. Water stood between the rows, and the ground where we walked was mushy with mud. "This rain will be very good for the cotton," Grandfather said, "but Choctaw will have to get a crew in here to chopping as soon as the ground dries out a little."

"The weeds will be very bad, won't they?" I asked.

"Yes. The same things that make cotton grow, make the weeds grow, too."

We came into the yard at the back of the garden and went on around by the plum thicket. "I'll bet it's still dry in there," I said, "let's see." And I plunged into the tunnel.

It had to rain very hard for a long time before the floor of the thicket became wet. In time, of course, the leaves became soaked and the water dripped on through, but often I had continued to play there, entirely dry, while a shower of rain poured down outside. Grandfather followed me and we came out into the dim room locked under the roof of the trees.

I think we both saw it at the same time . . . the umbrella opened and placed over the child's grave. It was an old, old umbrella made of black cotton. I think it had belonged to my grandfather's father, and it was a very big umbrella, made to be useful. The black canopy sheltered the small grave almost entirely, and the long, curved handle was propped with stones so that it would not slip. I slid my hand into Grandfather's, not so much frightened as puzzled. When I looked at him his face wore the strangest expression . . . . a shocked look, even a stricken one, as if he could not quite believe what he was seeing; and his hand into which I had slipped mine had no grasp in it. It was my hand that held. "Grandfather?" I whispered.

He looked down at me and then smiled. "Someone didn't want the little child's grave to get wet."

"Oh." I was touched by the thoughtfulness. "Wasn't that kind of them? Who, do you think?"

He shook his head. But I was remembering. "It was Grandmother! Don't you remember her boots and coat were wet? It was Grandmother, I'm sure."

"Perhaps."

It somehow made me feel very good toward her to think she had been so thoughtful about the little child. "But she needn't have worried, Grandfather. It doesn't get wet in here. I'll tell her."

"No. No, Katie. Don't say we've been here. Don't mention the umbrella to her."

"But why?"

"It . . . . it might make her unhappy. She would have told us if she had wanted us to know. Let's go, now."

Well, I could understand that, too. I sometimes did things about which I told no one, not because they were wrong but because they might seem queer to others. I told Grandfather, and it was the first time I had ever told anyone, why I always slept with my little brown bear in the wintertime, and never in the summer. My mother and father thought I simply liked to have him in bed with me, something to snuggle to, but actually I was convinced he was cold at night, when the weather outside was cold, and I could not sleep unless I knew he was warm, too. Oh, I could understand well enough if Grandmother was troubled by the rain falling on the little child's grave. I thought, even, I might always now be troubled by it myself. I had never before thought how it must have been; that a real child's body had been laid there, a body as real as my own. I shouldn't have wanted to lie in the rain, either. Perhaps that was why she was always so apprehensive when it looked like rain. It comforted me, however, to remember that the child need not entirely depend upon Grandmother's umbrella. The thicket was a much better protection.

Doctor Jim came that night. He was passing, he said, and saw the light in the parlor and thought we might be having some music. He wondered if he might not share it. Aunt Maggie was delighted to see him. It was she and I who had been doing duets at the piano, I picking out tunes with one finger in the treble, she following along with chords, and both of us singing. We had been singing a kind of silly little song:

Rufus Rastus Johnson Brown,
What you gonna do when the rent comes
   'round?
What you gonna say?
How you gonna pay?
What you gonna do on de Jedgement
   Day?

"Go on," Doctor Jim said.
But we left off the scoldings of Rufus Rastus Johnson Brown's nagging wife and I moved to the sofa. Doctor Jim sat down beside Aunt Maggie on the piano bench. I felt funny about him. It was not the disturbed feeling I had had at first, the mixed-up feeling

and the fear that Aunt Maggie might like him better than Adam. About that I was completely reassured. She had promised, and never in her life had Aunt Maggie broken a promise to me. What I felt now was an active dislike, beginning the day of the ball game when I realized that my father and grandfather did not like the man; and I understood too well the origin of their disapproval and dislike. I wished they had told Aunt Maggie. I thought she should know, so she wouldn't let him come any more, but I felt bound by their decision to say nothing. They had not asked *me* not to tell, to be sure, but I was certain that was because they had not thought it necessary. I had been included by my witness of what had occurred and what had been said. I did not differ with their opinions of Doctor Jim, but I did differ with their reasons for not telling Aunt Maggie. I thought them a little silly. Aunt Maggie would no more approve of Doctor Jim, if she knew, than they had done. So I was a little sullen about his appearance. At first I thought I would simply leave the room, haughtily, expressing my disapproval. Then I decided I had better stay. If he had been drinking again, I could at least run for Grandfather.

He seemed, though, to be all right. He wore the thin, black suit. I think it must have been made of bengaline, for it was slightly corded. "What were you singing?" he asked. He ran his hand over his hair, and felt the damp from the fog which had gathered after the rain had stopped. He had worn no hat, evidently. He took out his handkerchief and patted the edges of his hair, turning his head to reach the back.

"Oh, nothing," Aunt Maggie told him. "Katie and I were just fooling around . . . you know, having fun."

He tucked the handkerchief back into his breast pocket and moved to a chair. He leaned his head against the back of the chair and laid his hands on its arms, stretching out his legs. From where I sat, I could only see his profile. If I shut my eyes now I can see him again as he was that night, the hair crow-black against the rose velvet chair, his face shadowed but still somehow vitally alive, silhouetted against the light. I thought of those black cut-out silhouettes people used to do. There was a pair of them in my mother's room at home, and the doctor's face had the same clean, scissored edges, the nose, the mouth, the chin, cut thinly and neatly. "Will you sing for me?" he asked.

So Aunt Maggie sang. She began with some ballads, simple songs requiring little of her voice, trying it perhaps, testing it. Then, impatiently spreading her hands she said, "I need an accompanist."

Doctor Jim stood. "Do you have some scores?"

She looked at him questioningly and then turned swiftly to the stacks of music she kept on a shelf near the piano. She leafed through them quickly, choosing several things which she handed him. He glanced through them. " 'The Bohemian Girl' . . . yes. And . . . ah, yes, the Schubert songs, of course. Good. Fine."

He sat down at the piano, hesitated a moment, his hands hung over the keys, and then he curved his fingers and brought them down into deep, beautiful, crashing chords, as if, the indecision over, he would brook no reluctance on the part of the instrument to give its ultimate effort to him. Aunt Maggie, standing beside him, threw her head back and closed her eyes, her hands brought tightly together and gripped before her. From the chords, which had been so ruthless, his fingers ran quickly up the keyboard in an ascending arpeggio. "It is a good instrument," he said then. "Shall we try this first?"

Quietly, perfectly, he furnished the background for Aunt Maggie's voice. "I dreamt that I dwelt in marble halls." It is a too pretty song, of course, too sentimental, and the words are a little foolish, but that night it bloomed and unfolded into something exquisite. I had never heard Aunt Maggie sing so well before. It was perhaps the doctor's playing, following yet somehow leading her into better phrasing, bringing out all the

246

latent quality of her voice, urging it to a more sustained richness, which made her sing it so beautifully. She stood within the curve of the piano, embraced by it, her hands now loosely clasped before her, her head lifted, the pale blue of her dress flowing softly about her ankles. Back of her, the doctor, dark and intent, seemed joined to the piano, bound to it and part of it, the black of his head merely an extension of its shining ebony, and in the queerest way it seemed to me as if he, with the piano, embraced Aunt Maggie.

In the presence of great beauty I am always uncertain, drawn and at the same time repelled. I know so well how fragile a support it is for the soul, how demanding and at the same time how quickly forsaking; how thin and yet how imperative is its grace. Not knowing yet, I nevertheless was both glad and sorry when the song ended. I could have listened forever; and yet I could not have listened another moment.

The doctor dropped his hands from the keyboard. "Who was your teacher?"

"Werner."

He nodded. "That makes it final, doesn't it?"

"Yes." She turned away. "I did not want anything but honesty, you understand."

"From Werner you could not have got anything but honesty."

"No." She swung around toward him again,

appealing. "But there are times when I think I cannot bear it . . . when I must *make* it good enough, by sheer will and force, when I feel I must compel it . . . when I feel I *can* . . . I *will!*"

"Do you think I don't know?" he said, quietly enough at first, but his voice rose as he continued. "Do you think *I* don't know? I could *wring* what I need from this!" And he turned back to the piano smashing his hands down on the keyboard in violent discord.

Aunt Maggie put her hands over her eyes. "Don't . . . don't do that."

He reached up and pulled her hands down, looking long at her face. "Ah, Maggie. We are both cripples . . . that's what we are, cripples. Wounded and lame and limping, and flung aside." He laughed, then, and dropped her hands. "It does no good to hide your eyes. Come, shall we sing Ariel's song together, Maggie?" His fingers pecked mockingly at the keys and he made his voice a mincing falsetto, " 'Where the bee sucks there suck I: In a cowslip's bell I lie. . . .' " The tears slid down Aunt Maggie's face.

The doctor stood and put a finger under her chin, tipping her face with it. Then, quickly, he bent and kissed her, very lightly, very gently. "Forgive me, Maggie." He was gone immediately.

Aunt Maggie stood quite still for a moment. We could hear his footsteps on the front walk, rapid and quickly diminishing. When there was no longer anything to hear Aunt Maggie began slowly putting the music away. I slipped off the sofa and went to her. "He was terribly rude, Aunt Maggie."

I think she had forgotten I was there. She seemed to have to bring herself back from somewhere else. "No," she shook her head, "he wasn't rude, darling. He is only terribly hurt."

Sometime during the night I awakened, cold. The wind was blowing directly across my bed and I roused to lower the window. The wind had blown the fog away and the backyard was bright with the light of the late-rising moon; so bright that the trees and the fences were thrown back on the grass in shadows. One shadow was moving, though. When it came into the moonlight I saw that it was Grandmother, and she was carrying the big umbrella, now folded. I nodded. It was all right, now. The rain had gone away.

Twelve

Choctaw and I went fishing the next morning. As usual on Monday Lulie was washing and I was stalking her heels, helping or hindering depending upon one's point of view. Lulie always made me feel as if I were helping. She gave me small chores to do, let me splash around in the water, never told me I was in the way or to watch out I was getting wet. She talked to me, or listened to me talk, by the hour. I told her things that, as close as I felt to my mother and father, and to Aunt Maggie and Grandfather, I would never have told them, such as the way I was sometimes so certain I did not belong to my family at all, that I was an orphan and had been adopted by them. "I don't look like my mother and I don't look like my father," I told her. "Everyone says I don't look like anyone in the family at all. Do you suppose they found me somewhere, in an orphan's home, perhaps, and adopted me, Lulie?"

"Naw," she said reassuringly, "whut you mean you don't look like 'em? You gonna be the spitting image of your Aunt Maggie when you grow up. Same eyes, same nose, same color hair . . . you gonna be tall like her, too."

"Am I? But I'm dumpy and fat, now."

"You'll skin up one of these days. Lots of chil'ren is fat when they little. Commence growing up they don't know when to stop. You wait and see, you gonna be a nice, tall girl, like Miss Maggie. And you got a laugh just like her. Sometimes when I'se in the kitchen and hears you all in the sitting room, I can't tell which'n of you it is laughing . . . naw, you a Rogers all right . . . ain't no doubts about that."

It was such a relief to have pointed out the ways in which I was like someone in the family, and it was especially comforting to be told I was like Aunt Maggie. If I couldn't be beautiful like my mother, I would rather be like Aunt Maggie than anyone else in the world. Lulie always knew and said exactly the right things. Like the time I told her about feeling, sometimes, as I lay in the dark in my bed, that I was dead and lying at the bottom of a grave, of the terror of the dark and the grave gradually creeping over me until I felt smothered and choking and I wanted to get up and run and run and run, and that I had to hold tight to the bed to keep from it, make myself lie still, make my thoughts turn to something else; and that sometimes the effort was so great that I found myself wet with sweat, panting with fear and desperation. I remember that she looked at me with pity and put both arms around me. "Why you so scared of dying, Katie? Ain't nothing to be afraid of. Just close your eyes and die, that's all."

"But I don't want to die. I don't want to be buried in the ground. Why must everybody die, Lulie?"

"On account of that's the way the Lord planned it, Katie. He don't want nobody shuffling around in their old bodies up in heaven. He want to give 'em brand new ones . . . nice, sweet ones that'll float around like a cloud. He got plans for ever'body, Katie. You know what happens when you dies? You don't stay in the ground, sugar. You puts on your nice, new body and you goes up to heaven, and old Saint Peter, he open the gate for you and he say, 'Welcome to heaven, Katie, we is glad you've come.' And then he turn around and he tell one of the angels standing by, and he say, 'Here, Angel, give this little girl a nice, clean white robe with real good wings, so she can fly around light and fast. Make sure the feathers is real downy and fine, and give her a halo for her head. Give her one that'll twinkle like a star, all bright and shiny. And give her a harp, too, and mind, don't you go giving her no old second-hand one, you give her a nice, new one, real bright and shiny so she can play sweet, and you make ready a room for her in the best mansion we got.' That whut old Saint Peter say, and that whut happen when you dies."

"But suppose I'm bad and don't go to heaven?"

"You ain't gonna be that bad. You just do the best you can all your days, and the Lord, he gonna remember it. He just close his eyes to the badness in folks and look on the sweet ways. They ain't nothing to be scared of."

She believed it, all of it . . . and I believed it, too. When I said that terrible prayer of childhood, "Now I lay me down to sleep," and then the terror of dying before I awoke crept over me, I remembered the angel and the clean, white robe, the halo and the harp and I was a great deal more comforted by the clear-cut promise of Lulie than by all the theological abstractions of body and soul. It was my body that would die. It was my body I wanted resurrected, robed, haloed and provided with music. Lulie offered me the promise that it would be and I fended off the specter of death with her conviction. All children need angels. For that matter, most adults do, too.

Choctaw had built the fire under the big black kettle and had replenished the stack of wood so Lulie wouldn't run short during the day. He stood dusting his hands together, then. "Want to go fishing, Katie? Fish'll be biting mighty good today after the rain."

Lulie started laughing. "Bet you done got you a can full of worms dug up."

"I sure have. You want to go, Katie, run ask Mister Cap."

I wanted to go, of course, but I had come to believe that Lulie couldn't manage a washing without me. I looked at the huge baskets of clothing. "Well, this is washday, Choctaw . . . I don't know."

Lulie flicked her hand at me, dripping water. "Oh, you needn't stay to help me. You done helped a lot already, and I can do all right now. You run along."

Grandfather said I could go, so Choctaw rigged a pole for me and one for himself. He dropped a handful of hooks into his pocket and picked up the bait bucket and I shouldered my pole. "You ketch a nice mess of fish, Katie," Lulie told me, "but don't you go falling in the creek, and don't you go getting snake-bit, neither."

I looked at Choctaw. He must have told her about the time I fell in the creek, but I sniffed disdainfully just the same. "I haven't fallen in the creek since I was a small child," I told her, "besides, I can swim now."

"You be careful just the same."

We set off through the cotton field, Choctaw taking one row and I the one right beside it. The cotton was as high as my head now, and if I didn't look up at Choctaw I could easily pretend it was a jungle. I could pretend so successfully that my fishing pole became a gun and lions and tigers materialized on all sides of me until I was surrounded by them. At the shivering point, just as they were ready to pounce, all I had to do was look over into the next row and there was Choctaw striding along, his eyes on the cotton, a chew of tobacco bulging in his cheek. Choctaw never talked very much, and today was no exception. He walked along looking at the cotton, thinking maybe about it, maybe about the best place to fish, maybe about nothing. He rarely gave you a clue as to what he was thinking. And I, who chattered tirelessly to others, didn't talk much when I was with him. But I was never uncomfortable with him. It was more as if his silences made a cushion for one's own thoughts, and his presence reinforced them.

When we came to the creek he looked at the water in several places and finally chose a spot a little upstream where the bank was shaded by overhanging cottonwood trees and the water was fairly deep. Several logs had been caught near the bank and formed a breakwater. "You sit here on the bank, Katie," he told me, "and drop your line on the far side of those logs. Ought to be some good fish just laying there waiting for a worm."

He tied a small hook on my line and held out the can of worms to me. I looked at it uneasily, and then up at him. "Aren't you going to put the worm on my hook?"

"Nope. You want to catch fish, you got to bait your own hook."

It was almost as bad as letting the doctor take the piece of bark out of my hand. I reached for a worm several times, each time drawing back before touching them. At last I shut my eyes, made a quick dive into the can with my fingers, came up with something slick and wiggly, and by only looking through slitted eyes and by practially holding my breath I got him impaled on the hook. Quickly, then, so I couldn't see his wiggles I dropped him in the water. Choctaw paid no more attention to me than if I hadn't been there. He eased out on the drift of logs and dropped his line over on the other side.

We had our best luck the first hour. Each of us caught several perch and sunfish, and because his hook was larger Choctaw caught a few crappie. I had to take my fish off the hook, too, and I'm not sure that wasn't worse than putting the worm on. I felt so sorry for them. At the same time I took great pride in counting the ones I had caught on the string. Then the first rush was over and we waited long minutes between bites. Once Choctaw pointed up the creek and I saw a tufted bird flying over the water, whirling, turning, but never getting very far from the stream. "Watch him," Choctaw said.

I watched patiently, and was rewarded by seeing him dart suddenly and swiftly down and down, skimming the water, and then, a small fish in his mouth, just as swiftly zoom up and away. "Why, he caught a fish," I said in amazement.

"That's the way he gets his food," Choctaw said, "that's why he's called a kingfisher."

During the long, quiet times between bites now he told me about other birds, identified them for me as he caught sight of them . . . a peewee, a catbird, a killdeer, and others he did not know the name of, but knew their habits and could imitate their calls. He told me about the bugs on the water, too . . . the striders and the swimmers, and how they all warred on each other, and about the dragon-flies, the darning needles, he called them. And that was the day we saw the Red Admiral butterfly. Choctaw didn't know the name of it and neither did I, then, but we saw it hovering over a joe-pye weed and he told me to take a good look at it for it wasn't a common sight to see and I might never again see another one. "See the red marks on it," he said, "you'll see a lot of butterflies around in the summer, but I reckon that one is the king of 'em all. You can always tell him by the red bands. Ain't he the prettiest thing?"

He was exquisitely beautiful with the distinct red bands on his fore wings and the red borders on the hind ones, hovering gracefully as if he couldn't decide about the joe-pye weed, then suddenly making up his mind it wouldn't do and floating lazily away. "There's lots of pretty things in the woods and the fields," Choctaw said. "Never a day goes by a man can't feast his eyes." He chuckled. "Be nice if folks were as pretty."

"Oh, some of them are," I insisted. "My mother is . . . and Aunt Maggie is, and Lulie. I think Lulie is beautiful, don't you?"

He scratched his chin and looked at me thoughtfully. "Well, yes, she's right pretty. But she's shifty . . . changeable. You ever break one of them thermometer things and hold the little ball of quicksilver in your hand?"

I nodded, remembering exactly how the quicksilver had moved uneasily around in the palm of my hand, quick to move, uncertain of its destination.

"That's the way Lulie is," Choctaw said, "you don't ever know what to make of her."

"But she's good, Choctaw."

He squatted beside me and picked up a twig and started making drawings in the dirt with it. "I don't know if she's good or not. I don't know as I like her too well," he looked at me and grinned, "but I got a feeling I'm going to end up marrying that girl. I've not ever wanted to marry before . . . not ever cared one way or another whether I got married or not . . . but Lulie . . ." He threw the twig down and went to look at his fishing pole which he had propped against the bank. I thought he had finished talking, but he lifted the hook out of the water, inspected the bait and dropped it back in, and then as if he had forgotten he'd been talking to me he shrugged his shoulders and rammed his hands into his pockets, saying, "I somehow got to have that girl."

We went home soon after that with a fine string of fish. Choctaw cleaned them and Lulie fried them for supper that night, and even after they were fried I thought I could tell the ones I had caught. "I caught that one," I'd say, pointing to the one on Grandfather's plate.

"How do you know, Katie?" Aunt Maggie asked.

"Because it's so little," Grandfather said, teasing, "all the little ones, Katie caught."

But I was undisturbed by the teasing. It had been a fine day and I knew something that made me very happy. Choctaw was in love with Lulie, and everyone in love always got married and lived happily ever afterward.

Choctaw and Lulie, of necessity then, were going to get married someday and live happily ever afterward.

Thirteen

By the middle of the week following the rain Choctaw was able to start having the cotton hoed. He was having it done this year by a family of Negroes who had moved recently to a little farm across the creek in the bottoms. "They worked for Mister Adam last year," he told Grandfather, "and he said they were good workers . . . steady, he said, and you could count on 'em."

"How many of them are there?"

"There's the man, Willliam, and the woman, and they got six children big enough to help, three of 'em nearly grown."

"They ought to be able to handle it, then."

"Yes, sir, I thought so. Be a relief to have one family doing it . . . not have the work scattered out among several."

"Yes."

They came to work early one morning. They were in the field and ready to start by seven o'clock, and Choctaw was ready for them with hoes ground to a razor sharpness, and a barrel of drinking water set in the shade. A bucket and several gourd dippers were there, too. The Negroes, of course, wouldn't stop their work and walk all the long way down the rows to the drinking barrel. Choctaw would take water to them about every hour, and he would also trundle along a small grindstone with which to sharpen their hoes as they needed it. He could also keep an eye on their work. "Never was a field hand yet," he claimed, "did his best work unless the boss was looking."

I went to the field with Grandfather that first morning to watch them begin. I was surprised when I saw that the woman was the thin, ash-colored one who had played the tambourine . . . the one Lulie had called Sis Florine; the one who had brought the meeting to a climax that Saturday night by getting the shakes. She was even more gray looking in the daylight, but her intensity was gone and she was merely another Negro woman, shapeless skirts draggled with dew and her face almost hidden beneath a faded sunbonnet, lips puckered with snuff.

Each of the eight, the man, the woman and the six boys and girls large enough to work, took a row. The man appeared to set the pace, an unhurried one, and they all kept pretty well abreast. Occasionally when one of them struck an especially thick-grown place he fell a little behind, but one of the others usually moved over to help and soon they were caught up. There was a kind of practiced, lazy ease in the way they worked, the hoes sliding and scraping with a minimum of motion; even the smaller children had the same effortless-looking rhythm. Grandfather looked at Choctaw and they both nodded. "They'll do," Grandfather said.

I thought of the long days under the sun when they would be moving like a slow scythe up and down the rows. "Don't they get awfully tired?" I asked Grandfather.

"No," he told me, "not the way they work. They know how to save themselves."

"But it gets so hot."

"They'll drink lots of water and sweat a lot. You don't feel the heat too much that way. They'll just keep moving along, slow and sure," he chuckled, "like the tortoise. In two weeks' time they'll have the field clean."

We went back to the house then, passing by the shade tree where the water barrel was. There were four of the children who were too young to help, but of course they had had to be brought along. There were the twins, a boy and a girl, looking to be six or seven years old; there was a smaller boy, about three I thought, and a baby not yet walking. The baby sat on a quilt his mother had brought for him, playing with one of the gourd dippers. The others had been running about in some game of their own, but as we passed they stopped and watched us, shyly. Grandfather spoke to them, but none of them answered, just ducked their heads and edged closer together.

They were not so shy with me when I went back in the afternoon. Oh, at first they were, but I took my rag doll and a box of cookies. Food will break down almost any kind of a barrier between children, and soon they all had cookies in each hand, and the little girl was cuddling the doll. She crooned over it and smoothed its silk skirts, exactly as I did. "Wish I had me one just like it," she said.

"I wish I could trade you the doll for your baby brother," I told her. I was fascinated by him. He was as round and as brown as a chocolate drop, and fat and soft like a ball of dough. His head was covered with black fuzz and his big eyes rolled around alarmingly, showing irises as white as milk. When he laughed, which he did a lot, he had four teeth which looked like little kernels of white corn stuck in his pink gums. I stood him up and held him and he braced his stout little fat legs, wobbled about a bit and then pranced delightedly in a quick jig. All of us laughed at him, and the little girl shook her head. "I don't reckon Ma would want me to trade," she said, a little sadly.

"Oh, I was just wishing," I said quickly, "of course she wouldn't trade. He's so sweet."

"He's right sweet, but he's a heap of trouble . . . always puking and messing 'round."

He didn't smell very sweet, for a fact. He had sort of a sour and rancid smell, like woodsmoke and meat grease, but he was a fat, happy baby and he rarely cried. Florine came and nursed him once during the morning and once again during the afternoon, and he ate cookies, cold bread and even gnawed on meat bones left from their dinner in between. They brought their own noon meal in a big basket and ate it under the tree during the hour they took in the middle of the day.

I came to know the four smallest children very well, for gradually I got in the way of going out to play with them every day; at first I went only in the afternoons, but soon I was spending the mornings with them, too. The twins were Ruby and Tempy. The three-year-old was Buck, and the baby, for some reason, was called Ireland. Mostly they called him "the baby," however. We played hop-scotch, at which they were very good, being nimbler than I who was too plump to hop very well, but as young as they were, they were already beginning to learn the lesson which was a necessity for them to survive; they did not win too often from the white child.

Complacently I accepted what they were yet too unskilled to hide, for their efforts to lose were bumbling and obvious. I accepted the intention, and if it had not been offered it is not altogether certain I might not have demanded it.

I took my jacks sometimes, I was better at that than they, and with a dull knife we played mumblepeg. Every game in which skill was pitted against skill began with that solemn incantation, "Wire, briar, limberlock, three geese in a flock . . ." to see who would have the advantage of being "it." I was shrewd enough to know that said in a certain rhythm it always came out with the one you began with, and I recall struggling with my conscience to keep from cheating.

We played hide-and-seek, prisoner's base, and run, sheep, run, and of course we played house and had tea parties. Nearly always I was allowed to bring cookies or doughnuts or those crunchy little fried apple pies Lulie made, and it may have been that I was more welcome for the good things to eat I could provide, than for my own company. I may have been something of a tyrant, but they were glad, I think, to have someone else to play with, and they were generally kind and very goodnatured with me.

They were not always kind to each other, though. Frequently they quarreled, and sometimes they even fought, slapping and

266

pulling hair and kicking and screaming. Once they got into a fight and ended up pelting each other with cotton bolls. Cotton bolls can hurt when they are green and hard, and before long Tempy had Ruby streaking down the field, crying and yelling for help. He stood there hopping up and down yelling after her, sort of half singing, half chanting, "Run, nigger, run, the pattero'll git you; run, nigger, run, you can't git away!" Over and over he shouted it at her, until she was out of sight and safely hidden in the cotton.

It stuck so in my mind that I went marching into the kitchen singing it myself that evening. Grandfather looked up, "Where did you hear that, Katie?"

I told him. "What's a pattero, Grandfather?"

"A pattero is really a patrol . . . that's just the way the Negroes say it."

"Well, what's a patrol?"

"In the old days when a Negro ran away he usually tried to get up north where people would help him. But patrols kept watch and sometimes caught the runaways and sent them back home to their masters. They had a great fear of the patrols. That song goes back to those old days. It's not a very happy song." He told me about another song, too, "Foller de drinkin'-gou'd." He said, "You know the Big Dipper? Remember how it always points to the North Star? The Negroes called it the drinking gourd, and when they ran away they followed it north. They could keep it before them and find their way from one marker to another along the trail." To this good day I never, on a starry night, look at the Big Dipper that it does not become the drinkin'-gou'd, and the beckoning beacon to be followed on that long, black trail. That night the words of the songs, and the things Grandfather said had the effect of turning my skin dark and of sending me stumbling and hurrying out into the black night, searching the sky for the drinkin'-gou'd, following it, always running and hurrying and looking back, the heart beating fiercely, the breath coming fast and the legs stumbling with weariness . . . "Run, nigger, run, you can't get away." The bitter thing is that they have not yet got away.

Grandmother called us to supper and shiveringly glad to be myself again I forgot the songs, forgot Tempy and Ruby, forgot everything except my empty stomach and its need to be filled.

Sometimes Lulie went out to the field and hoed awhile. She liked to get out of the house and occasionally she had an hour or two in the afternoon when she could manage it. The children did not like her. When they saw her pass by they always stopped playing and watched silently. One day Ruby said,

"Mammy say she a bad woman."

"Why, she is not!" I was indignant. "She's as good as can be."

Ruby dropped her head and put her finger in her mouth. "That whut Mammy say. Say she sneak off from the meetin' an' go in the woods. Say ain't no good gonna come of it."

"She doesn't either sneak off from the meeting. She goes to the wagon the back way, sometimes. I was there when she did the other night."

Ruby spoke around her finger and I could barely understand what she said next. "Mammy say she sneak off. Say she go in the woods with a white man."

"She does not! What white man?"

"I do' know."

"Yes, you do know, too. What white man?"

"I do' know. Hones', I don't. Mammy jist say some white man."

"Ruby, you do too know. If your mammy knows she said who it was."

"No, she never."

"All right for you, Ruby. If you don't tell, I'll go back to the house and I won't play with you any more. And you won't have *any more* cookies and doughnuts."

"Whyn't you ask me?" Tempy said suddenly. "I don't keer to tell."

"Who?"

"That new doctor."

I think I had known all along, for I

remember I felt no surprise. I had to brazen it out, though. "Oh, the doctor . . . him. Well," and I told a deliberate lie, but I crossed my fingers as I told it so it wouldn't count, "he's been giving Lulie some medicine. She's been sick. I guess he was just giving her some more medicine or something, or maybe just seeing if she was feeling better."

Ruby took her finger out of her mouth and grinned. "Yeah, I reckon that was it. You come play, now?"

"Oh, sure. But you're very silly to think Lulie is bad. *She's* the one makes all our cookies and cakes and pies. I don't think she would make any more if she knew people were talking about her." I thought I might as well threaten in Lulie's name as my own.

"We not," they promised, "we not saying nothing 'bout her no more."

"You'd better tell your mammy, too," I said, adding grandly, "Grandfather just might not want somebody chopping his cotton that was talking about Lulie."

"Aw, naw, Katie. Mammy whup us. She whup us somethin' terrible do she know we tole. You ain't wantin' us to git a whuppin'?"

"Oh, well," I gave in, weak at the first mention of suffering, "you needn't tell your mammy then. But don't *ever* talk about Lulie again, you hear? Cross your hearts and hope to die!"

270

"Cross our hearts and hope to die."

I was worried, though, and I hung around Lulie in the kitchen that night until we were alone. I said I'd dry the dishes. It was a job I hated, but I had to talk to her. "What you pussyfootin' 'round about?" Lulie asked, grinning, when the others had finally left the room. "You ain't got no love for helping with the dishes, I know. You want something?"

I told her, bluntly, what Florine had said. She just laughed. "Florine, she just lying, that's whut. I ain't been sneaking off meeting nobody. Whut I want to sneak off and go in the woods for? That Choctaw cut my gizzard out did I do that."

"Not if he didn't know it," I said, shrewdly enough.

"Too much risk him finding out." She shrugged. "Besides I got more sense'n to go messing around a white man."

"I saw Doctor Jim getting back in his buggy the other night, myself, Lulie. And you *did* come out of the woods. Maybe he'd been in the woods, too."

She laughed again. "Wouldn't be surprised if he had. Man has to piss once in a while."

I was so shocked that I froze for a moment. That was a word one only saw written in chalk on sidewalks, or on the walls of public toilets. I think I had never in my life actually heard it said before. Then for some reason it struck

271

me as terribly funny and I began laughing. I could never dry dishes without getting the whole front of my dress wet, and in laughing the glass I was drying slipped from my clutch and shattered into a thousand pieces on the floor. "Now see whut you done," Lulie grumbled. "Go get the broom."

We swept up the broken glass. "Katie, honey," Lulie said then, "don't you worry your head no more about it. I can handle Florine all right. I can shut her up in a hurry."

"How?"

She giggled. "I happens to know that Florine's been sneaking off in the woods herself . . . with that banjo player. She ain't gonna talk much when I get through telling her whut I knows. Folks," she said darkly, "that lives in glass houses hadn't better throw no stones."

"I thought," I said, astonished at this revelation of sneaking off into the woods, "that you all went to the meeting to get religion."

"Oh, we does . . . we does. But," she giggled again, "they ain't as much diff'runce between the spirit and the flesh as you'd think. You get one worked up and the other'n is liable to get worked up, too." I felt I was getting mired down in a bog of dark reasoning beyond my understanding. I threw the dishcloth down. "You ain't through, yet," Lulie said.

"You finish," I told her, "I only wanted to

272

tell you about Florine."

"All right, then. You done tole me, and I done tole you. Run along, now."

I didn't believe her, though. And it was not so much that I didn't believe Lulie, as that I didn't believe in the doctor. But Lulie had convinced me of one thing. She didn't need anyone worrying about her. She could take care of herself very well.

When I went in the sitting room Aunt Maggie was just hanging up the telephone receiver. "Want to go to band practice?"

Of course I wanted to go to band practice. It was practically a certainty that I would want to go everywhere, but band practice was something very special. Grandfather looked up from his paper. "It's high time they were beginning. They've not too long before the Reunion now."

"Oh, more than a month, yet, Papa. That's plenty of time."

"Not if they learn something new . . . and I hope they do. But tell Adam for God's sake," he looked quickly at Grandmother, "for heaven's sake not to try that 'Marche Militaire' again this year. They'd better stick to Sousa."

"Yes, Papa." Aunt Maggie was behind him and she reached out and tweaked a thin lock of his hair up into a peak. "That was my doing, you know."

"It was a mistake." Grandfather smoothed

273

down the twist of hair.

"Yes. We'll stick to the familiar things this year . . . and, of course, 'Dixie.' "

Grandfather peered at her over his spectacles. "What's wrong with 'Dixie'?"

"Nothing. Not one thing."

"Always march to it in the parade . . . open the concerts and the ball games with it."

"Yes, I know, dear. Is it twenty or thirty times it is played during the Reunion?"

"Makes no difference how many times it is played." Grandfather rattled his paper irritably. "Confound it, Maggie, it *is* a Confederate Reunion."

"Of course, dear," and she laid her face against his, softening, I suspect, as she remembered that they were after all getting pretty old, those Confederate veterans and they would not be marching to the strains of "Dixie" or any other tune very many more years. The ranks were fewer each year. Time enough then for the valor of "Dixie" to die away.

It was just a small-town band, very uncertain and very noisy, sounding like and yet never quite achieving the smoothness of a German band. Only the tuba and the base drum could be counted on to oompah concertedly. There was a preponderance of trumpets and trombones, and two very rattly snare drums. They were most effective in the parades, where they rolled and flourished importantly. In the band concerts, given each night of the Reunion, they were apt to add merely a note of confusion. Adam played the trombone and, I think, he was better than the others. At any rate I was fascinated by the long, slender instrument and by the way he could bring forth such a deep, shivering slide from it.

The band would practice two nights a week now in preparation for the big event of the year, and many of the townspeople, perhaps I should say most of them, would drive out to the picnic grove to watch and listen. It was someplace to go and it was entertaining, and in a little town where not much happens, both are important. The bandstand was circular in shape and while the benches had not yet been brought out, and would not be until just before the Reunion, people took blankets and laprobes along to spread on the ground. They would gather and sit neighborly, gossip a little, exchange news, laugh a little at one another and immoderately at the antics of the band, which always clowned around a bit during practice. They would judge the improvement or lack of it in the music, and sometimes when the band played especially well, or played an especially beautiful waltz they would listen quietly, even dreamily, caught up in some magic maze of beauty.

The repertoire of the band was not as limited as one might think. It included most of the

John Philip Sousa marches, nearly all of the Stephen Foster airs, several of the Strauss waltzes, a polka or two, some schottisches, and, daringly, several ragtime pieces. I especially remember "Under the Bamboo Tree," because after the band played the verse, everyone joined in singing the chorus. Some of the words I have never forgotten . . . "If you lika me, like I lika you, we both lika the same. I lika say, this very day, I lika change your name. . . ."

I also remember "Bill Bailey, Won't You Please Come Home," because it had such an exciting trombone slide in the chorus. I can see Adam to this good day, red-faced, perspiring, tooting along with the rest of the band until time for the slide, then rearing back slightly and pushing that long, blue slide right out the end of the horn, beginning on a B-flat, I think, and ending on D . . . "She moans the whole day lo-o-o-o-ong! I'll do de cooking, darling, I'll pay de rent . . . I knows I'se done you wro-o-o-o-ong!" I waited for those slides, just as Adam must have waited for them, and a long shiver of delight ran down my backbone from the B-flat vertebrae to the D, and for some reason I always wound up giggling.

It was the kind of music the people wanted to hear; the kind of music the men of the band liked to play. I found no fault with it then, and I find no fault with it today. It was not great music, certainly, nor was it even especially well played, but it was something . . . a reaching out beyond the familiar and the routine. It was a passion, small and only meagerly recognized, but a passion nevertheless for some lustre added to life, some aching birth of expression, a part of the same ache which gives birth to all knowledge, to all beauty, to all effort, everywhere.

Adam came for us, but as soon as he had us settled on the ancient plaid robe he always carried in his buggy, he had to leave us. It was a very hot night with no breath of air stirring. There seemed to be no coolness even in the ground beneath the robe. Aunt Maggie fanned us with a broad palm-leaf fan, and I remember the slow, rhythmic movement of the fan back and forth and the gentleness of the stirred air against my hot face and neck. I remember that Aunt Maggie loosened the wristbands of her shirtwaist and pushed the sleeves up. "I don't care how it looks," she said, "I'm just too hot to care."

"It looks fine." The voice came from behind us and we both turned, startled. It was Doctor Jim, of course. It seemed to me he was always somewhere near, on the fringe of things, never quite joining and belonging, just sort of drifting around on the edges . . . the ball games, the Negro meeting, stopping at the house when he was in the mood, and now turning up at band practice. Well, of course it was his town, too, and he was only doing what everyone else did, more or less. But everyone else joined in, enjoying things. He seemed only to be looking on, making gestures. He folded his long legs and sat on a corner of the robe. "May I?"

"It's Adam's robe," I said grudgingly, ungraciously. Aunt Maggie poked me with the handle of her fan.

"Yes, I know," the doctor said, a little grittily. "And it's Adam's girl. That's what you really mean, isn't it, Katie?"

"Jim," Aunt Maggie warned.

"Oh, for heaven's sake, Maggie . . . if the child is perceptive enough to feel jealousy for Adam, she's too perceptive to be fooled by trying to ignore it. She's more honest than you are, at that. At least she admits there's a situation."

"She doesn't know anything about it."

"She doesn't need to know anything about it. She feels it."

"That's enough, Jim. There *is no situation.*"

"Very well, my lady. You hear that, Katie? There is no situation, so you needn't be a dog in the manger with Adam's robe. Ah," he began wheedling, "sweet Kate, pretty Kate, kiss-me-Kate . . . why don't you like me, Kate?"

When he used my *Taming of the Shrew* names, it softened me, reminding me of my father, but it flustered me to have him ask so directly why I didn't like him. I hung my head and muttered, "I like you all right."

"But not as well as Adam. Why don't you like me as well as Adam, Kate?"

With some last-ditch courage I determined he should know. "Because you're not as nice."

He drew his legs up and crooked his arms around them, resting his chin on his knees. "Well," he said, "I asked for it, didn't I? Maybe you just haven't known me as long, Katie. In what way is Adam so nice? He seems like a very dull fellow to me."

"Oh, no," I said, "he isn't dull at all. He knows all the same things we do, and the same people and he likes them, and he knows our jokes and he has fun with us."

"You see! That's just because you've known him longer, Katie. He doesn't know much about beauty . . . or things far away and beckoning, and he doesn't know much about the living pain a person may carry around inside him . . . he doesn't really know much about anything except Stanwick and the bank and baseball."

I was disgusted. He was pulling an old trick on me, and he was not really talking to me at all. He was talking through me to Aunt Maggie. Doggedly, though, I said one more thing. "He is very good."

"I see," he said, quite softly. Then he

chuckled and turned directly to Aunt Maggie. "I can't hope to match that, for obviously I am not good. But, oh, I have such lovely sins to offer!"

Aunt Maggie had been sitting aloof from all this, fanning a little, watching the band settling down, tuning up, acting as if she only half heard what was being said, but when the doctor turned to her she stopped her fan midway in a stroke and said, very evenly, "Irony does not become you, Jim."

"Doesn't it? I thought it did. It comes so naturally."

"It comes *too* naturally. It borders on bitterness. What do you expect to gain?"

The doctor dropped his chin again and mumbled against his knees. "Nothing. Nothing, really. You are so safely fenced around . . . by Stanwick and Adam and baseball games and band practices and that pre-Civil War atmosphere in your home . . . no, I don't expect to gain a thing."

Aunt Maggie's fan went very rapidly, but all she said was, "Hush, they're going to begin."

The men of the band, those who had worn them, had taken off their coats, but it was evidently very hot under the lights in the bandstand. They were all mopping perspiration, their faces glistening, Adam's especially looking very hot and red. I wished he weren't quite so homely. He so rarely looked as nice as he was, and tonight, his rough hair standing up even more unruly than usual, his ears sticking out big and awkward from his head, his collar loosened and much wilted, he looked just about as unprepossessing as a man could ever look. If a woman wanted a distinguished-looking man, one in whose appearance she could take great pride, it would never be Adam she would choose, because he would always look a little used and rumpled, a little ordinary and plain. The country farm boy was not hidden at all in Adam. But neither, of course, was his good business head hidden, nor his straight-hewn sense of purpose, nor his great joy in such simple and uncomplicated things as baseball and the band; and his goodness shone from his face as openly as his big nose and wide mouth and stubborn jaw. I could not help remembering, though . . . he doesn't know much about beauty . . . he doesn't know much about . . . oh, so many things that Aunt Maggie knew, music, travel, art, and Doctor Jim knew about them, too, and no man was ever handsomer than Doctor Jim. It was all so disturbing, in spite of Aunt Maggie's promise.

The band leader was a little fat German, Hans Schultz, who had a watch and clock repair shop. He also tuned pianos and gave violin lessons to the three or four pupils wanting them. It had been he who had organized the band in the first place, and it was he who bullied and sweated and cajoled them into giving some semblance of a musical performance. He scuttled about on the bandstand now, handing out the music. Doctor Jim had evidently not run into him before. "Who is the little fat fellow?" he asked.

Aunt Maggie told him. "*He* would know about that living pain you spoke of," she said, a little sarcastically.

"Not if he's leading the Stanwick band."

"Maybe that's why he's leading the Stanwick band. There are other things one may do with pain, you know, besides hug it to yourself."

"Maggie, preaching does not become you."

The band crashed into the opening bars of the "Washington Post March" just then. The doctor closed his eyes. "Oh my God. How can you bear it?"

"They'll get better, with practice."

"If they don't, they should be torn asunder."

There were some horrible discords, I must admit, and the doctor did not even wait for them to finish the first piece. He just suddenly unwound his legs and stood. "Goodnight, Maggie. Not even for love will I endure this."

I was glad to have him go, but Aunt Maggie sighed. "Oh, but he provokes me! He dramatizes everything so."

It was strange, I thought, seeing how the doctor had discussed Adam such a short while before, that Adam should speak of him on the way home. It was as if each man were deeply aware of the other. Adam and Aunt Maggie had been talking, naturally, about the band and Adam had laughed somewhat ruefully and admitted they were very rusty. "Hans has his work cut out to whip us into shape by the time of the Reunion."

"You need to play the year around," Aunt Maggie said; "you can't hope to be good with a few weeks' work each year."

"I know. I wish we could. I'd like it myself, but Hans hasn't the time during the winter, and we haven't the persistence to stick to it without him."

"Couldn't you lead the band yourself?"

"Me? Lord, no. I don't know enough music. I just barely manage to slide along on the trombone. I have much more enthusiasm than skill." Aunt Maggie laughed comfortably and said nothing. Adam then asked, "Wasn't that Jim Davis talking with you just before we began?"

"Yes . . . but he didn't stay long."

"He didn't like the way the band played," I piped up.

"Well," Adam said, laughing. "I expect we did sound pretty terrible to him. Doesn't he know quite a bit about music?"

"Quite a bit," Aunt Maggie said. "He

hoped to be a concert pianist."

"Wonder if we couldn't get him to help us out in the winter? Of course as long as Hans is interested, it's his band in the summer . . . but if Jim would be interested, he might . . . ."

"Darling," Aunt Maggie interrupted him, and she called him darling so rarely that it was somehow very strange to hear it, "darling, you're so very good, and you are also so very obvious. He wouldn't do it. He simply has to work this out for himself. I don't think you can help him. Not with the Stanwick band, at any rate."

"I suppose not. But it might do no harm to ask him . . . this fall, maybe."

"It won't do any good. He's too bitter, and he seems determined to remain bitter."

Always, later, Adam grieved because he said he should have tried harder to understand Doctor Jim. He said he had not been a good enough friend to him. "I feel so sorry for him," he said to Aunt Maggie that night.

"He would not appreciate your sympathy," Aunt Maggie said, and she laughed, rather shortly. "No one but you could possibly have a heart big enough to feel sorry for the man who is your rival."

Adam didn't say anything for a moment. When he spoke his voice was very quiet. "Is he? I'm afraid I didn't know that."

"In his own eyes he is."

"In yours?"

Aunt Maggie spoke quickly, "No . . . no, Adam."

"Then it's not important."

They were quiet for a long time, then Adam spoke again. "What was that you sang in church Sunday?"

" 'Cum sanctu Spiritu.' Why?"

"I liked it, very much. And you sang it so well."

"Yes . . . yes, I was in good voice, Sunday. It went well." There was another time of quiet, then Aunt Maggie said, "But it was not Sieglinde. Oh, Adam, if I could just have had a little success . . . just a little, I think I should not feel quite so badly."

Adam's voice was very gentle. "To me you are just as much a success singing *'Cum sanctu Spiritu'* in the Stanwick Methodist Church as you would be singing Sieglinde at the Metropolitan."

"You're sweet . . . but there is a difference, you know, Adam. There is a vast difference."

"I suppose so. But I can't think it is failure if one is simply not sufficiently endowed with a natural gift. If you have made every effort, if you have worked hard and tried with everything that is in you and the lack is in the endowment and not in your efforts, then I can't see it as failure."

"Suppose, Adam, when you went to the university with your heart set on learning banking and business administration, that you had worked just as hard as you had it in you to work, singleheartedly and without stint. And suppose with all your efforts it remained beyond you . . . you had to give it up. What would you have done?"

"I see. Well . . . I suppose I would have come back home and simply been as good a farmer as I knew how to be."

"With no bitterness for having failed? Be honest, now, Adam."

He laughed. "A little, I'm certain. Not bitterness so much, perhaps, as wistfulness. I don't suppose one could help that, but," he maintained stoutly, "when a thing is final there is nothing to be done . . . it simply has to be accepted."

"That's what I am trying to do," Aunt Maggie said.

"I know . . . and you are trying very wonderfully."

Aunt Maggie bent over me and lifted me into the seat more comfortably. "Let's get on home, Adam. Katie is nearly asleep."

Fourteen

It was on the Fourth of July that we had the battle and the barbecue and the fireworks. Five weeks of the summer had gone, and when I took stock, counting back and then counting ahead to what was left, I was uncomforted by the fact that twice as many weeks remained to me. "Nearly ten weeks, Katie," Aunt Maggie said, "that's a long, long time."

It did seem long . . . ten weeks, from Sunday to Sunday, and yet, knowing how swiftly the past five weeks had gone, I felt dismay. I had the feeling I must hurry and have immediately and quickly all of the summer, to store it up before it was lost so that I could *know* it belonged to me, so that I should have missed nothing . . . not a sound or a smell or a sight of this beloved place. I ran through the barns and the orchard, the plum thicket and the mulberry tree, a feeling of farewell already clutching at me, and a pall of grief already settling over me. I would *not* let the summer come to an end. I would *not* go away from these dear things.

Usually one must look back down the years to have such nostalgia for a place and a time, but I had it then. Perhaps I was already old, or perhaps I simply knew, without knowing that I knew, it was the best I would ever have.

The feeling lasted only a frantic hour and then I was caught up in the excitement of the day. There was always a barbecue on the Fourth of July. It was, however, not so important an occasion as the Reunion, and some summers my father and mother and I were not there for it. The custom went back to my father's boyhood. However hot the day, and it could be very hot indeed, a fire was built in the kitchen fireplace and chickens were spitted over it. Angie had turned and basted the chickens, roasting herself as well as the chickens in the process. It was Lulie's chore today, and since tradition did not sit so amiably on her she was grumbling about it. "Don't see why folks got to have chickens roasted on a day like this'n. Hot enough to lather a mule standing in the shade, and here I sits, stewing all the juice outta myself. Hand me that spoon, Katie, these damfool birds done got dry again."

"You said a cussword," I accused, handing her the spoon.

"I likely to say more, too, 'fore I gets through. They's times," she said darkly, "when I wishes I was back in Memphis."

"Pooh," I said, "what's in Memphis?"

"Whut's in Memphis? Why, lawzee, Katie, they's ever'thing in Memphis. They's big stores, and lots of folks, and places to go dancing, and," she winked at me, "they's places to go drinking, too, if that's whut you want. They's good times in Memphis, that's whut. And they sho' ain't much of 'em 'round here." She was spooning fat over the chickens as she talked, shielding her face from the heat with one arm thrown up. "Ain't much atall. I wouldn't never come, 'cept it suited my purpose to get out of town awhile."

"Why?"

She started chuckling, sitting back on her heels, and then she burst into cackling laughter. "Was a woman after me . . . say I took her man away from her."

"Did you?"

"How I know? Men is the easiest thing they is to take . . . mebbe I did. Anyhow, she pretty good with a butcher knife. 'Bout that time Mama passed on and I come to the funeral and Miss Emily asked did I want to stay on and work here. Looked like the hand of the Lord, to me, so I stayed on."

"It's not really so bad here, is it, Lulie? I

mean, you have a good time with Choctaw, don't you? Going to meeting and all? And you had to work hard in Memphis, too, didn't you? Aunt Maggie said you did." I thought it would be terrible if she went back, and I wanted to balance Stanwick against Memphis somehow.

She laid the spoon down and got up. "Yeah, I work hard there. And that steam laundry just about as hot as this fire, too." She shrugged, in a better humor now. "Naw, I don't reckon it so bad. I have me a good time wherever I goes."

"There aren't many colored girls in Stanwick as pretty as you," I pressed the advantage, "and that have as pretty clothes. And I guess there must have been hundreds in Memphis."

"They's a right smart of 'em, all right."

"You wouldn't hardly be noticed there if you had a new dress, would you? But when you wear a new silk dress here, *everybody* knows it."

"That's right. All they eyes just bug out I got so many. I got a new one for Saturday night . . . pink, pink as Miss Emily's Zephyr rose."

"You have a new one every Saturday night, don't you? And you don't have to spend your money for a place to stay and things to eat. You can spend it all on dresses if you like."

"That's right. Sho' can, and mostly I likes."

"And Choctaw . . . he's in love with you, Lulie."

"Oh, he just fooling around, I reckon. You can't tell nothing 'bout Choctaw."

"No, he told me. He said he was."

"When he tell you that?"

"The day we went fishing. And did you know that Choctaw is going to have his own farm someday?" That, I thought, would surely be the clincher.

"How come he will?"

"Grandfather is going to leave him a farm in his will . . . when he dies, Choctaw will get it."

There was exactly the speculative look on her face which I had hoped for, so I said, dryly, "It would be pretty silly of you, wouldn't it, to go back to Memphis and leave it all?"

She looked at me for a moment and then her face broke into a broad grin and she said, admiringly, "You just about the smartest thing ever I seen, Katie. How come you not want me to go back to Memphis?"

I hugged her tightly. "Because I like you."

She rocked me against those full breasts of hers and I felt them sway beneath me. "I likes you, too, sugar. I ain't gonna go back to Memphis."

I heard her telling Aunt Maggie about it later, leaving out the part about the woman with the butcher knife. "She the beatin'est

291

child. She gonna grow up and be one of them lawyer folks, Miss Maggie . . . or a witch or something. She know whut you thinking, and she turn it and twist it, and first thing you know you done tole her too much."

"I know," Aunt Maggie said. "She's spoiled, I'm afraid."

"No'm, she ain't spoilt. Ain't a spoilt bone in her body. But she odd. She got a lot of skin to feel with. She like a nigger that way."

I don't recall that Aunt Maggie made any answer, but I do remember thinking it strange that Lulie should know I felt things with my whole skin. I did, and I thought it odd if it was a Negro quality that my skin shouldn't have been black.

Grandfather and Adam and Choctaw were busy all morning at the barbecue pit. The people who were regularly invited wouldn't arrive until late in the afternoon. They would eat and then stay on for the fireworks, but it took a good portion of the day to roast a whole beef properly. I had hated to think of Choctaw killing the poor yearling . . . knocking it in the head and then slitting its throat; but once it was done I could quickly enough forget it and eat of it heartily. It was Choctaw's duty to keep plenty of hickory wood piled ready, and to run for various condiments which Grandfather invariably forgot. Adam lent a hand with putting up the tables under the elms, running errands for

Aunt Maggie and Grandmother, and making certain the fireworks were all in order. He would have charge of them that night. I went spinning like a top among them all, crazy with excitement, alternating between hot and cold and wondering *how* I could live until night.

That was partly solved when we decided to have the battle that afternoon. Everything was in order, the beef at the stage where it didn't need constant attention, the tables set, the salads and pies made, and we had finished eating what Grandmother called a "snack" of lunch. We were sitting under the mulberry tree, Adam and Aunt Maggie in the swing, Grandfather and I in the grass, when Grandfather said, "Katie, I do believe we could have the battle this afternoon."

I was instantly of the same opinion. Aunt Maggie looked at Adam and groaned and Adam laughed. "I can't think of a better time to have it than on the Fourth of July," he said. "We may have our battles mixed up, but patently the Fourth of July is a fighting day."

"Good a day as any other," Grandfather said, pulling himself up by one end of the swing. "The Madame won't let us have it on Sunday, and we're all together now. I'll go get the implements of war."

They were the flag, the plain one, not the silk one, it was saved for the Reunion; the campaign caps and hats, the sashes, field glasses, pistols and guns, and Grandfather's own sword. Adam said he'd go look over the battleground, which was always the orchard, and round up Choctaw. "Lulie, too," I told him.

"Lulie, too," he agreed.

Aunt Maggie sat on in the swing, keeping it in a very slow movement with the toe of one foot. She sighed. "Lordy, but it's hot. I wish these whingdings of Papa's didn't all come in the summer."

I barely heard her for I was trying to decide whether to be Newton Story, the color bearer of the Dixie Grays, or an aide to the general. Strictly speaking, General Johnston was not present in the sector in which the 6th Arkansas fought, but we pretended he was. Strictly speaking, too, the Battle of Shiloh lasted two days, but we ignored the second day which involved the retreat of the Confederates after the victory of the day before. We fought to victory and left it there. "Which was I last time?" I asked Aunt Maggie.

"Which were you what?"

"Was I Newton Story or the aide last year?"

Aunt Maggie thought. "I think you chose the sash last year."

"I think I did, too. Well, I'll be Newton Story this year." I was relieved to have it decided and secretly pleased. The aide got to wear a sash, a gorgeous scarlet one, as did the general, and he got to use the field glasses, but Newton Story was covered with honor.

He bore the colors and he had one dramatic line to say during the fighting. "Would you like to be the aide?" I asked Aunt Maggie.

"Yes," she said emphatically, "I certainly would. All I'd have to do is stand around with the field glasses and look important."

"Aunt Maggie! He has to take the general's orders!"

"Yes, but he doesn't have to crawl around in that high grass on his stomach and get all hot and sticky."

Then I remembered that Papa wasn't there. He was always the general. "Oh, dear. We don't have a general. Who will be the general this time?"

"Oh . . . I'd forgotten. Well, Adam or Choctaw, I guess."

I shook my head. "They don't look like a general." I was thinking of my father's tall, commanding bearing. It never occurred to me that there had been Confederate generals who were stocky, homely or ungainly. They were all heroes, and heroes were always handsome. That was both a law of the storybooks and of the Army of the Confederate States of America. Unbidden, Doctor Jim's dark height rose before me, and with a stricken conscience I suddenly remembered we had practically promised him he could take part in the battle this year. I wished I had not thought of him, nor remembered. It would be better to do without a general than to have him, although he was eminently suited for the part I had to admit. Had we truly promised? If I didn't say anything about it, and if Aunt Maggie didn't remember it . . . if she didn't remember, surely we hadn't made a real promise. I would just not say a word, I decided, just put it out of my mind. But even as I determined this I knew very well I could not do it. I wouldn't be able to put it out of my mind at all. It would stick there and trouble me all afternoon and would even spoil the fun. Life, I thought to myself bitterly, is very difficult. If you do what is right it may be unpleasant; if you don't do what is right, it is certain to be unpleasant. The horns of a dilemma are never comfortable. So, feeling very put upon I mournfully reminded Aunt Maggie of the drive to Thornberrys' and the talk with Doctor Jim about the battle. "Did we promise him?"

"Oh, dear, Katie, I think we did. I'll have to run call him right now. Of course he was coming for the barbecue anyhow, but . . ." she was scrambling out of the swing.

"Why was he coming for the barbecue?"

"Why, darling, Grandfather asked him and his uncle both, days ago. Doctor Clem always comes, you know that."

"Oh, all *right*."

"Katie, you have really taken an unreasonable dislike to him. You were downright rude to him at band practice the other night. Now, you *must* not behave so to him. He's a very nice person and we are fond of him."

"Grandfather and Papa aren't."

"What makes you say that?"

"They said he didn't have any principles. He told them the surest way to win the Reunion games would be to buy the other pitchers . . . and he was drunk at the ball game . . . and he . . ." I clapped my hand over my mouth, remembering too late. I had really done it now. I looked at Aunt Maggie anxiously, wishing I could recall my words, and hoping she wouldn't ask any questions. If she began questioning me I shouldn't be able to lie, not even with crossed fingers. It was all right to make up something and tell to other children, with crossed fingers, but not when answering grownups. I would have to tell her everything that had been said. She stood looking at me, smoothing the knot of her hair, which she often did when she was thinking. She didn't ask any questions, however, she just took a long breath and let it out. "He's heading straight for trouble if he won't even *try*. He can't afford to antagonize people so. Well, I'll go call him, dear. You'd better see if you can help Grandfather."

I must confess, however, that he could not have been more charming than he was on that day, and he made a splendid general. He was fully as noble looking as my father, just as serious, and he died just as beautifully. Not once, if he did, was there any evidence that he thought it all pretty silly. Of course he didn't say the lines right, at the last, but . . . well, I'll come to that. He wrapped the red sash, beginning now to split in the folds, carefully about him and set Grandfather's campaign hat squarely on his head. It was not so fine as a general's, but it served, with honor. He listened attentively while Grandfather explained the battle strategy. Grandfather still had his own copy of the map and he pointed out the positions on it. "This is us," he said, "Hardee's Corps, with Polk on our left, Bragg and Breckinridge on our right. We are Hindman's Brigade, 6th Arkansas, B Company, Chisholm Rogers, captain. On our immediate left is Cleburne; on our right, Gladden. There is a three-mile front. The order is to advance along the entire front and engage the enemy, sweeping him before us. The objective is Pittsburg Landing."

The barns were Pittsburg Landing, but the battle always ended when we came out of the orchard into the barn lot, for of course we never took Pittsburg Landing. We stopped with the capture of the Federal camps and Prentiss's Brigade. Grandfather issued muskets to Lulie and Choctaw. Lulie handled hers gingerly. "I is scared of guns," she said.

"Good Lord, girl, it's been forty years since

that musket was fired. It won't go off the way guns do nowadays."

Doctor Jim reached out and took the gun. "May I see it a moment?" He examined it carefully. "It's authentic, isn't it?"

"It's so authentic," Grandfather told him dryly, "that it was actually used in the Battle of Shiloh. Are you familiar with firearms, Jim?"

"They fascinate me. I love them."

"By George, you'll have to take a look at my collection. I've got a . . ."

"Papa." Aunt Maggie pulled at his sleeve.

"Oh, all right. Later today, Jim . . . remind me." He turned to Lulie again and Doctor Jim handed her the gun. "Now, Lulie, you line up there with Choctaw, watch him and do what he does. Now," he turned back to the doctor, "Adam is the artillery. He will support the advance." Adam had filled a wheelbarrow with corncobs and was ready. Grandfather then handed me the regimental colors, fixed to the standard.

I was shaking with excitement, praying that I would not let the banner touch the ground, and I would not forget Newton Story's words when the time came. I took my place. Grandfather settled his old visored cap firmly on his head, eased his sword belt and looked around. We skipped the preparation for the battle, the march up and so on. We began with dawn on Sunday morning, April 6, 1862, in the edge of the woods just south of the Corinth road and the Shiloh church house. We began with the command to dress on the colors. Choctaw stiffened and his eyes immediately snapped right. Lulie had a little trouble but eventually she managed a fair imitation. Grandfather walked down the imaginary line and stopped in front of them. He cleared his throat. "Gentlemen, remember you are the Dixie Grays. Do your duty today like brave men." Then he turned and whipped out his sword, poised it and then whipped it down, the command "Forward!" ringing out like the bark of a gun itself. I always got goosebumps at this point. So soon we would be meeting the enemy. We stepped forward briskly, but almost immediately we were engaged. Then came the firing, the dropping to the ground and the crawling, the advancing by short runs and spurts, Grandfather everywhere at once, flourishing his sword, barking out his commands. "Aim low . . . take cover . . . lie flat, but keep firing. A few rounds of grape, Lieutenant Crenshawe." Adam trundled up his wheelbarrow and began heaving corncobs. Grandfather peered through his fists as if they had been field glasses. The general's aide had the real ones. "Now, men," he cried, "up and advance!"

Behind us the general and his aide were tearing up and down the lines, encouraging, the general giving orders and the aide springing forward to carry them. Oh, it was not difficult to imagine the sound of twenty thousand muskets, the crash of the cannon, the smell of smoke, the flash of powder, the falling of the wounded, the yelling and the shouting and the running and dodging. My heart pounded loudly, the nerves in my fingers tingled and the wood of the flag staff became slippery with perspiration; my breath came quickly, but I remembered to keep the colors up, and to stay out front. We advanced, fell back, took cover, advanced again.

We were in the thickest of the battle, the firing from the Federals very heavy and momentarily the advance was halted, the men lying flat waiting. Grandfather yelled at me, and grasping the staff with both hands I plunged forward, planting the banner several yards beyond Choctaw and Lulie, and turning, shouted at them, "Come on, boys! See, there's no danger!" At the cue Choctaw and Lulie sprang forward and we swept the enemy before us. Oh, glory, I had not forgotten!

We were now overrunning the enemy's camp, flanking Prentiss and taking his entire brigade. We came out of the orchard in the flush of victory. But the victory turned sour in our mouths as the general's aide approached with the news he was dying. We rallied around him, where he lay gracefully on the grass. He leaned against the shoulder of the aide. Captain Rogers respectfully knelt beside him. "Where are you wounded, sir?"

With a long gasping breath the general said, "Nay, sire, I am not wounded, I am dead," and he went limp and lifeless. At this unexpected line, much to my consternation, Grandfather, Adam and Aunt Maggie exploded into shouts of laughter, and the doctor, supposed to be pale and dying, struggled a moment and then collapsed and joined with them. From Aunt Maggie's shoulder he looked up at them. "I could not resist it. I hope I did not spoil General Johnston's death scene."

"Oh, Lord," Grandfather said, wiping his eyes, "it was perfect."

"But General Johnston didn't say that," I insisted, tugging at Grandfather's sleeve. "He said, 'Well done, men. Press on. Keep after them.'"

"Well, sugar, that's what the doctor meant."

It didn't sound the same, but I supposed it was all right. Only I could see nothing funny about it. Papa always said the lines in a low, tense voice, and no one ever laughed. But it had been a fine battle, as fine as any we had ever had, and I no longer begrudged the doctor his participation. I felt, happily, that I had certainly covered both myself and Newton Story with fresh glory. We trooped back to the front yard where Grandmother had cold lemonade waiting for us. Grandfather and Grandmother sat in the swing and the rest of us ringed around them on the grass, I beside Aunt Maggie. I was very hot and she wiped my face with her handkerchief. "Wasn't Katie fine as Newton Story?"

"Splendid," Doctor Jim said, and everyone else agreed, Adam going so far as to say no one else had ever done the part so well. It was my moment, and I made the most of it, basking in the limelight, until the doctor said, "Did that really happen, sir?"

"Oh, yes. Why?"

"It sounds so dramatic . . . so emotional."

"It was a war of emotions," Grandfather said, dryly.

"Yes, I suppose so. You had that victory in your hands. What turned the tide against you?"

Grandfather told him. "Two things . . . the death of General Johnston, causing the command to fall on Beauregard, who was not a good commander. Johnston would have pressed on . . . Beauregard delayed and gave Lew Wallace and Buell time to come up and reinforce Grant. That battle was ours. It was one of the few times Grant was caught napping and we had every advantage . . . surprise, greater numbers and a terrain we knew. We threw it all away."

"But if Wallace and Buell were so near,

wouldn't they have had to be engaged anyhow, even if Johnston had not been killed?"

"Eventually, of course . . . but Pittsburg Landing would have been ours and the whole story might have read differently subsequently."

"I am told you are an expert on the entire war, sir. *Could* the South have won the war?"

"No. How it lasted four years under the circumstances is beyond my understanding. There *might* have been a small chance had we sold our cotton in the beginning and used the funds as a bank, and had we taken the war immediately to the North. Instead we hoarded the cotton in an effort to wring recognition from the European Powers and eventually had to burn it. And we let the war be fought on our own territory instead of taking it to Maryland and Pennsylvania soon enough. We waited for invasion, but war must be totally ruthless. We should have done the invading."

The doctor plucked a blade of grass and chewed on it thoughtfully. "Had you taken that chance, and had you won, it might have been very tragic."

"Yes, I think it would have been tragic."

Grandmother interrupted, saying vehemently, "How can you say that, Mr. Rogers? It would not have been tragic at all. We should have kept our own ways, our own homes, our own world! It was tragic to lose them! It is only because it was the will of God that I have ever been reconciled to it!"

"Well, if it is the will of God, Emily, it must have been a wise thing for us."

She was quite agitated, shaking the swing with her trembling, and her mouth was quivering as she attempted to speak. "I don't know. I just don't know. I don't question his purposes, of course, but I shall never understand some of them. There is so much of the Lord's wisdom that is beyond my understanding."

Grandfather tucked her hand under his arm. "There's a lot none of us understand, my dear. Come, it's almost time for the others to begin arriving. We'd better make sure everything is ready."

It was after the barbecue and the fireworks that Doctor Jim played for us. Everyone had gone but him and Doctor Clem and Adam. Stanwick people did not stay late, and I am sure it was not yet ten o'clock when the last of them had left. "Shall we go inside, gentlemen," Grandfather said, "and let a little peach brandy finish off the evening?"

"I should be going," Doctor Clem said. "It's past my bedtime, but . . . peach brandy did you say, Cap?"

"I can vouch for it," Doctor Jim said. "I have had a glass or two before."

"I can't resist it. Hang my bedtime. After all, this boy," putting his hand on Doctor Jim's arm, "is here to relieve me of night and early morning calls. He can worry about *his* bedtime now."

"Which I do, sir, except when invited to share Mr. Rogers's peach brandy."

We went into the parlor where Grandmother excused herself to send Lulie with the brandy. Catching her eye on me with a dubious look, as if she meant to call attention to the fact that it was getting late for me to be up, too, I straightened and tried to look alert and wide-eyed. I was tired; it had been a very exciting day, but I didn't want it to end by being sent up to bed while anything at all was still happening.

There was a little talk and then, inevitably, someone asked Aunt Maggie to sing. I think it was Doctor Clem. She was reluctant. "I am so tired tonight. One song, then . . . just one."

Doctor Jim went to the shelves where she kept the music. "May I choose? I saw something here the other night . . . a rare score of one of Mozart's songs . . . ."

"Oh, the *'Non so d'onde'?*"

"Yes . . . are you up to it?"

She made a little face. "It isn't one of my favorites."

"It is one of mine." He found the score and sat at the piano, loosening his fingers by rippling the keys, then he turned to the rest of us. "This originally was a Bach setting of one of the songs from Metastasio's *Olimpiade*. Mozart did a new setting especially for a girl with whom he was very much in love. I think it is one of the most moving things he ever wrote."

Grandfather moved a lamp to the piano and I remember that it threw Aunt Maggie into silhouette where she stood. I remember that her hair was rumpled, little curls springing loose on the sides and the knot loosened and slipping on her neck. I remember, too, that she was wearing the lilac lawn dress again, and that it was a little rumpled also, and smudged from helping Adam with the fireworks. But it would not have mattered what she wore when she began to sing; it would have immediately been forgotten, so purely, so beautifully did she sing.

> *Non so d'onde viene*
> (I do not know whence comes)
> *Quel tenero affetto;*
> (This tenderness of feeling;)
> *Quel moto, che ignoto*
> *Mi nasce nel petto,*
> *Qual gel, che le vene*
> *Scorrendo mi va.*
> (What is this new emotion
> That in my breast is stealing,
> This ice which so benumbs,

Burning through my veins.)
Nel seno a destarmi
Si fieri contrasti
Non parmi
Che basti
La sola pietà.
(Can pity in me awaken
This strife by which I'm shaken?
No, I fear
Pity ne'er
Such dominion gains.)

I think that was the beginning of my love for the Italian language, which deepened into love for the Italian opera. The language is music itself and is especially flexible for singing. Too often I hear only the guttural gurgle and bark of the German Lieder, and the sharp incision of the French. But then I am a romantic and not particularly musical. My ear must be pleased.

I do not know whether Adam understood the Italian words or not. But of course he did not need to understand the words to know that it was a love song. For that matter the doctor had told us it was, but the music also told us. It was passionately tender. Not for a good many years did I know the words myself and know why Doctor Jim wanted Aunt Maggie to sing it . . . sing it *for* him, as if it were he, the words telling her what he wanted her to know . . . sing it there before us all, but clothing it in the anonymity of words we could not understand. It still surprises me that she did it. Adam's face reflected only the gentle pride he always had in Aunt Maggie's voice, which because he was so undiscriminating had so little meaning beyond personal love and devotion. I think Grandfather did sense something of the undertone, for when the song was finished he rather quickly asked Doctor Jim to play, "Since Maggie is tired," he said.

"I'll be glad to," Doctor Jim said immediately. He did not ask what we wanted to hear. He seemed not even to think what he wanted to play. He plunged immediately into a movement of the Mozart *C minor Concerto,* explaining, "This will be a little thin without the orchestra, but I'd like to do it."

To this good day I do not know in what way Doctor Jim failed as a pianist. I do not know why he wasn't good enough. Perhaps if I could hear him now I would know, but it seemed then as if nothing marred his execution. He seemed to have both brilliance and feeling, and what appeared at least to be competent technique. It may not have been. I was much too young to judge, but I do know that when he had finished Grandfather said, "I feel as Beethoven must have felt when he said, 'Ah, we shall never be able to do anything like that.' "

Doctor Jim shrugged. "Beethoven

recognized the greatest genius of them all."

Aunt Maggie laughed. "You *do* care for Mozart, don't you?"

"Yes. He stands alone for me. Don't you?"

"Oh, yes. But I like him less well than you. I had to sing him, you know, and he can be terribly difficult."

"Yes, he made no concessions."

"It is a pity he chose his librettists with so little care."

"You think he did?"

"Well, do you think the libretto of *Così fan tutte,* or *Don Giovanni* for that matter, can compare with, say, the poem of Gluck's *Iphigenia in Aulis,* or Wagner's *Ring?* Don't they seem a little trivial?"

"Not at all. And I think he chose his librettists with extreme care. He, and almost he alone, saw that music must be concerned with human nature. He cared nothing for the spectacular, the huge, bulging drama. And he knew that human nature is dual . . . the good and the bad, the flesh and the spirit, the strength and the frailty. He could dispense with the trappings because he was so intent upon the great universal. Look at *Don Giovanni.* He did not see Don Juan as an individual. As an individual he was comic, with his thousand and three seductions. As Man he is all of Desire, the power of the flesh . . . of nature, never weakening through the ages, the motivation of life, the surging of the inner sea.

Take *Così fan tutte* . . . look at the humanity of the theme . . . the frailty of the two women who weaken under the pressure of the suit of the disguised lovers. Thus do all women, he is saying. Thus do all men. Thus is human nature . . . tragic, comic . . . divine, demoniac . . . weak, strong. Do you remember the fun of Figaro? Ah, he saw into the deepest heart of humanity. No, Maggie, he was never trivial."

"Well, perhaps not. But he *is* sometimes very frightening. That aria for the Queen of the Night, for instance. It is terrifying to me."

"Why?"

"I think it is because it appears so smooth and glossy on the surface, so serene, and yet you somehow feel that underneath he has hidden a bottomless pit of darkness. Night . . . and the music *is* night."

"Of course, it is the music *for* the Queen of the Night. But that again is part of his great genius. He knew that every man carries his own night around in his soul . . . he knew that beneath the surface, however serene and calm he might be, every man knows his own sin and suffering, his own fear and loneliness, his own knowledge of the certainty of death and the futility of hope. Mozart knew very well what was meant by '. . . the dropt curtain and the closing gate: This is the end of all the songs man sings.' "

"But that is horrible, Jim!" Aunt Maggie

shivered.

Adam spoke shortly and dryly. "That is Ernest Dowson . . . and drink, drugs, disillusionment and decadence."

"It may be," the doctor said, "but it is also truth. The curtain *does* always drop, Adam . . . the gate *does* always close. Man *is* always defeated. Life *does* end in death . . . and futility."

Adam leaned forward in his chair. "Life ends in death, yes, but not necessarily in futility. Something may have been done . . . something accomplished. And if nothing else, if a man has been valiant, he goes down with his own self-respect, and that is worth the battle. It is what gives dignity and meaning to the struggle."

"But why struggle, if it's all just dead-sea fruit?"

"Because the struggle is what is important. Michelet said it, 'le but n'est rien . . . le chemin c'est tout.'"

"If the end is not important, how can the struggle have any meaning?"

Both men were tense, leaning forward. "That is exactly it. The most perfect gift bestowed on man was the freedom to give life its own meaning, to make the struggle important for whatever end he can conceive. It is the man of sick mind, a Dowson, Verlaine, Baudelaire, Mallarmé, who sees life as dead-sea fruit . . . as futile."

"What do you think, sir?" Doctor Jim appealed to Grandfather.

Grandfather swung one foot over his knee and made a steeple of his fingers. "Oh, I think Adam has a point there. Of course, they wrote some beautiful things . . . there are some exquisite lines in *Romances sans paroles* for instance, and in Baudelaire's *Fleurs du mal*. There is no doubt they had a feeling for beauty . . . very sensitive . . . they could *sing*. The trouble is they *were* flowers of evil. It is unfortunate, it seems to me, that it has become the style to consider the pessimists the intellectuals."

"Aren't they?"

"Not necessarily. They may simply be the faithless."

Doctor Jim looked at Grandfather skeptically. "Can one be intellectual and have faith?"

"Oh, yes. As a matter of fact, it seems to me that the man who stops short of faith cannot actually be called an intellectual. I would be inclined to say that what the pessimist lacks *is* intellectualism. Oh, he has the mind and the temperament to question and seek, to probe and search, to discard dogma and old orthodoxies. But he comes out short because he stops with the discarding. When he comes out into a fatherless world, he accepts it hopelessly and looks upon all life as futile. He apparently doesn't see that what

he has been asking, after all, is a little childish
. . . a provable meaning of life, a cut and
dried purpose for it. 'Ah, what a dusty answer
gets the soul, When hot for certainties in this
our life!' Your man twists and turns and rants
at the realities of suffering, evil, injustice and
death. He wants them removed from the
world, and when he faces up to the fact that
they cannot be, he turns against all faith and
shuts himself into a dark, obsessed region of
frustration."

"But what faith is left to have?"

" 'The cry of the conscience of life.' . . .
faith in life itself. You know, Jim, some
people are born with a temperament which
accepts unquestioningly a deep religious faith.
Those persons are perhaps, very fortunate,
for their faith provides them a kind of shock-
proof cushion against the inadequacies of life
. . . a kind of solace and comfort. But there
are others, and I am among them, you,
apparently, and to some extent Adam, who
have had to think beyond the accepted orthodoxies. We are the ones who know early the
insecurity and the uncertainty of doubt, and
occasionally we stop at the kind of pessimistic
agnosticism of the poets we've been talking
about. If one goes further, however, it is quite
exciting to find that if one must do without
the old ideas, if one must with integrity admit
that there seems no defined reason or purpose
back of life, one has not necessarily discarded

all values. Simply because one cannot define the source of moral standards, it does not necessarily follow that the standards themselves are without validity. It is wise, intelligent if you will, to hold that goodness and honor, love, brotherhood, loyalty, are virtues in themselves whatever the source of their sanctions. If one can no longer say with authority that God intended men to be good and to love one another, it is still true that goodness and love are experienced values. It is still true that hate and war and sin are evil, also. For that matter, it is more exciting to me and perhaps even more valid to think that man himself is responsible for the conception of these values. No, what we must do is what the pessimist fails to do. We must turn with hope and exhilaration to the great challenge of using what we have."

"And exactly what do we have, sir?"

"Exactly? All right, since you put it that way. Exactly, we live upon a planet in a universe governed by laws that are unvaryingly dependable. They are not going to be set aside either to benefit or to punish the individual. They are neither just nor unjust, merciful nor cruel . . . they simply are. They will give us the sun and the rain, the wind and the stars, and life; they will at the same time give us earthquakes, fire, flood and death. They are completely indifferent and dispassionate. They are not friendly, or fatherly or loving . . . *but* they are dependable and usable. They kill us in the end, but so long as we are alive they are there, constant, and we may make whatever use of them we have learned to make. When we accept that fact, we may go a step further and say, 'What difference, then, does it make why it came about, or what its purpose is, or whether or not it has a purpose? Here is the universe, and here am I, alive in it, and I can make my life have meaning.' "

"No, sir," the doctor interrupted vehemently, "you cannot always. I cannot, by any power I possess, make myself a concert pianist, and that is all I ever wanted to be!"

"But, Jim, you are like the child who says if I can't have it my way, I'll not have it at all. Like the pessimist who says if I can't have life everlasting, without sin and suffering and injustice and evil, I'll have none of it. I say, you can make your life have *meaning,* but you've got to do it within the laws of nature. Apparently you can't be a concert pianist, but your life can still have worth."

The doctor lifted his shoulders and let them down again. "Go ahead, sir."

"Well, here is what challenges me. We are sure of only a few things. We are alive, and we live in a livable situation. As far as we can prove, exactly to use your word, the only purpose of life is to live it, to stay alive, and to create further life. Whatever meaning it

316

has beyond that, we ourselves must give it, according to one's own temperament and intelligence and conceptions of worth. There never has been one truth for all men, and there never will be. But one has to have faith in the process of life . . . and no pessimist ever really has it. He shrinks from life, hides in the corners of his mind, sings his sad songs and takes to excesses in his sorrow. The danger in the unredeemed pessimist, it seems to me, is in the fact that he leaves a treacherously beautiful flower of evil for other pessimistically inclined minds to seize upon. He leaves a bitter heritage."

The doctor looked down at his feet and moved them restlessly. He looked up and smiled, one-sidedly. "Well, sir, if *'Il pleure dans mon coeur'* it is at least something to have their company."

"Everyone's heart weeps at one time or another," Adam said, then, "but why should any man think that life should be made good or easy for him? For every individual born on this earth, life is going to hold grief and disappointment, failure and sorrow and death. The way in which one faces and meets them is the measure of the valor of a man. One doesn't have to take to drink and sobbing poetry. One can catch the tears and water roses. Good Lord, Jim, you of all people, a doctor, dedicated to easing suffering and saving life, ought to have hope."

"I didn't ask to be a doctor . . . I was made one, and if I save lives, for what do I save them?"

"That isn't for you to decide. If for no other reason, you save them to decide for themselves."

Aunt Maggie's eyes had moved from one man to the other as he spoke, resting now on Grandfather who sat erect in his chair, his small feet planted firmly in front of him, his hand combing his beard from time to time; moving then to the doctor who sat on the piano bench, leaned forward, his hands hanging between his knees, and from him to Adam, lounging loosely in his chair, his coat rumpled at the shoulders, his hair standing in unruly peaks. She had taken no part in the conversation. She had sat, looking on, watching and listening. But when Adam had finished she smiled at him suddenly, and he caught the smile and reddened as if she had touched him, rewarded him.

His uncle, who had gone to sleep while Doctor Jim was playing, awakened now, grunting and groaning and snorting, coming awake slowly and laboriously, blinking at the light like a startled old owl. "Hummmmph! Must have dozed off a minute." He stood, groaned at a kink in his back and smoothed down his hair and tugged at his coat. "What time is it, Jim?"

Doctor Jim looked at his watch. "Just on

the stroke of midnight, sir . . . the witching hour."

"Good Lord, what do you mean keeping those folks up half the night? Where's my hat? We must be going."

He began circling the room looking for his hat. Aunt Maggie found it on the floor at the end of the sofa and brought it to him.

"You mustn't blame Jim," she said; "he has only been one voice in a very interesting discussion."

"Oh? Why didn't somebody wake me? Like a good discussion myself . . . what was it about?"

Doctor Jim took his elbow. "You were napping too soundly, and we should be here till morning if we tried to tell you. Principally, though, I was being given a sound verbal spanking."

"You needed it probably. Cap, it's been a fine day . . . a fine one. Always look forward to your Fourth of July."

Adam was going with the two doctors and they all drifted to the door. Something was still troubling me, however, and I pulled at Doctor Jim's coat. He looked down at me. "Good Lord, Katie, you still up? What is it?"

"Did the girl marry him?"

"Did the girl . . . ?" He looked puzzled.

"You know . . . the girl Mozart wrote the song for? Did she marry him?"

"Oh . . . that one." The doctor ran his

hand around the rim of his hat. "No, Katie, she didn't. She had no sense of adventure, I guess. She married another man. One with more obvious means of success. You see, she wanted to be safe."

"Jim?" Doctor Clem called from the hall, "don't dally. Come along."

"Coming," and he followed his uncle out.

Adam, going last, smiled at Aunt Maggie. "It's been a good day."

She smiled, but her face was flushed and angry looking. "Yes," she said, shortly, "it has been."

When they had gone Aunt Maggie began fluffing up cushions, ordering the chairs, emptying the ash trays. Grandfather turned out two of the lamps and stood beside the other one, waiting. "He reminds me," he said, musingly, "of Dickens's Redlaw, the haunted man, hugging his griefs to his bosom, brooding on his melancholy."

"He reminds me," Aunt Maggie said, "of a spoiled child."

Grandfather chuckled. "Well, there isn't much difference, I suspect."

Fifteen

I seem to be remembering that summer largely by its events. But that is always the way. Remembering is mostly recalling events, for we seem unable to catalogue emotions and processes of thought otherwise. They have a way of floating off into thin air unless they are anchored to what was happening. One says, "My first remembered emotion was fear," and what does that tell. But if one says, "I was afraid of the little boy who lived across the street when I was a child. My first memory is of seeing him coming down the street and of running to hide in a bed of leaves piled under a tree; of burrowing down into the leaves and pulling them over me, of lying there, my heart drumming in my wrists, my throat tight with panic." The emotion is recalled, tied to the event, and a great universal has been stated, that life begins with the first remembered feeling, anchored to the first remembered event.

Looking back I can see how tenuous and yet how tensile was the thread upon which each had his hand that summer, following it to its destined end, where it met, tangled and snarled with all the other threads. But then it was merely the summer, hot as only southern summers can be hot, a little lazy, a little timeless, moving day by day through a pattern of people doing familiar things in familiar ways. The staccato emphasis which my memory gives it was not present . . . nothing was present but the morning sun, shining each day on the jeweled grass, the south wind lifting the broad, flat leaves of the mulberry tree, the cool moisture under one's feet of the brick paving of the grape arbor, the acid heat of tomatoes eaten from the vine, the wild, running freedom of the calves in the pasture, the crackle of Lulie's breakfast fire and the smell of hickory smoke mixed with bacon browning. And in this pastorale of sights and sounds and smells we moved in a daily routine, broken only now and then by a happening not scheduled, by some thing unforeseen.

It was after the barbecue but before the baptizing that Aunt Maggie went up to the city with her friends, Fanny and Mary Gardner, to the concert. *Carmen* was to be given at the Opera House, and they were terribly excited about going, I remember. There was some talk of me going, too, so that I could spend the night with my parents, but in the end it was decided it would be better if I didn't go. "It will just make it more difficult for Katherine," Aunt Maggie said; "she's grown used to having Katie away, now, and to see her and have to let her go again would be hard for her."

"Yes," Grandfather agreed, "best leave things the way they are."

I wanted to go, but at the same time I had been away so long now that even my memories of home had grown so dim as not to pull strongly at me. I was afraid, too, that once there my mother and father might not allow me to come back with Aunt Maggie, and the very best part of the summer might be missed. So I was content not to go.

The doctor went, too . . . but not with Aunt Maggie. I remember that he called her during the afternoon before she was to leave on the evening train. Evidently he had not known she was going with Fanny and Mary, for he had called to ask if she would go to the concert with him. She had explained. "But we'd love to have you join us," she had told him. "My brother, Tolly, will be going with us, so you wouldn't be the lone male in the crowd."

But he had said no, rather brusquely we

gathered, for Aunt Maggie had turned from the phone more than a little provoked with him. "He can be so ill-mannered," she said. "He said he didn't care to hear *Carmen* with a bunch of cackling women."

They had gone and returned, Aunt Maggie full of the music of *Carmen*. I recall that she went around for several days singing some of the arias. She had also done some shopping, which had been exciting, for she found new materials and patterns for some dresses; and she had enjoyed being with my parents, had given them my messages and brought me theirs. My mother was well, doing splendidly; my father was also well, but, she thought, a little nervous as the time of confinement drew nearer. "He is in that state," she told Grandfather and Grandmother, "of wishing the whole thing had never been begun, of being certain it was ill-advised, and at the same time of being jubilant that Katherine is doing so well and apparently is going to bring it off this time."

"When that boy arrives," Grandfather said, laughing, "he'll forget he ever had a moment's uneasiness."

"Yes," Grandmother said, looking up from her knitting, "it is a very easy thing for men to forget. After all, they have so little to do with it."

Aunt Maggie shrugged. "Well, Mother, bearing children is pretty much a woman's job. Tolly can hardly help it if his part is relatively small."

Grandmother stood suddenly, her face working. "It is the most grotesque . . . the most uncouth . . . I could have planned a better scheme of reproduction myself . . . a child could have planned a better one." And with her usual way of ending a conversation, she had swept out of the room.

Grandfather had tugged at his beard. He had cleared his throat as if starting to say something, then had picked up a newspaper as if thinking better of it. And Aunt Maggie, after a wordless moment, had turned to me with some further news of home.

It was several days after that that I saw the attic door open one morning. I was on the back porch helping Lulie string beans. It was cool there, the porch shaded by the trees, and a pattern of light and shadow moving with the breeze across the brick walks. The beans were cool, too, and still damp from the dew. They slid under one's fingers. I wasn't much help, for I concentrated on trying to pull an unbroken string down the entire side of a bean, and for every one that I finished, Lulie did a dozen; but it fascinated me, the way trying to peel an apple whole has always done. Lulie was telling me about the baptizing to be held Sunday. Baptism to me had to do with babies being taken up to the front of the church and sprinkled with a little dash of warm water. "You mean," I said, incredulous, "that the people wade right into the creek?"

"They sho' do," she said, nodding her head vigorously, "and the preacher, he plunges 'em clean under the water. Just washes they sins right away."

I was immediately worried. "Is that the best way to be baptized?" Maybe my sins hadn't been sufficiently washed away.

"I do' know as it's the best way, sugar. Ever'body think diff'runt 'bout it. We does it that way."

"We just sprinkle."

"I reckon that's all right. Some folks believes so, leastways. Just happen we doesn't."

"Well, I guess it must be all right . . . my father and my mother think it is, I guess."

"They the ones to say, Katie. You too little, yet."

"I don't know . . . I have a lot of sins, Lulie."

She peered at me and then started laughing. "You got sins? Whut sins a little girl like you got?"

"Oh, a lot. I sometimes think bad things . . . sometimes I tell things that aren't *really* true . . . and I'm very vain, Lulie. I love pretty hair ribbons and nice silk socks. You think I'd better be baptized your way, too?"

"Naw . . . you just wait, Katie. You been sprinkled your mama and papa's way. You needn't to worry till you get growed up."

"Is Choctaw going to be baptized, too?"

"Naw. He say it just be wasting water. I don't reckon Choctaw ever will get religion. He too much white."

"I want to go." But immediately, remembering the camp meeting, I qualified it. "If it's in the daytime, I want to go."

"Oh, it'll be in the daytime. Couldn't see to dip folks in the dark. I figured you'd be wanting to go. I done tole Choctaw we just as well be fixing on it."

"What did he say?"

"Don't make no diff'runce to him. He say he hope you don't get sick no more."

"I won't. Where are they going to have it?"

"Down by the bridge. It's a nice, sandy place down there, and the water ain't so deep. I reckon we got enough strung, now, Katie. I'd best get 'em on to cook." She stood, gathering the beans into the fullness of her apron. She was wearing a pretty calico print dress, yellow with little red flowers. It reminded me that I had intended to ask her about making Topsy, the rag doll, some more clothes. "Do you have some scraps of that dress?" I asked her.

"This 'un? I reckon. Why?"

"Topsy needs some new dresses. That green silk one is getting pretty dirty."

We went into the kitchen and she dumped the beans into a big pan and poured water over them. "You run find her and we'll go up to my room and see. I got lots of scraps and you can pick out the ones you want. We make her all the dresses you want."

She stood on tiptoe to reach high on a shelf for a saucepan in which to cook the beans. When she reached her petticoat showed beneath the hem of her dress. It was bright red. "O-o-o-oh," I said, "what a pretty petticoat? Did you make it? Let's make Topsy one like it!"

She lowered her arm suddenly and pulled at her dress. She turned and looked at me, scowling. "Don't you say nothing 'bout this petticoat, you hear? Don't you say a word!"

"Well, of course I won't if you don't want me to, Lulie. But why? It's such a pretty one."

"Mebbe that's why . . . on account of it's too pretty." She started giggling. "You wanna know where I got it? I tell you," she whispered, "if you cross your heart you won't tell."

I crossed my heart solemnly.

"The doctor brung it to me from the city last week." She said it triumphantly and she raised her dress so I could see all of the petticoat. I looked at it, not liking it so much any more. "Why?" I asked.

"Why? Why not? I tole him I wanted one

328

is why. He going to the city, I tell him to bring me a red petticoat. He done so."

"Men don't buy women's petticoats for them."

"He do . . . for me," and Lulie tossed her head.

I had a sinking feeling in my stomach. All I knew about love-making between people was kissing and holding hands, but I was certain Lulie and Doctor Jim had been doing that . . . and that they still were. Why that was wrong between the doctor and Lulie I didn't exactly know. It was all right sometimes . . . with Aunt Maggie and Adam, for instance, or my mother and father . . . and the right and the wrong of it didn't trouble me greatly. What did bother me, and bother me very much, was the fear that Choctaw would find out and either have nothing more to do with Lulie, which would be disastrous since I intended for them to marry, or he might become angry enough to do what she herself had said, cut out her gizzard. "You better be careful," I warned her worriedly, "Choctaw would sure be mad if he knew."

"Don't I know it? But I'se careful. Real careful. Don't you worry your head about it. You go get your Topsy doll now."

Topsy was upstairs in the bedroom and I ran to get her. Now, a child needs no more than an open door to make it imperative for him to investigate, so when I came to the top of the stairs and saw the attic door open I had to see who was there, and why the door was open. No one was there. I had only to stick my head inside to know that, but what I saw drew me into the room as inevitably as if a magnet had been pulling at me. The little tin trunk had been moved to the center of the room and its lid lay back, open, against the floor. I had to see what was in it.

Step by step I ventured in, a kind of shivering fearfulness accompanying me. It was Grandmother's trunk, I was certain, and she had left it open, for Aunt Maggie was at the post office. It could only have been Grandmother who had been there. She had pulled the trunk out of the dark corner into the middle of the room where it was light. Gingerly I edged closer, holding my breath as if the trunk must surely contain something terribly dangerous, or evil. I don't know what I expected to see, but I should not have been surprised at anything . . . poison snakes would not have surprised me, even. Something about the trunk, something secret and dark and musty, was evilly fascinating.

But when I came near enough to see, there were only clothes in it . . . baby clothes, of all things. I let out my breath, gustily, and all the tension went out of my chest and shoulders. All the fear and fascination of the unknown, the smell of evil, went with it and I sat down beside the trunk to look at the small things folded and packed in layers of tissue paper in it. They were very old, at least they seemed so to me, yellowed and oddly out of date. I picked up the little dress which lay on top. It was long, very long, very full-skirted, with rows of lace insertion set in, and hundreds of tiny tucks between the rows of lace. The skirt was gathered onto the smallest yoke I had ever seen, and it, too, was tucked with tiny, patient stitches. I laid it aside and began lifting out other things . . . dozens of other things, little petticoats made of the sheerest lawn and some of a fine, thin flannel. There were more dresses and stacks of little woolly shirts. There were beribboned small sacques and jackets, little bonnets, small knitted booties . . . everything a baby could possibly need. I was enchanted. They would just fit Topsy, I thought, and I ran and brought her to see.

I had no feeling of doing anything wrong. I had never been told not to bother things in the attic, saving Grandfather's uniforms and the flags and other war mementoes. Those were sacred, I knew, but they were also kept apart. There was no precedent in this situation, and a child, when faced with something new for which there is no pattern, is not aware of temptation. I would never have pried open a locked trunk. But finding it unlocked and open, and full of old clothes which I had always been allowed to play with, it never occurred to me that its contents, too, might be sacred. I stripped the green silk dress off the rag doll and struggled to slip one of the baby dresses on her. It was a tight fit, but it went on finally and buttoned. If Grandmother would let me have them, I thought, Lulie and I wouldn't have to make her any dresses. There were enough here for several dolls. I held her up and smoothed the folds of the long skirts and then hugged her ecstatically, laughing at the incongruity of the black doll in the lovely, long dress.

"What are you doing in that trunk, Katherine?" I had not heard a sound, and Grandmother's voice, speaking so suddenly behind me and so coldly, frightened me. I jerked around, clutching the doll. She was standing just inside the door, and I had never seen her look more stern, more angry. Her face, usually so calm and colorless, was splotched with red which ran up from her neck in ugly streaks. She said again, "What are you doing in that trunk?" I think ice could not have been more cold than her voice.

I was badly frightened. I knew that somehow I had done something terribly wrong. In my fright I stammered. "I was . . . I was just putting . . ." but the lump in my throat choked me and I had to swallow. Even so I found I could not go on.

"What are you doing with the baby clothes?"

I struggled to speak through the clamped feeling in my throat. "I found them here . . . in the trunk. It was open, Grandmother. I was putting them on my doll. See, they just fit." I held the doll up for her to see. She closed her eyes for a moment and a kind of shudder ran all through her. "Take the dress off the doll immediately, Katherine."

"Yes, ma'am." I set to work, my fingers trembling. I was very awkward with it and Grandmother did not offer to help. She simply stood there and watched. I had to tug at the dress to get it over the doll's shoulders.

"Don't pull at the dress, Katherine," Grandmother said sharply, "you'll tear it."

"No, ma'am." Tears were scalding my eyes and beginning to overflow, but I did not try to wipe them away. I peered through them and worked as carefully as I could to get the dress off. I had never been spoken to so unkindly before. I had been corrected, of course, many times. I had been scolded and even, on occasion, punished. But there had always been kindness in the voice which scolded, and the knowledge of love unabating even in punishment. I had never before been pushed to the outside edge of love . . . felt its entire withdrawal. It was that sense of withdrawal, of isolation, which devastated me and reduced me to tears . . . to forlorn tears. I finally got the dress off the doll.

Grandmother came across the room, then,

and going to a stack of old newspapers she took one and unfolded it, placing it on the floor. "Put the dress on the paper," she said, "it will have to be laundered."

I looked at her, astonished. "It isn't hurt, Grandmother. It isn't soiled at all, see?"

She just pointed at the paper. "Lay it there. Did you put anything else on the doll?"

I dropped the dress on the paper. "No, ma'am."

"Are you sure?"

"Yes, ma'am, I'm sure. Just that one dress."

"Very well." She knelt then and began folding the other clothing which I had disarranged. One by one she laid the small garments back in place. Her face no longer showed any emotion, but her hands were trembling a little. She laid the things in carefully, not hurrying, but not lingering, either. When she had put them all in place she covered them over with a piece of tissue paper, closed the trunk and locked it. Then she dragged it back into the corner. I had stood, watching, not knowing what else to do, afraid to offer help, afraid to say anything. Grandmother paid no more attention to me than if I had been one of the chairs nearby, until she had finished. "Never touch that trunk again, Katherine. Never, do you understand?"

"Yes, ma'am. I won't ever touch it again."

Oh, no . . . not for a million dollars would I ever touch it again. Something inside me was shaky, something in my stomach, and I wished I could run to her, fling my arms around her, say I was sorry and be comforted. But I could not. It would have been as comfortless as hugging an icicle.

"You had better go to your room, now, and I suggest you study the Fifty-First Psalm and learn it by heart."

"Yes, ma'am."

There are nineteen verses in the Fifty-First Psalm. It begins, "Have mercy upon me, O God, according to thy loving kindness: according unto the multitude of thy tender mercies blot out my transgressions. Wash me thoroughly from mine iniquity, and cleanse me from my sin. For I acknowledge my transgressions: and my sin is ever before me."

I did not mind learning the Psalm. It would not even be difficult for me, but I minded terribly being condemned a sinner and not even knowing how I had sinned. As I chanted the words over, transgression, iniquity, sin, they sounded fateful, hopeless of appeal, and I felt doomed. The tears poured down my face and blotted the page of the Bible. If I did not even know what I had done, what terrible, awful thing I had done, how could I be forgiven? Never in all my life have I felt more forsaken than I did that hour in my room. My father and mother, dear and understanding, were far away. Aunt Maggie was downtown. Grandfather was somewhere about the place. I was alone with my enemy, and I did not know whether it was myself or my grandmother.

I had learned the Psalm but was still sitting quietly, subdued, hunched into the cushions on Aunt Maggie's chaise longue when there came a tapping at the door. It pushed open a crack immediately, and Lulie's scowling face peered around the edge. "Your grandmother say you can come down, now. To the kitchen. Whut you *do*, Katie?"

I started sobbing again and she came flying into the room, gathered me up in her arms and sat with me, rocking me back and forth. "Now, now, don't you cry. Don't you fret no more, sugar. Lulie got you now. Ain't nothing gonna hurt you. Miss Maggie be home in a minnit. She not gonna like you being shut up in this room all morning. She gonna be awful mad with your grandmother. I gonna tell her, you wait and see, I gonna tell her. Mean old bitch. That whut she is . . . mean old bitch . . . mean, mean, mean."

"No, no, Lulie," some loyalty came crowding up, "no, she isn't mean, Lulie. But I don't *know* what I did. I was just playing with some old baby clothes in the attic . . ." Freshly the injustice pushed up inside me and I cried more bitterly.

Lulie rocked and patted me, crooning

336

wordlessly but very comfortingly, until I had checked the tears. "You come, now. Let Lulie wash your face. Your eyes all red and swelled up."

I allowed myself to be led to the washstand where Lulie bathed my face and eyes with the cold water. The worst was over now and I felt controlled and calmer. "I suppose," I said, "when Grandmother tells Aunt Maggie, I'll be in disgrace with everybody."

"Naw. She got more sense, Miss Maggie has. She be awful mad with Miss Emily, though, I bet."

"I don't know." I felt my lip beginning to quiver again. Aunt Maggie had never been angry with me . . . but neither had Grandmother before. If people could be so unpredictable, one could trust no one, then.

Lulie jerked her shoulders and drew her eyebrows together. "I knows. Miss Maggie settle all this."

When I went into the kitchen, however, Grandmother was very gracious. She held out her hand and I went to her. She smiled. "Katherine, I was too severe. I was too annoyed. You didn't know. Those clothes, my dear, are your own father's and Aunt Margaret's. They are very precious to me. I keep them in the little trunk, which was my own trunk when I was a little girl. I couldn't bear for anything to happen to them. No one ever touches them but me. No one knows

. . . I was just so shocked when I saw you with them.''

A child does not hold a grudge. He goes much more than halfway in forgiveness. It is so relieving to him to be restored to grace, to hear the kind voice again, to feel loved once more. Nothing, nothing is so terrifying to him as to feel unloved. I could have bounced with joy, could have spun on my heels. It was so wonderful not to have Grandmother angry with me. I offered her all my contrition. "I didn't know, Grandmother, and I'm sorry. I won't touch them again."

"I know."

"I learned the verses. Shall I say them to you, now?"

Abruptly she stood. "No. No, there's no need. But they aren't bad verses to know. We are all sinners and transgressors." She released my hand and walked to the door. After a long, long moment she went on, "I, among the greatest."

Lulie told Aunt Maggie, of course, but I don't think Grandmother did, and I do not know whether Aunt Maggie talked to Grandmother about it. Some of the horror which she felt was still reflected in her face when she talked to me about it that night, reflected also in the warmth of her arms about me, and in the gentleness of her voice as she tried to explain, to reassure, to comfort. "It's all right, Aunt Maggie," I told her, and it *was* all right at that time. But I am not sure such things are ever quite all right, that a child does not forever bear a scar from such wounding.

Sixteen

I did not go to the baptizing with Lulie and Choctaw, however. At first Aunt Maggie had said I might, but on Saturday evening she changed her mind. She and Grandfather and I had been to the ball game that afternoon and we had come home very hot and sticky and dirty. We had also come home very jubilant because we had won again. Grandfather was now positive our troubles were over. The new pitcher, Gorchek, had seemed to give the whole team fresh spirit and even when he didn't pitch they played better. "We've got 'em licked, now," he said triumphantly, "we've sure got 'em licked."

Lulie helped Aunt Maggie bring up our baths and when we had finished she came back to empty the water, take away the soiled towels and hang fresh ones. She was going about her tasks, humming, breaking now and then into snatches of words. Aunt Maggie and I were quiet, both of us hurrying a little because we were late. Lulie broke off her humming to say, "I sho' hope it don't rain tomorrow. Be a shame, wouldn't it, if just as we get the picnic spread it'd commence pouring down."

"It certainly would," Aunt Maggie said, automatically, and then catching the sense of what Lulie had said, she said, "Picnic? I thought this was a baptizing tomorrow?"

"Yessum, it is. But they's to be preaching in the morning, and dinner on the ground. The baptizing comes in the evening."

"Oh, well, Lulie, I don't think Katie can go, then. I didn't understand about the picnic."

"Oh, Aunt Maggie!"

"No, Katie . . . no, absolutely not. Come on, now, let's do your hair." I sat on the bench in front of the dressing table and Aunt Maggie began unbraiding my hair. "There's no telling where all that food would come from, Lulie, there'd be no way of knowing how clean it was, or anything. It just wouldn't do at all." She undid my braids briskly and began brushing my hair. My head jerked with the vigor of her brushing. She and my mother both brushed very hard. They thought it made the hair glossy and healthy. I always had to hold my neck very stiff.

"I could just not eat," I said, hopefully.

"You? Not eat?" She laid the brush down and began braiding one side, laughing at the very idea of me not eating. "I'm afraid that wouldn't work, darling."

In the mirror I caught Lulie's eye and pled with her silently. I needn't have worried. She didn't give up easily, either. "Well, I gonna take dinner, too, Miss Maggie. No need spreading it with the rest. I be careful and see Katie just eat our own fixings."

Aunt Maggie reached over my shoulder to the box which held my ribbons. Her hand hovered over it. "Let's see . . . you're wearing your white dotted swiss with a blue sash. Blue ribbons or white, Katie?"

"Blue, please, Aunt Maggie, if I promise not to eat a bite except Lulie's. . . ?"

"No, dear." She tied one blue bow and began braiding the other half of my hair. "No, Lulie and Choctaw would miss most of the fun if they didn't spread their dinner with the rest. That wouldn't be fair. You wouldn't really want them to do that, would you?"

The truth was, I would have, without a moment's hesitation, but put that way of course I had to say no. In the mirror I could see that Lulie was looking her scowliest, eyebrows beetling, mouth sulky. "Won't be no fun noway . . . knowing Katie here at home eating her heart out wanting to go so bad. I reckon I not relish a bite I put in my mouth."

"Oh, yes, you will. And Katie won't be eating her heart out. She doesn't like hearts. She likes fried chickens." Aunt Maggie finished the second braid, tied the bow and spread and plumped both of them until they stood out like stiff, fat little pillows. "There you are . . . braids as smooth as silk, bows as perky as Christmas."

I peered at myself and wiggled my eyebrows to loosen them. It was a peculiarity of mine to want my braids as tight as possible. I could not abide a loose or sloppy braid. As a consequence sometimes I felt as if my scalp extended down to my eyes, and it was only with effort I could wrinkle my forehead or raise my eyebrows. I said thank you and got up from the bench. Aunt Maggie sat down and began taking the pins out of her own knot. Her reddish-brown hair, released, tumbled over her shoulders and fell slowly down to her waist. It was very thick, a little rough, not too fine, and while it did not curl, it had a deep, rippling wave which always shone as if it had just been freshly washed. She picked up the brush and tilting her head to one side a little began the hard, brisk strokes which made the hair crackle and fly. From under the wing of it she looked at me and caught her lower lip between her teeth. Then she smiled. "No need to feel bad about it, Katie." I surged with relief. It was going to be all right. She had thought of something. She stopped brushing and turned to face me. "Tell you what . . . we'll ask Adam tonight if he won't drive us out for the baptizing. I think I'd like to watch it myself. Wouldn't that be fun?"

Well, of course it would have been more fun to go with Lulie and Choctaw for the whole day, but it was certainly better to salvage the baptizing than to miss it. "That'll be fine," I said, and seeing I was not unhappy about this solution, Lulie's face cleared.

Adam was with us for supper as usual on Saturday evening and later went with us to choir practice. It was a rather long practice, for they were working on a new anthem. It was a friendly group, the Methodist choir, and with perfect good nature they went over and over the anthem, doing their best to satisfy Aunt Maggie. I think I have not said that she not only sang in the choir, she was the director. There were no trained voices in the group, but as so often happens in such groups they had a sense of music which was flexible and teachable. Little by little under Aunt Maggie's direction they were learning not only to sing, but to know what they were singing and why. There was a lot of hard work that night, but along with it a good bit of joking and laughing. During the times of rest there was the usual flutter of talk, exchange of news, the common interest in the baseball team and its success, and one sensed a growing excitement in the nearness of the Reunion and all the plans for it. Families with members scattered all over were beginning to make ready for their homecoming, for everyone who had been reared in Stanwick and reared on the tradition of the Reunion made an effort to get home for it. There would be new in-laws to welcome, new babies since last summer, and older sons or daughters who for one reason or another had had to miss a year or two, might confidently be looked for this year. "John is coming . . . all the way from California, and he's bringing the whole family. I don't know where we'll put everyone, but we'll manage. Just think, there'll be twenty of us at home together!"

There was a feeling of responsibility about the band. "We've got to do something about those uniforms. They're beginning to get very shabby." There was anxiety about the leasing of the concessions, the condition of the picnic grove and how much work remained to be done on it, how soon to cut the grass in the ball park and so on. It was small-town talk, not world-shaking, not even terribly important, but it had the warmth that all family talk has, the personal concern widened to the responsibility of the group, the common bond of a community enterprise.

Going home Aunt Maggie and Adam spoke of it, laughing a little at the idiosyncracies of

345

some, knowing them from far back and expecting them, finding them amusing in a rather loving sort of way. "Fanny and Mary," Aunt Maggie said, "are determined their father shall not roast a whole mutton for the Reunion this year. They say they will pay someone to steal the goats first."

"They'll never get away with it," Adam said, chuckling, "they'll be eating roast mutton during the Reunion as long as there is one."

We were walking slowly, the stars moving with us, so close to us that over the trees they seemed to be fiery blooms stitched among the leaves. "I suppose so," Aunt Maggie said. "Nothing changes much in Stanwick." Adam's pipe glowed occasionally and bubbled when he drew on it, and the smell of it was mellow. Aunt Maggie's starched skirts swished against the grass at the edges of the walk. Lamps glowed in the windows of the homes we passed, and the deep-set lawns, dark under the trees, were sparkled with the lights of hundreds of fireflies. "It isn't so bad a place," Aunt Maggie went on, "is it, to make out one's life . . . Stanwick."

"No."

"Oh, it will always be a small town, stodgy, dull at times, commonplace, provincial, insulated, even ugly. Everybody knows everyone else's business. Everybody talks about everyone else; but everybody sort of joins together, too, gets worked up and excited about something like the Reunion, the big Christmas tree, the baseball team, the band . . . and the weather and crops. If there's a drought and a crop failure everybody is hurt, some more than others, but no one escapes entirely. The fun and the failures are all sort of common property, aren't they? I've just been thinking . . . walking along here, knowing every home we pass, the people in them, their problems, the kind of things they enjoy and want . . . there's old man Hughes back there, paralyzed, in bed for three years now, Sallie and her mother tied to the house . . . I don't suppose there is a day someone doesn't run in with fresh bread or cookies, or a little pat of butter or some eggs, or just to sit with him and let Sallie and her mother get a little rest, run downtown a minute. If he lives another year, or three, or ten, someone will keep right on running in to help out. The Clarksons next door . . . the whole town knows how she worries about his drinking . . . the whole town keeps an eye on him for her, sort of watches over him and rescues him, so she won't be too badly hurt by him. The Millers, here . . . everyone is so glad their oldest boy has got such a good job in the city finally . . . everyone knows how badly they need the money. And by and large everyone was very good to Maggie Rogers when she came home from the east, a failure. No one at all said, or even implied she didn't have what it took. They said, it's nice to have you home again, Maggie. We missed you. No one is ever alone in a small town, is he? No one is so small he wouldn't be missed. Everyone is important in his own way. I was just thinking, too, how different it is in a big city. How one lives in a little cubicle, not an individual at all, just one little pebble on a very large and stony beach. If a wave rolls in and washes you away it doesn't matter much at all. Your little cubicle is immediately occupied by another pebble and no one ever knows or cares that you are gone. You aren't missed by anyone. Because you have never really been needed. You might never have been, for all the good you do. You float around on the streets, go in and out of offices, go to the theater, eat at restaurants, and the only thing that is real is yourself. There are thousands of people all around you but they don't count, to yourself or to one another, except when they get in your way. They are like the scenery on the stage. They're alive, yet they don't have life, because they exist in such a mass."

Adam did not speak for a little while after she had finished, and then he said, "I think you are trying to convince yourself that life can be endurable for you here in Stanwick, Maggie. You know too well that there is another side of the picture . . . that there are things one can find only in the city, without which the world would be very poor . . . great music, for instance, the best of the stage, literature, the heart of banking and commerce, trade and industry."

"But you would not be happy anywhere else, Adam."

"Why?"

"Oh . . ." she laughed, "you have, essentially, a small-town heart, dear."

"What is a small-town heart?"

"Oh, many things I suppose . . . one that loves one place, one people, one corner of the earth where your foot feels at home . . ."

"I don't think that's valid, Maggie. There are many people who would feel very lonely outside the city . . . who would miss its noise and hurry and crowds and being part of something big and bustling and who would feel very insignificant if they were lifted out of it. I think it depends in the long run on what one is doing, and on what one wants. If I were doing work which I loved, I believe I could make any corner of the earth home."

Many years later I was to remember that conversation, and to wonder that Adam should have known so well, even then, what he could do. But Aunt Maggie simply laughed again. "You won't have to, darling. I shall be perfectly happy, here."

There was another silence, which Aunt Maggie broke finally. "Jim is one of those with a big-town heart eating itself out for the city."

"Yes."

"He went up to see *Carmen,* you know."

"Yes . . . I knew he was going."

"He must have made a very big night of it. He brought a woman to the performance who, so Tolly says, everyone in town knows is not quite respectable . . . a widow with a little money, who likes a form of gaiety not exactly approved by the best people."

"Was he offensive to you?"

"Oh, no . . . we only spoke. He was obviously drinking, also. Why does he do such things, Adam?"

"Probably because no one cares much whether he does or doesn't."

"But there's his uncle . . . Doctor Clem cares."

"Maggie, what's an uncle? Besides he resents Doctor Clem."

"Why should he resent Doctor Clem?"

"Don't you know why he studied medicine? Hasn't he told you?"

"No. He's never spoken of it, except in that slighting way he has. I just supposed he took it up when he learned he couldn't become a pianist . . . sort of second-best choice."

"Well, in a way he did . . . but Doctor Clem was mixed up in the whole business. He furnished the money for Jim to study music, but he always wanted him to study medicine

350

. . . wanted him to come here and follow him. In a way I suppose it was Jim's misfortune that Doctor Clem never married and had children of his own. He settled all his hopes and dreams, the ones he would have had for a son, on Jim. When Jim wanted to study music he was impatient of it, didn't like the idea at all, but finally provided the money for it . . . with a promise extracted from Jim that if it didn't work out he would then go into medicine and come here. That's what happened."

"Did Jim tell you all this?"

"Oh, no. Doctor Clem did. You know how he is . . . as good as gold, but dogmatic, opinionated, intolerant. Studying music was just plain foolishness to him. He told me about it long ago. He still owed the bank a little when I took over after your father retired. I suppose he thought I should know why he was still paying off such an old note, and such a large one. Between educating Jim musically and medically, it came to a sizable sum."

"I should think Jim would feel a little gratitude, instead of resentment. He *was* given his chance, after all."

"I doubt he knows Doctor Clem had to borrow. He probably thought the old man was pretty well off . . . had money saved, never having married and so on. But, even if he did know, gratitude is a thing hard come by. It is usually tied to obligation . . . to the bitterness of having to accept favors. We rarely feel it pure and unmixed.''

"You did . . . to my father. You took Tolly's place when he decided to leave Stanwick.''

"Ah, but not out of gratitude. I wanted to be a banker from the start. Your father did a lot for me, but he never tried to make me over into something I didn't want to be. Sure, I'm grateful to him, because he gave me the opportunity to be what I wanted to be. But your father didn't say he'd help me if I'd be a banker. He let me do the choosing. Perhaps if Doctor Clem had just left Jim alone when his music came to nothing . . . or if he wanted to help further had told him to try anything else he wanted to try . . .''

"It wouldn't have hurt Jim to stand on his own feet, would it? I think it would have turned out just about the same. He's just temperamentally one of Papa's pessimists.''

"Maybe so. People are strange, aren't they? We're all made up of our fathers and mothers, and their fathers and mothers, the influences of the home we grew up in, the town and its people, the influence of teachers and institutions . . . it takes a lot to make a person what he is, and no one of us ever knows exactly what another one is. At best we can only attribute causes and feelings and actions to what we know of ourselves. We're bound to misjudge, hurt and cripple, even with the best intentions in the world."

Nothing could have shown Adam in purer profile than his contrast with Doctor Jim . . . all of his fundamental saneness, integrity, gentleness, goodness, were thrown in sharp relief by the doctor's passion, pessimism, fatalism. And yet, remembering, I can see how Aunt Maggie might have ambivalent feelings about each of them. The one was a part of the old familiar pattern of things, steady, rock-ribbed and earth-bound, as comfortable as a well-worn shoe, with little of himself left to be discovered. The other was unpredictably exciting, gypsyish, with, perhaps, a broad streak of the black sheep in him; but there was never anything dull or familiar about him, and there was the strong bond of their similar experiences in music. Oh, I can see it well enough, and even understand it. What I cannot understand is how Aunt Maggie could have so misjudged Adam.

We had come home. I had to remind Aunt Maggie about the baptizing, but Adam promised to take us, and we said goodnight.

Seventeen

When I remember the Negro baptizing that Sunday afternoon it is with mixed feelings. I cannot help having a certain tenderness for that little girl who was so earnest, who carried such a disproportionately large burden of worry, and who felt no ludicrousness at all, at the time, about what she did. At the same time I remember it with much amusement. It *was* funny. As an adolescent I was terribly ashamed of it. I carried the memory of it around with me, hidden well out of sight most of the time, recalling it only to wince blushingly at my stupidity. I have had to take a good bit of teasing about it at one time or another most of my life. But time has mellowed the entire incident now and what I principally recall is the motive. That, at least, was unimpeachable.

Fox Fork circled Stanwick in a long, lazy loop, very like the coils of a rope laid carelessly around it. In some places it nearly touched, as down by the railway station. Back of my grandfather's it was at least a mile to the creek, and at either end of town it was several miles to the bridges. But one could not leave Stanwick in any direction without crossing the creek, save on the west, and there was nothing over that way but the first of the hills. The bridge where the baptizing was to be held was south of my grandfather's, which meant we did not have to go through town. We simply turned left on the road, as we had done the night I had gone with Lulie and Choctaw to the camp meeting. The brush arbor itself was not far from the bridge.

It was the last of July now and the full heat of the summer was upon us. It had been some weeks since the rain and the dirt road had become dry and powdery. It had been churned to a fine dust which lay several inches deep, and with every passing vehicle it was stirred into thick, turgid clouds. The weeds alongside the road were covered with dust and were even bent under its weight. I remember identifying the weeds as we rolled along, making a kind of chant of their names . . . ironweed, wormweed, ragweed, dock . . . ironweed, wormweed, ragweed, dock . . . saying them in time to the beat of the horse's hooves. They looked unkempt and disreputable, slatternly and trashy. They would not again this year bear their height proudly and greenly, for from now on until the fall the rains would only wash them meagerly, and within a day or two the clouds of dust would roll over them again.

Ahead of us the heat lay over the road, dancing and shimmering like water seen through an imperfect glass. The glint of it hurt one's eyes and the feel of it against one's face was like the heat from Lulie's oven door. Even the leaves on the trees which occasionally shaded the road were wilted, hanging disconsolately and limply by their stems. Adam's mare jogged along, but any pace was enough to bring out a lathery foam under the harness straps. I watched the breeching and crupper straps slide back and forth greasily and wondered if the horse were very uncomfortable. I should have been, I thought, pulling a heavy buggy in all that heat; but she seemed not to mind, plodding steadily along, switching her tail and now and then tossing her head against the flies.

The sun beat down on the buggy top and made it smell like melted oilcloth. It also made it feel like a frying pan turned over our heads. Aunt Maggie fanned listlessly with her big palm leaf. "Why we do these foolish things," she fretted, "I'll never know. It would have been much more sensible to stay at home out of the heat this afternoon."

"But much less fun," Adam said, smiling at her.

"Besides," I put in, "you . . ."

"Promised!" she and Adam said with one voice, laughing.

"Well, you did," I said defensively.

"And you just remember, my love, that on a day hot enough to fry eggs on the sidewalk we kept that promise."

The road curved in a wide bend around the edge of a low, swampy place which was really an arm of the creek called the slough. It rarely had more than a foot of muddy, sluggish water in it, and it was full of old cypress knees and water-soaked logs. It was also full of cottonmouth snakes, and it was doubtless the breeding place of millions of mosquitoes. As we came around the loop of the bend we saw a horse and buggy drawn up by the side of the road. "That's Jim's rig," Adam said. "Wonder what he's doing out here."

When we drew abreast of it we saw that the buggy was empty and the horse tethered to the limb of a low-hanging tree. At about the same time we saw the doctor standing on a log extending out into the slough. He had a pistol in his hand and was sighting down his outstretched arm. He saw us at about the same time, but he motioned with his other hand and continued sighting. When he fired there was a splash of water, a brief but convulsive heaving, and then the surface of the swamp was still. "Got him!" he cried triumphantly, dropping his pistol arm.

"Snake?" Adam asked.

The doctor nodded and came toward us. "One of the biggest I ever saw. Big around as my arm. God, but those things explode when they're hit! Like firing into a cream puff." He looked excited, his face flushed and his eyes brilliant.

"How'd you happen to see him from the road?"

"Didn't. I come out here and look for them when there isn't anything else to do. Some afternoon I kill as many as half a dozen within a hour."

Aunt Maggie shuddered. "What a way to spend time."

The doctor shrugged. "Well, it's better than sitting in an empty office waiting for calls. Better than making most of the calls, for that matter. Do you shoot?" he asked Adam.

"A little. We have pretty fair bird and duck hunting later on. I like to get out once or twice in the fall."

"Come try this baby. You've never handled a sweeter gun. I just bought it when I was in the city the other day."

Adam looked at Aunt Maggie and she nodded. "Go ahead if you like. We've plenty of time."

He wrapped the reins around the whip socket and clambered out. The doctor handed him the pistol . . . I have no idea what kind it was. I only remember that to me it looked ugly, long-nosed and deadly. Adam took it and looked it over. "Must have cost quite a bit."

"Plenty," the doctor said. "How about the knot on that log over there for a target?"

Adam looked at the knot and then at the doctor, and laughed. "Are you fooling? I couldn't hit that knot with a rifle!"

"Go ahead . . . try."

Adam raised the gun and aimed it, fired, and while water splashed beyond the log there was no splintering of the knot. He fired again, missed, and then handed the gun back to Doctor Jim. "I'm not that good," he admitted ruefully.

Doctor Jim raised the gun, took aim very steadily, fired, and the small knot disintegrated before our eyes. Adam looked at him. "Man, that's real shooting."

The doctor whirled the carriage, laughing. "Firearms are a hobby of mine. I'm crazy about them. Shooting," he said dryly, "is the one thing I figure I'm practically perfect at."

A crane, hidden until then by the reeds on the far side of the swamp, and now startled perhaps by the firing, suddenly took to the air, his wide, snowy wings beating heavily for speed and height, his long ungainly legs folded sweepingly behind him. He flew directly toward us, his long neck stretched and straightened. The doctor turned swiftly and raised the gun again, and before we knew what he meant to do he had fired and the crane went plummeting to the water. We watched it fall, the big, beautiful bird that had been so confidently and freely air-borne, watched it fall in one swift heavy plunge, and then disappear in the muck and the mud of the slough. I remember putting both my hands over my eyes at the last, so I wouldn't see it hit the water, and I remember Aunt Maggie's sharp, indrawn breath. Then there was just silence . . . a kind of echoing silence in which the sound of the gun and the felt thud of the water when the crane hit were both still mixed. When Adam spoke his voice was thick, but quite controlled. "That was a bit unnecessary, wasn't it? We had already seen evidence of your marksmanship."

"Couldn't resist it," the doctor muttered, "perfect target." He moved toward his own buggy, the gun hanging from his hand. "Well, it was just a bird."

"But it was a beautiful bird," Aunt Maggie said, then, hotly, "and it was alive and free. There wasn't any reason for you to shoot it. It isn't as if it had been a game bird. It was just cruel . . . just wanton killing."

The doctor drew his shoulders together. "It doesn't matter, does it? I shot without thinking. Didn't you ever do anything on the spur of the moment? I'm sorry . . . . if that helps any."

Aunt Maggie leaned forward and began unwrapping the lines. "Adam, please . . . let's go."

Adam got in and we drove slowly on down the road. Neither she nor Adam said anything. I sneaked a quick look at each of them. Adam's face was very red and his jaw was set hard, with little bony bulges, as if by keeping it very tightly clenched he might avoid boiling over. Aunt Maggie's brows were drawn together as if her head ached, and she kept biting her lower lip, and all the while she was fanning furiously. They were both disturbed, angry, and, I think now, they were confused. They could not understand the impulse that had shot down a beautiful, free-flying thing simply for the sake of shooting. Its deeper implications were so dark that they could not follow them. I came closer to understanding it myself, for they had grown out of the impulses to cruelty with which a child is still familiar. I knew what it was like to feel the sudden necessity to destroy. I had felt it and obeyed it more than once, as when seeing a perfectly harmless worm crawling in the dust I had felt compelled to step on it, mash and crush it, feel some kind of godlike power rise up within me, and then seeing it bruised and lifeless had wept over it, not knowing the source of either my compulsion or my tears; or as when, knowing full well the exquisite tenderness of Rastus's ears, I had deliberately pulled them, tormented her, listened to her cry and then just as senselessly hugged her head close to me and patted and loved her. The impulse to cruelty has to be civilized out of us, and often then remains only very thinly under control.

When we came to the bridge and the place of the baptizing we saw that both banks of the creek were crowded with people, the Negroes on the far side, the white people, who had come as we had come, out of curiosity, on the near side of the bridge. The Negroes sat on the grass, the sand, on logs they had dragged up, anywhere at all, in row after row clear down to the water's edge. I had never before seen so many Negroes gathered together. We sat, the buggy drawn to one side of the road, looking for a few minutes. "Good heavens!" Aunt Maggie said, "I didn't know there were that many Negroes in the county!"

"You didn't?" Adam said. "Forty per cent of the population of the county is Negro."

"Well, the whole forty per cent must be here this afternoon."

"Most of them, I suspect. An all-day preaching with dinner on the ground will draw them like flies to molasses."

It struck me how very much like a bouquet of flowers they looked . . . the women and girls in their bright colored dresses, the men in white and colored shirts, all massed together, clustered, all having, however, chocolate-drop centers. The dark faces were like the brown centers of black-eyed Susans, or the small, wild sunflower we called "niggerheads." If I closed my eyes a little bit, squinted hazily, I could shut out the features of the faces and see nothing but color, red, green, blue, yellow, and the brown-black centers. If I moved my head rapidly, they whirled, ran together and blurred, like the bits of color in a kaleidoscope.

We did not cross the bridge. There was no place very near the creek to leave the horse and buggy, so Adam turned around and drove back a short distance into the woods. "This will be too far for you to sit in the buggy," he told us, "but there's no help for it. There's too big a crowd."

"It doesn't matter," Aunt Maggie said, "we can sit on the bank."

Upstream from the bridge a little way the creek came flowing around a bend. It eddied toward the far bank in the curve, shelving under it and making a pool which barely had a current the water ran so slow. The bank was steep just over the pool, but it sloped away to a flat beach, white, sandy, and almost level, just below. From the beach one could wade into the pool, the water gradually deepening. Eventually it would be quite over one's head, but there were no dangerous holes or treacherous suctions in the floor of the pool. It was flat, hard rock which slanted slightly, but increasingly and deepeningly toward the center. One could always stop at any desired depth. Here in the pool, which was not entirely clear but was clearer than the rest of the creek, was where the baptizing was to be held.

Adam found us places on a little point of land which overlooked the curve of the creek, but which made us upstream and across, of course, from the pool. The people to be baptized were gathered on the long, sandy beach. The women and girls were dressed in white or in light-colored dresses; the men wore white shirts with whatever trousers they didn't mind getting wet. No one was robed except the preacher, and in him I recognized the same tobacco-brown man who had led the singing, praying and speaking at the meeting. He was standing now, facing the group of people on the beach, leading them in singing. Their voices came to us across the creek, high and quavery and a little sad. I kept wiggling and squirming, trying to find Lulie in the crowd of Negroes across from us. Everything was happening over there, and I felt exactly as if I were sitting in the top balcony, far to one side at that, when I very much wanted to be in the front row.

A man with a tall staff started wading into the water, feeling ahead of him and searching the depth with the staff. It looked rather silly to me to be walking so dramatically and slowly, head upraised and thrown back, feeling for depth when the water came only to his ankles yet. But he was an actor, the center of the stage for the time being, before a very large audience. He appreciated the drama of his situation and made the most of it. Very slowly, very cautiously he moved into the water, as one called and compelled, as one bearing a prophet's mantle, seriously, solemnly. And then, as I watched the man, in the corner of my vision, as one frequently does see clearly, I saw Lulie. I should have seen her immediately, I thought, for she stood out so clearly to me now among the white and lightly dressed women that I didn't see how I could have missed her. It was a case of not being able to see the forest for the trees, because Lulie was wearing her red and yellow print dress and now that I saw her, she was like a sore thumb, swollen beyond life size. I couldn't help giggling over it. Not for anything in the world would Lulie have dressed like all the others. Even in her baptizing she had to make herself different, handsome; she had to dress so all the men could see how bright and shiny was her golden skin; she had to arouse the envy of every woman there; she had to be Lulie, the city gal. I did so understand how she felt, and in some inexplicable way I thought it pretty wonderful of her.

I wondered, rather idly, if she had the red silk petticoat on, but the wonder turned to certainty almost immediately. She wouldn't pass up an opportunity to show it off. But with the certainty came a great uneasiness. If she went into the water with that petticoat on, her dress would float on top of the water when she was baptized, and everyone would see the petticoat. Choctaw would see it! It didn't occur to me that by now Lulie might have thought of some perfectly logical explanation for the petticoat to give Choctaw. I was just suddenly convinced that she hadn't thought how her dress would float, revealing it, and I was equally sure that Choctaw would know the doctor had brought it to her and he would be very angry and that we might never see the end of the trouble that red petticoat would cause. I scrambled up. I had to get over there and warn her. "Where are you going?" Aunt Maggie said, as I wiggled past her.

"I'm going over where Lulie is," I said, not stopping. She might not allow me to go if I stopped.

"Katie!" she called after me, but I was running now, having found a clear aisle back of the people. I knew she might come after me, or send Adam, and that I had no good explanation, or at least none that I could give, for what I was doing, but I felt a very real urgency to get to Lulie. Maybe I could warn her before Aunt Maggie came after me.

I flew across the bridge and down the bank, dodging in and out among the sitting Negroes, coming finally to the beach and pulling up, out of breath, beside Lulie. They were singing "When the Roll is Called up Yonder," and in the back row of the twenty or so people to be baptized Lulie was standing, her hips swiveling in time to the music, her eyes closed, shouting out the promising words, caught up in the rapture of being there when the heavenly roll was called. I poked her in the rear unceremoniously, "Ps-s-s-t, Lulie!"

She jumped and opened one eye, peering down at me without losing a syllable of the song or missing a beat of the rhythm. When she saw who it was she opened the other eye, widened them both, but shook her head at me, warning me that this was no time for conversation. But it was all the time I had. I tugged at her elbow, hissing again, "Ps-s-s-t, Lulie!"

This time she jerked her elbow loose, doubled it and rammed it sharply into my chest, mumbling at me out of the side of her mouth, "Go 'way!"

She very nearly knocked the breath out of me and it made me so angry that I boiled over. Doubling up my own elbow I dug it into her ribs violently. "I *won't* go away! Have you got on your red petticoat?"

But she wasn't listening to me, and she wouldn't stop singing, and the preacher was leading the first of the people into the water. I sat down on the sand, and trying to make myself very small, hiding as much as I could of what I was doing by hunching my shoulders, I lifted the hem of her dress. She had it on, all right. I gave it a jerk, hoping to loosen the button at the waist. Ladies' petticoats in those days were made on a band which buttoned around the waist. It just depended on how tightly that button was sewed on whether I could yank it loose or not. Lulie hitched at her waist and kicked backward at me. They were now going, without any pause, from the roll call into "When the Saints Go Marching In," and two assistants to the preacher were leading out of the water the man who had just been baptized, while two more were leading into the water the next man. I calculated. Standing where she was, Lulie would be among the last to go. It would give me time to keep on jerking on the petticoat, and I could think of nothing else to do; so I would yank, Lulie would twitch, without missing a note, kick vaguely at me as if I were a horsefly buzzing at her heels, and I would wait a few seconds and yank again. I really think no one paid any attention to me right then, for there was too much ecstasy over the baptizing, too much shouting and singing, and, too, there was a press of people all around us. Once in the water, however, the spotlight would be focused on Lulie, and the baptizing was going alarmingly fast. The preacher, with his two assistants, was wasting no time, and the outcoming convert met the ingoing candidate with dismaying regularity. The men were all finished now, and the women were starting and if the petticoat was any looser I couldn't tell. I began yanking a little oftener.

I truly didn't mean to go into the water with Lulie. I hadn't thought beyond trying to get the petticoat off of her before she got into it. But as the line shortened she had moved forward, a foot at a time, and I, without noticing, had inched my behind along in the sand, following. The first thing I knew she was wading in, and I, clutching the petticoat for another yank, was pulled in, too. I had either to turn loose, then, or go ahead. I went. I recall having the despairing feeling that perhaps I could hold it down in the water. How strange it looked for a little white girl to wade into the deepening water with Lulie did not immediately occur to me. I was intent upon one thing, and with the blindness of children feeling such intensity, I simply hung on. Lulie, ecstatic and in an emotional delirium which had her waving her arms and shouting at every step, never even noticed me. Deeper and deeper we went. As it became apparent to the people on the banks that I was going all the way with Lulie the singing faltered, then someone, not understanding but probably fearing a scene of some sort, started it up again. I have never to this day forgotten what the song was. "We are . . . climbing . . . Jacob's Ladder . . . we are . . . climbing . . . Jacob's Ladder . . . we are . . . climbing . . . Jacob's Ladder . . . Soldiers . . . of the . . . Cross." It is an old Negro spiritual, the tempo very slow, dominated by the rung-by-rung effect of the climbing tune. On and on it went through all of its dozen verses.

The preacher advanced to meet Lulie and stopped her in water not quite up to her waist. I was up to my shoulders, but I think I would simply have closed my eyes and gone right on over my head had it been necessary. I was still clutching the petticoat, hanging on to it, weighing it down. Aunt Maggie told me later that when she saw me going into the water with Lulie she was simply paralyzed. For a few seconds she had just sat there, in a sort of frozen inertia, not quite believing what she saw. Then she had grabbed at Adam, at the same time trying to get to her feet. "We've got to get her out of there!"

But Adam, chuckling, had pulled her back down. "Leave her alone, Maggie. Whatever it is, the child knows what she's doing."

But Aunt Maggie, looking around, had begun to see the hidden mouths, hear the sniggers and muffled laughter, and to her first horror was now added embarrassment. All the white people, the townspeople, the family friends were watching, were all beginning to laugh, and she said she wished devoutly for a deep, wide ditch in which to hide herself. More than that, however, she wished she could jerk me out of the creek at once, by the hair if necessary, and switch my legs thoroughly for me. She said she was never so provoked in her life. I can imagine it.

The preacher, meeting us, looked at me. "Who is this child, Sister Lulie?" He had to ask her three times before she began to come out of her state of bliss. Then she looked at me as if she had never seen me before, amazement and rising fear almost blinding her.

I told him myself, finally. "I'm Katie Rogers."

"Whut you doing here?"

"I'm holding Lulie's petticoat so it won't float."

He was speechless, as well he might be, and he looked peeringly first at me and then at Lulie. Lulie's head was hanging low. "Katie, you done got us both into trouble. Whut you do such a thing for?"

Slowly, then, I began to realize what I had done . . . that I had got us into a situation where there was no explanation I could possibly give, to anyone at all, that would not do more damage than good. Not to anyone could I explain, sensibly and reasonably, why it had been necessary to hold Lulie's petticoat. Anything less than the truth was silly, and to prevent the truth being known was the sole reason for the whole ridiculous affair. It took a great deal, however, to defeat me, and immediately my mind began working, fast and hard. "Just baptize me, too," I whispered.

"Little girl, I can't do that. Your folks be mad, do I do that."

"No, they won't. I promise they won't."

"You just turn around and the menfolks'll take you back outta the water," the preacher counseled.

"If I turn loose of Lulie's petticoat," I hissed at him, "it'll float. Something terrible will happen if it floats. Go ahead, baptize me, too. Everybody's going to notice, if you don't."

"They done notice," he muttered.

"Well, go ahead, then. Hurry!"

Lulie was completely broken. She stood there, waiting, afraid of the preacher, afraid of me. The song from the Negro side of the creek droned on. Finally, taking courage, the preacher lifted his eyes to the heavens, raised his hand, and dunked us both under at once. I had only to bend my head a little, but Lulie made a nice splash. Then we waded back to the shore, I turning loose of the petticoat before we reached shallow water. Lulie was mumbling. "Whut I gonna tell Miss Maggie? You done ruin my baptizing, Katie, and got me in the worst trouble with Miss Maggie. Ain't done me no good at all to get my sins washed away. Just got me a load of new ones to carry. Whut I gonna say? Whut I gonna do?"

"Just say you didn't know I was there."

"That's the God's truth," she said.

"And just say you didn't know anything else to do but let me go ahead and be baptized."

"And that's the God's truth, too."

"Well, then," I snapped at her, "just tell it . . . and next time don't wear that god-damned petticoat!"

She was too miserable to notice what I had said, but it gave me eminent satisfaction to use the worst swear words I had ever heard at her. Her and her red petticoat, I thought angrily. It would have been good enough for the vain, silly girl if I had just let it float and let Choctaw see it. Fine thing, the kind of appreciation one got for making a fool of oneself . . . for by now I knew very well that was exactly what I had done.

Eighteen

I stuck stubbornly to my story, first with Aunt Maggie and Adam, and then with Grandfather and Grandmother. No one could shake it at all. "I just wanted to be baptized with Lulie," I said, over and over again. Aunt Maggie and Adam had let it go at that and I had been taken home immediately to be dried out. Adam had let us out at the gate without coming in himself. "I'll be over after supper," he had told Aunt Maggie, but engrossed with me she had simply nodded and scurried me and my dripping apparel down the walk ahead of her.

Grandfather and Grandmother had reacted typically. Grandfather, after one stunned moment, had collapsed into a chair and had then leaned his head back and laughed until the tears rolled down his face. "Katie, you are the most unpredictable child I ever saw in my life! Baptized . . . with Lulie! For God's sake, what next?''

Grandmother was horrified. She followed Aunt Maggie and me upstairs and stood there fussing and fuming while I was stripped and got into dry clothing. Her light, brittle voice was like little bits of broken glass showering down all around me, tinkling annoyingly and persistently. She kept on and on. "What on earth came over you, Katherine? What *did* you mean by behaving so? It was so common, so coarse . . . to go into the creek with a Negro servant and allow yourself to be baptized by a Negro preacher! Don't you have any sense of the seemliness of things? Didn't you think how it looked? What got into you?"

"I just wanted to be baptized," I muttered sullenly. "It's been a long time since I was baptized, Grandmother, and then it wasn't all over. I was just sprinkled. Lulie was going to be baptized and I just thought I would, too.''

"Well, if you had to be baptized you might at least have told us and allowed us to have it done in our own church . . . with a little dignity. I never heard of such a thing. What will your father and mother say?''

Aunt Maggie was drying my hair with a towel. I peered out from under it at Grandmother, who was marching up and down a corner of the rug. "They won't say anything,"

I said, on certain grounds there, "or if they do they'll say if I wanted to be baptized with Lulie it was all right."

"Yes," Grandmother said bitterly, "that's just what they *will* say, I suppose. They have no more sense of propriety than they have taught you to have. This, Margaret," and she turned to Aunt Maggie, "is what comes of all this free thinking of theirs. I have always said that Katherine and Tolliver were spoiling the child. She isn't controlled, she's encouraged to think and to do things no other child would even dream of doing. She's practically allowed to run wild, and you and your father encourage her in it when she's visiting here. Now, see what's happened!"

"Well, what has happened, Mother? Nothing very terrible, as far as I can see."

"You don't think making a laughingstock of herself and of us is anything?"

"No, I don't." Aunt Maggie threw the towel on a chair and picking up the brush, began brushing vigorously. "Oh, it's a little embarrassing, yes, but I don't think it's important. She's a child, and no matter what children do, they don't make laughingstocks of themselves. People are going to laugh, of course, but down deep in their hearts there isn't going to be a soul in this town who will be making fun of Katie. They will be laughing fondly, I think. So we can just forget that side of it. And another thing, Mother, if Katie wanted to be baptized and chose this time and this way to do it, I think we should respect her actions. Katie may not be able to give us a logical reason for what she did, but I, for one, am willing to believe she had one and let the whole matter drop right there."

Grandmother sniffed and started walking toward the door. "Well, then, you can just do whatever explaining needs to be done. I wash my hands of the whole affair." Her skirts swished against the door frame and she was gone.

Not until then did I begin to feel the least twinge of guilt over the matter. I was provoked with Lulie and I felt foolish, but not guilty. Now, however, it made me very uncomfortable to have Aunt Maggie express such confidence in my motives. The troubling voice of conscience told me I ought at least to disabuse her of her faith in my goodness. But I could not do that without telling the whole thing, and, rationalizing, I told myself that the true reason was just as worthy. I wished, however, I could just burst out with all of it to Aunt Maggie. I didn't much think she would mind Lulie's red petticoat, and I was certain she would understand how important it had been that Choctaw shouldn't learn of it. But, still, I reasoned, adults were so peculiar, so illogical and unreasonable, so given to unpredictable actions and angers and disturbances, one could never be sure about the most dependable of them, and she just might be very angry with Lulie. So I just squirmed uncomfortably and let the moment pass.

I felt a little buffeted by the storm of Grandmother's scoldings, however, somewhat wind-blown and ruffled, and more than a little weary of the whole experience, so that when Aunt Maggie had finished braiding my hair and I was free to go, I was glad to escape the house. I wandered out into the front yard and drifted aimlessly over to the mulberry tree. I sat in the swing, setting it to moving with my toes, and I swung idly back and forth for a few minutes, wondering why I should feel so unaccountably sad and, for the first time in weeks, a little homesick.

Lulie had not yet come back and I had the feeling that the entire day had all at once deflated. The sun was well over into the west by now and the air was almost unbearably still and heavy with heat. Without even thinking, moving restlessly rather, unable to stay in one place for very long, I climbed to the top of the tree and settled myself on the chairlike limb. The tree was cool against my back, and against the bare skin of my legs, and when I laid my face against it, it felt almost damp with coolness. It had a very soothing effect upon my ruffled feelings and I sat there, absorbing the coolness, conscious of weariness in every bone of my body, and drooping sleepily as the emotional disturbances of the afternoon drained away. I did not notice when the sun set, nor that the swing and the lawn below the tree were beginning to turn gray with the fading light. I think I actually slept a little, or else drowsed and dreamed in my drowsiness, for I remember seeing very clearly an image of my mother, slender and lovely again, holding the new baby brother swaddled in a blanket in her arms, and my father standing near her, the two of them talking. I could not hear what they were saying, though I tried, but I could hear my mother's voice, and then, answering, the deeper voice of my father. The dream faded very slowly, my father and mother simply becoming invisible, but the voices kept murmuring, and suddenly I was conscious of where I was, that it was twilight and the voices of the dream were real and were coming from directly below me in the swing.

It was Aunt Maggie, of course, and I moved to start climbing down, thinking Adam had come a little early. But the man's voice was raised suddenly and I knew it was not Adam at all, but was Doctor Jim, and I knew, too, that I should not clamber down and interrupt them. There was too much urgency in Doctor Jim's voice, and when I heard what he was saying I was too frightened to move. "But you know," he was saying, "you know very well, Maggie, that I am in love with you . . .

that I have been in love with you almost from the beginning. You can't deny that."

"I do deny it, Jim," Aunt Maggie said slowly. "It was stupid of me, perhaps, but I didn't know. Not at first, at any rate."

"But how could you not have known? From that very first night when I heard you singing 'Kathleen Mavourneen' . . . how could you not have known? What did you think? What went on in your mind?"

"I don't know. Oh, I thought you were dramatizing the whole thing . . . it was all mixed up with music and the east and remembering . . . and you were always so ironic. I think, perhaps, I just thought you were playing with the notion of being in love."

"I see." The doctor's voice became very rough. "And what were you doing? Playing with the notion of being in love, too? It has been with your permission that I have seen you so often, you know."

"I don't know . . . I don't know!"

"Well, I know. You love me, just as I love you. Look, Maggie. Neither you nor I belong in this town . . . among these people. Marry me . . . Marry me tomorrow and let's go away from here. I don't have to practice medicine here. I can hang out my shingle anywhere. Let's go back to the city. I can make a living, with the medicine, if necessary . . . but together maybe we can do what we both want to do. Maybe together we'll find

that one or the other, or perhaps both of us
. . . think, Maggie, think what it would be
like! To be back where there are people
again, where people really live! No one here
lives . . . the people here are clods . . . they
only exist. They get up and eat and go about
during the day and go home again at night
and eat and then go to bed. That's not for us,
Maggie. That's for the slaves of the world.
Think of listening again to real music! Think
of the noise and the life and the bustle and
the crowds, the excitement, things happening.
Think of *living* again, Maggie. Let's do it . . .
let's do it tomorrow! It would be mad and
wonderful and wild and it would be the most
fun in the world. Oh, I'll set your heart to
flaming, and you'll sprout wings as free as
mine, and as wicked, and we'll do wild, insane
things which only gypsy violins know about!
Maggie? Maggie, will you?"

His voice was so persuasive, so charged with
passionate eagerness, so flaming itself, that
it brought a beating lump to my own throat,
and looking straight down I could see, very
dimly, that Doctor Jim was holding Aunt
Maggie in his arms and was kissing her. I
could not bear what was happening and the
tears welled over and slid slowly down my
face. I could think of only one person, and I
kept saying his name over and over to myself,
pleadingly . . . Adam . . . Adam . . . as if
by repetition I could make his name a spell

381

to ward off the doctor's magic. Oh, I had known, had always known he meant danger to Adam, boded no good for Aunt Maggie and carried in himself the destruction of happiness for both of them. Now she would go away, forever away, and Adam's heart would be broken and nothing would ever be the same again. It wasn't fair, I thought. It simply wasn't fair. The pathos of it nearly overcame me and I was within an inch of falling into the middle of the embrace below.

Then, out of the silence Aunt Maggie spoke, chokingly, "No . . . no . . ."

"I will not let you say no!" the doctor cried, and the swing creaked crazily as he tried to put his arms around her again.

But she pushed him away. "No . . . it would not *be* what you say it would be. It would not be adventure, nor anything gay and wonderful and fine. Oh, at first, yes, maybe. But I know what it would turn into . . . a cubbyhole and friendlessness and burnt-out hopes and ashes, and in the end you would hate me and I would hate you, and we should sink into desperation and hatred together. It isn't good enough. We don't love enough and we aren't good enough to make it fine and wonderful. I am going to marry Adam, Jim."

"You think you and Adam *are* good enough to make a fine and wonderful life together, is that it?"

"Adam is."

"So you'll marry him . . . and spend the rest of your life in this sinkhole! You can't possibly mean that's what you intend to do."

"It's exactly what I intend to do. I've been silly and foolish, hugging my dreams to my heart, deluding myself, pining over lost hopes, and refusing to face what lay straight before me. I haven't a voice, I never did have and never will have one, and I am going to quit feeding on false dreams. I am going to marry Adam, and I am going to give up that silly job in the post office, and if they will let me I am going to teach Stanwick's young people to sing a little better in their church choirs . . . that's a worthier ambition than being second-rate myself . . ."

But the doctor was laughing and the swing creaked loudly. When I looked down the dark shadow, which was all I could see of him, was standing before Aunt Maggie's white dress. "How noble of you! How very noble of you . . . Oh, God, the things a good woman can think of to justify herself! I have certainly been mistaken in you. This is where you belong after all, isn't it? You belong here so much that you crawl into the first safe hole you find, in order to stay here . . . marry a man you don't love . . ."

"I *do* love Adam . . . in a way you wouldn't understand . . ."

"Oh, sure, the childhood playmate sort of thing, the good, solid citizen type, the friend of the family, the safe, sure, hellishly dull banker. Well, marry him . . . marry him, and grow fat on your own boredom!"

"You're being intolerably nasty!"

"I'm being honest. Well, it serves me right. I shan't ever look for comfort from your kind again. Goodnight."

There was a soft swish over the grass and then the clip of his heels on the stones of the walk. The gate banged, and then there was quiet except for Aunt Maggie's weeping. Whether she wept for him, for herself, for Adam, or a little for all of them, I did not know. It grieved me to hear her, but mostly I was very tired of sitting in the tree and wished she would go in the house so I could get down. I was also very hungry, and now that the doctor was disposed of I thought we might as well forget him and have some supper.

Nineteen

What, if anything, was said to Lulie by Aunt
Maggie or Grandmother about the baptizing
I don't know. But I do know that Lulie herself
had plenty to say to me the next morning. I
was allowed to sleep late and Aunt Maggie
had already gone to work, Grandmother was
busy and Grandfather already out about the
place when I breakfasted. Lulie lit into me
like a house afire. It was not, however,
because she had been scolded or made to feel
uncomfortable. It was because she had had
time to ponder the whole affair and she was
highly indignant with me for not giving her
credit for having more sense than I apparently had. At least she pretended to be
indignant. "You think I a plumb fool?" she
growled at me, sprinkling brown sugar on my
oatmeal and pouring about twice as much

cream over it as I would have done. "You think I ain't got no sense at all? You think you got to bother your piddling little head over my red silk petticoat? Think I be baptized in it 'thout making sure of something? Whut I do 'fore I got you to take care of me, huh? How I get along? Whut I do all my life 'thout you? You tell me that, Katie Rogers! You so smart, you tell me that!"

"Where'd you get the brown sugar?" I asked, paying no attention to her scowly face thrust over my shoulder.

"None of your business," she snapped.

"You got it out of the big chest, that's where you got it. You stole it. Grandmother keeps it locked away to make caramel pies. One of these days you're going to be so smart you'll smart yourself into some trouble you can't get out of. You'll be needing somebody's help, then. Besides, you don't need to steal to get on the good side of me." I went right on eating the brown-sugared oatmeal, loving every rich, sweet, buttery bite of it. I didn't look directly at her, but out of the corner of my eye I watched to see what would happen and she got just as helplessly furious as I had thought she would.

"Who trying to get on whose good side?" she yelled, stomping one foot and flapping her hands against her hips, almost beside herself. "I ain't got no call to have to get on *nobody's* good side, I'll have you know, Miss

386

Priss! I gets along my own way, it make no diff'runce who like it or not. I ain't caring 'bout you. And taking half a cup of brown sugar ain't no stealing. I just help myself a little. You the beatin'est kid I ever saw. First you shame the living daylights out of me right in front of all my friends and church folks, wading into the creek hanging on to my petticoat, then when I tries to be nice to you, in *spite* of you butting in where it was strictly none of your business, you . . . you . . ."
She was sputtering by now and flailing the air with her arms. I grinned at her and she stopped to take a deep breath. She pointed a finger at me. "You just trying to get me mad, that whut you doing. Just trying to get me mad and get my mind offa that baptizing. Well, you ain't gonna do it. You just listen to me, Katie Rogers, and you learn a thing or two. Wasn't no more need you hanging on to that red petticoat yesterday than nothing in this world. You think Choctaw ain't never see that petticoat before? You think I ain't done tole him first thing about that petticoat? I done tole him first crack outta the box Miss Maggie brung it to me when she went up to the city the other day. That whut I tole him and that whut he b'lieves. Had he see it yesterday wouldn't of made no diff'runce. So you ain't so smart, after all."
I felt pretty deflated. I might have known she was shrewd enough to think of every-

thing. It made my behavior seem even more silly and useless. But I would have died before admitting it, so to hide my chagrin I seized upon one thing she had said and scolded her roundly. "When did Choctaw see your red petticoat? He's got no business seeing it! Ladies don't let their petticoats show except when they gather them up to step across something, or high up."

Lulie snorted. "I ain't no lady. Whut the use of having a red silk petticoat if I gonna hide it all the time? And it's some more ain't none of your business when Choctaw see it. But," she giggled suddenly, "he never seen it on account of me stepping across something, or up high, either!"

I had spooned up the last of the oatmeal and Lulie brought me bacon and eggs. "How'd he see it then?"

"You too young to know," she said, smirking.

Lulie could fry the most beautiful eggs in the world. She spooned butter over them and they turned a lovely, golden brown and there was none of that pale, sickly white look that boiled eggs have. I took a bite of muffin and egg and then, with my mouth full, said, "What did he do, turn your skirts up?"

She was pouring herself a cup of coffee and she stopped and looked at me. "What you know about turning skirts up?"

"Oh, it's in a book of Grandfather's. Some

soldiers one time, a long time ago, got drunk and tore up a town and went around turning up the girls' skirts. Seems pretty silly to me, but I guess it made the girls giggle and run. Some of the boys at school like to tease and make the girls giggle and run, but they don't turn up our skirts. Except," she had brought her coffee and sat down at the end of the table with it and I leaned toward her confidentially, "except once a boy ran behind Susan Price and flipped up her dress and you could see her panties. But that's the only one that ever did."

Lulie stirred her coffee slowly. "What she do?"

"Susan? Oh, she told the teacher and the teacher made the boy stay after school for a week. She said it wasn't nice. You shouldn't let Choctaw, Lulie."

Lulie studied me, and of course I know now that it must have been very difficult for her to believe I was as innocent as I sounded. But I truly was. The trouble was that I read so much that I had a surface knowledge of and familiarity with many things about which I had very little understanding, and I had a huge vocabulary of woefully mispronounced words which I understood not at all. I gave the impression of knowing a great deal more than I actually did. Now, I knew well enough and understood why Choctaw would have been jealous of Doctor Jim and would have been very angry had he known the doctor had brought Lulie the red silk petticoat. Jealousy was within the realm of my experience; but I certainly did not understand why Lulie could ask for it and get it, or what hateful implications would have underlain Choctaw's jealousy. I had no more idea than a jack-rabbit of what was actually involved.

"Well, Choctaw ain't turned up my skirts, missy. I ain't letting him. Maybe us gets married some day. Time aplenty for turning up skirts then. I just teases him along a little. You wanna know, I turn up my own skirt, show him. Just turn it up so he can see the ruffle."

She was telling the truth. When it was all over it was evident that she had never allowed Choctaw to be free with her beyond a certain point . . . that she expected to marry him and that she lured and enticed him toward the wedding point with her denials of herself.

I went on eating and Lulie stirred her coffee, then sipped, testing its heat. She made a face at the taste and shuddered. "I sho' mess up that coffee this morning. Wonder Miss Emily didn't say nothing 'bout it. Taste like burnt feathers."

I looked at her, surprised. "It tastes all right to me."

"Oh, you ain't got enough coffee in that slop they lets you have to know. All it do is color the milk a little. But it ain't good coffee,

390

I can tell you that. It taste terrible." She sipped again questioningly and shook her head. "Must of boiled it too long. They scold you much 'bout the baptizing?"

"No, not much. Grandmother did . . . some, but Aunt Maggie made her quit."

"I figured Miss Maggie wouldn't let 'em fret you much. You know what I hear her tell Miss Emily and Mister Cap this morning?"

"What?"

"She say she gonna quit her job at the post office and her and Mister Adam gonna get married."

"Oh, I knew that."

"When you know that? You ain't tell me."

"Well, I just knew it since last night. I sure am glad she isn't going to marry Doctor Jim."

Lulie turned her cup in the saucer and studied the design of the flowers circling the lip. "Whut make you think she might?"

"Oh, he wanted her to. He tried to get her to run away with him . . . to New York, I think," and I told her about being in the mulberry tree and overhearing them.

"Whut she say?"

"She said she wouldn't do it . . . said she was going to marry Adam."

Lulie kept turning the cup in the saucer, but she nodded her head. "Miss Maggie smart to take Mister Adam and not the doctor. He handsome, but he bad. He just break her heart, him. He no good for a woman like Miss

Maggie. She too nice a lady."

I nodded, agreeing. "What did she tell Grandfather and Grandmother?"

"Whut I say."

"Did she say when they were going to get married?"

"Not 'zactly when. Said him and her decided last night and he wasn't gonna rent his place next year on account of they would be living there theyselves. Reckon it'll be the fall when they gets married, when the renter moves out."

I was so provoked. I had been too tired the night before and had gone to bed right after supper, so I had missed the most exciting thing that could possibly have happened. "Wouldn't you know," I said, exasperated, throwing my napkin down on the corner of the table, "they'd pick the very night I was too sleepy to stay up? I always miss the most important things!"

Lulie chuckled. "Don't look to me like you miss much of anything. You got your nose stuck into everything happen 'round here, and you know more'n's good for you." She took a last swallow of her coffee, and then her eyes rounded in surprise and she grabbed the napkin I had thrown down and, clutching it to her mouth, ran for the back door. I watched her in amazement, then, understanding, ran to hold her head or bathe her face or give what comfort I could. Being sick at your stomach was no joke, and a person always needed a little help. The coffee, I decided, must surely have been terrible and I was glad my cup had been more than half milk.

Twenty

Aunt Maggie had been right, of course, about the way the townspeople would take the baptizing. There was quite a bit of teasing about it, a lot in fact, and while it was all good-humored and I had sense enough to realize that, I didn't enjoy it much just the same. I particularly felt foolish now that I knew it had not been necessary. I grew very tired of having everyone I met for a few days stop, look at me with twinkling eyes and begin chuckling. Inevitably they said the same thing, "Well, well, Katie . . . hear you've turned Hardshell Baptist . . . even been dunked." I fussed a little about it, but got no sympathy from anyone. Aunt Maggie simply said, "Well, if you do things that are odd and queer, Katie, you have to expect curiosity and some comment."

"It's my own business," I grumbled.

"Nothing is every entirely one's own business," Grandfather told me. "Whatever you do, all your life, is going to touch and affect others. Don't hide behind an excuse like that."

But it was soon forgotten because we were all excited about Aunt Maggie's news and, in addition, we were soon caught up in a more immediate excitement.

Having made up her mind Aunt Maggie moved promptly, and she told the postmaster on Monday of that week that she would be leaving as soon as he found someone to replace her. That was an easy thing to do for there were half a dozen young women he could ask, and, since we were in the last week of July, the two of them decided she could leave at the end of the week so the new girl could begin work on the first of August.

Her last week in the office went by swiftly. Each day she came home, burdened with and laughing over the load of personal things she had gradually accumulated there and was now having to bring home; an extra umbrella, a pair of rubbers, a hat which she vowed had been hanging on the hatrack for over a year, scissors, pens, ink and so forth. "I feel like a squirrel having to move a store of nuts," she said.

It was all very strange and upsetting and exciting, this business of Aunt Maggie and

Adam planning to be married in November . . . the first of November was the date they had set. But the thing that seemed the very strangest to me was that suddenly Aunt Maggie and Adam were acting so silly about one another, Adam especially behaving foolishly. He phoned her every morning just as early as he thought she would be up, and sometimes before she left the house he would phone again, and she would stand at the phone and laugh and murmur into it softly so we couldn't hear for half an hour at a time, as if they would never get through talking. Some days he could come home with her at noon, carrying things for her, and they both would be laughing, Aunt Maggie with a kind of nervous breathlessness that was entirely unfamiliar to me, and Adam with his face red and his eyes shining . . . and Aunt Maggie had such queer moods. One minute she'd be talking and laughing a blue streak, and the next she would be very quiet and her face would look sad and sometimes her eyes would fill with tears, and she'd have to brush them quickly away. And she behaved so oddly when we met Doctor Jim out anywhere. He never came to the house any more, but sometimes we saw him downtown. He always spoke very pleasantly, if anything more pleasantly than usual, bowing low . . . but Aunt Maggie never did more than nod at him. You'd have thought she didn't know him well at all.

Adam came every single night, now, and usually he ate supper with us. Instead of sitting by me, Aunt Maggie always sat on Adam's side of the table and they were forever holding hands, and Adam would forget to eat sometimes. You could speak to him a dozen times and he wouldn't hear, and once he took bread three times on his plate without even knowing it. They would get up from the table and wander out into the yard to the swing and they didn't care who saw them with their arms around each other.

"What is the matter with them?" I asked Grandfather one evening when they had left the supper table without eating enough between them to feed a bird.

"They're in love," he said to me, laughing. "Is your nose out of joint, sweet Kate? Just be patient with them, and don't bother them any more than you have to. Give them a chance to talk and be alone together."

"Oh, I don't mind," I said, airily, "it's just such a silly way to act."

Grandmother was brushing the crumbs off the table and setting the dessert around. "Katherine is right," she said shortly, "they are behaving ridiculously. It isn't proper for them to make love so obviously."

Grandfather pulled at his beard and pursed his mouth, eying Grandmother. "Well, I don't call the family the public, Emily. Neither of them would have the bad taste to show affection in public, but times have changed and there are fewer inhibitions in young people nowadays. I see nothing wrong in their being affectionate before us . . . rather nice, I'd say. I'm glad to see it. And it stops far short of making love."

Grandmother reddened. "I don't like to think of Margaret marrying at all. I wish she wouldn't. I wish she would be contented just to stay with us."

"I don't," Grandfather said briskly, "that's the last thing I wish for her. I'm very glad she's decided to marry Adam soon . . . the sooner the better, I say. Every woman needs to marry, and Maggie will make a good wife and mother."

Grandmother laid her spoon down, carefully placing it on the serving plate beside the bowl of custard as if it were important to have it laid just so, and she wiped her mouth with her napkin, then folded it and slipped it through her napkin ring. She leaned back in her chair. "That," she said, then, precisely and neatly, "is exactly what I wish to save Margaret . . . being a wife and mother."

Grandfather pushed his own plate of custard away from him suddenly and rose, shoving his chair back impatiently and noisily. His face was very red now, above the beard, and the fretwork of small veins around his temples stood out corded and hard. I knew he was very angry and I sat very small, not wanting to be included in the scene. He flung his napkin down. "That's the most arrant nonsense I ever heard, Emily. Margaret has decided for herself. You are not to say one word to her, do you hear? Not one word!"

Grandmother dropped her eyes, but said nothing. Grandfather leaned against the table, looking at her. "Don't try to poison your own daughter's happiness, Emily."

Grandmother stood, too, then, and picking up one of the dessert plates started with it to the kitchen. At the door she turned. "Very well, Mr. Rogers."

She went on through the door and Grandfather sighed deeply, rubbed his hand across his mouth and pulled the corners down, then seeing me he smiled. "It's always hard for a mother to see her daughter be married, Katie. Your grandmother is going to miss Aunt Maggie very much."

I nodded my head. "You'll miss her, too, though . . . but you are glad."

He looked down at the toes of his shoes. "Of course . . . of course I'll miss her . . . and of course I'm glad. Aunt Maggie must have her own happiness. And I'll have one girl left, anyhow." He swung me to his shoulders. "Katie will be here a good many years yet." He hugged me very tightly, "Ah, Katie, that's what grandchildren are for, to fill up all the room in empty old hearts . . . to keep them from rattling, you know, in their last days."

"Don't . . . you make me sad," I said, squeezing his neck, "your heart isn't old."

"Why, of course it's not," he said, laughing, "it's as young and gay as yours. Keep it that way, Katie."

"Oh, I will, I will!"

He put me down and took my hand. "We have something very important to do now." He looked at me quite seriously. "Can you help with something very important?"

"Of course I can."

"Very well, then. It is only ten days until the Reunion, now. We have to go up to the attic and get my uniform out of the trunk and make sure it is clean and ready for the parade, and we have to get out the flag and see if it needs mending, and we have to get out my sword and polish it."

"Are you going to let *me* help?" I couldn't believe it. Oh, I had always watched Grandfather lay out his uniform and the old silk flag which lay swathed in its folds of tissue paper all year, and the sword I had handled many times. We used it each year in the Battle of Shiloh, as we did some of the campaign hats and caps and some of the old guns. But the uniform . . . the flag, never had I touched them save very gently, with just a fingertip perhaps. Always there had been the admonition, "Don't handle these things, Katie. These things can never be replaced."

"But of course you are going to help. You're getting to be a big girl, now, Katie."

I closed my eyes very tight and said Thank you, God, and then hunched my shoulders to keep the shivers of excitement from shaking my whole body. It was exactly as if I had a chill and I was cold and hot all at the same time. All my life I have been glad I was big enough to help . . . once. I can think of nothing so fine or so wonderful that I would trade it for the memory of that hour in the attic with my grandfather.

I remember how the light lay across the attic floor, and how the very last rays of the sun shone through the windows, setting dust motes to dancing and twisting. I remember how Grandfather laid back the top of his old trunk and spread papers on the floor to protect the things he would lay out. First came the hats and the sword and the regimental colors. These were familiar things. He handed them to me and I put them on the papers. Then he lifted out the coat of the uniform and took it out of its wrappings. It was badly worn and stained with stains which nothing had ever removed . . . earth, and blood and sweat. There was nothing fine about it. It was made of a very rough material, coarsely woven and scratchy. It was gray. He held it a moment, looking at it, then he ran a hand over the front of it, smoothing it. I remember how his hand looked, old, knotted arthritically at the joints, the veins on the back of the hand standing up purple and corded, but the hand in movement was gentle and remembering. He smiled and gave the coat to me. Almost without breath I took it and, in imitation, ran my own hand over its front. It was a heavy coat and it drooped with its own weight. I remember its heaviness in my hands, and I remember that when, involuntarily, I hugged it against my face, its coarseness scratched against the skin. In the palms of my hands and on my cheek I have the feeling of that rough gray coat yet, and I am glad to have it there. I laid it down with the other things and took the trousers when he passed them to me.

Next came the flag. Grandfather did not unwrap and hold it up. Its silk was grown so old that he feared its own weight might tear it, so he laid it in its wrappings on the floor and then pulled back the papers and the old white sheet in which it had been swathed. He spread the sheet and then unfolded the flag upon it, and there it lay . . . the stars and bars, the flag of the rebellion, the flag of the lost cause. He laid a finger on it, searching, and he looked up at me and smiled, crookedly. "You know, Katie, I love the Stars and Stripes, and it's a very fine thing it is our flag to this day . . . but a man somehow never forgets a flag he has fought for. To love this flag is nothing to be ashamed of. We were wrong, but we believed we were right, and a man must fight for what he believes. When I die I want to be buried in that old gray uniform, and I want this flag laid on my coffin. Not that they have any military meaning or any military glory any more . . . but to me they signify my life's intentions . . . to live by what I believe and to die, believing."

I didn't understand the deeper meaning of what he was saying, of course, but I *felt* what he meant, and I knew it was good and right. "Yes, Grandfather." And when the time came he *was* buried in the old gray uniform, and his coffin was draped in the stars and bars.

"Come, it's growing dark up here," he said, then, and we gathered up the things, I being allowed to carry the flag itself. The attic had turned dim and dusky, and I remember that Grandfather threw the clothing over his arm and picked up the sword. I remember that he waited for me at the door and shut it behind us when we had gone through, and I remember that very carefully we went down the stairs, I ahead, Grandfather following. I remember feeling as if I were leading a parade myself, a solemn, grand parade, with the colors flying and the band playing, my feet spurning the ground and my head touching the clouds. That's what it was like to be Chisholm Rogers's granddaughter, helping him get ready for the Confederate Reunion, carrying the flag for him, fine and important, almost bursting with pride and splendor.

The next day we had news of such importance that everything else was dwarfed by it. Several weeks before, Grandfather had written the governor asking him to be the guest of honor at the Reunion and the principal speaker on the opening day. Shrewdly he had guessed that this would be a good year to ask the governor, for it was an election year, and the Reunion would offer him an opportunity to appear before the people of several counties, on an important occasion when what he had to say might be heard with greater appeal. But the governor had not replied immediately, and Grandfather had, of late, begun to sizzle a little. "He might at least have acknowledged my invitation," he had grumbled.

Adam had thought the fact that he hadn't answered meant that he was considering coming. Apparently Adam was right, for on Saturday morning, just ten days before the Reunion itself, his letter of acceptance came. He would be delighted to come, but he regretted he could not stay overnight as the guest of Captain Rogers. He would arrive on the morning train and would be at the disposal of the committee for the entire day, but he must leave on the evening train.

There promptly began a great hubbub and stir. Grandfather went into session with the committee and began to plan the program for the day. A welcoming committee must be appointed to meet the train. A special platform must be built in front of the bank to serve as a reviewing stand for the governor during the parade. The parade must be rescheduled to form and march immediately after he had taken his place on the stand. He must then be escorted to the picnic grove. They must get more bunting for the bandstand, and a state flag. The address must be delivered in the morning, for the ball game was already scheduled for the afternoon. Should the address begin at eleven, or eleven-thirty? It was going to be a very close thing, and if the train were only a few minutes late everything would be thrown out of kilter. Grandfather held conferences with the conductor, went carefully over the train's schedule and got his promise that short of a natural catastrophe over which he could exercise no control, he would deliver the governor promptly and on time to the split second. He, personally, would make certain that the engine was gone over thoroughly so that it could not develop any trouble, and a picked crew would bring the train down.

After the address the governor would be

Grandfather's guest at the big picnic dinner. It was the custom for everyone to bring dinner, to spread it on picnic tables and to eat in large family groups, with a great deal of visiting back and forth between groups. Grandmother promptly went into a dither about the picnic dinner. There was never any question about it, it was always an abundance of fried chicken, baked ham, three or four kind of salads, pickles, breads, cakes and pies, but would that be fine enough for the governor? Shouldn't she have something more elaborate, something a little more spendid? Grandfather impatiently told her that a picnic was a picnic whether a governor was present or not and for heaven's sake to keep it plain and simple. After all, the governor had been raised on a farm, too, and would probably enjoy fried chicken and baked ham.

There would be the ball game in the afternoon, and Grandfather and Adam thought the governor should be invited to pitch the first ball. The committee agreed, so Grandfather made a note of it. "But you remind me, Adam. I'll have so much on my mind that day I'm apt to forget it."

Following the ball game he would be brought to our house to rest, then he would have supper with us. There was a great deal of discussion as to whom to invite for the supper, and some distress as Grandfather realized that to have anyone at all would be to hurt those left out. It was finally and regretfully decided that supper would have to be kept a family affair. Adam insisted that even he be left out, but Grandfather would not have that. "You are in the family already," he said, "of course you'll come."

Grandmother was made happy when Grandfather told her to do what she liked about the supper, make it as fine and as fancy as she pleased, and she and Aunt Maggie immediately put their heads together and began to plan the meal.

There was still more discussion as to whether or not he should be taken back out to the ball park for the band concert after supper. It would make a very full day for him, and he would probably rather not, but, as Adam said, it would mean such a lot to old Hans and the other men in the band if he would hear them play. It was finally decided that if they began the concert half an hour before they had expected to, there would be time, and surely politicians were accustomed to a full schedule.

Everything discussed, everything decided, Grandfather began to pull the strings which were to bring order out of chaos, although on the surface it certainly looked as if he were only creating more. He was hardly ever at home that last week. He was dashing around collecting the materials for the programs, conferring with the printer, the carpenters, the merchants, the minister who was to give the invocation, running up to the city for flags and bunting and some crystal of my mother's which Grandmother insisted she must have for the supper, checking with Adam about the ball club's uniforms, checking with the committee who were finding homes for the visiting veterans to stay in. Aunt Maggie said he was exactly like an angry hornet buzzing around, getting into everybody's hair, stinging first this one and then that one into more action, and frazzling his own hurrying wings in the process. But I have never seen him happier. The Reunion was his pet and his love and this was to be the most important Reunion of all. It seemed to me that even his beard crackled with excitement as he flew about and he kept the road between our house and town stirred up with a dust that never settled.

At home, Grandmother was causing almost as much confusion. She decided that every one of the downstairs rooms must be thoroughly cleaned, for the governor would be received in the parlor, would rest in the guest room, dine in the dining room, "And," she said, "it would be just like Mr. Rogers to take him into the bedroom to show him one of those old guns of his. To be on the safe side, Margaret, we must clean them all."

So carpets were taken up, carried out,

beaten and swept, curtains were taken down, washed, ironed and put back, furniture was moved and rubbed down and dusted; even the walls and the floors and the woodwork were washed and waxed again. Choctaw worked until he had a crick in his back and all of us ran and carried and shoved and pushed and bent and stretched until each night we went to bed groaning. The worst of it was that Lulie was still ailing. "She must be coming down with chills and fever," Grandmother grumbled, "she's got no more energy than a sick cat. And right now when we need her the very worst way! That's just the way of darkies. You can't depend on them, not for a single moment, you can't. They turn up puny and ailing right when you need them most."

Lulie helped, of course, but it was true she didn't feel well. She went about sort of listlessly, taking such a long time to do the simplest piece of work that Grandmother was forever at her heels, picking at her, scolding, nagging. Malaria was a common thing in that section of the country in those days. All of us took quinine regularly through the summer and fall, and having had it myself I could sympathize with Lulie. It was no fun. Lulie's skin seemed to have lost tone and instead of glowing with its usual beautiful shiny gold, it had dulled and tarnished. Sometimes it seemed to have a greenish cast to it, although that was usually when she had eaten something that made her sick. Grandmother didn't know about those times, because Lulie would leave the room as if nothing were wrong, not hurrying at all, only I, knowing, able to tell that she was by sheer will controlling her nausea until she was well out of sight and hearing. She was not so careful with me, and that was why I knew she had had more than one bout with the nausea. "What makes you sick, Lulie?" I asked her after half a dozen times.

"The devil," she said shortly, "the ole devil's whut makes me sick." Then, warning me with her face all scowly, "Don't you tell! Don't you tell a soul, not even Miss Maggie. You tell and I pack my clothes and go 'way."

"Well, I'm not going to tell," I told her, "why should I? But why don't you take some medicine and get well? What do you keep on being sick for? Have you been skipping your quinine? Grandmother said she bet you had. You act just like my mother before she has a baby. But of course you couldn't be going to have a baby. You're not married yet."

"You shut your mouth," she snapped at me, putting her face down close to mine, her eyes slitted small and narrow and her mouth puckered. Her breath had the foul, sour smell of illness. I drew back a few steps. She followed me, catching my arm and shaking me a little. "You mind your own business,

Katie, hear? Don't you go butting in no more. You get into bad trouble you does, I promise!"

I pulled my arm free, indignant. "Don't put your hands on me that way, Lulie . . . and I don't care whether you ever get well or not. Just go ahead and be sick. I only meant to help, but you can just puke your insides out for all I care now. I'll not ever hold your head for you again or bring you a fresh towel. I don't know what's got into you. If you don't take your quinine you ought to go see the doctor. Besides being sick you're as cross as an old bear, and I don't like you very well any more."

We were out by the garden fence and she suddenly leaned against it, catching hold of the palings with both hands and letting her head rest on her hands. "Oh, God, I in trouble, Katie. Real trouble . . . trouble I ain't never counted on. I ain't meaning to be cross with you. Ain't meaning to be ugly and ill with nobody, but I so worried, and I sick." She raised her head and looked up at the house, her eyes puzzled and clouded. "Ain't nothing like this ever happen to me before . . . don't know why it do now. Plenty chances, since I sixteen . . . don't never happen . . ."

Not having the slightest idea what she meant, I patted her shoulder. "Well, go see Doctor Jim. He'll fix it."

She looked down at her apron, smoothed it across the front and then picking up a fold of it started pleating it. She stood there, pleating, smoothing, repleating the fold of apron, thinking, studying, puzzling. Then she started chuckling. "I do that, Katie. I go see Doctor Jim. He get me into this mess, ain't nothing but right he get me out. I go see him right away." She straightened her apron. "I gotta go iron them curtains. My God, that starch smell under the iron sho' make my stummick turn. Just got two more pairs, though, and I be through. I gonna do something about this, right away. Ain't gonna fool 'round with it no more. Miss Emily be catching on pretty soon. Come on, Katie, you can hold the curtains straight while I irons 'em."

"Are we friends again?" I didn't intend to hold curtains for her otherwise. It was much too hot and disagreeable a job unless we were friends.

"Sho' we friends. Ah, Katie, I sorry to be so cross. Don't pay me no mind. Next week I be fine again, you see. I be chipper as a frying-size chicken. Won't be sick no more."

"Well, I sure hope so. Everything's so upside down with Aunt Maggie going to be married, and the governor coming, and the Reunion almost here, and you sick, and Grandmother turning the house topsy-turvy . . . sometimes I think I'll be glad when it's all over . . . the whole summer, I mean."

"Naw, you don't mean that. Ever'thing gonna be all right, Katie. I be fine pretty soon. The Reunion . . . it gonna be fun, all that parade and the picnic and the governor coming and all. Naw, you just feeling kind of misused a little. You ain't wanting the summer all over, you know you ain't wanting that."

No. No, I didn't really want that, but I was piqued and hot and tired. Lulie soothed my ruffled feathers and, it may be, soothed her own and we went back inside the hot kitchen to take up ironing the curtains once more.

Twenty-One

There could not have been a more perfect day than the Monday on which the Reunion began. It was hot, of course, but that was to be expected in August. The important thing was that the skies were clear and sunny and there was not even a hint of rain. Rain would have been catastrophic, but no one really worried much about it, for in all the history of the Reunion it had never been known to rain on Opening Day. On the second day, yes, occasionally there had been showers, but it was as if the opening day had been especially blessed and marked for fair weather. So that while occasionally someone remarked, from habit, I hope it doesn't rain, no one really thought it would.

The early hours of that morning were filled with a rushing about. There seemed to be, at the last moment, ten thousand things to be done, and not nearly enough hands to do them, although Grandmother had Florine in to help Lulie. If Lulie had seen the doctor, it hadn't done any good, I thought, for she was as listless and ill as ever, and she hadn't become as chipper as a frying-size chicken at all. If anything she was even more morose and sullen. "I guess it takes longer than a week for medicine to make you well, doesn't it?" I said to Grandmother that morning. She was making salad for the picnic dinner and she answered absent-mindedly, "Sometimes."

"Lulie said she was going to the doctor so she wouldn't be sick any more."

"Well, I hope she went. I'm getting very tired of all this. Katie, set this bowl on the table for me. I've got to start the chickens."

I took the bowl from her hands and carried it carefully to the table. "She said it wasn't anything but right he should help her. Said he got her into all this mess. I don't see how she could."

But Grandmother was getting out the big iron skillets and she clattered them onto the stove without replying. There was such a lot to do. The chickens had to be fried, the salad had to be made, the cakes had to be iced, and all the food had to be carefully packed. Then Choctaw would take it, and Lulie and Florine, out to the picnic grove in the wagon. The house had to be left spotless, and we ourselves must be dressed and on the platform in front of the bank by ten o'clock. Grandfather was up and away from the house very early, leaving us with warnings not to be late, and the rest of us, even I, rushed and hurried and scurried right up to the moment Adam called for us.

I remember, however, the calm that came over Grandmother once she had taken her place in the surrey. Adam helped her in, she spread her skirts about her, touched her hat with one immaculately gloved finger, glanced down her bosom as if making sure of her brooch and watch, then she straightened her back and shoulders and she left behind her all the cares and duties of the house and became a gracious lady, with nothing more arduous before her than the pleasant task of meeting the governor.

I was invested with something of her calmness and pride, and on the back seat beside Aunt Maggie I imitated her, smoothing my stiff plaid taffeta skirts, flicking a speck of dust off my patent leather shoes, straightening a sock, and then sitting with straight back and shoulders like hers. Never had I felt it so important to look and behave well as I did that morning; not all day, for once we got out to the picnic grove I could abandon dignity and run wild if I liked, but for meeting the governor, for watching the parade, it was terribly important.

The main street had been roped off from traffic for the morning, and we approached the bank from a roundabout way, coming up in back of it by a narrow dirt lane. Adam left the surrey in a vacant lot there, and we walked around to the front. The governor was already on the stand when we arrived, and it is odd but I do not recall much about how he looked, except that he was a big man, and I retain the feeling of having looked up at him when he took my hand as if he were a great way off. I remember, too, that he had that gracious poise which seems to be an inherent possession of successful politicians, that he bent low over my grandmother's hand and Aunt Maggie's, spoke softly and easily, laughed often.

Adam left us almost immediately, for of course he had to play in the band and march in the parade, and we were seated. I remember that the railings of the platform were draped with bunting, and that the chairs were those hard little folding chairs which tip over easily. I recall that I nearly came to grief with mine, for the parade, as are all parades, was late starting and I kept peering down the street to see if it was coming. My chair tipped with me once and I had to grab hurriedly at the railing to keep from sliding to the floor. Aunt Maggie reached out to help me and when I looked up at her, she frowned a little and shook her head. I was embarrassed at having to be warned at this important moment.

I think the parade was a little late because of Adam having to call for us, but it could not have been delayed more than ten minutes. To a child, however, it seemed an hour. As best I could I waited, bubbling with anticipation, wondering once rather horribly if I could be going to have go to to Greenland and immediately putting the dreadful thought away from me. That could not happen now. It would be too awful. I resolutely watched the people, of whom there seemed to be an endless number. The street was packed on both sides as far up and down as one could see, and they were remarkably patient, talking quietly together as they waited, their voices, joined, making a kind of buzzing, humming sound. The oily smell of the street was very strong under the hot sun, and while there was a canopy over our heads on the platform, it seemed merely to press down the simmering heat. Aunt Maggie passed Grandmother a fan, and she waved it gently, not disturbing the governor's conversation.

Suddenly there was a shout from far up the street, which was picked up quickly and relayed group by group, coming at last to us. "Here they come! Here they come!" And there was a surging of the crowds toward the middle of the street. Very faintly we could hear the band. I could not see and I could not sit still another moment, I positively could not. I slid to the floor and stood, holding to the railing, craning my neck. "I can't see, Aunt Maggie! I can't see!"

"You will be able to see nicely when they come nearer, Katie. The people will fall back as they come on."

But I wanted to see right then. I wanted the very first glimpse of them. "Can't I please stand on the railing, Aunt Maggie? You could hold me so I wouldn't fall."

"No, Katie . . ."

But the governor, bless him, interfered. "Of course she can stand on the railing. Here, Katie," and he swung me up and stood me on the railing directly in front of him, steadying me himself. It was perfect, and down the street I could see the flags flying.

Gradually the music became louder and we could hear the sound of feet marching. Little by little the people who had surged to the middle of the street gave way before the van of the parade, and it passed through like a ship plowing the waves. Now they were at the end of the block . . . we could hear the music plainly. We could see the color bearers . . . the crowd was shouting. They came nearer and nearer. And then the crowd directly to either side of us fell back and they were crossing the depot road, almost in front of us now. There were the colors . . . the Stars and Stripes, and the stars and bars, side by side, fluttering in the breeze, and the man who carried the Stars and Stripes wore a uniform as gray as the one who carried the stars and bars. The governor snapped to attention. The strains of "Dixie" were loud and clear, now. "I wish I was in de land ob cotton, old times dar am not forgotten, look away, look away, look away, Dixie land." It made chills like cold fingers chase each other up and down my spine.

Next came the regimental colors of the 6th Arkansas, fluttering boldly and beautifully, and then . . . and then came Grandfather. Oh, he was so handsome, so erect, so soldierly, his eyes straight forward, his face so stern and unyielding, even his beard having a sudden and patriarchal dignity. His campaign hat was set very firmly and squarely on his head, his coat was buttoned to the chin, and his sash, the golden satin one we never played battle with, tied securely about his waist, the sword clattering at this side with every step. He marched alone, of course, as a captain should, at the head of his men, and if, instead of a company following him, there were only five old men, he marched at their head all the more proudly. The five old men had been at Shiloh with him. As they passed the reviewing stand Grandfather drew his sword, and the eyes of the old men snapped right. The Governor returned their salute.

Next came the colors of another regiment, and another straggling handful of old men. Behind them another, and another, until, in all, the veterans of six southern regiments had passed. They did not straggle as they marched, or shuffle tiredly. They stepped out valiantly and vigorously, and one old man, who had evidently been a drummer, carried his drum with him and rolled a pretty flourish as he marched. The band brought up the rear, still playing "Dixie." Only "Dixie" was played during the parade. And that was it. That was absolutely all of it. There were no drum majors or majorettes; no merchants or local citizens filling out with numbers; no school children, no local chapters of lodges. There were just the scraps of six regiments, twenty-nine old men in all. Last year there had been thirty-three. Next year there would be perhaps twenty-five. They were all that were left to us of the Confederacy. They marched by us and our hearts beat faster and our eyes filled with tears. The band passed, and played on . . . "In Dixie land I'll take my stand, to lib and die in Dixie; Away, away, away down south in Dixie." The sound of the marching feet grew fainter and fainter, and the sound of the music diminished in volume, too. It was over . . . it was all over, and I felt as if something vital in me had gone marching with them and only a husk of myself was left standing behind.

I am a middle-aged woman and, I hope, I am reasonably sensible. But each of us is the inheritor of an emotional climate, a temperament and an environment. We are the product of many things. To this good day I cannot hear the strains of "Dixie," played by a military band, that I am not returned to my childhood, to the smell of an oiled dirt street, the heat of an August day, the tramp of marching feet, the sight of flags flying and proud colors streaming in the breeze, but above all to the look and the feel and the smell of those rough gray uniforms on old men who once wore them youngly. It has nothing to do with any kind of rational thinking. It has only to do with feeling, and I have been glad, always, that I was born soon enough to see the last of them, and proud that I was born of them. Somewhere in my soul, it must be, I take my stand alongside them.

The rest of the day followed the planned program, and in my memory it has become a kaleidoscope of fried chicken, pink lemonade, balloons which I constantly burst and which Adam or Choctaw constantly replaced for me; little rubber balls, attached to an elastic string with which people went about hitting one another; striped canes and little whips, boys and girls paired off walking wanderingly about hand in hand, licking at ice cream cones; the smooth round and round of the merry-go-round and the heaving motion of the shiny black horse with the golden mane which I rode; the repetitive strains of "Over the Waves" which came silkily from the organ in the middle; the swoosh of air going over the top on the Ferris Wheel, and the downward fall, leaving one's stomach behind.

Those were the only rides on the grounds, and the concessions were leased by local lodges and church organizations, so that there was not a professional carnival look about the fairway. It wasn't much of a picnic, really, I guess. But to me it was fairyland.

And that opening day was a happy one. The governor's speech went well. Stanwick won the ball game, Grandmother's supper was superb, the band played splendidly and when the night train bore our distinguished guest away that evening, everyone could sigh tiredly and say, "Hasn't it been perfect? Simply perfect."

There was nothing at all to warn us that we had only one day more of happiness left to us.

Twenty-Two

The second day of the Reunion was never quite as glittering and exciting as the first. That was only natural, of course, for the peak had been reached. But it had its own merits in a kind of relaxed, happy enjoyment of the day. The tension of the opening day had passed and there seemed to be a slower flow of time. It was more like a big gathering of home folks, and a slow drifting of visitors from one group to another. Each family staked out a place for itself under one of the big trees, and the out-of-town members, especially, wandered from one group to another. There was more talk, more laughter and a renewal of old ties. I remember how Grandmother sat, like a tiny queen, in her chair under the shade of a great elm, and held court. She herself never went about visiting, but there was always a crowd about her and Aunt Maggie and Grandfather. There was less hurry about the day and we could all drive out together, for there was no parade. There was again the big picnic dinner, but it was somehow less sumptuous than the one the day before, although it usually fed more people, for there was always Grandfather's urging, "Have dinner with us."

The third and last day always had the feeling of farewell in it . . . a little sad as friends went about saying goodbye. "It's been wonderful. We'll see you again next year." There would be no next year for so many of the old ones. We didn't know it, but there never would be a next year . . . we never even got to the third day of the Reunion, for it was on that day that Grandmother found out about Lulie.

It was inevitable, of course, that she should find out. Once too often Lulie was sick, and time ran out on her and she could not hide it.

As a matter of fact, though, we were all a little sick at what happened. It was the last day of the Reunion. We were all keyed up, especially Aunt Maggie, Grandfather and I, because Stanwick had won a ball game and lost one, and today was the big day. I had been lying awake since before daybreak myself when I heard Aunt Maggie stirring, heard her bed creak as she tried to slip out of it, and had whispered to her that I was awake and wanted to get up, too. "All right," she said, "but let's be very quiet. Grandfather and Grandmother will be asleep yet."

We crept down the stairs and into the kitchen and then felt very foolish creeping along with our shoes in our hands, for the fire was going, a pot of coffee was bubbling on the stove and Grandfather was sitting at the table with a steaming cup in front of him. "Come in, come in," he said, chuckling at us, "and join me. You couldn't sleep, either, huh? Too much excitement. I've been awake since before daylight. Maggie, we'll have to pitch Gorchek again today. There's no other way."

"He'll be too tired, Papa."

"Well, it's a better risk to pitch a tired Gorchek than any of the other men. I've made up my mind, and I'm sure Adam will agree. Oh, I don't know how good you'll think this coffee is, but at least it's strong . . . and hot."

"It smells wonderful," Aunt Maggie said, and she got down cups for herself and me. I slid onto the bench along the wall and she brought the coffee and sat beside me. I circled the cup with my hands and felt its good warmth, sniffed its heavenly aroma and tasted its good, hot strength. "Um-m-m-h, it's fine, Grandfather. It's as good as Lulie's."

"Oh, it'll do. I guess I've not forgotten how

to boil a pot of coffee yet."

Rastus whined at the door and Grandfather got up. "It's foggy and damp this morning," he said, "and she's chilly. Believe I'll let her in for a few minutes." He opened the screen and Rastus slipped in. It was time for her puppies and she was heavy and clumsy, her beautiful slim body awkwardly misshapen. She was short of breath and panting. Grandfather stooped and patted her. "It won't be long, now, girl. Not much longer and then you'll be free of that load you're carrying. Go lie down by the stove and get warm . . . that's a good girl."

"When are they due, Papa?" Aunt Maggie asked.

"Any time, now."

In the excitement of the Reunion I had completely forgotten Rastus and the puppies. "But, Grandfather," I said, "they may come while we're at the picnic grove! What will she do if we aren't here?"

"Oh, Rastus is an old hand at having puppies. She'll know what to do. She won't need us."

"Won't she need a doctor?"

"Well, if she has some trouble we'll get the vet. But she never has had any. Rastus is a good breeder. We'll keep an eye on her, though."

We heard a stirring above us, a thumping and bumping and the sound of feet moving across the floor. Grandfather looked up. "Sounds like Lulie's getting up."

"Yes, Mama told her last night to get up early this morning. There's so much to do."

As if speaking of her had materialized her, Grandmother came into the kitchen just then. She was already dressed to go to the picnic grove, beautifully groomed in her black taffeta dress with its tiny white lace collar and cuffs. At her neck was the cameo brooch which she always wore, and on her bosom was pinned her gold watch. Her hair was, as always, perfectly dressed, not a pin loose, not a hair out of place and it was as white and lusterless as the collar and cuffs of her dress. She was like a porcelain figurine, exquisite and beautiful. As a concession to the kitchen she had a big apron tied about her waist. It was as purely white as her hair. Grandfather stood as she came into the room. "Well, Emily, I thought you might sleep a little longer. Will you have coffee with us?"

She waved her hand impatiently. "No, no. You know I never eat in the morning, Mr. Rogers. Go on . . . sit down. I have a thousand things to do, and I'll just get on with them. I'll not bother you at all . . . just go on with your coffee. Isn't Lulie down yet?"

Aunt Maggie answered her. "No, but she's up. We heard her moving about. I imagine she'll be down in a few minutes. Can I help, Mother?"

"Later, perhaps, Margaret. Not now. But I do need Lulie." She stepped to the doorway that led up to the room overhead. "Lulie? Lulie! Are you coming?"

"Yessum . . . I'se coming right this minute. Just starting down the stairs."

"Well, hurry."

We heard Lulie close her door and then there was the sound of her feet, a little heavy and fumbling in the dark of the enclosed stairway. Grandmother turned away. Just as she did, Rastus stretched, yawned, clambered to her feet and lurched clumsily across her path. Grandmother stumbled over her, but did not fall, recovered her balance and looked sharply to see what had been in the way. Rastus stood looking up at her, her tail wagging indolently, her round-barreled body grotesque in its heaviness, her breath panting shortly and her tongue lolling droolingly out of one corner of her mouth. Grandmother peered at her unbelievingly and Aunt Maggie drew in her breath sharply.

As she recognized the dog, saw her puffed, swollen body, there swept over Grandmother's face a look of such hatred and repugnance, such distorted loathing, as to convulse every feature and twist it into a grimace. She backed away from Rastus as if she had been something unclean and filthy. Her hand, outstretching, touched a broom leaning in the corner and before we could possibly know what she meant to do she had clutched it and begun beating the dog with it, hitting her again and again, sweeping the broom down viciously, chasing the dog which instinctively ran, circling the room looking for shelter, yelping with pain. Not a word did she say, she simply kept chopping away at Rastus, and with remarkably good aim, hitting her almost every time. Grandfather, who was at first as paralyzed as Aunt Maggie and I, sprang up when Rastus ran under the table and grabbed the broom loose from Grandmother's hand. "Emily, have you gone mad? What in the world has got into you! Stop that this instant!"

Grandmother faced him, trembling. "That dog! What is she doing in the kitchen? Who let her in? I won't have her in the house, I tell you! I won't! I won't!" Her face was still working, her mouth drawn into a grim line which quivered, and her eyes were widely dilated and as black as night

Grandfather set the broom in the corner. "I let her in. It was damp and cool outside this morning and she was cold. It's very near her time. She hasn't done any harm and I'll put her out right now. But you may have hurt her badly."

He knelt and called to Rastus who crept, cringingly, toward him. "It's all right, girl. It's all right, now. Don't be frightened . . . it's all right. Poor girl. Poor dog." He felt all over her, satisfied himself that no immediate harm had been done, then led her outside, going himself to take her to the barn.

Grandmother stood in the center of the room where he had left her, one hand tremblingly hiding her mouth. It was then that Lulie, who had evidently been standing at the foot of the stairs looking on, broke into a run across the room trying to reach the outside door. Perhaps it was the scene she had witnessed, perhaps it was the warmth of the room, or the odor of the coffee, perhaps it was a combination of all of them, at any rate she didn't reach the door in time and a vile eruption spouted out of her mouth, between her fingers clasped over it, down her chin and the front of her dress and onto the floor. She moaned and glanced down, but she kept going.

Grandmother looked at the stain of the vomit, looked at Lulie's fleeing back, looked at Aunt Maggie, and then she dropped into the chair which Grandfather had left empty at the end of the table. Her face was now drained of all the color with which her rage had flushed it, and it seemed wizened and shrunken and pale. She drew in her breath and let it out with a sigh. "Lulie is pregnant, of course," she said on the outgoing breath. "I don't know why it hadn't occurred to me before." She leaned her elbows on the table and laid her head in her hands, rubbing her temples with the palms, shaking her head a little from side to side. "My head aches so . . . I can't think. It hurts, Margaret." She lifted her head and looked up, around the room, a bewildered, confused look in her eyes. "Why is everyone going to have a baby all at once? Everyone . . . everyone is having a baby! Katherine . . . and Lulie . . . and even Rastus. There are babies everywhere . . . everywhere I look . . . all over the room . . . all over the house . . . every-where! Even in my sleep I see them . . . they float around in the air, little, pink, babies . . . sweet, beautiful babies," her voice dwindled off, gently. Then she sat up straight. "But babies aren't sweet and beautiful. They aren't ever sweet and beautiful. Margaret are you going to have a baby, too? You mustn't, Margaret, you mustn't! It isn't nice."

"Mama!"

But just as Aunt Maggie started to say something else, the bewilderment and confusion died out of Grandmother's eyes and she spoke clearly and briskly again. "How stupid of me. I'm sorry, Margaret, forgive me. It's my head. It aches so often. But Lulie is pregnant . . . of that there is no doubt."

I was so confused. "How can Lulie be going to have a baby?" I said. "She isn't even married."

Grandmother looked at Aunt Maggie and then at me. She stood. "You answer her,

Margaret. You agree with her father and mother that she should be told these things. Find an answer for her, now. My headache is intolerable. I'm going to my room."

Aunt Maggie and I sat on at the table. I remember feeling as I sat there, that everything that had happened had been part of a very bad dream. It was so unreal that it couldn't have been real. None of it fitted into anything possible and for it to have even the semblance of possibility it should fade gradually away as dreams do, and I should awaken in my bed in Aunt Maggie's room. I remember picking up a spoon and holding it, rubbing my finger over its slickness, thinking, This is real, this spoon is real, I can feel it . . . so it must be true. But even if it was true there was no sense to it, any of it. Like the fuzzy fringes of clouds in the air, the incidents floated raggedly before some wind of terror which blew about us, which blew coldly but without reason. Why should Grandmother have beaten Rastus? Why was Lulie going to have a baby? Why did Grandmother care? Why did she think babies weren't always sweet and beautiful?

Aunt Maggie moved and then she got up and took the empty coffee cups to the sink. "Katie, dear, I think I had better find Grandfather. Will you see if Lulie is all right, and if she is will you tell her to start breakfast and perhaps you'd like to help her. If she doesn't feel well enough, you can come out to the barn and tell me and we'll work it out. Dear Lord, such a morning! I don't feel as if I could ever eat again, but," she laughed, "I suppose meals must be cooked and eaten no matter what happens."

"Yes, ma'am." I felt very small, very young, very dwindled, but I took hope at this effort to re-establish something usual and normal. Actually the things which give us courage all our lives are those small daily things which must be done, come what may. The world may crack and split in two, but we must get up in the morning, eat, wash dishes, go to work, grow weary and sleep again. The small functions of life hold it together.

I didn't have to look for Lulie, however. She must have been waiting outside, hoping everyone would leave the kitchen, for when Aunt Maggie had gone she slipped in the door and stopped at the water shelf. She poured herself a glass of water and sipped at it, shuddering even at the feeling of water in her mouth. I told her what Aunt Maggie had said. "I feels all right, now," she said sullenly, setting the glass down. "I fix breakfast all right. Whut they say, Katie? Reckon they caught on."

"Caught on to what?" I felt cold toward her. She had deceived me.

"Caught on I'se making a young'un. Reckon they wants batter cakes this morning?"

434

"Aunt Maggie didn't say. You didn't tell me you were going to have a baby."

She was getting out a mixing bowl, big spoon, flour and so on. "Wasn't none of your business, as I could see. Besides, you too young to know." The sifter grated as the flour went through, it being warped a little on one side.

"Oh, for heaven's sake, Lulie. My mother told me about babies long ago! Only she must have left something out, because I don't know how in the world you can be having a baby when you aren't even married. Mama said married people had babies. Are you and Choctaw already married and keeping it a secret?"

"No, we ain't already married and keeping it a secret. Just wish to God we was." She turned around and shook her apron at me. "And you just hush up, Katie. Folks has babies whether they is married or not, but you *is* too young to know and I ain't gonna be the one telling you, so you can just shut up 'bout it."

I watched her pour milk into the flour and begin to stir the batter, her hips swinging with the motion of her arm. I thought about what she had said. "Can anybody have babies, then, Lulie?"

"Well, they got to be girls, silly, but if they girls they can."

This, I thought, was becoming serious.

Maybe something just sort of floated around in the air. "Could I?"

"My God, Katie! No, you ain't big enough yet."

"When will I be big enough?"

She turned again, the bowl of batter in her hands, and looked at me. "I done tole you to hush up. You don't, I gonna go right upstairs this minute and I ain't gonna fix you a bite of breakfast."

But she didn't fix anyone breakfast that morning.

It was like a converging of forces, the way they all came into the room at once, Grandmother through the dining-room door, Aunt Maggie, Grandfather and Choctaw through the other one. Lulie, seeing them, set the bowl of batter down and backed into the space between the cupboard and stove, like some poor, wounded animal which has been cornered. Grandfather spoke first. "Lulie, some things need to be straightened out here. Miss Maggie has told me about you. I, thinking immediately that Choctaw was to blame, went to him. I meant him to marry you at once. He denies it flatly, and insists upon facing you. I think you'd better tell us the truth."

Never had Choctaw looked more Indian than at that moment. He had been feeding the stock, and there were still wisps of hay on his clothing and the smell of the barn about him. He stood just inside the door, his face darkly, implacably stolid. There wasn't the faintest evidence of what he may have been thinking or feeling. He was like a red-brown rock. He had fastened his eyes on Lulie the moment he came into the room, and he never took them off of her. Neither did he say a word.

Aunt Maggie sank into a chair, her face drawn and sallow looking, the dark circles which always appeared when she was tired or under stress, smudging her eyes. Grandmother stood just inside the door to the dining room, her small hands lightly clasped in front of her. All of us, of course, were looking at Lulie. Her skin had that ghastly greenish cast to it, like brass tarnished with mold, and she stood, stooped a little, holding to the corner of the cupboard.

She would not answer . . . just stood there, looking at us, at bay, hunted. Grandfather went to her. He put his hand on her shoulder. "Lulie, we aren't monsters, you know. No one is going to hurt you. We'll take care of you. But this is all very mixed up, and you are the only one who can straighten it out. Is Choctaw to blame for this? Is the child his?"

She shook her head then, her frightened eyes looking at Choctaw. She had to swallow in order to speak, but she managed it. "No, sir. It ain't his. He telling the truth."

"Of course it isn't his . . . don't be an idiot,

Mr. Rogers." Grandmother spoke briskly and swished past Grandfather to the end of the table. She leaned over it toward me. "Katherine, what was that you were saying about the doctor?"

I shrank back, so frightened all at once that my teeth started chattering. Aunt Maggie put out her hand. "Don't, Mother . . . don't . . . ."

Grandfather turned, startled. "Is Katie here? Get her out at once, Maggie."

"No," Grandmother said, "Katherine has the key to this whole affair. I mean to get to the bottom of it. What was it you told me the other morning, Katherine . . . about Lulie and the doctor?"

And so I had to tell it. I would have given anything if I could have recalled those casual, so unimportant to me, words to Grandmother. But now they had caught up with me, and I had been taught never to lie. I sent Lulie one anguished look. I hoped she knew I could not lie. Imagining things was one thing, fibbing with crossed fingers to other children was one thing, but when one was asked directly about something by an adult, one never, never lied. So I had to betray her. It didn't help that I was compelled to . . . it was still betrayal, and I was sick in my soul over it.

Grandmother's questions were so astute that nothing was left hidden, and when it was revealed the meaning was all too clear . . . that Lulie was with child by Doctor Jim, and that she had tried to get him to cause an abortion. "Did he?" Grandmother whirled on her.

"No'm. He wouldn't. Say for me to get Choctaw to marry me."

Choctaw turned on his heel, saying the only thing he had to say. "I don't take no white man's leavings." And the door slammed behind him.

Well . . . now it was all in the open, and it was an old, old story . . . a bright girl and a white man, and nothing to be done about it.

Some kind of order was restored to the day. We did not, of course, go to the Reunion. Grandmother went to her room, complaining of feeling very ill. When she had sent Lulie upstairs, Aunt Maggie went to see if Grandmother needed her. Grandfather went to find Choctaw. I disconsolately tried to wash the dirty cups and saucers and nibbled hungrily on cold cookies. I also wept in the dishwater. It seemed to me nothing would ever be happy and right again. I wanted to go home. I thought this would never again be the bright, warm, lovely room it had always been. I wished I could forget it all.

Both Grandfather and Aunt Maggie were back in the kitchen soon. Grandfather was worried. Choctaw was nowhere on the place. "He isn't anywhere near the house, at any rate,' he told Aunt Maggie. "I'm going to walk over to the creek, and down around the lower fields. I don't want him running wild, the mood he's in. If he cared for Lulie at all, and I think he did, he's bound to be pretty cut up over this thing. I'll be back for lunch, and then, I suppose I'll go out to the ball game. How's your mother?"

"Papa, it's the queerest thing. She undressed and got into bed, saying her head was aching terribly, and I went to get a glass of water to give her a sedative. When I went back to her room she had already gone to sleep. She was as sound asleep as a baby . . . deeply asleep, for I called her and even shook her to try to waken her enough to take the sedative. She didn't rouse at all."

"I suspect she's exhausted from all this emotional upheaval. Just let her sleep. It will do her head good, anyhow." He looked closely at Aunt Maggie. "You don't look too well youself. You'd better lie down awhile, too."

"I'm all right. I just feel a little . . . all gone, inside."

"I know. It's rather a surprise, isn't it? I suppose, though, it shouldn't have been. It fits in with the other things we know about Jim. Thank goodness you never let yourself get involved with him. There's that to be grateful for, at any rate."

Aunt Maggie's head bent. "Yes."

But I could see that her hands shook as she put a cup and saucer up on the shelf.

Grandfather could not find Choctaw, and when he left to go to the ball game he was still very uneasy about him. "I've been uptown, looked up most of his friends, been to all his usual haunts . . . no one has seen him at all. I don't like it, Maggie."

"Papa, there's no use worrying about him. He's gone off alone. He'll get drunk, and then he'll sleep off the drunk and be all right."

"I hope you're right. Well, I've done all I know to do."

The house was very quiet when he had gone. It seemed to have lost all its life. Aunt Maggie lay on the couch in the sitting room, or wandered restlessly about, not being able to read or to sew or even to talk. Whatever she was thinking or feeling, it was deep within her, and it made her brooding and sad and silent.

Along about the middle of the afternoon I crept slowly up the stairs to Lulie's room. Half a dozen times I had got as far as the door to the stairway, but my courage had failed each time and I had turned back. But I kept being pulled toward it, and finally, one slow step at a time, I crawled up. Lulie's door at the top was closed, and I almost turned back again, rather than knock. Some final courage, however, screwed me up to the act, and I tapped very lightly. She answered, "Come in."

I slid inside the door, half expecting that when she saw who it was she would be so angry she would order me out of her sight. But the wonderful thing was that she sat up in her bed, held out her arms to me and smiled. "Ah, Katie, I so glad you come. I been so lonesome . . . so sad." Even when I cried and said I was sorry, she bore no grudge. She just rocked me and told me never mind. "You not to blame," she said, "not you. Can't hide nothing like that long, noway, sugar. It all right." It was so wonderful to know she still loved me.

When Grandfather came home some of his worry over Choctaw had left him. It had been a fine game, Gorchek had pitched well, and we had won. His spirits had risen considerably with the victory. "Adam said he'd stop by before going out to the band concert, so I told him to come for supper. That all right? I thought perhaps you'd like to go, too."

"Of course, Papa."

So that is how it came about that Adam was there when the rest of it happened.

Twenty-Three

Even now as I must write these words my pen falters. I did not realize when I began that recalling all of the details could still be so painful. I had thought the years had had their way with the grief. But I find the tears falling freshly now, my words blurring, the paper spotting.

Aunt Maggie recovered something of her composure as she bathed and dressed. I remember that once again she wore the lilac lawn, but that instead of the girdle which matched the dress, she wound a deep purple velvet sash about her waist, tucked it in and pinned it with a small cluster of pink roses she took out of the vase on her dressing table. She rubbed her cheeks and complained that they were so pale . . . but I remembered that her eyes were bright and shining. She looked very beautiful to me that night.

I think afterwards both Grandfather and Adam felt that if he had taken Adam into his confidence, something might have been done to prevent at least a part of what happened. But he did not. When Adam arrived there was no hint that anything had gone awry. Grandfather had told him earlier merely that Grandmother was not well, and that had been accepted as the reason for our not coming to the picnic. Adam asked about Grandmother, was told she was sleeping, and we went in to supper. We had supper at the usual summer hour, around seven o'clock, because the band concert would not begin until eight-thirty. No one thought of disturbing Grandmother for the meal. It was not even discussed. Grandfather had said that he would stay at home so Aunt Maggie might go with Adam. Of course, I was going, too.

We had sat down to the table. It was a very light supper which Aunt Maggie had concocted mostly of scraps of the picnic dinners, and cold except for a casserole of fresh corn and tomatoes. Adam had told us about the ball game, jubilant because they had won again, and he and Grandfather were deep in a discussion of the game, Adam going over a score card with him, when suddenly there was Grandmother standing in the door to the sitting room. She looked very white, but rested and she smiled at all of us and spoke to Adam. "Don't get up, please. Go on with your supper. I just want to speak to Margaret a moment." Then she stepped back into the sitting room.

Aunt Maggie rose, went round the end of the table, laying her hand lightly on Adam's shoulder as she passed behind him, giving it a little pat, saying, "I'll be right back, dear."

I'll be right back, dear. Those were the very last words she ever said . . . to Adam, or to any of us. I'll be right back, dear. She never did come back. Instead we went to her.

She was gone quite a long time, but we continued to eat and Grandfather and Adam continued to talk. I even heard the gun, but didn't know what it was. It was muffled and sounded more like a very far-off thud, something falling, perhaps, or even a very remote echo of thunder. I said nothing about it, for it didn't disturb me and it raised no questions in my mind. I was listening to Adam explain some technicality of the game to Grandfather.

Then Grandmother came back, and the gun, one of Grandfather's, was still in her hand. It was a new, fairly modern revolver. She came into the room, laid it on the table and turned to Grandfather and Adam. "Margaret will never be married now. Margaret will never be a wife. She will never have to bear a child. I have killed her."

Those were the last rational words she

spoke, for almost immediately a bewildered look crossed her face and she tilted her head as if listening. "What a terrible storm, Mr. Rogers. The thunder hurts my ears!" She clapped both hands to her ears and rocked from side to side. "I can't bear it to thunder like that! Don't you hear it? And the rain . . . and the rain and the rain. Make it stop, Chisholm . . . make it stop!"

Grandfather had sat as if turned to stone at her first words, but when she began about the thunderstorm he jumped to his feet and ran to her. "Emily! Emily, it is *not* storming! Listen to me, Emily! Listen! See?" and he led her to the door, "see the sun is barely set and the sky is clear. See, my dear, there isn't a cloud anywhere. It isn't storming. There is no thunder."

But she wouldn't look. She stood there, rocking and rocking, her poor, tiny shoulders shriveled together, her hands to her ears, her face drawn and withered. "I can't bear it. I can't bear it. But I put the umbrella over Margaret, Chisholm. It mustn't rain on Margaret, or the baby. They mustn't get wet, Chisholm. Oh, the poor, poor baby . . . Margaret's baby . . . out in the rain. Help me, Chisholm! Help me, it mustn't rain on them. Make it stop!"

"Oh, God!" Grandfather turned her about, taking her shoulders and shaking them. "Emily . . . where did you get that gun? How did you get the cabinet open? What have you done? What is this all about? What do you mean about Margaret?"

Something penetrated the poor wandering mind at the mention of Aunt Maggie's name. "She's in the plum thicket, Chisholm. I buried her there. Don't you remember? But it won't rain on her. I put the umbrella over her. I won't let it rain on her, Chisholm. I'll take such good care of her."

Adam had stood up and he now came around the table, running. He went past us and through the kitchen without stopping. Grandfather took Grandmother's hand. "Emily, show us."

"Of course, Mr. Rogers."

She led the way, out through the kitchen, down the path by the garden fence, stooping into the tunnel of the plum thicket. Adam was already there, standing beside Aunt Maggie. She *was* dead, of course. Adam had made certain. Grandmother *had* killed her. And then she had arranged her carefully on the stone slab which covered the little child's grave. She had folded her skirts meticulously about her, and had crossed her hands on her breast. From the velvet sash she had taken the pink roses and had tucked them in Aunt Maggie's hands. In the dim light which penetrated the thicket we could see it all, unbelievably awful and terrifying. But the most awful thing of all was that she had raised the big black umbrella and had propped it so that it furnished a canopy over Aunt Maggie's head. And the most terrifying thing of all was the sweet, wistful way in which she knelt beside Aunt Maggie and straightened a wrinkle in the hem of her skirt, then looked up at Grandfather and said, smiling as innocently as a child would have smiled, "She is safe, now, Chisholm."

A child usually meets grief so unarmored, so ill-prepared to deal with its suddenness and force, because all grief is sudden to a child. But mercifully I did not yet feel anything except an awful fear of my grandmother. I shrank away from her toward Adam, and he put his arms about me and lifted me and held me. I think if she had touched me just then I should have died, quite literally. I had the quivering feeling that she was unclean, repulsive, and I would not even look at her except askance.

Some kind of numb calm seemed to have descended over Grandfather and Adam, too. I suppose it was the absolute unreality of the whole thing. I remember that they simply stood there, looking at Aunt Maggie . . . that neither of them touched her, neither of them seemed even able to believe it was she. Then Grandfather rubbed one hand over his eyes. "Merciful God, this is surely a nightmare. Surely I shall waken in a moment. Surely,

surely such things don't happen."

Adam wet his lips. "I'm afraid it has, sir. Hadn't we better get Miss Emily back to the house, and call Jim or Doctor Clem for her? and . . . and, I suppose Ed Lowe."

Grandfather looked at him dully. "Ed Lowe? The sheriff?"

"Well, Maggie hasn't . . . died naturally, sir."

"Oh, dear Lord, dear Lord!"

Grandmother peered into his face. "Are you not well, my dear?" she asked solicitously. "Does your head ache, too? Come with me, Mr. Rogers. I know exactly what to do for a headache. I have them all the time, you know." And as strange as it sounds, it was she who turned and led us out of the plum thicket.

Doctor Clem came and got Grandmother to bed and to sleep, but by the time he had got there Grandmother no longer knew Grandfather or any of us. She had retreated entirely into a dream world of her own and she thought she was again a little girl and that Grandfather was her own father. "She is completely insane, Chisholm," Doctor Clem told my grandfather. "She may come out of this sleep a raving maniac, or she may simply remain in that dream state."

"Will she never be sane again?"

Doctor Clem shook his head. "I don't know. No one knows. No one can tell about these things, positively."

During this time Adam had awakened Lulie, and she had come down. The three of us sat in the sitting room, Adam holding me. "Lulie, something should be done about Katie," he said once, "she shouldn't be mixed up in all this."

"I will not go to bed," I said, putting my arms tightly about his waist and holding on. "I will not! You can't make me go to bed!" I would not have gone upstairs just then for anything in this world or the next. Not even with Lulie would I have gone. I was frantic at the very idea. Adam was my rock and my shelter and I was not going to turn loose.

"All right, Katie. All right, you shan't go to bed if you don't want to, dear."

In truth Lulie was not much good to us. She was too frightened. She kept rolling the whites of her eyes up and mumbling, "Be me next, be me the old bitch shoots."

Finally Adam told her, "Shut up, Lulie. She isn't going to shoot anyone. She's sick. Go fix Katie and me something to drink . . . some coffee or tea, cocoa, something . . . anything."

"No, sir," she said stoutly, "I ain't going in that kitchen by myself. I go fix you something does you go along. Not by myself, I ain't going."

"All right," he said again, and let it go.

When I think of how he must have been

hurting inside during that time, how his own grief must have been so raw and gashing, it is a miracle to me that he was able to keep controlled. Not once did he cry out for himself, and inside he must have been crying constantly. Not once did he say an ugly word against Grandmother, and he must have been thinking many. Not once did he rail against the circumstances, and surely he must have been feeling their horror. All he did was to sit and hold me, quietly, comfortably, patting my shoulder or my cheek occasionally, asking in his deep, soft voice, "All right, Katie?" And I *was* all right, because it was Adam who asked it and who at the same time answered it for me.

But we were not yet done with horror, or it was not done with us, it matters not how it is said. The telephone rang, I think it was around nine-thirty by that time, perhaps a little later, nearer ten, it isn't very clear to me and none of us could remember later. Adam answered, setting me down in the big chair as he got up. Grandfather and Doctor Clem were just coming from Grandmother's room. I was listening to them as they talked, crossing the hall. I knew Adam was saying Yes, yes, and I was aware before I turned to look at Grandfather that his head had dropped so that his chin rested almost on his chest, but the doctor was telling Grandfather just then that Grandmother was hopelessly insane. And when he had finished, he said, "Someone must be with her constantly, Chisholm. She cannot be trusted alone for a waking second. She should be, of course, put . . ."

Grandfather waved his hand. "That is out of the question. I will not have her in an institution. We'll get a nurse from the city. I must call Tolly at once." He turned toward the phone, where Adam was just hanging up the receiver. "Were you calling someone, Adam?"

"No, sir. That was Jim. He called to say that Choctaw had tried to break into his office a little while ago, that he was drunk and armed, brandishing that knife of his, and that he had just shot and killed him. He had already called the sheriff, but he wanted to tell us himself."

Those were the things which happened to us on the third day of the Reunion. Our world was split in two and it came crashing down around our ears.

Twenty-Four

If they thought I did not understand many of the details of what went on the next day, they were right; but I was there . . . that fact was inescapable. And I took in a great deal more than they thought I did, and more than I myself realized at the time. I know that many people came and went during the day; that shocked as they were, even horrified, kindly women brought in food, and offered to give me shelter. I remember my own fear that I would be made to go with one of them, and how I clung tenaciously to Adam's hand and pled not to be sent away, and how he refused to allow it. "She has already seen and heard too much," he told Grandfather, "there is no use trying to protect her now. She will feel better with us." How blessedly he understood.

Adam himself was calm, but only he perhaps knew the effort it cost him. I have never forgotten that all day his face looked as if it had been pasted on over the bones, stiffening as it dried, entirely smoothed of any expression, except, perhaps, endurance. I have never forgotten that his eyes looked as if a fire had burned itself out in them, cold ashes only being left. He could not control those things, but he could and he did control his voice and his manner. He was competent, quiet, thoughtful, kind . . . oh, it was more than kindness he showed that day, it was loving kindness. He was with us the entire day, of course, the bank being closed.

My father came on the morning train, bringing with him a nurse, and vaguely I sensed that my grandmother was very, very ill, that she had never recovered consciousness and that they were all deeply worried about her. Doctor Clem never once left the house during the day, and he rarely left her room. Somehow, even after Papa came it was still Adam to whom I clung. Papa had not been there. He had not seen what we had seen, or heard what we had heard. He was not close to me just then. Adam was still my rock.

When Aunt Maggie was moved to her own room, I do not know. It must have been some time in the night, for very early the next morning I was told not to go upstairs again, not at all for anything, and Lulie tearfully moved my clothes and personal possessions into the guest room downstairs. I had been allowed to sleep on the leather couch in the sitting room, for no one knew what to do with me, and neither Adam nor Grandfather went to bed at all that night. Lulie told me as she moved my clothes. "You and your papa gonna sleep downstairs now."

I was very glad, very glad we were to sleep downstairs and that I was to be in the same room with Papa.

I remember that the house was very quiet, that people spoke in soft voices, that there was a kind of grieving sound in all the voices, even when they spoke of completely normal things, and I remember the dropped eyes, the sad faces, the handkerchiefs and tears. They were kind people, but in that day grief was not hidden, and the voices quivered and the tears flowed freely.

At some time during the day Choctaw's body was brought home and Grandfather had him taken to his own room over the carriage shed. They thought, he and Papa, that Choctaw would have liked it best that way. I think it was when I saw Choctaw's body being taken to his room that I felt the first wave of grief . . . I could feel it for Choctaw, but I was still numb about Aunt Maggie. Poor, dear Choctaw . . . he would never plant his long rows of cotton again; he would never flirt with Lulie or marry her; he would never go fishing with me and tell me about the birds and the Red Admiral butterfly, and warn me that if I was going to catch fish I had to bait my own hook; he would never shine the surrey again, or drive the wagon down to the woods lot. He would never, now, farm his own hundred acres. It was real to me that Choctaw was dead. I could feel him dead, and my child's heart hurt over his going. I hoped he would like heaven, but I somehow doubted he would like it as well as the farm. I could even weep for Choctaw, but that Aunt Maggie was dead was not yet a fact to me.

I know now that Adam never did believe Doctor Jim had to kill Choctaw. He said, many years later, "He wanted to kill him. He liked to kill. It didn't matter if it was a man. He could have disarmed Choctaw. He was staggeringly drunk. It would have been easy to disarm him. No, Jim liked to pull a trigger and listen to a bullet thud home. He wanted to kill."

"Do you think it was true that he didn't know it was Choctaw?"

"Oh, that . . . yes, it may have been. He didn't wait long to find out who it was. Had it been me I think he would have pulled that trigger just as quickly."

During the afternoon, also, word came that the coroner had found that Choctaw had been killed in an attempt at armed robbery and that Doctor Jim had shot in self-defense.

Nothing further, of course, would be done. No one at all said a word about why Choctaw had actually gone to Doctor Jim's office. It was never mentioned that in anger and grief he had drunk himself into a fit of insane jealousy, that he had gone with the intention of killing the doctor. We knew it, but telling it would not have brought Choctaw back; nor would it have changed the coroner's verdict. It might have changed the words "armed robbery" to "an attempt at murder," but the essential facts would have remained the same. A good man, except when he was drinking, a good, decent, dependable man, three quarters Indian, one quarter Negro, had been plundered of his love, and he had done what the age-old instinct of his race told him to do with his enemy, and he had been killed in the doing. Nothing could help Choctaw, so the doctor's secret remained a secret known only among us.

Arrangements must have been made for the two funerals, for when my father called my mother that night he told her Aunt Maggie's funeral would be the next afteroon. Choctaw was to be buried in the morning. She seemed upset about me, as well she might be, and Papa let me talk to her to reassure her. He was quite uneasy about her, for the time was very close now, and he was torn between the necessity for his presence at Grandfather's and his anxiety about my mother.

I went to sleep at the supper table that night. Weariness had accumulated to the telltale point, and in the middle of a bite, almost, I succumbed. The supper had consisted largely of food that had either been brought or sent in, but Lulie had served it as nicely as usual. No one ate very much, not Grandfather or Papa or Adam, but my appetite was increased if anything, and I think I ate more than usual, at least until my eyes closed. "Poor little tyke," Papa said as he lifted me out of my chair and I roused enough to hear him. "I'd give anything if she hadn't seen all this. I hope it hasn't made too deep an impression."

I do not know what time it was when I awakened and became frightened. The room was dark, but there was a slit of light under the door. I called to my father and when there was no answer I slipped out of my bed and went to the big double bed in which he would be sleeping. The bed was empty, and feeling further fear I opened the door and crept into the hall. The light came from the parlor, and I felt immediate reassurance when I heard voices in there. I did not mean to listen. I had no intention of listening at all. I wanted only the comfort of the sound of their voices and the warming light streaming from the door. I think it is understandable that I should have dreaded being alone. I hunched down against the wall, meaning only to stay there a moment and then go back to bed. But I did listen, of course. Grandfather was talking. " . . . demands an explanation and I have the only key to it. You have a right to know. There are women who don't like being wives, you know . . . and mothers, and you'd have to know all the elements of their nature and environment to know why. They just don't. But Emily's mother was one of the most strait-laced, narrow-minded, bigoted women that ever lived. That certainly had something to do with it. Emily wanted to be married . . . her pride would never have allowed her not to be. Every girl married, as a matter of course, and I was devotedly in love with her, perhaps flatteringly so. At any rate she could not have borne not to marry . . . so when I paid such ardent suit, she accepted me. I think she was one of the most exquisitely beautiful girls I ever saw . . . so tiny, so perfectly made. I loved her almost to the point of worship. But she could not hide, not even at the very first, that she did not like the physical side of marriage. She thought it gross and bestial, and she was affronted by what she called its indignity. It did no good for me to say that love gave it dignity. It remained for her an animal thing, ugly, sinful even in marriage, and uncouth. It made her ill. I have seen her shrunken and white and struggling with nausea. It was . . . it was very pitiful."

There were long halts between the words, as if he were hunting for them, turning them over and looking at them, and then choosing between them. "She never tried not to hide it. She couldn't have, but she did have a very strong sense of duty, and she had absorbed the notion from her mother that however distasteful a lady might find her conjugal duties, they nevertheless remained duties which a lady performed."

There was a quite long silence and my eyes drooped. Then Grandfather began talking again. I smelled smoke so I knew he had been lighting his pipe. "And now, I'm afraid what I must tell you will hurt you, Tolly. She never wanted children. I don't think she was afraid of any part of it . . . she simply hated all of it. And she did not particularly like children. I don't know what part of her pregnancies she hated the most. The human body was itself repulsive to her, and I think she particularly felt disgust when it became evident to the whole world that she had participated in what she called 'carnal knowledge.' She felt a deep shame, and she would never allow herself to be seen after it became evident. She hated the child within her, the conception of it, the necessity of its delivery. There was nothing fine or beautiful to her in any aspect of birth . . . it was one long wallowing in shame and indignity, and you know how increasingly it spread from humans to animals and even to plants. She could not bear to be reminded of the processes of reproduction. It was almost pathological in her from the beginning."

I heard him stir in his chair, heard him sigh deeply. "Well, after Maggie was born I hadn't the heart to disturb her for . . . for over two years. Being a man, though, and a most imperfect one, eventually I did. We had been rather close during those years, partly I suppose because I made no demands on her, and I thought perhaps she had grown more . . . well, more willing. She had not. On the contrary she had supposed I knew she did not want any more children, and that I would therefore never approach her again. When I left her that night she was more ill than I had ever seen her, positively sick with horror and disgust. She looked at me with loathing and hatred, and I vowed it would never happen again. The two double beds made their appearance shortly afterward, as you remember them most of your life, Tolly. I kept that vow, but unfortunately she had conceived. She went almost wild when she knew it. She kept to her room for days and days, and she would not speak to me. And finally, in some way I never learned, she caused her own abortion. I have always suspected that she made Angie help her. You have always known that the child buried in the plum thicket was our own baby . . . and you were led to believe it was buried there because we wanted it near us. Actually it never attained maturity. It was, I think, not more than five or six months along. Your mother insisted upon the burial there . . . whether to remind herself of her own guilt, or whether in an effort to punish me, I have never known."

I do not know how even as strong a man as my grandfather could have told such things in that quiet, even voice of his. It never broke at all. It simply went on telling the terrible truth. There were pauses, it is true, long pauses, and the sound of his breath indrawn, but he always went on.

Adam spoke then. "Did you ever have any idea at all, sir, that her mind was going?"

Grandfather seemed to be taking time to think. "No, not really. Oh, there have been evidences that she was feeling guilt very strongly. She had begun lately, just this summer, going to the attic to fondle the baby clothes . . . the ones she had used for both Tolly and Maggie and would have used again for the new baby. And of course she had grown increasingly frightened of thunderstorms. Just a few weeks ago, too, Katie and I found the umbrella over the little grave during a rainstorm. It shocked me . . . but she was so normal in every other way. No, no, it never actually entered my mind that she was slowly losing her grip. I wish to heaven it had!"

"Well, it never does, does it, sir? In families, I mean? After all, it's just not conceivable that one of our own can . . . can, well, go violently insane. It always happens to someone else."

"Like death. No, I suppose it doesn't, until we are brought up short. Finding out about Lulie must have touched the whole thing off . . . Lulie's desire for an abortion . . . Emily's sense of guilt over her own. She was a very religious woman, you know . . . very dogmatic and strait-laced, and probably no amount of rationalization could remove that stain of having taken life from her. The whole thing must have come crashing down about her ears all at once. But even so her obsession did not leave her. Sex was unclean, and Maggie must be saved from it."

I heard a sound which I knew was my father striking his fist into the open palm of his other hand. It was a thing he did when he was nervous, tired or distraught. "If only Katie hadn't known . . . or if only she hadn't said anything . . ."

"Katie is just a child, Tolly. She had no idea what Lulie had meant. She didn't know what she was telling your mother."

"Oh, I know, I know. But it was that little hint which set Mother to thinking . . . touched it all off."

"Your mother was heading for this breakdown, anyhow, Tolly."

"I know that, too. But she might never have learned of Lulie's effort to get rid of the child . . . the whole thing might have taken a totally different slant . . . Maggie might . . ." and then there was one of the most terrible sounds one can ever hear . . . the sound of a grown man weeping, reduced finally by pain to blind, agonized tears, stripped defenselessly to the final submission of grief.

I crept back across the hall to my own bed, and lay shivering, even though the night was very hot.

So I learned the awful thing I had done . . . the whole chain of terrible events I had so unwittingly set in motion . . . *that,* I have never forgotten. Oh, I know, I was a child . . . I didn't know, I couldn't be held accountable. But if I had not been such a smart-aleck child, so nosy and curious, so determined always to be in the thick of everything I wouldn't have known about Lulie and the doctor; and if I hadn't felt always such a need to be important I would never have spouted off so unwisely to Grandmother. I had always to contribute my own bit of knowledge, had always to be noticed. It got me in the end this lifelong burden, which began that night. Mercifully I was not too aware of all the implications, then. I only knew that, miserably, I was caught up in the current of the tragedy, that somehow, unknowingly, I had played a part in it. There was so much I did not yet understand, so much that was too confusing.

I went to sleep clutching the small comfort of my grandfather's quiet voice, "She is just a child, Tolly. She didn't know."

Twenty-Five

The full weight of my own personal grief had a slow accumulation, beginning with a kind of hysterical realization of loss the next day. I did not go to either funeral. In those days children were taken to funerals, but neither my father nor my grandfather thought it wise, and they gave no care to what the townspeople would think of my absence. But I was allowed to decide whether or not I should see Aunt Maggie when she had been brought, in the casket, down to the parlor. I chose to look at her, and it was Adam who took me into the room. I have never forgotten a detail . . . the dimmed room, the flowers, the slow-burning lamp, the bronze sheen of the casket in which she lay . . . and finally, Aunt Maggie herself, looking not asleep as they had told me she would look, but quite dead, quite unfamiliar, quite gone away from us all. I forgot all about heaven and angels and haloes and harps, all about souls and spirits gone to their eternal abode. I saw only what had been my beloved Aunt Maggie and knew only that today, soon, she would be where no one would ever see her again, and she would be alone there and forever alone. The burden of it was so unbearable that I flung myself on Adam and began sobbing uncontrollably, began even screaming against the very idea of it, began that rage of all rages the most futile, against that fact of all facts the most inexorable.

Adam carried me hurriedly from the room and took me to my father, who called the nurse. She very sensibly did not try to soothe me. Instead she gave me a sedative and I was drowsy and unperceptive most of the day.

Papa and I went home the following day. He could not stay longer because of my mother, of course.

My grandmother lived only a month after Aunt Maggie was buried. She lived that month like a hibernating animal, sleeping, rousing very slightly but knowing no one, being fed by the nurse, sleeping again. And finally her heart simply quit beating. It was, perhaps, best that way.

The baby brother had been born during that month, but my mother had not been strong enough to go to Stanwick for the funeral.

Papa went, of course, and afterward he brought Grandfather and Lulie home with him. Lulie was to stay with us, but Grandfather would not. Papa had asked him, "What are you going to do now?"

"I?" Grandfather said, "Why, exactly what I have always done. The cotton has to be picked this fall. It must be planted again next spring."

"You are going to stay on at the farm, then . . . alone."

"Of course."

"How will you manage? Choctaw is gone . . . Lulie, Maggie . . . everyone. Papa, you know we should love to have you stay with us."

"Yes, I think I know that. But I have my own home, Tolly. I belong there. There's no need for me to clutter up your and Katherine's life. I have my own place to fill, there are things for me to do. I'll manage."

Just before Grandfather left to return to Stanwick, my father asked him one question, very gently. "Papa . . . how was it possible for you to live during all those years, so admirably . . . to make them count?"

All the greatness of my grandfather was in his reply. "Possible? Why, Tolly, one doesn't think about the possible and the impossible, you know. One goes along, does the best he can. You think it's been a tragedy? Well, there were times when I was younger when I thought it was pretty bad myself . . . when I was around your age. But the thing is, one can't have life whole. At best we must deal with fragments, little things, one thing at a time . . . little pieces of happiness or sorrow; little bits of joy or grief; little shards of grace or ugliness. One has to put them together, glue and paste and stick all the little pieces together as best one can, to give meaning to the whole. The cracks nearly always show, but in the end they are part of the whole, too. You must not blame your mother. She was a great lady. Much of what we had as a family, and we had much, you will remember, we owed to her strict sense of discipline, even to her inflexibility. She graced our home exquisitely, and gave it order and a very loving beauty. I may have set the course for us, but as strange as it may sound, it was Emily who kept it steady. She was the hinge upon which everything hung."

One other thing happened about that time. It concerns Doctor Jim. He came to the city shortly after he had killed Choctaw . . . within a month, as I remember. And immediately after arriving he married the wealthy widow. After that he neither practiced medicine nor played the piano any more. Instead he spent her money, was flagrantly unfaithful to her, and gradually drank himself to death. Drink and sobbing poetry were his portion.

He must have died with the words, "Il pleure dans mon coeur," still engraved upon his mind, and his heart must have wept considerably more after Aunt Maggie and Choctaw were killed.

Grandfather did stay on at the farm, and he carried on as much as possible in the way he was accustomed to doing. With Lulie gone, he got Florine and her husband to move over with him, the husband to do the work Choctaw had done, but never in the loving way Choctaw had done it, Florine to take care of the house.

We never had another summer at Stanwick. There was never another Reunion. For the next spring, trying to help William with the plowing and the planting, Grandfather was caught in a chill spring rain, took a deep cold which rapidly developed into pneumonia, and he died within a week of taking the cold. That summer, when I was eight years old, was the end of a whole way of life.

When I was eighteen, Adam and I were married. He was called to an important position in a bank in the city several years after that summer, and living as he then did, a neighbor to us, my two younger brothers and I thought of him as a member of the family. I do not know when the love I had always felt for him began to change into something deeply personal. I am not sure it did change. I think it simply grew. He watched me grow up, helped me to grow up. He was in our home the night I went to my first dance, indeed it was he who drove me and my escort to the dance in his car. He took me to my first football game. He sat with the family in the front row the night I was graduated from high school, and I carried the roses which he had sent. It was on his shoulder that I wept when my heart first broke for love. . . . There has just always been Adam, giving me the rock of his presence and his sheltering love. And during the years of our marriage it was somehow a wonderful thing to turn to him, to lay my head on his shoulder and to remember that it had lain there when I was a child, that there was nothing about me he did not know and understand, that he had been a part of my life as far back as I could remember. It was a little like never having to grow up.

Oh, I am aware of the psychological terms which might be used of our marriage; there was, after all, twenty-six years' difference in our ages. I know the meaning of the words transference, substitution, association. I know that by the time I was eighteen I was very like Aunt Maggie, fully as tall, as ample-bosomed, with the same red-brown hair, long thin nose, deep-set gray eyes. I know that. But the important thing is the way we felt. If

Adam's love for me was a continuing of his love for Aunt Maggie, if at times he looked across the room at me and his heard cried, Maggie! . . . I have never minded . . . his heart was big enough for us both. But mostly I have not minded because I have loved him for us both. I have been both myself and Aunt Maggie to him, willingly and gladly.

We had thirty beautiful years together. We reared a family of fine children . . . with Lulie's help. She went with me when Adam and I were married, and she was never again very far from me. She never married and she never had any more children. Her little boy, who was a beautiful child, remarkably like Doctor Jim, was with us until he reached his teens. Some wanderlust took hold of him then, and he left, returning only rarely to see his mother. We lost all touch with him after he became a man, and I do not now know what ever became of him.

Something wild and free was quelled in Lulie that summer, and she was quieter, more subdued, more earnest afterward. Oh, not that she became entirely tamed. Lulie could never do that. To this good day she has a temper, can scowl fiercely at me and scold as if I had never grown past my childhood. But she knew what she had done, and she knew it had cost her a good man, and had cost him his life. But it has been one of the good things in life to have had Lulie beside me all these years.

Adam rose in banking circles to positions of increasing importance, and as he rose it became my duty and my life to follow him farther and farther afield, until finally during the last great war we found ourselves in London, Adam at the head of an international financial group. He went very far, and there have been times when I have thought, sorrowfully, how Aunt Maggie would have loved the kind of life we had.

It was to bring him home that I went to Stanwick last summer. I thought he would have liked to be buried there. He never said so, there wasn't time; for he died as my grandmother had died, his heart simply stopped beating one night in his sleep. But I thought he had gone so far, he would like to rest, finally in the little cemetery in the family plot where Grandfather, Grandmother and Aunt Maggie lie. I wish I could have been certain. He lies beside Aunt Maggie, but there is room for me on the other side.

Isn't there?

in life to have had Lulie beside me all these years.

Adam rose in banking circles to positions of increasing importance, and as he rose it became my duty and my life to follow him farther and farther afield, until finally during the last great war we found ourselves in London, Adam at the head of an international financial group. He went very far, and there have been times when I have thought, sorrowfully, how Aunt Maggie would have loved the kind of life we had.

It was to bring him home that I went to Stanwick last summer. I thought he would have liked to be buried there. He never said so, there wasn't time; for he died as my grandmother had died, his heart simply stopped beating one night in his sleep. But I thought he had gone so far, he would like to rest, finally in the little cemetery in the family plot where Grandfather, Grandmother and Aunt Maggie lie. I wish I could have been certain. He lies beside Aunt Maggie, but there is room for me on the other side.

Isn't there?

The publishers hope that this
Large Print Book has brought
you pleasurable reading.
Each title is designed to make
the text as easy to see as possible.
G. K. Hall Large Print Books are
available from your library and
your local bookstore. Or you can
receive information on upcoming
and current Large Print Books by
mail and order directly from the
publisher. Just send your name
and address to:

G. K. Hall & Co.
70 Lincoln Street
Boston, Mass. 02111

or call, toll-free:

1–800–343–3806

A note on the text
Large print edition designed by
Bernadette Strickland
Composed in 16 pt Times Roman
on a Mergenthaler Linotron 202
by Modern Graphics, Inc.